The 4 Phase Man

ALSO BY RICHARD STEINBERG

Nobody's Safe
The Gemini Man

Richard Steinberg

The 4 Phase Man

Doubleday

New York

London

Toronto

Sydney

Auckland

PUBLISHED BY DOUBLEDAY
a division of Random House, Inc.
1540 Broadway, New York, New York 10036

DOUBLEDAY and the portrayal of an anchor with a dolphin are trademarks
of Doubleday, a division of Random House, Inc.

All of the characters in this book are fictitious, and any resemblance
to actual persons, living or dead, is purely coincidental.

Library of Congress Cataloging-in-Publication Data

Steinberg, Richard, 1958–
The 4 phase man / Richard Steinberg. — 1st ed.
   p.   cm.
I. Title.   II. Title: Four phase man.
PS3569.T375492A615   2000
813'.54—dc21   99-26632
CIP

ISBN 0-385-49259-6
Copyright © 2000 by Richard Steinberg
All Rights Reserved
Printed in the United States of America
May 2000
First Edition

10   9   8   7   6   5   4   3   2   1

To Shawn Coyne,
editor and guide,
Who fights for what he believes and, luckily, believes in me

A one phase man's a keeper;
Two phase man's no sleeper.
A three phase man's a man of old;
But a four phase man's worth his weight in gold!

—CIA verse

The 4 Phase Man

In another world, at another time, they would've been hailed as angels or damned as demons. Songs would've been written, stories handed down, their likenesses reproduced into the finest art of their period.

Considered good or calculated evil, they would *most certainly* have been noticed.

But not today.

Today they are hoarded like gold and food in a poor and starving land. Hidden from the light, denied existence—simply and completely *not there.*

But they *are* there.

Men of cold intellects, colder viewpoints, and an implacable relentlessness beyond conception.

The *Four Phase Men* of whispered legend and mythic shadows.

Since the creation of modern intelligence agencies there have been only seven of this special breed. Men who could, by themselves, carry out all four pestilential skills most prized in the unacknowledged black wars of our times.

Gather intelligence.

Carry out counterintelligence.

Implement the highest technological forms of warfare.

Kill . . . dispassionately, cleverly, cleanly, and without trace.

The four phases of modern intelligence field operations.

Seven . . . *Four Phase Men.*

Seven men who had risen to the heights (or depths) of the black ops world. Whose very presence made the world's governments nervous, their masters confident, and all who knew about them very much afraid.

Seven men in sixty-three years.

And in the early days of a century that threatened to make the twentieth seem to be a time of rampant peace and tranquillity, only two left. No longer under anyone's command and control; no longer tethered safely to flag, God, and country. Now outside, looking in.

At us.

Phase One

Intelligence

One

There was no place left to go.

But the sun was going down, the weather turning, and the soldiers had lately begun to enforce the curfew. So *Aegri Somnia* (The Sick Man's Nightmares), the only place in the district that a stranger could go without questions being asked, it would have to be.

The hostess just inside the taverna's door never looked up from her paper. *"Ti alismonitos ehos."*

"Mu fanatay tsutayros." The man dropped some gold coins on her table. "That a good enough sound for you?"

At the American-accented English words, the woman looked up. Tourists almost never came to this part of the island. "Who you?" she asked cautiously, her cigarette dangling from her upper lip.

"Xenos Filotimo."

The old woman laughed; using the moment to study the flat expression, the callused hands, the knife in the climbing boot. No emotion or feeling came off the big man. Just a blank, somehow foreboding wall.

But with the curfew, rich Americans or English (and they all were rich, she thought) were few and far between. The soldiers and the mercenaries, well, they had their own places. And the local toughs were too busy running from the soldiers—when they weren't robbing unwary European and American college students —to bother with a place where they had to pay.

So this man who spoke Greek like a Greek, but reeked of America and closeted disaster, was unusual.

She made up her mind.

"To look, ten thousand and more," she said as she assessed his nonreaction. "To rent, fifteen thousand and more. To stay night is . . . more."

"Thay prape na mirasto to domatio mu me aluis skorpeues?" The man tossed thirty thousand drachmas (about $100 U.S.) on her table. "I hate scorpions."

"No scorpions here, sir." The woman quickly counted the bills before sliding them off the desk into a drawer. Next to a loaded and cocked Tokarev. She left the drawer open as she smiled up at the man.

"Filoxenia, Xenos Filotimo. Parea," she said in broad welcoming tones, then stood and unlocked the door behind her. She held up three arthritic fingers to the bartender inside. "Only scorpions are those you bring with."

She relocked the door as soon as the man had gone through. She instantly picked up the phone to call the taverna's owner.

A man like that, he would want to know about.

It took a long moment for the man's eyes to adjust to the dinge of the place. Lanterns and lamps on the walls gave off a mixed red and green tone. A few candles flickered on fewer tables, occupied by maybe six or seven people in the near dark. The sound of a bouzouki strumming softly somewhere floated over the place, neatly mixing with the odors of Greek tobacco, burned lamb, and sex.

"Milk."

The bartender nodded, then poured a glass of the thick, barely chilled goat's milk. He hesitated as he handed the glass across the bar. He'd seen the type before: men who could go from docile to violent in moments. Men past caring, the *aeiramenê doupêsen* they were called in the islands.

Walking corpses, devoid of human emotions, compassion, or clemency of any kind.

Xenos slowly swirled a sip of the sweet liquid in his mouth

before swallowing. He briefly closed his eyes as his scarred neck pulsed with the effort. A smile played across his lips, then was instantly exiled as he opened his eyes.

"You want now, mister?" the bartender asked carefully.

"*Amesos.*" He took another sip of the milk. "Not a child, *parakolutheô*? A woman." His voice was hard, stone, inhuman.

"Understand." The bartender swallowed hard, picturing what lay ahead for the woman he selected. What lay in store for *him* if he chose wrong. He waved to the back of the room and three women came forward.

They wore the long slit skirts and tight button-front sweaters that were the virtual uniforms of the whores of the islands. Maybe in their thirties, maybe older, they all looked at least fifty, and an old fifty at that. Their practiced smiles, pale olive skin stretched tight, their eyes all begging *"pick me, I need to feed my family."*

He selected the cleanest of the group. The one who preened the least, arched her back the least, seemed to *care* the least.

"Bring the milk."

Carrying a pitcher of the milk in a bowl filled with ice, she led the way to the back. *"Emai Eleni.* I make you real happy," she said tonelessly, in a rehearsed fashion, as they climbed the stairs to the second floor. She let them into a small room with a bed, chair, dresser with a radio, a crucifix, and a tiny mirror.

As Xenos walked to the heavily curtained window to look out at the street below, the woman knelt in front of her crucifix, mumbling a nearly silent prayer for strength and forgiveness. Then she stood and looked over the stranger. "What do you want me call you?"

Xenos allowed the curtain to fall back as he turned to her. "That's not important." He dropped his pack on the floor to the side of the bed.

He reached out to her, gently stroking her cheek with the back of his hand, surprised by the real softness there. She turned her head into his hand, professionally but effectively; like a kitten arching into its owner's caress.

He inhaled her hair, her fragrance, felt her warmth. Slowly slid his hand down her neck, finding she had already unbuttoned the old, worn sweater—she probably always did, to keep it from being torn. His fingers found her firm smallish breasts, slid over her warm nipples, felt the regular, completely detached beating of her heart.

"Jerry?"

"Yeah, boss!"

"See you a moment?"

The boy—barely a man—jogged over to the older man. "What d'you need, Herb?"

The older man gestured at a nearby couch in the half-empty rec room. "Got something to show you."

Jerry looked pained. "God, it's Sunday, man. Can't we put off more training videos until . . ."

"Now, son." Herb's voice was the perfect mix of professional discipline and paternal disapproval.

Jerry sighed, then sat down.

"I thought you'd be interested in this," Herb said simply as he started the video. "Thought you might learn something."

The picture on the projection television resolved itself into a small bedroom. A woman in her forties lay naked on the bed, holding out her arms to someone off camera.

Then a nude, erect Jerry walked in front of the camera.

"Hey!" someone from the back of the room called out. "Dirty movies!"

"Herb," Jerry said in a pained whisper, "turn it off. Please," he begged.

But Herb just pointed at the screen as a crowd gathered round.

On the screen Jerry first sat on the bed, then gingerly lifted himself over the woman. He fumbled around, trying but failing to enter cleanly, requiring the woman to reach down and guide him in.

"Hey, Goldman," someone in the crowd called out. "I never knew you was Jewish."

"Need some help there, did you, Jerry?" from another.

The boy/man shrunk in his seat as his image continued to awkwardly be helped by the woman. "God, Herb, please!"

The image froze, then was shut off.

"Gentlemen," Herb said, looking at the blank screen, "may we have this room?"

A minute later they were alone.

The older man took a deep breath. "She's one of ours. One of our little, I don't know, tests?" He shook his head. "One you failed."

Jerry couldn't look at the man.

"You are never alone, Jerry," the man said firmly. "Never off duty." He paused. "Never safe."

He looked into the ashamed boy's eyes. "Jerry?"

"Yes, Herb?"

"For you to be what we know you can be," he said gently, "for you to do what we know you can do, you must never let up. Never take unnecessary chances. Never"—he hesitated—"allow ANY vulnerability."

He smiled supportively. "Do you understand, son?"

"I . . ."

"We never get second chances, my boy. Never."

"I understand," the mortified but committed boy muttered.

"Good, son. Good."

"Mister? Mister? What you want?" she whispered. *"Possos?"*

"Lock the door." She did, as he sat on the bed. "Now take off your clothes."

She slowly undressed.

Xenos lay back on the bed, propped against the pillow, his heavy boots pushing against the fragile footboard. He didn't undress, didn't move, just lay on top of the covers . . . watching.

Her blouse. Her skirt. Her skin.

No reaction, no reaching out to her or quickened breathing; no masturbation or vulgar commentary.

Just his eyes darting back and forth along her body. Probing. Examining. Devouring.

"Turn around," he whispered.

Shrugging, she did as she was told.

"*Ayfaristo,* Eleni. Thank you."

The man's voice seemed to trail away as if he was momentarily transported away from the small brothel into a place of, well, Eleni couldn't really describe it. But she knew it must be a better place than she'd ever seen. Then, like a horse throwing off flies, he was back.

He nodded toward a chair after a few long minutes. "Put that by the door and sit down."

Puzzled, but sensing the barely suppressed violence of the man, she did as she was told. Then watched as the man fished around in his boot. He pulled out a wad of drachmas and the biggest knife she'd ever seen. He loosened his shirt, unholstering a large chrome and steel revolver.

Petrified, she felt like screaming for help; stopped only by an unreasoned logic that no sound would ever escape her lips if she tried. And the certainty that she would be dead a second later.

Xenos noticed her discomfort, shook his head sadly, then tossed her the wad—50,000 drachmas, almost three times the going rate for all night. He turned on his side, put the knife under the pillow—still gripped in his right hand—cocked the gun, then laid it across one of his boots.

"If anyone tries to get in before morning," he said in a tired voice as he closed his eyes, "you stop them. For at least thirty seconds. *Parakolutheô?*"

She nodded. "I . . . understand."

"If you don't," he said through a yawn, "pray to your God that they kill me." He settled himself more comfortably on top of the bed. "You can get dressed if you want to."

And he was asleep.

She quickly dressed, never taking her eyes off his sleeping form. No matter how he tossed or turned (and his sleep *was* deeply troubled), the right hand never came out from under the pillow and the expression on his face never reflected any of the inner turmoil that his body clearly spoke.

Eleni readjusted the chair so that it was jammed under the

doorknob as a brace against any unexpected opening, then moved to the window, barely moving the curtain aside to peek down at the street as twilight crept across it.

Every ten minutes or so, she would move to the door, listen closely to the sounds of urgent couplings in the rooms around hers, to soft footfalls on the threadbare carpet; to anything that might spell a threat.

And she did that for the remainder of the night.

Praying and wondering in equal measures throughout.

The dream came right away, before his breathing could shallow and even; before his body could settle and unwind. As always, it came with blinding speed and life-crushing impact.

He stood in the sanctuary of the hundred-year-old temple. The men in their dark suits, gray beards, *tallisim* and *kepas* in place, swaying to their own rhythms as the ancient prayers were recited. An odd cacophony of English, Yiddish, Russian, and German mutterings rising out of them.

Upstairs, the women sat. More still, more controlled than the men; they prayed with equal fervor but less demonstrably, as was the tradition. The old women in black, the middle women in navy or pale blues, the young women and girls in a few bright colors. But all had their shawls over their heads, their hands cupped over their eyes, their mouths moving almost silently with their prayers.

Xenos would move among them, looking into their eyes, tasting their breaths, inhaling the women's soapy-clean fragrances, feeling the submerged power of the men. He stood for the longest time by his mother—who couldn't have been there, since she had died years before—watching as she tried hard to suppress a grin of pride and, well, ownership, in her son below. It was the one comfort in the dream. A mother that he had barely known approving, supporting, loving.

He would move to his father, sitting proudly, stiffly, on the dais next to the president of the synagogue. His freshly altered suit —worn only for the most special occasions—paling in comparison to the other man's. But he prayed with more fervor, with an extra something that had been reserved for this moment when he would sit in front of the congregation. A proud father's one and only embracement of his son's accomplishments.

Xenos would reach out, try to touch the old man with the scar across his forehead from a soldier's rifle butt. But he could never quite make it. Somehow, no matter how close the dream allowed him to move, it was never close enough. So his fingers would stretch and reach and beg; but never find the man whom he most wanted to please, whom he had most disappointed.

Then he would find himself standing beside his younger self.

Thirteen, clear-eyed, acne-strewn innocent face, studying the ancient text spread before him. Sneaking glances up to the balcony at his sister; to the side at his father; out at the men who knew the text by heart and who would criticize or praise his performance for years to come.

And he heard his voice—breaking and cracking with youth—singsonging the age-old words with as much feeling as he could. Praying that his fear of screwing up couldn't be heard between the Hebrew and Yiddish.

"*Vayomer, a'donai el Moishe. Koh tomar, el b'nai yisroyel. V'mru chi, ani, a'tem re-etem; keey, meen ha'shmiem.*"

Then it began.

A slight trickle of blood from his left cheek where a knife would one day almost take his eye.

A crack and distortion in his right arm where grenade fragments one day would destroy much of the bone, requiring three operations to repair.

Flames and the bittersweet smell of burning human flesh rising up from the floor, mixing with naphthalene from the napalming that he would barely survive.

As the blood and pain continued to leak out of the seemingly impervious boy all over the holy text, the faces would appear.

Iraqi, Russian, Palestinian, Vietnamese, South American, European, and Asian faces that just floated in the carmine-stained mist; quietly taking in the destruction of the boy who—as a man—would take their lives.

Or cause their lives to be taken.

They never spoke, never revealed so much as an expression or thought in their dead eyes. But they floated and they watched the piecemeal devastation of Xenos's younger self.

Then all froze; all became stilled and quiet.

Xenos turned to his father, as he knew he must. For he was no mere observer in this dream/horror. He was dragged along on its vicious current with no more power to alter its path than he'd had to alter his own.

The old man stood, walked over to the boy, gently smoothed a vagrant lock of hair out of the now blind but still clear eyes, then turned to the man that the boy would, must, become.

"I have no son," he said sadly yet firmly. He gestured at the slowly immolating boy. *"He* was my boy, my life, my future." He sighed as his eyes locked with Xenos's. "You're just a corpse. A dead man. A stranger to me now and forever."

He reached up, violently tearing the lapel of the best suit he'd ever owned. Shaking his head, crying unheard tears, then covering his eyes with his right hand as he began reciting the ancient prayer of mourning.

"Yis'kadal v'yiskadash, shme raboh. There be some who have left a name behind them; whose remembrance is as sweet as honey in all mouths. People will declare their wisdom and the congregation will tell of their goodness.

"And there be some who have no memorial; whose names have vanished as though they had never been. They lie at rest in nameless graves. Their resting places in far-off forests and lonely fields are lost to the eyes of their revering kin. Yet they shall not be forgotten."

The old man lowered his hand, staring deeply into Xenos's sad eyes. And the old man's voice was firm as stone and hard as iron.

"My son is lost to me, now and forever. His name will be vanished, his memory as though he had never been."

Then, as if on cue in this kaleidoscopic horror that haunted Xenos virtually every time he closed his eyes, the mother he had never known stood beside them, crying deeply, her voice begging.

"No! Avidol, don't do this! He is your son! You cannot—"

"I have no son," was the old man's simple, pained, inelastic reply. "He is a stranger to me. *Yis'kadal v'yiskadash, shme raboh.*"

And the scene would grow dark, insubstantial, as Xenos would reach out—through—the image of his father. Would be racked with a soul-deep pain that threatened to do what countless evil men's bullets could not do.

Destroy the man he had become.

As the scene would shimmer, blink from existence, then repeat itself in even greater strikes of torment and anguish.

He awoke with a start, instinctively grabbing the person he sensed above him by the neck, pulling the person down, his knife pressed hard against the exposed throat.

"Emai Eleni!"

A quick glance around the tiny room confirmed that they were still alone.

"What is it?"

"Soldiers," she whispered urgently. "Downstairs!"

"Have you seen the bastard or not?" the lieutenant spat out in Greek through his thick Cypriot accent as two enlisted men held the bartender's arms behind him.

"I know nothing," the bartender slurred out from somewhere in his battered face.

A baseball bat to the groin was the lieutenant's response.

As the man collapsed to the floor, the soldiers began kicking him.

The lieutenant casually turned to the nearest prostitute, a trembling girl in her early twenties.

"Listen, grandmother," he said to the old woman in broken English so that he would not be understood by his men. He may have been speaking to the old woman, but his eyes never left the girl in front of him as his bat began to work its way beneath her skirt. "We do business here. I give you piece of commander's reward, yes? You get rich, I get richer, an enemy of the state is removed, and your girls stay . . ." The bat lifted the skirt, then tore it away. ". . . Charming. *Parakolutheô?*"

A commotion upstairs caught his attention and he drew his

pistol. The soldiers with him cocked their weapons and looked nervously at the stairway. An almost endless moment later the bodies of the two soldiers who had been sent upstairs came rolling down.

Blood still spurting from gaping wounds in their throats.

"Attention!" the lieutenant ordered. But it wasn't necessary. His men couldn't have been more aware of the gore and threat in front of them if they'd tried.

It came from two weeks of "hunting the Devil."

"Attention," the tense man called out in Greek. "This is Lieutenant Kazamakis of the Cypriot Provisional Guard. You will immediately surrender all weapons and slowly come down the stairs, hands above your head."

No answer.

Knowing what his men did not, he repeated the order, in English this time.

"Yeah, right," came the slow atonal reply.

The soldiers shivered at the lack of humanity in that voice. Some overturned tables or moved into the cover of doorways. Others crossed themselves and prepared to die.

"If you do not surrender immediately, we will be forced to come up and get you," the lieutenant said with less strength than he would have liked.

"The stairs are in front of you. Come ahead." A pause that seemed to last many lifetimes. "I'm waiting."

"Spiros, Hector! *Ketagatay kati!*"

But the men the lieutenant had ordered forward just looked at each other, looked at their friends' bodies in the stairwell, then slowly shook their heads.

Before a reprimand could be issued, new orders contemplated or screamed out, a new sound filled the room.

Heavy footsteps coming *down* the stairs.

The lieutenant grabbed the old woman, holding her in front of him as a shield. Men crouched, lay flat, their fingers pressing on the triggers with ninety percent of the force necessary to fill the air between them and the stairway with a solid wall of lead.

"Don't die for this, boys," Xenos's voice called out from very near the bottom of the stairs. *"Tota esos na say afisso na zis."*

One of the soldiers near the back of the taverna dropped his weapon as he ran out the door. *"E zoe enai glikeah!"*

"Open fire!" the lieutenant screamed, and the air was shattered by the remaining seven AR-15s emptying their clips into the wall by the stairway.

After ten seconds of violent noise, a silence filtered into the place. No one moved. No one spoke. Everyone prayed that it was over.

Silently the lieutenant ordered two men forward to check it out. When they hesitated, he carefully aimed his pistol at them and gestured again. With more caution than any of the others had ever seen before, the two men reluctantly crept forward, into the stairwell.

Less than a minute later they returned, carrying an empty pair of climbing boots and a small cassette recorder.

"I'm still waiting," Xenos's voice said calmly from the tape player.

"Shit," the lieutenant muttered, a moment before he felt the cold steel of Xenos's knife pressed against the base of his skull from behind.

The men gasped at the man in stocking feet who held the knife to their officer's head and pointed a gaping .44 Magnum at the rest of them.

"Order them to drop their weapons or you die first," Xenos said in a voice very much like the devil's, the lieutenant thought in an instant.

"English no good," the lieutenant stammered out in an attempt to buy time and think of something.

Xenos smiled spasmodically. "You understand well enough."

The lieutenant was trembling so hard that he was almost impaling himself on the rock-steady knife. He instantly issued the order. "Do it for God's sake!"

Most of the men did as they were told.

Two didn't.

"Release lieutenant," one of the last yelled out, "or we kill you and others!" He leveled his rifle at Xenos.

Xenos looked almost sympathetically toward the young, cleanest cut of the soldiers. "Don't die, boy. Not for him. Not over this. This has nothing to do with you. *Tota esos na say afisso na zis.*"

For thirty seconds the standoff held, then the young soldier's finger began to tighten on the trigger.

The shot that exploded through the room lifted the soldier into the air, slamming him into the wall; his life created an abstract on the clay as he slid to the floor, already dead.

"Dumb," Xenos whispered as the last armed soldier threw his guns across the room.

"Dureté!"

Xenos whirled around, almost pushing his gun into the face of an old man, who instantly paled. But the younger man who had called out the name was standing behind and to the side of the first man.

"You going to shoot everyone today?" He laughed. "Or just your old friend?"

"You ain't that good a friend, Franco."

The young man laughed again. "You got that many in this room you can be so picky?"

Xenos shrugged as he lowered his gun, and allowed the old man—the taverna owner—and his sons, who were waiting outside, to round up the surviving soldiers and lock them in the cellar.

"What are you doing here, Franco?" Xenos asked as he poured himself a glass of goat's milk five minutes later.

The young Corsican sniffed at the pitcher, turned up his nose, then grabbed a nearby bottle of ouzo. "You know this is a safe haven for my group." He took a deep drink of the acidic wine. "Just walking the property, like you Americans say."

"No."

"I haven't asked you anything yet."

Xenos turned to the bar's mirror to study Franco's reflection. "The answer's still no."

"There's no trust left in the world, Dureté. No trust." He stepped out of the way as one of the soldiers with his throat cut was dragged out of the taverna. "Something I should know about?"

"I thought you knew everything."

"So did I."

They drank in silence for a few minutes as the room was cleaned of all traces of the short-lived battle. The wall and floor were being scrubbed, fresh clay applied to the walls, tablecloths torn for gags.

"Okay," Franco finally said. "I heard *some* things."

Xenos just poured himself another glass of milk.

Franco studied the man he'd known for ten years, but knew almost nothing about. "Like I know that half the fucking Cypriot Army is looking to exterminate Xenos. And that the local Greek militia has orders to stay out of it." He raised his eyebrows. "I must admit, that did pique my interest."

"I killed the Cypriot commander's son," Xenos said simply.

"Yeah, I heard that too." The briefest of pauses. "Any particular reason? If it can be told, of course."

Xenos took his gun from the bar and slid it into its holster. "How long can you hold these guys?"

"How long do you need?"

A deep sigh. "The son, and some of his friends, were running charters for college kids in the islands. Then stranding them here on Naxos, robbing and torturing the men, raping and sodomizing the women. Shooting videos of it and selling it to other tourists."

"So?" Franco seemed completely unaffected, almost bored.

"I found their last charter. Including a nineteen-year-old girl who died naked and bloody in my arms."

Franco looked into his associate's eyes. "I can hold them as long as it takes to get you off this rock." He smiled broadly. "Of course there's going to be a price, *amico mio.*"

Xenos put his knife in his boot, threw his last roll of bills on the bar, then started for the door. "No, *grazie.* I can take care of myself."

Franco roared with laughter. "Of that there is little doubt!"

He put a hand on the bigger man's shoulder. "But let me do this for you. It'll make it easier for me to ask you for my favor."

Xenos shook his head. "I thought I already said no."

"There are all *sorts* of no's." He followed Xenos out onto the predawn street. "And the job is in New York. Don't you have family in New York?"

Xenos stopped, with his back to the Corsican. "I don't have any family," he almost whispered, his dream gnawing at his consciousness. "In New York or anywhere else." He started off.

Franco watched him for a few seconds. "But *I* do, Dureté! I came to this Godforsaken rock because of this. To find you! You can at least hear me out. You owe the Brotherhood that much." He immediately regretted saying it.

Xenos turned around, slowly walking back to Franco. His face a frozen nothing mask. A soulless, blank evil.

"Io non devo niente a nessuno! Capito?" His voice was hoarse, choked with violence and black possibilities. "I owe no one a *fucking thing.* Not anyone."

But Franco never backed down, never took a backward step.

"You owe us at least the courtesy of listening." He paused. "For that we will guarantee your safety off this island and back to Toulon."

Xenos thought about it. The hills of Naxos were impassable and crowded with blind canyons, caves, and ancient labyrinths. He could easily avoid the army until calmer heads prevailed and the pressure came off.

But how many more young soldiers with an overdeveloped sense of duty would he have to kill between then and now?

"You have a car, Franco? Or we going to have to walk?"

Franco nodded slightly in silent understanding, then held up his hand. A minute later a windowless panel van rattled to a stop. "Do I *ever* walk, *amico mio?*"

Five minutes later, after giving explicit instructions to the taverna owner and assuring him of his group's protection against reprisals, Franco climbed into the van beside Xenos.

"I got a boat at Mikolas."

Eighteen hours later, under cover of darkness, Xenos Filotimo sneaked aboard the fishing smack *Orphelin* and, with the tide, escaped into the warm waters of the Mediterranean for the long voyage to the French port of Toulon.

Once clear of the waters off Naxos, the big man stretched out on the foredeck, his backpack as a pillow, and closed his eyes.

But he didn't allow himself to sleep.

The streets of Georgetown were about as different from the Greek islands as possible. The first frost of the year clung to the barren trees and bushes; the grass on the rolling hills was browning up, and people frowned with the sure and certain knowledge that winter was in offing.

But the streets of the Washington, D.C., suburb were no less dangerous than those outside the taverna.

The two people saw each other at a distance, walking diagonally toward each other on two of the quaint paths that bordered the university. They both adjusted their pace to ensure coming together at the right point at the right instant. As they both did their sums in their heads.

Do I recognize any faces or cars?

Does anything appear different from how it should be?

Any windows open, exhaust coming from parked vans, workmen on power poles?

Any reason at all to walk on by?!

As they came to the intersection of their paths, the older of the two checked the time. The younger yawned. A moment later they fell into step alongside each other as they began to meander through the carefully manicured university paths.

"Do you need to come in?" the older asked.

"No," the younger replied. "I'm clean."

"Do you need to deliver anything?"

"No."

"Are you intact?"

The younger one hesitated before answering. "That's what I'm here to find out." The voice was brittle; scared but under tight control.

"Are you intact?" the older one repeated, insisting that this rendezvous go by the numbers, as had countless clandestine meetings before.

Sighing, the younger replied, "I've detected no changes in the flow across my desk, in my assignments. My phone was clean as of 0930 today, and I've detected no surveillance."

"Very well."

They turned into a darker corner of the grounds, to a narrow strip of grass that wound between two buildings.

"So," the younger one began without further explanation, "am I intact?"

The older one shrugged. "We believe so."

"Thank God."

The older one smiled. "God and *Canvas*."

"Sure." The younger one stopped for a moment.

"Is something wrong?"

"I don't trust him. Where he is, what he's doing for us; he could make us all very, uh, exposed."

"The cost of doing business, I'm afraid," the older one said simply. "But Canvas's loyalty is based on money, and we cannot be outbid for his services, rest assured of that."

"He knows a lot."

A shrug from the older one. "A necessary evil. Canvas is a consummate professional and must have access to all sorts of information in order to do his part in this."

A long silence.

"Does he know me?" The younger one's voice rose with anxiety.

The older one smiled reassuringly. "He no more knows you than he knows anyone with whom he is not *directly* involved. He has detailed information only as far as his specific assignment goes and no further." The smile vanished. "In any event, the knowledge he does have dies with him at the end of the operation."

"And when is that?"

Now the older one sounded tense. Barely. "Access is not what we had hoped for, there has been *resistance* to the suggestions. But we hope that the affair can be concluded within six months." The briefest of pauses. "A year at the most."

"A year's a long Goddamned time," the younger one whispered as a student moved past on a bicycle. "And it's been getting worse since the, uh, *thing*."

The older one nodded in agreement. "The incident *was* unexpected. Unfortunate. It might've even been catastrophic, but Canvas performed admirably on that score." The older one smiled warmly. "I think we can return to the original timeline now."

"I'm not so convinced," the younger one said brusquely. "You only know them academically. I deal with them every day."

An expression of deep disquiet passed across the worried face. "They could just be laying low, waiting to be sure of what's what and who's who. These are vicious, cunning, unpredictable bastards and I am *not* about to put myself further at risk until you *know*! Not *think*!"

The older one sighed. "Well"—it was said in a carefree tone— "Canvas has removed our source's options. The psychs agree with his assessment; and I am content." A smile peeked out. "As long as we maintain our leverage, the source will continue to be most compliant. With that in our hands, we cannot be surprised."

"What about the French kid?"

"No longer an issue. He comes from nowhere, has no family, no ties in this country. Was a loner in his. No one will miss him. Canvas has been most thorough." A genuine laugh. "And I understand *you* have put certain other checks into place, just in case." A light laugh. "Pure overkill. No one will come looking."

The younger one nodded. "You're too damned pleased with yourself."

"I see the big picture, and the pieces falling into place," the older one said simply. "I'm not *pleased*"—he wheezed out the word—"just confident and encouraged."

"You be confident and encouraged. Me? I'll stay paranoid. And we'll see which of us is left standing."

They continued on, just two more people speaking in quiet abstracts in a city that thrived on them.

.   .   .

Xenos hated abstracts.

Oh, he could think in them, analyze them fairly effortlessly, extrapolate almost infinite conclusions from their colors and shapes. But he had lived in the abstract for too many years, and now longed for solid, immutable definition instead.

Which was largely why he had chosen Toulon as his second home.

The old French naval station, the harbor that sheltered over half of the Mediterranean's smugglers, the modern city built along the edges of the old city, all masked the rock-solid heart of the French town.

Like Naxos, Toulon was carved from the mountains that surrounded the harbor. It could be tough, unyielding, attacking. It required its residents to be equally hard in return. Strong men and women who made their own rules, then lived strictly by them.

And the heart of this stubborn, bullheaded, unyielding population was the fifteen hundred members of the Corsican community.

That they ran the harbor and the bulk of the city beyond was a given. That the token forces of French Naval Shore Patrol, Metropolitan cops, and GIGN thugs would deal only with the non-Corsican community was also a given. Payoffs were made, penetrations were made, *arrangements* were made. And the Brotherhood—that most violent, most feared, most insular organized crime group in Europe—ran the Corsicans.

From his earliest days in Toulon, Xenos—known to them as Dureté ("the hard man")—had known the rules and had made his own arrangements with the Brotherhood. He would leave them alone, not interfere with any operations or plans, would assist them in those things that they needed a non-Corsican for (they had checked out the tough man's virulent reputation . . . then apologized for the intrusion).

In exchange they would lend their protection to a small farm on the cliffs above the city.

The Clinic of the Broken Children.

In its forty-five beds lay the shattered remnants of fifteen years of war in Afghanistan. Boys and girls—none over twelve—missing arms, legs; blinded or deafened; massacred all.

How they found their way from the mountain passes (where they would've died) to the small clinic on the French Gold Coast (where their destroyed bodies and minds would be healed) was never explained or inquired into. Simply accepted as the right of a man whom the Brotherhood considered completely trustworthy in a deal or a fight.

And it would be watched over during his long absences.

But now, as he stood on the edge of the cliff looking out at the crystal-blue Med, Xenos wondered—not for the first time—what would happen to the clinic if he ever failed to come back. Breathing in the salty, slightly fishy air, he forced the thought away from the present and turned back to Franco.

"Answer's still no."

Franco shook his head sadly. "He's a good boy, Dureté. Sharp as a tack and also bright. It's not like him. *Capito?* He's going to be a big Chaillot attorney one day. Or maybe on Wall Street in America. He's not in the rackets. Boring, squeaky-clean."

He laughed a forced, somehow painful laugh. "Hell, he even took another name and life so my Brothers and my reputation wouldn't hold him back."

"I'm not a family counselor. If he doesn't want to talk to you . . ."

"It's more than that, I'm telling you. He's not the kind to run off. Not for pussy, not for money, no way! And no one's seen him in a week."

Xenos shook his head. "Go yourself."

"You know I can't. No member of the Brotherhood is safe in New York without permission from the Mafia's Commission. And to get that, I'd have to tell them about Paolo. They'd never believe he wasn't in the rackets. It could start another war."

"Jerry!" a small girl squealed in delight as she came limping up. "Jerry! *Regardez moi!*"

Xenos turned as the little girl displayed her brand-new artificial arm to him. With a pride and dedication that only the small can have, she opened and closed the metal hand, even pulled a cigar out of Xenos's shirt pocket when he kneeled to hug her.

"*Merveilleux*, Gabi. *Superbe*." He kissed her on the cheek. "How are you today, fair lady?" he asked in slow, deliberate English.

She concentrated hard. "I am well . . . *monsieur*."

"Sir," he corrected gently.

She nodded fiercely. "I am well, *sir*. How are *you* today?"

"Very well." He kissed her again as a clinic sister came up to shepherd her back to the group playing on the lawn. He took an envelope from the nurse as he watched the little girl go.

"X-ray machine's breaking down again," he mumbled as he read. "That's another fifteen grand, easy."

Franco suddenly brightened, stood, walking over to Xenos, reading over his shoulder. "And I noticed that the ward is over-crowded."

Xenos nodded. "They just keep coming. No end to it. No end." He started to walk away, then stopped. "What are you offering?"

Franco smiled his convincingly sincere smile. "A new, state-of-the-art X-ray machine and a new ward . . . say twenty beds."

"Forty-five beds."

Franco nodded. "I misspoke. A new *forty-five*-bed ward."

Xenos looked at the man suspiciously. "You don't have those kinds of resources."

"The Brotherhood does; and will stand behind my pledge."

Xenos walked very close to the man. "What aren't you telling me?"

There was no point in lying any more, and Franco played his last card. "*Mio fratello* he is, shall we say, a *project* of the Brotherhood. They sponsored his college entirely. Over six hundred thousand francs."

Xenos suddenly understood. "And they're making you responsible."

Franco grimaced as he nodded. "Paolo repays the Brotherhood with services after he is become a lawyer. Or I must, well . . ."

"And if I find he's run off with the money?"

"Then it is between us. *I Fratelli*. But," Franco hurriedly added, "the Brotherhood does not believe he has stolen from them. Their concern is for his safety in a city like New York."

"For the moment," Xenos finished.

"They feel you can be trusted to find and return the money," Franco said, ignoring the comment, "if the worst has happened. Or to help Paolo if he has gotten into some kind of trouble." He shrugged deeply. "He is my brother, Dureté. I would go if I could, but that would only cause more troubles." He hesitated. "My family. Do it for family."

Xenos walked to the cliff's edge, looking out at the storm clouds building across the calm Mediterranean waters. "There might be some problem with my getting into the U.S. I'm not real popular over there." He shook his head at the clouds. "In a lot of places."

Franco walked over, smiling. "If there is one thing the Brotherhood knows how to do, it is getting things into and out of places."

Less than twenty-four hours later Xenos Filotimo drove across the New York/Canadian border.

For family.

Two

It was New York.

Loud, run-down, alive. People jammed the sidewalk five abreast, seemingly unaware of the people around them. It was dirty and proud, private and loud, unforgiving and compassionate beyond measure.

It was New York, and Xenos loved every inch of it.

Although he hadn't set foot there in a decade, it was the one constant in his world, a place that wouldn't change no matter what. And he easily found his way to the student apartments outside of Columbia University.

The street was filled with the odd mix of working poor, welfare caste, and enthused college students that you might expect for one of the world's great universities that was located on the border of one of America's great slums. So, amidst the coloration of so many, he had no problem slipping into the building.

Phone calls from his hotel had provided little more than he had been told in Toulon.

Paolo DiBenetti (known to the college as Paul Satordi) had been a good student, an activist in the university social scene, with a job as a bellman at a midtown hotel on weekends. He also did some freelance research through the university's Alumni Association.

And he had not been seen on campus or at his jobs since two days after his return from spring break.

That he *had* returned was witnessed by an occasional girl-friend, people at the hotel he worked at, by his work contact at the Alumni Association.

But that had all been preliminary to this visit to the boy's apartment.

Xenos casually strolled through the building's dark corridors, smiling through his own college memories at doors with obscene or amusing signs posted on them. *No entry without pizza! Naked girls only need apply.* And *Don't fuck with me; I'm a seminary student!* People passed him, paying no attention to the man with the backpack and the casual air. It was a building of interchangeable students, transients, and constant changes that went unnoticed.

Everything seemed more than ordinary enough.

At the door to Paolo's apartment, for the first time Xenos tensed. A nosy neighbor, curious friend, or wandering security (minimum-waged, unarmed) could vastly complicate things. But the boy had chosen a room at the far end of a dark corridor, near the fire escape, with no apartment directly in line with the front door, on the hot or cold side of the building, depending on the time of year.

In classic Corsican style, it was a place that few would just wander by.

Although he had a key supplied by Franco, Xenos took his time outside the door . . . studying.

It was typically worn pressboard, probably hollow, showing hundreds of routine scratches and nicks. The knob was slightly discolored brass-metal, with scratches around the keyhole. The dead bolt was much the same.

For more than a minute Xenos studied that door, the frame, the wall around it, his mind clicking into analysis mode without being asked.

Something was wrong here, and his instincts wouldn't let him move until he knew what it was.

He closed his eyes, pictured the door that was only inches away, tried to break it down into individual components and constructs; tried to see inwardly what he couldn't see with his eyes.

Fire escape.

The window at the end of the corridor with the fire escape had no coverings of any kind. The wall on the apartment side showed the effects of thirty-plus years of direct sunlight eight months a year. And the sun shone equally brightly on the door.

Which was still dark, not dried out, fresh despite the superficial signs of wear and tear.

For the next twenty minutes Xenos checked the ends of all the other corridors of the building that corresponded to Paolo's end of the building. All the doors were faded and dry.

Paolo's door had recently been replaced.

Returning to the apartment, he pulled a small set of what looked like opera glasses (that oddly came together at a point in the front) from his pack. Checking to be sure he was alone, he pressed them up against the one-way peephole installed in the door. The prism-reversal imaging system (developed by the United States Secret Service) allowed him to reverse the qualities of the peephole's optics and get a fish-eye look into the apartment.

It seemed empty.

After carefully looking over the entire perimeter of the door, and not wanting to take the time and have the visibility that running an ion meter over the door frame would involve, he was convinced the door was unalarmed. Using the key, he let himself in.

"Six-eight."

"Go."

"We have a shake at target."

"Specify."

"Single individual. White male, forties. Baggy clothes, Yankee cap, shades, backpack."

"Will relay. Tag Indigo One. Continue observation."

"Six-eight."

The place *was* empty. As empty as an apartment could possibly be. No furniture, curtains, carpet, possessions of any kind. No marks on the floor where furniture might've been. No stains, dirt, cobwebs, nothing. As devoid of identity as any place had ever been. As he moved through the living room, kitchen, and one bedroom, Xenos's sense of *wrong* dramatically increased.

Even new homes, freshly built and never occupied, were less empty.

Xenos had personally emptied enough places over the years in precisely the same way to understand the message behind it. Someone—maybe Paolo, maybe not—wanted nothing left behind that could trace him or give hints of what had happened.

And there *was* the door.

Maybe the kid *had* run off with the money, and knowing that the Corsicans would send someone after him, was taking no chances. That was the simple answer, but Xenos hated simple answers.

So he continued to wander the small rooms.

He pulled out a small camcorder and began to video the room, the view from each of the three windows. He opened the traps on the drains and bagged the small amount of sludge he could scrape from the almost clean pipes. Moved the shut-off refrigerator, tested the floorboards for hollows, leaned out the window and checked the outside of the building around it.

Nothing of note.

Finally he reached into his backpack and pulled out a lineman's test phone, plugging it into the phone socket.

Surprisingly he got a dial tone.

"That's not right," he mumbled as he unplugged the phone, and plugged in a palm-sized—less than half-inch-thick—plastic box with an LCD readout. "Not right." He pressed some buttons on the box, then watched the display.

212–473–3749

"Why go to all this trouble and leave the Goddamned phone . . ." He pressed a different sequence of buttons.

96.3265%

Xenos smiled without realizing it. He began to enter another sequence. "Now, what's drawing off less than four percent of your natural impedance, little fellow?"

Tracer Line Confirmed

The smile remained frozen as he began to enter a final, longer sequence. Then he quickly gathered his equipment and left the apartment.

"Six-eight."
"Go."
"Indigo One on the move."
"Seven-one will pick up Indigo One on exit."
"Six-eight."

It would take several hours for his invisible electronic hunter to follow the signs, cut its way through the digital brush, and locate the receiver on the other end of that tracer line. Hours during which little else could be done. So Xenos found himself driving randomly through the early afternoon traffic; allowing the car to find its way as his mind floated over the problem.

Franco had no reason to lie, so Paolo wasn't involved in the rackets. But he still might have picked up—over the years—the skills of disappearing and covering his tracks. It was a natural thing for someone that close to the Brotherhood.

But it didn't feel right.

The young Corsican masquerading as a French student might have been uncovered by the local Mafia, kidnapped and killed as yet another chapter in that two-hundred-year-old feud. But the Mafia had never been known to professionally clear a victim's apartment.

And there was the door.

And there was the tap.

Only a professional, someone very good, would've thought to replace a door that had been kicked in or forced. The doors in the building were flimsy at best, easily manhandled. But would just as easily show the violence done to them.

Maintaining a tracer tap on a line that had no phone or modem attached was also a pro's touch.

Take someone by force or guile, expunge all physical evidence, then leave an active tap in place. Not to listen to calls that could never be placed, but to determine who might be calling the young student. And, by extrapolation, who might be looking for him.

It was a thing Xenos might've done, *had done,* in his not-distant-enough past.

He pulled out of the Brooklyn–Battery Tunnel shaking his head.

"There's got to be another answer," he mumbled as he looked around. "Got to be."

Ten minutes later he pulled to a stop on Linwood Avenue, convincing himself that he was looking for conspiracies out of habit, not evidence. Paolo DiBenetti was born to the Brotherhood, whether he was an active member or not. He was a law student at one of the top law schools in the world, so he was not only intelligent but sharp. He *could* have thought it through as part of an elaborate scheme to steal the nearly $100,000 the Brotherhood had given him for his education.

Xenos wanted to believe that, desperately! It would've removed all pressures, made the job easier. It would've allowed him to avoid that part of his personality—which he'd exiled to a tightly bound place within himself—to stay tautly under control. For him to maintain at least the counterfeit peace that he'd so barely established in the last years.

But instinct and experience make for impassable arguments and waking nightmares of the bad old days.

Getting out of the car, he put aside the contradictions, the questions, looked around, then sighed.

He hadn't intended to come here, in fact had promised himself he wouldn't. But he wasn't all that surprised that he'd ended up in front of the old apartments built above the storefronts.

Pulling his cap down low over his large sunglasses, he started down the street.

As a black Lincoln pulled to a stop a half-block back, the passenger snapping pictures of him through a telephoto lens.

"I'll be right with you," the teenage boy behind the counter said as he finished with some paperwork.

The small printing shop was largely empty. An old man was copying a Lost Cat poster on the Xerox machine; an overnight courier was emptying the drop-off box. Somewhere behind the thin partition that separated the lobby from the shop, a heavy press could be heard running, and the smell of warm ink and toner filled the place.

"What can I do for you?" The boy was seventeen, maybe older, and smiled a familial smile.

"I'm looking for Sarah Goldman."

The boy looked mildly curious. "This about an order?"

"It's personal."

"Got a name?"

"Filotimo."

The boy looked him over carefully, then hesitantly stepped behind the partition. *After* locking the cash register. A minute later a woman in her mid-thirties in jeans and a sweatshirt came out.

"You wanted to see me?"

He took off the sunglasses.

She froze. "My God," she whispered. "My God." Sarah quickly looked around, not frightened . . . *careful*, then gestured toward the street. "I'll be back in a few minutes, Bradley." She followed Xenos out before the boy could form the obvious question.

They walked together silently for half a block, Sarah openly staring at Xenos, shaking her head but saying nothing.

"Is it safe for you here?" she finally asked.

Xenos shrugged. "There is no *safe*."

"Jesus," she mumbled. "Jesus."

They turned into a small park, walking over to the swings, where some small children were playing.

"If this creates a problem for you," Xenos said after another awkward moment, "I'll leave."

"No!" Sarah almost yelled in a panic.

Xenos smiled, looked around, took off his shades and cap, and held his arms wide. A moment later he held her tight against him in a hug he hoped would never end.

"Twelve years is too Goddamned long, big brother." Sarah weeped as she kissed him. "Where you been, huh?"

Xenos hesitated, then indicated a nearby bench. "Don't ask questions like that." He smiled bitterly.

"Dope," she said with an equally large grin.

"Princess," he shot back, trying to ape her human emotion and warmth.

She stroked his face. "I have so much I want to ask, need to say."

"Later."

She looked doubtful. "Will there be a later?" There was the slightest hint of accusation in her tone.

"I'll try."

For the next ten minutes Sarah talked of her life, her son, her ex-husband, all the meaningless things that she could think to avoid the thing that was always there on the rare moments that they saw each other.

Xenos feigned interest, responded with generalities about the Greek islands, France, with no specifics intended or asked for.

Finally, painfully, the inevitable lay before them.

"Will he see me?"

"He hasn't changed," she said glumly. "And I'd bet my last dime—if I had a dime to bet—that you haven't either."

Xenos concentrated on the street. "You might be surprised." His look turned solemn. "I really need him to see me."

"Jerry"—she took his callused hand in hers—"it's sixteen years."

The big man moved his mouth, nothing came out. Then a deep breath. "Seventeen. I just need him to see me, to talk to me." His eyes followed a cable TV truck as it slowly moved past.

"Why now?"

And his nightmare demanded attention. "I, well, he's getting old. I can't let him go before I . . ."

Sarah hugged him. "I'll try, Jerry. That's all I can do, you know?"

"Yeah."

They started walking back to the shop.

"So where can I reach you?"

"I'll call you when I can."

Sarah laughed bitterly. "I know what that means."

He thought for a moment. Analysis: she needs something, some *human* reaction to reassure her that everything's going to be all right. A simple, distinct gesture of reassurance.

"Always remember," the instructor had droned on, "that simple eye contact is one of the most powerful tools in the perfect lie. Combined with intimate, nonsexual physical contact, it defeats all doubts and suspicions. Assuming your tone is reflective of the act."

He looked at the one student in the room. "Goldman! Demonstrate!"

Jerry got up, walked to the front of the room, then turned to the instructor. "Uh, what do you want me to . . ."

"Lie to me."

"Big lie," Herb called out from the back of the otherwise empty classroom, where he and five other instructors were watching.

The young man turned to the instructor, nodded, then smiled. A thing that exploded across his face and out of his eyes.

"God, I love these classes!" He reached up, stroked the instructor's cheek as his voice dropped low and sincere. "Seriously, I love them."

Herb applauded. "Good. Be a little less forceful, though, and don't repeat yourself, son." He winced at the thought. "Repetition reeks of falsity."

The boy nodded, then turned back to his instructor.

Xenos took Sarah's chin in his hand, lifted her tearing eyes to look into his, then softly stroked her cheek. "It means, I'll call."

Another kiss, a rib-rattling hug, and he was gone.

Sarah Goldman watched her older brother, the idol of her early years, walk down the street, wave, then get into his car. Wondering all the time if this time, for the first time, he would stay long enough to help repair their shattered family. Silently crying, she watched him start the car and drive off.

Not noticing the black Lincoln pull out behind him.

. . .

"Where'd he go? Where'd he go?"

"I don't see him. But relax. In this traffic he's probably as stuck as we are."

The two men in the black Lincoln stared through their windshields at the ocean of yellow cabs and town cars that surrounded them. They'd followed Xenos back into Manhattan, through Columbus Circle into midtown. But now, in the late afternoon traffic, they were separated from their target.

"I'm getting out." The passenger opened his door and hurried up Fifty-third Street, scanning the traffic as he went. Suddenly he saw Xenos's car double-parked across the street. He dodged the barely moving traffic, crossing over to examine the empty car.

"Shit!" He looked all around, then started as he recognized Indigo One casually walking down an alley. He pulled out his cell phone and hurried behind.

"Seven-one."

"He's headed across to Fifty-fourth."

"Stay on him. I'll swing around and pick you up when I can. Report back every five minutes."

"Yeah, yeah!" He shut the phone and continued on. But when he looked up again, Xenos had disappeared. "Shit!"

The man ran down the alley, desperate to get to the Fifty-fourth Street side in time to see where his target had gone. Ten feet from the alley's exit, he was suddenly pulled from his feet and slammed into the side of a Dumpster.

Then an iron hand grabbed him by the neck and smashed his face into a brick wall.

"I don't know you, friend," Xenos said coldly as he shoved the broken, bleeding man behind the Dumpster. "But I'm going to."

Twenty minutes later, as the driver slowly cruised Fifty-fourth Street between Seventh and Eighth Avenues for the third time, cursing the traffic, his partner, and anything else he could think of, he dialed a number on his cell phone.

"Yes?"

"Seven-one, I think we have a problem."

"You do," Xenos said to himself in the next car back as he listened on earphones attached to a small parabolic microphone mounted on the dashboard. "You most definitely do."

It took the better part of an hour for the driver of seven-one to make his way across Manhattan and into Queens. He finally pulled into a key-entry subterranean garage in a sixteen-story office building. Xenos parked across the street at a hamburger stand, bought a burger, and sat, watching the building.

It seemed ordinary enough. Doorman, concierge desk just inside the lobby. Gold-tinted, shaded windows. Usual aerials on top. But there was little traffic in and out of the building, no cars or cabs pulled up, and uniformed, armed security guards patrolled the exterior, seemingly on a fifteen-to-twenty-minute orbit around the building's perimeter.

Ten minutes after they'd arrived, the car and driver he'd followed from Fifty-fourth Street pulled out of the garage. But Xenos never moved. The man in the alley—most likely now in the emergency room of a hospital—had merely been a surveillance agent. Who for and why, he didn't know, would definitely have told if he had.

So Xenos had followed the man's partner, assuming something as important as an operative's disappearance would have to be reported in person. Xenos was now interested in the building, *not* the other man.

"Big Goddamned haystack," he mumbled as he plugged a cell phone into a laptop. He quickly brought up the program he needed, then prepared to speed-dial Paolo's apartment. If his electronic hunter had worked, the laptop would dial in, retrieve the data, then activate an electronic bullet that would fry the circuits of whoever was listening.

If it didn't work, well, he'd probably change hotels anyway.

He pressed the enter button on the phone and laptop simultaneously, then watched the display.

Connecting
Connected

Retrieving data
Shot fired
Connection terminated.
Working . . .
Tracer tone activated at 1437:39
Tracer killed at 1437:58

Xenos smiled spasmodically. Somewhere, someone was going to be real pissed. If they didn't need a doctor for the blood coming out of their ears when his cybernetic sniper sent a 500 dB shrill squeal through the phone line before destroying the circuitry of any listening device on the line, then they sure as Hell would need a new tracer.

He waited patiently while the slow laptop processed the information it had retrieved from the device in Paolo's apartment.

40°45.57′ N
73°49.90′ W
135′

It took less than a minute for the tracking program to plot the coordinates and display it on a map.

13520 39th Ave
Flushing, Queens, NY

The building Xenos was watching.

Somewhere on the tenth, eleventh, or twelfth floor of the building was the location of the tracing device.

Ten minutes later, after parking his car behind a deserted car wash, he casually crossed the street.

Valerie Alvarez also watched the building. Sitting in her car a half-block down, she stared up at the eleventh floor and sweated. She knew what was going to happen, and knew there was nothing she could do about it.

Now.

But if there was a God—and she was long past blind acceptance of that fact—there would come a time, a place, a moment when she could release the pent-up anger, frustrations, and animal fury that she held so tightly checked.

And then . . . God (if he existed) help them! Because there were two things Valerie knew well. One was people.

And the other . . . getting even!

A sigh then a check of her watch. Five minutes to three. Time to go.

She dropped the car in gear and drove to the building's garage intercom. She pressed the numbers and waited.

"Yes?"

"Hyacinth," she said in as strong a voice as she could muster. The next few hours would not be pleasant. They would be filled with psychic pain, humiliation, and bone-crushing fear. But she'd be damned if she'd let *them* know it.

"Pull up by the elevators, level six. You'll be met."

The gate rolled up and she drove in.

Four men were standing by the elevator banks on the bottom level of the garage. Three she'd never seen before; but then *they* seemed to have almost unlimited personnel. The other she knew too well.

She got out of her car, leaving the door open and the engine running, as she knew would be expected.

"Congresswoman," the fourth man said politely.

"Smith."

They stood there for five minutes while two of the men covered every inch of her car. They searched, probed, used monitors of some kind, as they examined it all. Finally they were done. One of the men got in and drove away, while the other returned to them.

Smith walked to the end elevator, punched in a code on a keypad, then motioned her in as the doors opened. The four of them rode up one and a half flights, then the elevator was stopped.

"I believe you know the procedure, Ms. Alvarez."

She took a deep breath, stared daggers at Smith, then spread her legs shoulder width apart and held her arms out to her sides.

While two of the men began to strip her—examining her clothes closely as they went—she never blinked or reacted in any way, except by maintaining the icy stare.

"Lovely, as always," Smith said politely as he was handed her bra.

"Go to Hell."

Smith smiled. "Perhaps, one day. Perhaps after you take me to Heaven?"

She simply stared on.

Valerie ignored the leers, the lingering gropes, the mumbled comments as the men finished their thorough search of her. Then she dressed quickly as the elevator restarted.

"Have you been working out, Congresswoman?" Smith smiled.

"Felt like it," one of the men whispered to another.

Valerie turned toward him. "Get a life or an inflatable girl-friend, asshole," she snapped out. Then she turned back to Smith. "You've had your show. Now give me mine!"

"Making demands?"

She took a step toward Smith. "I don't say another word—to anyone—until I see it," she said in low tones.

If the notion hadn't been so absurd, Smith thought Valerie might be ready to tear out his throat with her teeth. He slowly reached into an inside pocket and pulled out a photograph.

"You'll recognize today's *Times* headline," he said as she took it from him.

She studied the picture, her expression softening as she looked at the small frightened faces, at the huge bruise on the boy, at the all-too-recognizable pain in the girl's eyes.

"Bastards," she mumbled.

The rest of the ride was accomplished in silence.

They trooped out on the eleventh floor and moved down the corridor to their left, Valerie never looking up from her photo.

None of them noticing a thin, blue-sheathed fiber-optic cable slide up and out of the elevator's ceiling.

· · ·

Crouching on top of the one private elevator in the building, Xenos ignored the whirring of gears and cables rushing by. He sat there calmly, riding up and down several times without realizing it. His body might be trapped by the confines of the elevator shaft, but his mind was elsewhere, wandering through the more-complex-by-the-moment problem. Reviewing what had happened. Analyzing, interpreting.

Planning.

The doorman and concierge might have been easy marks, might have been people of high integrity. He'd never bothered to find out. But a security guard—now lying handcuffed and unconscious in some landscaping by the side of the building—had been another issue.

The man was more than run-of-the-mill minimum-waged security. He'd been sharp, obviously trained, carrying a backup piece on his ankle and cell phone in place of a radio. But men like that were anachronistic to Xenos; dinosaurs trained to think and react with one-dimensional thinking.

And Xenos lived in a *three*-dimensional world.

The man's uniform had been a close enough fit, and his keys easily interpreted. Xenos had let himself in through a garage fire door, then made his way to the lobby by a back hall. Pulling his hat low against the closed-circuit cameras that seemed to be everywhere, he casually waited for the first up elevator, then pressed the buttons for floors nine through fourteen. Noticing that eleven wasn't listed on this elevator's control panel.

He left the elevator between the seventh and eight floors.

Jumping from elevator to elevator while in motion required not only timing but luck. Like moving through a maze, he waited to leap lightly from his *up* to the next *down*. To the next up. Finally landing crouched and ready for detection and flight on the secured elevator.

From on top he could easily see the camera installation that monitored the inside of the car, so he never considered getting in. Just rode up and down for fifteen minutes, waiting.

He knew that the guard would be missed at some point—with

no idea exactly when that would be. But the road led from the apartment to the tracer; from the tracer to the men, from the men to here.

Next stop, the eleventh floor.

He'd witnessed the humiliating search of the congresswoman. Had heard the words, noted the tensions. But he'd noted much besides.

The men—though vulgar and coarse—had restrained themselves to a large extent.

The man in charge—Xenos thought "Smith" as an alias showed a lack of imagination and he stored that fact away—was far from the casual air he exuded. He was a man under careful control, born from someone else's orders. A greeter and delivery-man—not a boss.

The congresswoman had stood up to the search with poise and controlled anger. She showed no resistance, cooperated when asked, but seemed less intimidated by the men than by some threat they held over her.

The way Smith had held the photograph, it was clear that he considered that threat to be an immutable trump card. Almost like the key to Fort Knox.

And from the behavior of all of them, this wasn't the first time the scene had played itself out.

Was playing itself out . . . on the eleventh floor.

He still didn't know the connection between what had happened and Paolo DeBenetti. Or even if there was one. The men and Alvarez might be part of some other mystery, nothing to do with Corsicans or missing students. Maybe someone had leaked. Hell, there were more than enough groups within the *community* that wanted him back in the fold.

Or dead.

It *was* very likely that word had leaked about his search for the boy. That old cells—hungry for an old familiar body—had merely set the tracer in place to find and locate the man on top of the elevator. Alvarez and their hold over her might even be peripheral or unconnected to an effort to bring him in or take him out.

Two disparate intelligence operations run out of the same head-quarters, having nothing to do with each other.

But coincidence and survival were uneasy lovers at best.

His decision made, he lightly grabbed the service ladder, allowed the elevator to slide out from beneath him, then eased into the crawlway above the eleventh floor.

If anything happened to him—and it usually did, he thought with bitter humor—any events during the next twenty-four hours in the private elevator would be captured by the video tap he'd installed in the elevator's camera cable. Captured and relayed to the VTR in his car. And if he didn't check in with his "safety"—a double-blind contact that the Corsicans had provided called Quattro Cani—the car would be privately lo-jacked, and the tape sent to Franco in Toulon.

What happened then, Xenos didn't care about. Because if it happened, it meant he'd be dead. The nightmare, the pain, the wandering finally over.

Overall, he thought, a not-wholly-undesired solution.

The smallish conference room was clean, designer-decorated, comfortable, but utilitarian. Alvarez sat on one side of the table, calmly going over some files, as three men sat across from her waiting patiently. It might have been a legislative conference or the reading of a will.

Smith stood in the corner, watching the scene, bored, his mind turning over the problems he had to deal with after this meeting was over. Nothing major, just the routine of being middle management in a sophisticated multinational operation.

"Congresswoman?" one of the men at the table prompted.

Valerie closed the file, then looked up. "It's mostly right. I think he called it the 'Apple Blossom colloid,' though. Not 'collaboration.'"

"You are prepared to attest that this is a fair and accurate representation of the statement made by Source 24601 to you on the twenty-third?"

She sighed. "I am."

"Then will you please write words to that effect on the bottom of the last page and then sign the document."

Valerie did as she was told, then sat back. "Is that it?"

One of the men smiled warmly. "I hardly think so. There's still the matter of Source 24601's movements in the hours between your meeting and his end."

"Goddammit! We've covered that three times before!" For the first time in the last two hours her anger had a voice. "I told you everything I know, gave you everything you want! For two God-damned weeks!" She slapped the tabletop hard enough to make the file bounce and Smith step forward.

Another of the men waved Smith back.

"We appreciate your cooperation, Congresswoman. And we understand your schedule conflicts. But we must be—"

"Cooperation?!" She jumped to her feet hard enough for her chair to topple backward. *"Mentirosos!* You're not getting another word until I get what you promised!"

Smith came up behind her, grabbing her shoulder, trying to force her down into another chair. Her elbow flashed back, pounding into the side of the man's head. He toppled backward as though he'd been shot.

Before he could regain his balance she grabbed his left arm, twisting it violently inward and back. His head smashed down onto the edge of the table, his mouth seeming to bite the wood as his arm painfully gave way from the pressure.

Smith's muffled scream filled the room as Valerie pulled his Glock 9mm from its shoulder holster, released him, then worked the slide. A moment later she was pointing it at the shocked men across the table.

The men from the elevator came rushing in, guns drawn, but froze when they saw their boss sprawled in a bloody heap across the table, and the gun unwaveringly moving from one of the men's heads to another.

"Put the gun down, bitch!" one of the elevator men screamed out.

Valerie ignored him, concentrating her aim on the center man across from her. "It's over," she said in low, deadly tones.

The man simply nodded seriously. "If you wish," in a slight German accent.

"Kill us," another said casually, "and it *will* end. We will be dead, and a moment later so will you."

"But go to your grave knowing this," the third added. "Your son—so young, so strong—will die in inconceivable pain over a long period of time. Your beautiful daughter"—he pulled a school picture of the young girl out of a file—"will be given over to men like Mr. Smith here. And when they are done with her—if she survives—her death will make your son's look pleasant."

The German-sounding man smiled. "Pull the trigger," he said in an almost inviting tone, "and take that with you to eternity."

For long seconds the gun remained steady, then slowly, almost painfully, it began to shake. She didn't resist as it was pulled from her hand.

"*Gusanos,*" she moaned as she was forced down onto the table beside Smith.

A woman came in, ignored the scene, handing a slip of paper to the center man, who put on his glasses to read it. "Get him out of here." He gestured at Smith as he began to read.

"Sir?" The gunman holding Valerie on the table looked uncertain.

The German-sounding man handed the note to one of the others as he accepted a new note from the woman courier.

"Congresswoman Alvarez," he said without looking up from his reading. "Normally I would allow this—this outburst—to pass with only the warning you have already received."

He handed the note to his colleague who had passed on the first note. "But this kind of behavior cannot be tolerated at this stage of our relationship."

He thought for a moment. "You are free to go," he suddenly said. "But there will be a price. To you. To your son. Perhaps to your daughter. And you will not know that price until next we meet."

He began to confer in whispers with his two colleagues, then noticed she was still standing in front of them. "Good day, madame."

Valerie was led/dragged from the room, silently crying—a wilted version of the woman who had arrived.

After five minutes of quiet discussion, the other two men left the room as the German-sounding man picked up the telephone that was plugged into a random scrambler. He dialed a number, waited, then entered the correct code for that day and hour.

"Canvas," a slightly accented voice said across the electrically cleaned line amid chirps, whistles, and static.

"This is number five."

"Yeah."

"I have just been informed that Apple Blossom's man has been located in an intensive-care ward at Columbus Hospital. He is in a coma."

"I know," Canvas said brusquely. "He'll be dead before midnight."

"Most efficient."

"Why you pay me, sweetie." An angry pause. "Was there a *reason* you called?"

"A guard, one of *yours,* has been reported ten minutes overdue from his rounds."

A long silence. "Let me talk to Smith."

"Mr. Smith has been"—he paused as a one-word note was passed to him from a colleague—"*incommoded* for the present."

Another silence. Then: "I'll take care of everything. Leave the building, go to safe house number four, and wait for my call."

"As you say, Canvas."

The line went dead.

Nine hours later, just after midnight, and after four thorough searches of the building by reinforced guards and after the unconscious guard had been found, revived, and questioned, Xenos emerged from the eleventh-floor crawl space.

It was a simple matter to climb down the service ladder to the basement, let himself into the service dock, and leave the building. He never encountered any guards, but it wouldn't have mattered if he had.

They would have simply and silently died in the night. Their last sight an angry man covered with grime carrying a nylon backpack.

Few answers had been found. Far more questions had been asked. And he still had no idea if the operation he'd stumbled into had any concrete connection with the disappearance of a nineteen-year-old boy who owed the Corsican Brotherhood either $100,000 or a law degree. But he did know two things, engraved in granite and in his mind.

Someone—the Corsicans, Paolo, the interrogators, maybe even Alvarez or someone yet unknown—was dragging Xenos back into the life and world that he'd forsaken years before out of a need for spiritual and moral survival.

And for that, *someone* had to pay.

The next morning, he arrived in Washington, D.C.

Three

The Longworth House Office Building is dark at the best of times. Its dark woods, high ceilings, windowless corridors, too few ceiling lights with every third bulb removed for energy conservation, long ago caused it to be dubbed "the Congressional Cave." It is a place for new members of the House on their way up, old members on their way out, and the usual one-termers that came and went every session.

But it *was* close to the House Chamber, closer to the main pressroom, and photogenic as Hell. So a few of the truly powerful members treasured their suites there for the limelight that existed just beyond the cave's mouth.

And Valerie Alvarez was one of those.

She almost always smiled as she walked past the pressroom—lingering to go on the record on whatever. Smiling seductively, shaking her head sagely. Generally winning friends and admirers from those gray individuals who had been assigned—or sentenced—to cover the House of Representatives.

Marks—one and all—for her to play to her advantage . . . as she always had.

Maybe that defined her, some of the willingly used thought. The "bitch on wheels" who would do anything, say anything; persuade, finagle, seduce any opponents to her goals.

Or perhaps it was more complicated than that, her defenders in the media would argue. Possibly what she was, who she was, had more to do with who she'd been. That to understand the successful—high-flying—politician, you needed to look first at the strength at her core; the resilience and perseverance and resolve of the woman who had raised herself from almost nothing to the highest corridors of power in the land.

Or, wind and weather permitting—a misogynist establishment and a media hungry for sound-bite caricatures permitting—she was more than all of that.

Or less.

Even Valerie didn't know for sure.

The result of a clumsy date rape or seduction (her parents never did agree on which), Valerie had been born into the kind of poverty that liberals weep over and conservatives deny.

That neither ever does anything about.

Her father was a drug dealer, gang member, and violent alcoholic. Her mother, well, was a victim. No other words ever seemed to fit the young girl's first memories.

For years she'd watched helplessly as her father beat her mother unconscious, whipped her brothers with a studded leather belt. Came to *her*—crying, drunk, her siblings' blood on his torn T-shirt—calling for his little girl to "hold your daddy. Show me how much you love me."

Then he died.

Shot dead with his own gun as he lay in an alcoholic stupor on the couch. The police merely shrugged it off; another meaningless minority death. Bad for the precinct's statistics, true; otherwise insignificant.

But liberating to the little girl.

The boys in the neighborhood quickly found Valerie when she reached her teens.

Tall, well developed at an early age, an inner arrogance and strength both drew them to her and kept them at a distance. Sex was just another challenge for her to master, as she had school and athletics. The mechanics of it grew quickly boring—pushing, shoving, vocalizing—but the possibilities for control, for the power that that control implied, *that* ignited her far more than any foreplay or awkward fumbling in the back of cars.

It was in college, though, that the wild girl began to see a world beyond the moment; a prospect of greater things, better places, and new forms of power that were unavailable to uncultivated, uncultured members of society.

So she reinvented herself.

As the five or six reporters—their pads and camera crews at the ready—waited for Congresswoman Alvarez to arrive, they continued their recent game of speculation.

"Fund-raising scandal," one said.

"Secret abortion," another proclaimed with certainty.

"An affair with the president" was the most popular, if least believed.

But, whatever the reason, her drastically lowered profile was beginning to cost her in the most important way possible . . . she was down in the polls.

Valerie was considered to be the leading Democratic candidate for the upcoming New York gubernatorial race. A liberal who was well liked by the party's conservatives, with strong ethnic appeal and a charm that guaranteed her the larger upstate towns, she seemed formidable competition.

Seemed, until two weeks ago.

The photogenic politician had dropped from sight. Her carefully orchestrated sound bites on almost every night's newscasts dried up. And—on the House floor—the normally articulate and appealing woman had become inexplicably monosyllabic.

The rumors had started almost immediately . . . the consensus being that she was remodeling herself for her race for the Governor's Mansion.

After so long an absence from her usual limelight, the growing crowd of press was anxious to see how she would emerge this time.

At Columbia, a school she'd chosen for convenience and the sheer challenge of admission, Valerie learned the world was round and possibilities endless.

If you weren't a half Puerto Rican street girl with a penny-ante criminal record and no connections.

So the reconstruction began.

Appeal was taught to become grace. Sexual manipulation metamorphosed into psychological influences. And sensing that the sorority system would find her out, she concentrated on athletics. Running track, swimming, she could display herself in *acceptable* ways, connecting with the star jock or influential professor.

Who, *amazingly,* always brought out more in her—in the bedroom or the classroom—than she'd *ever* thought herself capable of.

Most important, her strength and native capability were concealed from some, flaunted to others. Allowed to be discovered or nurtured; coaxed out or challenged. It was a flawless, if aimless, performance.

Until one day—in a class on "Political Brinksmanship in the Late 20th Century"—the prize suddenly became clear.

She married the attractive, *connected* but weak—and white— assistant professor in her senior year.

Moonlighting as a consultant to various successful candidates, her husband explained to the eager young woman the intricacies of modern politics. The art of the favor. Why people contribute money or time. What makes a good speech or a bad one.

The roots of real power.

She virtually inhaled the lessons from the man she didn't love, but liked well enough. And she gave to him an emotional adoration, a sexual triumphancy that he had never known or hoped to know.

It was enough for him, though he would have *liked* to be loved as well.

Then, without expectation or warning, with no intent and definitely *not* part of her master plan, Valerie fell in love.

His name was Drake; red-haired, blue-eyed with a smile that could melt any heart, he was born after a difficult pregnancy and nineteen hours of labor. But from the moment his mother first held the squirming baby in her arms, Valerie was changed.

Her son—and an equally adored daughter three years later— became her reason for existence.

They would never know the world of their mother!

The realm she would create for them—within their home and

without, in the real world—would be shining and pure. Using the gifts of her birth—rage, relentlessness, cunning, intelligence, and ambition—she would carve out that world.

With nothing and no one—including their unfortunate, understanding father—getting in the way.

She had to work full-time at two jobs as a cocktail waitress and cabdriver to support them, her husband's salary never being near enough for the growing family. She became adept with a .38 along the way, practicing whenever she could, so that her babies would feel *and be* as safe as she had made her brothers and mother.

She faced more obstacles than she believed possible, but five years later she became the first Latina elected to the Community College Board of Trustees.

"Am I that late, Barb?" Valerie asked as she got out of the elevator from the garage.

Barbara Krusiec, Valerie's chief of staff, fell into step alongside her boss. "Not if you'll go on the record on the coal subsidies report."

Valerie handed the younger woman her briefcase. "Draft a statement for release."

"A press availability would be better."

"No."

"But . . ."

They pushed their way through the press that was calling out questions. Not a smile, not a frown, not ignoring . . . exactly. But Valerie never slowed or said a word as she and her staffer moved on.

She stopped at the private entrance to her office. "No press in the office, right? Not until further notice." She checked her hair, then let herself in.

Waving to her staff, she moved through the cramped corridors lined with file cabinets and junior staff. "Nothing but the essentials, right?"

Krusiec shook her head. "It's your funeral," she said offhandedly, then immediately regretted it as her boss stiffened. "Uh, light schedule this morning."

"Run it." Alvarez plopped down behind her desk, vacantly sifting through the overnight faxes, letters, and e-mails.

Krusiec opened her clipboard. "Senator Pierson wants fifteen minutes to talk about the IMF."

"After lunch."

"The Speaker's invited you to his exercise group . . ."

". . . in hopes of seeing me sweat through my shirt. Next."

Krusiec made a note to politely turn down the invitation. "No votes or committee meetings, but you are supposed to review the latest reports from the Intelligence Committee's staff on the Source 24601 testimony, as well as meet with the minority counsel on the next steps to be taken."

For the first time, Valerie seemed to be paying attention. Rapt attention.

"I don't want to see any new reports on that issue until further notice," she almost snapped. "And blow off counsel until next week." Seeing the surprised look on her closest assistant's face, she forced a smile. "I mean, hey! This thing's been dominating way too much of my time as is, right?"

The younger woman had never seen her boss so desperate for a supportive answer. It was in the tone of her voice, her body language, the look of begging in her eyes. "Whatever you say, boss." She looked down at her list, mentally crossing off the next four things on it. "What about hometown visits and photo ops? You've got three scheduled for this morning. And there's a fourth that's a walk-in."

"I don't know . . ."

"You can't just disappear entirely, no matter what's going on!" Krusiec allowed her disapproval of the current state of things to show. To her surprise, Valerie smiled.

"Okay. Down, girl." She laughed in a forced way. "But no one with an agenda, right?"

"Not a problem," her assistant said with genuine relief. "They're all tourists and loyalists. And I'll screen the walk-in myself."

A moment later Valerie was alone in the big office. Trying hard to concentrate on the latest *Congressional Quarterly* and not stare into the eyes of her children that seemed to beg her from the gold frames on her desk.

A quiet divorce after her first election to Congress had little impact on her rising career.

An articulate, attractive minority woman—and the doors on the left quickly opened for her.

A single mother, working to support her children, who was a gun ownership advocate caused the doors to the right to fly open and invite her in.

A subcommittee chair before the end of her first term.

A seat on the National Security Committee in her second term.

National campaigner for other candidates in her third.

Now, in her fourth term, she sat on the House Select Committee on Intelligence.

But she always had time for her children. They had the run of her offices, knew she would never miss a recital, a game, an important moment for them. They were the passion and the center of her existence.

And while she fought for the secure, safe, and glorious world that she dreamed of for her loves' future, she never forgot the past.

Bringing flowers monthly to her mother's grave.

Shooting for an hour each week at a Virginia firing range.

Life had finally become what she had always longed for.

Accomplishment.

Acceptance.

Control.

Until just over three weeks ago.

"You understand, Mr., uh, Smith," Krusiec said, "that the congresswoman is an incredibly busy woman. It really would've been best if you'd called ahead for an appointment." She didn't like the look of the man in the ill-fitting suit across the conference table from her.

"I appreciate that," Xenos said easily. "But I still need to see her."

Krusiec looked at the mostly blank information sheet she'd had the man fill out. "I'm afraid that without more detail, the best I can do is put you with one of our general caseworkers." She started to reach for the telephone.

Xenos shook his head. "If I said it was a matter of life and death?"

"I'd say whose, and you'd still have to wait. This is a busy office, we deal with so-called life and death issues every day of the week; and without more information from you, the best I can do is put you with . . ."

". . . a caseworker. So you said." He stood, apparently to leave. "You really do a good job of guarding the palace doors."

"That's my job," Krusiec said as she moved past him to open the door to reception. "Next time, call ahead. It'll make things . . ."

But when she turned around, Xenos was gone, the door to the inner office area opened, and nightmares flashing through her head.

"That the last of them, Barb?" Valerie asked as she splashed water on her face in her private bathroom.

"Afraid not, Congresswoman," Xenos answered flatly.

Valerie snapped up and spun around. "Who the Hell are you?"

Xenos heard a commotion coming toward the office. "I know about Queens," he said just before an armed Capitol policeman and Krusiec burst into the office.

"I'm sorry, Ms. Alvarez," Krusiec hurried out. "But this man just got by . . ."

Valerie ignored her, staring into the hard eyes and set expression. "It's okay, Barb." She hesitated. "Please leave us."

Krusiec looked confused, angry, and suspicious. All at the same time. She reluctantly left the room with the policeman; confused by Valerie's manner and the way she and the man never looked away from each other.

Valerie moved behind her desk, slowly sitting down. "Who are you?"

"Names aren't important," Xenos said as he moved to a chair across from her.

Valerie shrugged, the act casually covering her dropping her hands to her lap. Her right hand easily finding the familiar diamond-etched butt of the .38 Cobra taped under her desk. "You said something about Queens? I represent a district in Manhattan." Her finger closed on the trigger.

Xenos wasn't sure how to proceed, was still uncertain of any connection between this woman and the DiBenetti boy, other than the building in Queens. But her reaction—so carefully casual—made him begin to believe that he was on the right track.

"You met with three men in a building at 13520 Thirty-ninth Avenue in Flushing yesterday afternoon. You were strip-searched prior to the meeting, knocked a guy's teeth out during the meeting, then were released after threats against your children."

His answer was the unmistakable click of a .38's hammer being cocked. A moment later he stared into the barrel.

"You bastards were never supposed to contact me here," she said in an almost growl. "What the fuck do you want?"

"I'm not with them, whoever *they* are."

Valerie held the gun at arm's length, steadily aiming between the big man's eyes. "I'm getting real tired of your game playing. Now say whatever the Hell it is you're supposed to say and get out!" She took a deep breath. "Or there's going to be an accident."

Xenos's smile—relaxed, open—shocked her. "Really?" His voice was almost humorous.

It was so odd a reaction—not mocking or overconfident, just, well, amused. She quickly recovered.

"The gun is untraceable," she said in simple, deadly tones. "You burst in here, past my assistants and staff. I tried to placate you, but you pulled a gun. We struggled, it went off."

"You really expect anyone to believe that?" The man seemed genuinely curious.

She shrugged. "Whatever, you'll never know. You'll just be dead."

The briefest pause as she gauged his nonreaction. "Now you

either give me their message or tell them that I won't be intimidated anymore. I'll do what I said I'd do. But that's it!"

Xenos shook his head. "I'm not with them."

Something, some indefinable thing, made her hesitate. "Convince me."

"The way I see it," Xenos said as he casually looked around the room, "you're either a traitor"—he paused as he concentrated on one of the many certificates on her wall—"or you need a friend."

He stood up, slowly, deliberately, conscious of her gun's tracking him as he moved across the room to read the parchment more clearly. He took the framed diploma off the wall. "I didn't know you went to Columbia."

"You have one minute," Valerie said uncertainly. There was something different about this man, stronger than the others she'd dealt with in the obscenity that her life had been in the last nineteen days. "What's where I went to college have to do with anything?"

"Paul Satordi worked for the Columbia Alumni Association doing contract research work," he said without turning around.

"Paul?" She allowed the gun's aim to waver, slightly. "How do you know Paul?"

Xenos turned to face her, sure of his ground for the first time since arriving in the States. "I can help you."

Valerie was feeling torn in two. This could all be some horribly sadistic game or trap perpetrated by the bastards who now owned her, body and soul. Just another control play to further humiliate and trap her within their malignant grasp.

But there was something else standing in front of her as well. An indescribable strength and anger in the man who so calmly regarded her. An inner power and confidence that seemed to be willing to lend itself to her, for her. Perhaps a ray of light at the end of the blackest tunnel of her life.

But the faces in the pictures on her desk pleaded with her to be careful.

She lowered her gun. "If you have nothing else to say, I think you'd better leave now."

Xenos took a step toward her. "Tell me about Paul."

"I haven't seen Paul since before spring break," she said honestly. "I don't know who you are, or how you know what you know, but please leave."

He studied her, saw the strain, the worry, the commitment.

"Please leave and don't say or do anything with whatever you may think you know."

Xenos stood very still for long moments, then barely nodded. He let himself out of the office, almost colliding with Krusiec just outside the door.

"Valerie," Krusiec asked softly, "are you okay?"

"No," Valerie said as she picked up the photograph from her desk and walked into her bathroom. "Not at all."

Even with the sun reflecting off the marble and asphalt all around him, Xenos felt cold. Like all the warmth was slowly but steadily being sucked out of him. Routine had become a puzzle, that puzzle—a cloudy *something*. A metaphorical fog bank that was closing in on him in an inexorable claustrophobic push that was forcing him more and more back to who he had been.

Who he had sworn to never be again.

The shadow of a missing Corsican student and a blackmailed member of Congress grew all the more ominous with the sound of a familiar voice behind him.

"Helluva place for a dead man to show up, Jerry."

"What's one more dead man to you?"

"On other days, in other places, not much. I grant you that." There was a pause while Xenos felt the author of the voice draw nearer. Close enough to reach out and strangle the life out of. "But this is one of those *special* days, it seems." A light laugh. "You still remember those days, don't you, Jerry?" The voice seemed to genuinely care about the answer.

Xenos never turned to look into the cold familiar eyes. "Go away." There was death in the sound.

The much older man in the thousand-dollar suit just smiled casually. "When one of my favorite people comes to town?" He laughed, with the sincerity of a man who *seemed* to understand human emotions. "Now, what kind of friend would I be then?"

"We were a lot of things, Herb," Xenos said as he turned to face the man, "but I don't remember *friends* being one of them."

Herb shrugged. "Semantics." He nodded down DuPont Circle. "Walk with me, Jerry." He set out as if expecting a recalcitrant puppy to fall into place.

After a moment, Xenos came up alongside.

Herb pulled the stub of a cigar from his jacket and began chewing it. "You see," he began without preamble, "we naturally get nervous when one of our corpses turns up inside the Beltway. Especially when we find them talking to Congress."

"I imagine you would." Xenos was completely relaxed . . . and aware of the two men who had dropped in behind them when they'd started off; as well as the two men just out of listening distance up ahead. He just assumed a car somewhere behind. "Faced any interesting hearings lately?"

Herb gestured up at the Capitol dome. "They're more interested in immolating each other than us, these days. Been kind of restful actually." He began chewing again until a tourist family moved well past. "Until this morning."

"Sorry to wake you."

"I'm sure you are, I'm sure you are. But the thing is, well, I *am* awake now, you see. That's the problem."

Xenos stopped and faced the man who he once thought of as a savior and now saw only as the devil. "We done with the word games?" Herb shrugged. "Say your piece and leave."

The older man shook his head sadly. "You've lost all sense of grace and charm in your Greek hills." He sat down on a marble bench, looking up at the much bigger man. "I've been asked to give you a message."

Xenos laughed. "Since when are you a messenger boy?"

"Since this morning, it seems."

"I don't believe it." Xenos sounded almost sorry for the old man. "Who's the message from?" He sat down beside him.

"Don't really know, myself. But it comes from so high, I get nosebleeds just thinking about it." The briefest of pauses. "If I allowed myself to think about it, that is."

Xenos had never seen the man look anything but confident.

And he didn't look *un*confident now. Just *less* confident. It was an impressive sight. As if Mount Rushmore had suddenly grown a new head.

"What's the message?"

"Son, you're in it deep this time," Herb said in a cautionary tone. "You're shaking someone's tree hard enough for them to worry about all-ever falling out." He took out the cigar and gestured at the forest of government buildings around them. "Look around, Jerry. What do you see? What do you smell?"

Xenos just stared blankly at the man, wondering vacantly if the shot would come from the tourists taking pictures on his left or the teens making out on his right.

"What you smell," the old cold warrior continued slowly, "is fear. This city was founded on it. Fear of offending the wrong person, or of not puckering properly to another. Fear of being passed over, fear of being singled out." He leaned in so close Xenos could smell the sausages he used to share with the man every Thursday afternoon. "Fear of being discovered."

"You used to preach fear," Xenos whispered. "Used to call it the great safety."

"Not this kind of fear. What we're talking about here, Jerry, is stupid fear. The kind that makes otherwise sane people do crazy things. Things they'll regret later, make private grievings over, but finite, *permanent* things." He shrugged. "No one is safe when that kind of fear starts going around. It's like an airborne virus passed from a man on the street, to another on a telephone, to a man in a tiny office. Eventually working its way up the line until even the Eunuchs in their corner suites have caught the contagion." The briefest, most spasmodic frown. "And when they catch it, son, the only cure is kill."

For the first time, Xenos saw something else in his old boss's eyes. Something he would have bet his life (and had many times) could never exist within this man.

Doubt.

"That your message?"

Herb gestured with his cigar, and a black town car rolled silently up. "No," he said simply. He stood up, looking down at the one man he'd thought he'd never lose, then lost. *"My* message is far simpler."

He put the cigar away, pulling a plane ticket out of the same pocket. "Your flight leaves in two hours, nonstop to Athens." He turned and walked over to the open car door. "Don't miss it."

When the car door didn't close, Xenos got up and walked over. "And?"

"What did you do in New York?"

"You tell me."

"I wish I could." He was silent for a minute. "Care to tell me what you told Hard-Ass Alvarez just now?"

Xenos remained silent.

Herb shook his head, closed the door, but lowered the window. "Don't ever change." He laughed lightly. "Stay pure forever, son. It's what you do best."

Xenos handed the ticket back to the old man. "Message rejected."

The old man took the ticket and put it away. "You still don't get it." The engine started. "The message was in a 9mm that I never ordered to fire." The car started to pull away. "The ticket was from me."

As he listened to the whines and whistles of the electronically swept line, the man entered the access code he needed. But before hitting the enter key, he carefully looked around the empty office— the office he'd ordered emptied immediately after getting a report on the encounter outside the Capitol.

As satisfied as the paranoid man ever was, he took a deep breath, then pressed a key.

"Canvas," came the static-filled answer after two minutes.

"This is Apple Blossom," the man whispered through a haze of confusion.

"Clarify."

The man spoke in a shouting whisper. "I say again, this is Apple Blossom, Apple, copy?"

"Line clear. Go ahead," was the emotionless response.

"Apple Blossom reporting, latest results are insufficient, insufficient, copy?" the man said, remembering Canvas's open distrust for anything but the most general comments over even secured lines.

"I warned you about going official."

"I don't need recriminations, I need solutions."

A silence on the other end of the line.

"We'll bring in Hyacinth for another talk. We could use the updates anyway."

The man looked doubtful. "And the other thing?"

"Yeah, well." An unexpectedly long pause. "He'll be extra."

"Whatever you say."

Light, somehow malevolent laughter drifted across the clean line. "Of course, darling. That goes without saying, now doesn't it?"

Four

Xenos fumed during the entire flight back to New York. The more he got into this *favor,* the worse it got. And the meeting with his former boss had only confirmed his worst suspicions.

Herb Stone was a man who never owed anyone favors; who instead acquired them like a housewife does coupons. He was the epitome of the old-line intelligence bosses: a man with few if any morals; no emotional attachments to anything; and no restraints of any kind on what he might do or whom he would do it to.

So it was soul-shocking to see him forced into a position he clearly detested. That of hired gun for an unknown boss. But it *was* typical of the man to disobey—no, that was wrong—*misinterpret* orders he disagreed with.

He would've killed Xenos for many reasons, could probably have listed half a dozen or so instantly if asked.

But he would never do it just to "follow orders."

Xenos only hoped, without really knowing why, that the old man wouldn't be killed for his momentary bout of ethics.

Which led directly to the problem at hand.

The tap Xenos had placed behind Alvarez's diploma had revealed that a half hour after he'd left her, she'd received a call from her tormentors. Although he'd only heard her side of the conversation, it was enough. Her hurried orders to her staff immediately afterward were clear enough.

She was headed back to New York, most probably to another meeting with the men from Flushing. And she would most likely be carrying some classified papers with her. She'd called "the committee repository" to request access to "Bureau updates," before catching her flight.

She'd added one other piece to the puzzle as well.

On the plane, Xenos played back that part of the tape.

ALVAREZ: "When was the last time you talked with that boy from Columbia?"

KRUSIEC: "Which boy?"

ALVAREZ: "Paul Satordi. The one who was doing the IRT research for us."

KRUSIEC: "I don't know. Couple of weeks ago, I guess. Why?"

ALVAREZ: "When, exactly?" Her voice had gone low and cautious.

KRUSIEC: "Uh, I guess it was around the time you spoke at the Ellen's Fund banquet."

ALVAREZ: "He was there?"

KRUSIEC: "Don't you remember? He worked at the hotel where we were staying?"

Alvarez's voice had almost been indecipherable; it had gone so sad and mournful. "Oh God."

As he considered this newest piece, viewed in context with the rest of the continually bizarre tableau, Xenos decided what to do.

As soon as he got off the jet shuttle, he placed a cell call. An hour later his Corsican contact in New York arrived at the airport.

They wandered among the kiosk food stands and souvenir shops, weaving their way through the sporadic crowds that surged through the plush terminal. The big man talked, the little man listened. For the better part of an hour Xenos reported what he knew, what he thought, drew the connections wherever and however he thought they lay.

Quattro Cani made few comments, asked fewer questions. Merely listened, nodded, and shook his head.

"When I leave this airport," Xenos finally said, *"finito. Capito?"*

"Lui è morto?"

"Sconosciuto," Xenos said unemotionally. "But whether he's dead or not, he ain't a runner. I'm sure of at least that much."

"That will please his brother." A pause. "And frighten him."

"I understand."

"And this Alvarez, she is definitely involved?"

Xenos hesitated. *"Sì. Non disposto, mal disposto.* But, yeah." They turned off into a relatively empty alcove where they could talk more freely, away from the deplaning tourists and businessmen they'd wandered into.

"Willing or not, she must be made to cooperate," the Corsican said offhandedly.

"None of my business."

A broad, charming smile, so similar to Franco's that for the briefest moment Xenos wondered if it was taught to all members of the Brotherhood.

"Would you be willing to, uh, *facilitare* her cooperation? For appropriate remuneration, of course."

But Xenos had already turned his back and was starting to walk away.

"Just keep your end of the deal," he called over his shoulder as he mixed with the crowds.

"We have already broken ground on the new ward, Dureté," Quattro Cani called after him. Then, looking around to be sure he hadn't been spotted—his death warrant if seen by the wrong eyes—he wandered away in the opposite direction.

To make his calls and set his plans.

Plans—more or *less* venomous depending on how the game was going—were also being laid in the den of a quiet home in Georgetown.

Senator Rod Buckley carefully lined up his next shot while waiting for his two guests to finish pouring their drinks. "Three in the corner," he said as he concentrated.

"Five hundred says you blow it," Lane Kingston, former congressman and current director of the Peace Corps, called out.

"If gambling weren't illegal in this state," Attorney General Jefferson DeWitt said, laughing, "I'd take you up on that."

Buckley simply smiled, pulled back the cue, and easily made the difficult bank shot. "That," he said with a self-satisfied grin, "is called grace under fire."

"That's called damned lucky," DeWitt said as he poured himself another drink.

"Lucky *is* graceful," Kingston said between bitefuls of his sandwich.

"More pearls of wisdom from the only M.A. ever to flunk philosophy."

"Pearls before swine," came out hoarsely—half word, half sandwich.

For almost ten years these three men had casually insulted, prodded, harassed, or needled each other in their once-a-week "our nights." It was a ritual that none of the men would miss, although none deeply enjoyed either.

Brought together by politics and life, the men were considered by many to be the next generation of leaders in the Democratic Party.

Brought together by common appetites—for food, challenges (physical and intellectual), women, and ambition—the men considered themselves the cream of their generation, poised on the verge of assuming their destinies.

Brought together by George Steingarth—the lame duck president's closest friend and personal adviser—the men were being *considered*.

And all of that combined with the free-flowing beer and liquor to be deeply intoxicating.

Actually they had a great deal in common.

Under fifty, athletic, intellectual, charismatic, all had been Rhodes or Westinghouse scholars, had attended college in the U.S. and abroad. They spoke several languages, were fanatical sports fans, and had an almost boyish admiration of women.

All women.

They were slightly more conservative on national security issues than the rest of the party, but quite liberal on social issues. All three were married to trophy wives, had trophy kids, trophy careers, and a natural sense of humor that carefully hid their goals.

Most important, they all *knew* they'd been chosen—by God or the party, it didn't much matter since none of them really believed in either—for great things.

So in the thralls of their burning desires—for power, pleasure, and destiny—they'd found each other. Once a week to have no secrets, no hidden agendas. To share, to help, to prop each other up.

One day, they all knew, one of them must step to the fore and take up the trappings of his personal destiny. But until that day, they would be there for each other.

Or so the other two would be led to believe.

"Rod," Kingston asked, "what d'you hear on PANCON '03?"

"Dead in the water." Buckley grimaced as he made another shot. "Never get out of committee."

"Why?"

"Women's lobby."

DeWitt shook his head. *"Person's* lobby, please."

Buckley laughed. "Well, certain *persons* have had it in their head that the grants are antiwomen in nature."

Kingston glanced at a *New York Times.* "Are they?"

"Probably."

"You going to fight it out?" DeWitt looked over his *friend's* shoulder at the front-page article.

Buckley shook his head. "Wrong fight, wrong time."

"Even with this?" DeWitt tossed the paper onto the pool table.

Buckley glanced at it, then made his shot, around the paper. "We've seen headlines like that before." He chuckled. "They're essentially meaningless. Like when the *Post* called you—what was it? *The Beltway Bad Boy?"*

DeWitt shrugged. "Only my *very few* enemies think me abrasive, really."

"Yeah," the senator agreed. "Your friends *know* it. And what about you, Laney? I seem to remember a *Sun Times* piece that used the phrase *perniciously ambitious."*

The man who enjoyed a 78 percent approval rating among college students (especially coeds) smiled. "Like that's a *bad* thing."

"Didn't CNN call you something like the senator from Fantasy Island?" The attorney general laughed while taking a closer look at the photograph that accompanied the headline.

"My point exactly." Buckley threw down his cue on the table, then picked up the paper. "The media in this country select hot button phrases like"—he read the headline aloud—*"Puzzling Disappearing Act Plagues Congresswoman,* then forgets about it ten minutes later, when someone else gets caught with their pants down."

"I wouldn't mind seeing old Hard-Ass caught with her pants down sometime," Kingston whispered as they looked at the photograph.

"Fucking Alvarez is such a pain in the ass," Buckley said angrily, "I doubt I could get it up over the agendized bitch."

Kingston pointed at the paper—a photograph of Valerie at a White House function in a clinging evening gown. *"Fucking* Alvarez is exactly what we're talking about. Think about it."

As he looked at the color photo—the one Alvarez always attacked the paper for using instead of her more conservative "official" portrait—the senator's hand slipped down to his crotch. "Point taken."

Both men looked at the attorney general.

"Being a gentleman and a lover/protector of the fairer sex," DeWitt said, "I will, of course, withhold comment, beyond this."

He walked over, took the paper, seeming to consider the picture carefully. "Congresswoman Alvarez represents all that is best in America today," he said in his politician's voice. "Successful legislator, mother, community activist. I applaud her accomplishments and eagerly look forward to working—closely—with her in the future."

"I can just imagine," Kingston said with a leer. "You got something going with her?"

"He wishes." Buckley shook his head at the shorter attorney general. "What makes you such a feminist all of a sudden?"

DeWitt raised his eyebrows. "Obviously, my lecherous friends, you haven't seen the latest polling data. Women between eighteen and forty-nine consider me 'boyishly engaging.' And I am nothing if not devoted to my supporters."

"Bullshit!" Kingston—notorious for his temper—shouted. "You telling me you wouldn't fuck Alvarez given half a chance?"

DeWitt smiled comfortably. "Of course I would." He stopped suddenly as there was a knock on the door, and his aide let himself in. "But I would do it politically correctly," he said easily, then turned to the younger man. "Yes, Michael?"

Michael Culbertson, personal assistant to Attorney General DeWitt, knew full well what these evenings were about—alternately sharing the guarding of the door with the personal aides of the senator and the Peace Corps director. But he understood his role and where it could eventually leave him as well. So he suppressed any expression, beyond basic pleasantness, as he began.

"Mr. Attorney General, gentlemen, Mr. Steingarth has asked me to inform you that the fight is about to start. The fighters will be coming into the ring shortly."

"Yes!" Buckley called out. "I've been waiting all week to see this! That Mendoza's a mean motherfucker."

DeWitt followed him toward the door. "But Hollander's got the speed, man. Boxer over slugger every time."

"Screw it," Kingston said brusquely. "Raw power over finesse any day."

And they were gone.

Michael spent the next ten minutes straightening up the room, putting away the bottles, making sure any notes, papers, crude sketches, were either burned in the elaborate brick fireplace or returned to briefcases. Finally he crawled beneath the pool table, retrieving a small cassette recorder.

Because Michael had ambitions of his own.

"Tonight is going to be different."
Valerie was shocked that the words were said out loud. For the

last nine hours she'd been thinking the thought, enabling the thought, but had never even whispered the words. Fear of their real meaning had kept her silent. But sitting in her car in the isolated Long Island field had somehow brought the reality of it to her.

And they had found their voice.

For the fifth time since she'd parked, she checked the specially secured briefcase issued to senior members of the Select Committee on Intelligence.

Strictly for transporting extremely sensitive or classified documents, it was lead-lined, contained a chemical incendiary device that would instantly reduce the contents to ash if the case was improperly opened. As well as a few other "nuances," the designers had called them. Things that would've made James Bond jealous. Things that had actually been inspired by those movies. Cartoon gimmicks that government and private sector engineers had brought about to terrifying realities.

They'd been all too willing to give it to her, along with the extraordinarily classified papers it housed. She was the ranking minority member, chair of the subcommittee dealing with the Source 24601 defection, and an acknowledged expert on the subject. Hell, she'd even been a part of the team that had initially debriefed the former communist colonel when he'd defected.

Unquestioned credentials for any and all files in the case.

Despite that, Valerie had been as cautious in obtaining them as she'd ever been in her life.

She'd asked for seven files unrelated to those she'd been ordered to bring to the meeting; files on things from Chinese missile throw weights to the color combination on the shoulder flashes of the Moscow Militia. But the files *they'd* wanted—classified FBI and CIA reports on Source 24601's recent assassination and his unfinished allegations about a penetration in the U.S. intelligence establishment—were there as well.

She certainly thought about *not* taking them, had no intention of ever turning them over to the bastards that had destroyed her life. But prudence and routine demanded that she go through the motions. Who knew who else had been trapped (voluntarily or not) in the conspiracy? So she had established the record. All files properly signed out for in triplicate, with two witnesses each.

Then the short flight to New York.

She assumed she was under constant surveillance, although she'd never detected any. These weren't the kind that made themselves obvious. Mailing the letter had been the trickiest part of all; a feat only accomplished by driving in circles—to be sure she wasn't followed, as ordered—and a less-than-thirty-second stop at a Thirty-seventh Street mailbox, just before driving into the Queens–Midtown Tunnel and her fate.

As she waited for the obscenity to finally play itself out, she went over that twenty-three-page letter, her middle finger raised at the world that had finally defeated her.

The first part had been a mere recounting of facts: dates, times, what names she knew, what locations. And, of course, *his* name. The bastard chief interrogator, the one she *would get,* if no others.

The next bit was more detailed: physical descriptions of the nameless ones, as-close-as-could-be-recalled accounts of each of the interrogation sessions, what they knew, what they wanted to know. Then there was a little conjecture, Valerie's sense of what it all meant. The last part, the shortest part, was her . . . *explanation* was as good as any word for it.

I love my country and would never have voluntarily betrayed it. And I pray that this, my final testament, will in some way undo the damage I may have done. It doesn't lessen my guilt any, but you will—I hope—understand that what I did, I did as a mother. And my weakness was my love for my children.

I realize now that they were doomed from the start, that I was naïve and visionary to think that this could end any other way than it has. My prayers, constant and unheard it seems, will continue to the end, that when they realize what has happened, they will be merciful and grant my son and daughter a quick, painless end.

Do not think too badly of me, as a member of the noblest

institution in the world—our government—or as a mother, a job I did with love, if not well. My only solace is the certainty that I will be saving lives—perhaps a great many—when I take as many of the bastards out with me as possible.

When I join my children in whatever comes after this planet of pain and heartbreak.

Valerie Elena Maria Alvarez

Valerie wiped a tear from her eye as the headlights of a panel van pulled to a stop twenty feet away. She kissed her favorite photograph of her and the kids—the one taken when they were all so young and unaware of the dark and gooey place that the world truly was—then placed it beneath a statue of Jesus on the seat beside her.

She opened the car door with strength and a will dedicated to one, deadly purpose. It invigorated her, filled her with fire and potency.

"Forgive me, Jesus," she mumbled before stepping steadfastly —and finally—forward.

In Brooklyn, Xenos was also thinking of finality and ending things.

He stood outside his sister's apartment looking up at the argument in the window two stories above, and realized that this all had to end. If he was ever to sleep soundly, peacefully again, if he was ever to heal and begin the process of recovery, it must start tonight.

He'd called his sister shortly after leaving the airport. The plan they'd arrived at was simple enough, and—in fact—the kind of thing he might have laid on had the event been an attempted assassination rather than reconciliation.

1. The subject will be lured to a location that is known to him as safe and hospitable. In a neighborhood he knows well and is completely comfortable in.

2. The subject will be engaged on a subject that is sure to

anger him, cloud his judgment, give no real alternative but to leave the location at a known time, through a known route.

3. The killers will lie in wait in a position from which they can view the subject's arrival and the signal that indicates the subject is on the way out.

4. The killers will then place themselves in a position where the subject *must* move past them.

5. The kill.

The argument seemed to wane, move away from the window, and, for the barest moment, Xenos hoped that a confrontation on the street would be unnecessary. But his sister's reappearance at the window doomed that hope stillborn. As agreed, she shook her head and lowered the blind.

Quietly, with years of training and condition, Xenos moved through the shadows. The old man would turn left when leaving the apartment building. He'd head for the bus stop at Twenty-fifth or the subway at Grand. Either way, he had to pass by a five-foot space between two buildings.

As though it had been prepared for him, Xenos slid noiselessly into it and began to wait. Five minutes, no longer, he told himself. Then they would be on.

Three minutes later the old man casually walked past the space and Xenos silently stepped out behind.

Sensing more than hearing the intruder's approach, the old man stopped. "I have no money," he said with the slightest hint of an accent.

"It's me, Papa," Xenos said softly.

The old man stiffened. "No," but it was said as a prayer he hoped would go unanswered.

"It's Jerry, Papa. I want, I need to talk to you. To set things right."

For the longest time it seemed as if the old man was about to turn around. Almost as if his body tried turning—physically fighting the old man's will—but somehow couldn't overcome his iron resolve.

"My son is dead."

"I'm right here, Papa," Xenos begged. "Just turn around and look at me, please!"

The old man involuntarily shuddered. Then slowly he stiffened again. "My son was a murderer and a thief and a looter and a pillager."

"No, Papa." Tears rolled down the big man's cheeks.

"My son is dead. I have said Kaddish, I have helped prepare the way for his soul to God's side. I will not look upon or traffic with his doppelgänger."

Xenos grabbed him and spun the old man around. "Look at me, damn you! I *am* your son! You taught me to play the piano, to sing. You were the one who was always there for me! Please, God, I need you here for me now!"

But the old man's eyes remained squinted tightly shut. "My son is dead."

Xenos released the old man, seemed to sag, almost deflate. "I don't sleep, Papa." His voice was sad and pained, more like a child's than a man's. "I see their faces, all their faces, Papa. They're all there. Everything you always said. They just stare at me, mock me." He dropped his head; his shoulders curled in; in every respect the image of a man beyond exhaustion. "Judge me."

For the briefest flicker of a second, the old man barely opened his eyes wide enough to see the son, the man, he felt almost a physical longing for. He felt his hand start to reach up . . .

He spun around, tightly closing his eyes and stalking away.

"You are a ghost! A phantom of my son who has been sent to mock me! I deny you!"

"Papa," the too familiar voice called out in the night.

But the old man continued on.

Then a screeching of tires, a shot, and the old man—a veteran of too many gang wars and pogroms in his life—dived into a store-front doorway. When the sounds stopped, moments later, he cautiously looked back out at a completely deserted street.

Deserted except for a shining blackish stain near the space between the buildings.

He slowly walked back—propelled by something more than instinct and less than certainty—stopping by the stain, crouching down, touching it with his tobacco-stained fingers to confirm for his eyes the horrific truth his heart already knew.

Staring into his bloody fingers, his anger—at himself, at his son, at the world that had come between them then and now—boiled and raged, finally finding voice and fury.

"Bastards! Give me back my son!"

Phase Two

Counterintelligence

Five

"Stupid."

The impeccably dressed older *European* gentleman opposite the big man in the back of the limousine looked over at the comment.

"Excuse me?" he asked.

"You heard me right enough." The big man's tone was full of contempt and disbelief.

A second man merely shrugged. "The situation was thrust upon us."

"We did what we could," a third added. "When that failed, we relied on your talents."

The big man shook his head. "You made it worse by not letting me handle things from the start. If you had, Goldman would be dead and Alvarez would be, well, compliant at worst."

"But, Canvas, you *didn't* kill Goldman."

"Of course not, you stupid carp! After your pointless games, I have to find out how far operational integrity has been compromised, don't I? Who he's working for and what he's told them and why. Christ!" he spit out. "If you'd just blown the bugger away when he came out of the college prick's apartment, I wouldn't be missing Liverpool v. Man U." He began to gaze out the window at the passing farms and fields. "Good bloody match it was going to be too."

Silence settled over the car.

"Wö xihuan dàifu häo xîe de," the first man whispered casually as he checked his watch.

"Duì," the second responded while seemingly obsessed with a loose thread on his jacket sleeve.

The third smiled in the direction of Canvas, who never looked away from his window. *"Nî néng jièsháo xiё shéme líangcài ma?"*

The first yawned. *"Wô xiâng bâoxiân."*

"Gentlemen," Canvas said in a quiet voice, "before you start talking about my *relative quality,* or getting *insurance* against my possible failure, I think you should know two things."

He turned to face them, his eyes cold, narrow, his body virtually emanating death and destruction. "First, you'll only get one chance at severing our relationship. Fail that and *I* start the severing."

He leaned back, seeming to relax as he returned to studying the countryside. "Second, I understand that gutter slop you like to speak. So no secrets, right? *Wô dông le."*

"Our apologies, Canvas." The European bowed slightly toward the big man.

"Forget that and tell me about this new Alvarez bullshit."

"It is not *bullshit."* He clearly disliked the word. "It is an ultimatum, and it is most complicated."

"You must remember," the third man quickly added, "that options available to us in other circumstances are unavailable now."

Canvas poured himself a drink. "And why is that?"

"An unscheduled disappearance of a high-visibility member of Congress; visible, unexplained wounds or injuries; or worse—a death?" The Second shook his head. That would raise our profile to an unacceptable level."

"Unacceptable," the European repeated. "Ms. Alvarez has reasoned the situation most clearly, I'm afraid."

"We'll see," Canvas said as he stretched. *"I'll* see."

For over ten hours Valerie had waited. Constantly evaluating, watching, waiting.

Should I do it now?

Are there enough of them here—the right ones of them—to really hurt?

Have I gotten all I can?

After the usual, routine humiliations, she had been driven for hours—she thought to somewhere in Connecticut. There she'd been searched again, insulted again, and eventually brought into the presence of her three, usual interrogators.

But there'd been something different about it this time. The men in the car, the guards and others in the corridors of this carefully unmarked building, all seemed tenser, nervous, taut. At first she thought they had sensed her plan, or had somehow discovered it outright. But she quickly realized it was something else.

As they'd waited to be let into the conference room where the questioning would take place, she noticed two heavily armed guards in front of a door at the far end of the corridor. She saw the covert, worried looks of the others as they glanced in that direction, then whispered among themselves. But she'd had little time to analyze or guess at the cause of their discomfort.

The questioning had begun simply enough, routine questions about surveillance and suspicions that opened each session. Her secured briefcase had been gingerly placed on the table in front of her—the men obviously aware of its intricate booby traps. No one mentioned it throughout the meticulous beginning. It was simply silently acknowledged as her interrogators checked off their lists of the routine Q&A that they lived by.

Finally the preliminaries were over and the main event began.

"Congresswoman, have you retrieved the reports we requested?"

"I have."

The first man—the German she couldn't look at without undisguised rage—had nodded toward the briefcase. "If you please."

"No." Her voice had been firm but carefully controlled. She must play for the moment, that instant when she had won all she could and not an instant sooner.

The man sighed. "Need I remind you of the consequences to your—"

"You don't have to say anything, you traitorous bastard! When this is over, I'm going to see that everyone knows who—"

The German looked exasperated. "They will *know* nothing. Not if you care anything for your children, madame. Now *open the case.*" He was barely controlling his anger.

"Not till I get some things first."

The third man actually smiled. "What do you expect *us* to give *you?*"

It was hard, the hardest moment of her life, but she kept her voice calm and reasonable. "I want my children released immediately. They're to be taken to the home of Speaker Wilson. I'm scheduled to call there at ten in the morning. If they're not there, then it's all over."

"What, precisely, is over, Ms. Alvarez?"

"All of this! You get no more from me—not personally, not documents. Nothing. Not till I get what I want."

The man shook his head. "You will not sacrifice your children."

Valerie took a deep breath. "If they're not there, then they're probably dead already." She paused. "And you'll have no more hold over me."

"We'll have you," the third said simply. "And we will have the contents of your case. That might well suffice."

Valerie actually managed a laugh. "Who do you think you're talking to? *Ratas de cantarilla incontinente sin dientes!*" she sneered. "If the KGB couldn't ever open one of those without destroying the contents—with all their techno know-how—what the Hell are you second-raters going to do?" She laughed openly, fully; in relief and fear of what might happen next, sure. But also a laughter born of a final freedom of action.

The laughter shocked the men behind the table, who quickly consulted with each other, then with a bandaged man, Mr. Smith from the last session.

"*You* can open it," Smith finally lisped out from behind swollen lips and a black eye. "And there's lots we can do to you." He came around the table toward her.

"You learn slow, Zippy," Valerie said softly as she evened the weight on her feet, took a more solid stance, gauged the diminishing distance between them, as the man approached.

Smith nodded. "But I do learn." He seemed to look past her. "Jimmy."

She never heard the man come up behind her, punching her in the side with a hammerblow that bent her over. The man pulled her arms back, forcing her to bend over the conference table, her face less than a foot from her frowning interrogators.

"Open the case, Ms. Alvarez," the German said softly. "Spare us all this . . . unpleasantness."

"*Chingatè, enaños!*" She felt Smith come up behind her, tearing at her jeans, pushing the other man away as she flailed behind her; praying to grab a hunk of hair, an eye, anything that would inflict pain.

"Open the fucking case," Smith spat out in a hoarse leer as he tore her panties off. "Or I'm going to do you ugly and for hours!"

As she heard the man begin to undo his belt, as the men across the table looked on in mild discomfort, her briefcase was pushed in front of her.

"All right!" But her cry seemed unnoticed by the man behind her as he lifted her higher on the table and began to spread her flailing legs.

"Mr. Smith!" the German called out angrily.

Reluctantly the man backed off.

Valerie slowly pushed herself off the table.

"Please cover yourself, Congresswoman," the Second said solicitously. "Then open the case."

Out of the corner of her eye, she saw Smith angrily panting as she pulled up her jeans.

"This isn't over yet, bitch," he muttered beneath his breath.

"Too right," she mumbled back, then turned to the case.

Standing it on its end, she dialed a combination into one lock, then a different number into the other. There was an audible click, and a wave of relief around the table.

Then Valerie spun around, the handle of the case coming off in her hand revealing two large, pointed spikes. She plunged them deep into the right side of Smith's face.

The man's pained screams were more animal than human and they filled the room and corridor beyond. He collapsed on the floor, rolling around, blood covering his face and forming abstract art on the pale yellow carpet.

Valerie was wrestled back onto the table, held painfully in place by two men.

But her interrogators were stunned into silence by her smiling face, bent up toward them, speaking in a quiet, almost satisfied tone.

"Not till I get what I want."

But that had been ten hours ago. Ten hours spent locked in a small windowless empty office. Handcuffed, gagged, but somehow satisfied. Because she knew that soon the waiting and the planning and the praying would be over, and the end would come.

For all of them.

She looked up as the door was opened. Two of the men from earlier walked in—tense, worried looks on their faces—followed by a big man whose face revealed nothing.

The new man looked her over casually, then shook his head. "Unbelievable," was all he said as he turned to leave. Then he stopped, walking back into the office, crouching by Valerie. He reached over, gently pulling down her gag.

"So the boss finally shows up," Valerie rasped out of her too dry throat.

"In a manner of speaking." He gestured at her cuffs and she was quickly unlocked. "You're a tough little cow, I'll give you that."

Valerie cautiously stretched, then stood, after the big man stepped back. "Have my children been released?"

Canvas smiled. "I bet you're dying to know." He stepped toward her, leaning close, whispering in her ear. "*Wonder for a bit longer, sweetheart.*"

He easily caught the kick that was aimed at his crotch, held her by the ankle for a moment, shook his head like a parent who'd caught his child in a foolish lie, then simply tipped her over onto the floor.

"I like spirit, Valerie. May I call you Valerie?" As she scrambled to her feet, he spun backward to his left, catching her too-slowly-thrown punch at the elbow and throwing her forward. Again, she ended up in a pile on the floor. "But there's a time and place for it." He shrugged as she got up more slowly, more cautiously, this time. "And this is neither the time nor the place, right?"

He reached out so suddenly that Valerie was unable to do anything as she was shoved back against the wall, an iron grip squeezing the life from her throat.

"We'll talk later," Canvas said casually after a full minute of her breathless struggling.

Then he was gone, leaving a chilling presence, like bad after-shave, in the air behind him.

"Where's Smith?" he asked after the door had been locked behind them.

"Lying down," one of his escorts reported flatly. "One of the meds sewed up his face, shot him with some painkiller and shit. But I figured you'd want to talk to him before we sent him to a hospital."

"Yeah."

A minute later they were in the improvised infirmary where Smith—half his face concealed by a bloody bandage—was drinking Dewar's from the bottle.

"I've got to go to the fucking hospital," he said in a pained mumble when he saw Canvas.

"Well," Canvas said easily, "that's not really necessary. Is it, love?" He casually took a gun from the waistband of the man next to him and fired three times into Smith's forehead.

He handed the gun back and started out. "Where you been getting these guys?"

His assistant merely looked away.

Canvas sighed as they left the room. "All right." He wiped his eyes as if he was exhausted and faced with one final odious job before he could rest.

"Let's go pay our respects."

. . .

Xenos had drifted in and out of consciousness for hours. Pain racked his body, nausea roiled in his stomach, and he'd lost all sense of time. He couldn't move, whether because of the ropes that held him to a ceiling beam or not he didn't know.

He *hoped* it was the ropes.

So he hung there—five inches off the floor—and waited. The next move belonged to the other guys.

The door opened, and a guard ordered the two interior gunmen out. After casting a nervous look up at the seriously wounded man, the final guard left. A moment later Canvas came in.

"Morning, Jerry."

"Who's that?" The brighter light from the hallway obscured his view.

"Has it been that long?" Canvas closed the door behind him.

Xenos concentrated on the man who came a step closer. "Oh," was all he finally said.

The two men—English and American—sat quietly as their Russian defector instructor finished his lesson.

"Remember, never believe yourself to be smarter, more able or better trained than your subject. It is leverage, *not experience or talent, that moves mountains."*

The man bowed at the head, then left the small classroom.

"Waste of time," Colin Meadows said as he closed his notebook.

Jerry shrugged. "He made some points."

"Granted. But all common sense, really."

The two young men got up, left the building, and began walking through the landscaped grounds of Shweinfurt Intelligence Annex Beta, only one kilometer from the Wall.

"I think most of this stuff is common sense, Colin," the American thought aloud. "I mean, think about it. You need something from somebody, they don't want to give it to you . . ."

"And physicalizing could just radicalize them. Yeah," the Englishman said simply. "Like I said, waste of time."

They sat down on a bench watching a volleyball game between two teams of French and American servicewomen.

"You really believe in all this Four Phase stuff?"

Jerry yawned. "They believe it, or they wouldn't have spent the last year and a half training me, I guess."

"Two years for me." Colin slicked back his hair. "An' all they done is convince me of what I knew already."

"Which was?"

The stocky twenty-four-year-old Brit smiled. "That I am different from everybody else." A spasmodic smile flew across his face. " 'Cept maybe you, Jer. And if they want to make me more different, and I can make a living off it, why not?"

The lean twenty-two-year-old American nodded sadly. "I always felt it too. But I'm not in it for the money."

"Why, then?"

Jerry was quiet for a long time. "I want to make things, I don't know, better maybe."

Colin looked disinterested. "Whatever, mate." He concentrated on two of the women standing by the side of the game, toweling their firm bodies. "But I say we put some of their bloody awful lessons into practice."

"What do you have in mind?" Jerry asked as he followed the man's gaze.

"That we practice a little leverage to see if we can't get those birds' legs in the air."

Jerry nodded enthusiastically as the fledgling Four Phase Men moved toward their first real . . . targets.

"Game on."

"Is it morning?"

Canvas smiled warmly. "Always is somewhere, right?"

"I suppose." Xenos studied the man below him. He was unarmed, casual, relaxed, and completely in control. A bad sign. "How you been, Colin?"

"Fair. And yourself? How you been?"

"You tell me."

Canvas ignored him, instead pulling up a chair, sitting down, and lighting a cigar. "When my man got taken out so easy, that should have told me." He laughed. "And I got audiologist bills from what one of your toys did to my listener." He shook his head. "That's a new one on me." He shook his head. "You know, between you and the bitch, the insurance copayments on this thing are going to break me."

"Pity."

Canvas looked up sharply. "Not from you, old son. Never from you."

Xenos wet his lips. Canvas noticed, then gave him a drink of cold water from a pitcher nearby.

"Still chasing rainbows?"

Xenos exhaled deeply. "Ain't no rainbows anymore," he almost whispered.

The sitting man seemed shocked to the core. A wounded look that seemed to say that the blue sky had just been discovered as truly plaid.

"I don't believe it," he said quietly. "Not you. Not ever." Canvas stood and began pacing. "You're a constant of the universe, Jerry. Like the moon's orbit or flowers in spring." He chuckled. "You and me, old son. Sides of a coin."

He came so close that he brushed Xenos's chest—almost intimately—as he looked up into the burned-out eyes. "The White Knight on the side of the demons. The Black Knight on the side of the angels." He reached up, tenderly wiping sweat out of the hanging man's eyes. "We defined each other. We *were* each other."

"Ancient history."

Canvas gave him another drink. "Not history. We're the last two, you know. For at least our generation." Canvas's voice became veiled and choked with emotion. "Not history. *Legend*."

Somehow, Xenos managed a weak laugh. "I retired from the legend business."

The standing man regarded the hanging man closely for some minutes, then turned away—physically and emotionally. "I honestly *thought* you'd retired, Jerry. I'd heard you'd told them all to shove it where the sun don't shine and disappeared. Somewhere in the Med, I'd heard."

"I did."

Canvas shook his head as he turned back to face him. All emotion banished from his face. "You don't look retired to me." He moved to more closely examine the wounds to Xenos's exposed back and chest. "Looks like a through and through shoulder and a nick on the old collarbone. Must hurt like a nasty bugger." He shook his head as he studied the blackening wounds. "My people treating you all right?"

Xenos nodded. "More or less."

"More, I should think." He looked into the hanging man's eyes. "The *less* comes later."

"Pleasantries over, Colin?" Xenos asked in a conversational tone.

"Afraid so, Jerry. Afraid so. You're about to become an object lesson for the Honorable Ms. Alvarez." He hesitated. "Unless you want to tell me what she told you. What you know and who you're working for."

Xenos grimaced in expression and pain. "I don't think so."

Canvas took a deep, somehow sad breath. "No," he said softly. "I don't suppose you would." He started out of the room.

"Colin?"

"Yeah?"

"My father . . ."

"He's fine. We all know about you and him."

Xenos seemed to relax. "Thanks, man."

"Don't mention it."

Five minutes later Canvas returned with two brutes and Valerie. Then the beatings began.

The knock on the door almost catapulted Avidol off the couch. But he hesitated, waiting to be sure Sarah and Bradley were in the other room by the fire escape, before opening it. A short old man chewing an unlit cigar stood outside, an insincere smile on his face.

"Reb Goldman?"

"Yes?"

The man held out his hand. "Herb Stone. I'm a friend of your son."

"I don't know you," the old scholar said carefully.

"No? I'm not surprised, really. You haven't exactly spoken to Jerry a lot lately, have you?"

Avidol continued to ignore the outstretched hand and the un-dangerous face beyond it. "Where is my son?"

"Yes, well . . . that's what I'd like to talk about." He pushed past the barely resisting man. "Lovely apartment," he murmured perfunctorily as he sat down on the couch.

Avidol sat across from him. "What have you done to my boy?"

Herb looked genuinely shocked. "Me? I assure you I've done nothing to him at all. At least not lately," he said more to himself. "In fact," he continued in a stronger voice, "I'm worried about him myself."

Suddenly memory attached itself to the wrinkled face and the aged voice. "We've met before, Mr. Stone. Yes? Many years ago, when you came to steal my son." Anger dripped from the old man's voice. "Deny it!"

"You have a marvelous memory, Reb Goldman. I'd forgotten that myself," he obviously lied. "But better we discuss the present than the past."

"The two are joined," Avidol insisted. "If you had not cor-rupted my jewel then, you would not be here now."

"Interesting point, but—"

"Say what you have come to say, then leave. You and your kind are not welcome here."

Herb leaned back, relaxed. "Now I am intrigued. What *kind* am I?"

"Where is my son?"

"Answer for answer, Reb Goldman. Isn't that what the Tal-mud says?"

Avidol jumped up, would've struck the man if not for a life's dedication and discipline. "Do not," he warned in a cold voice, "*ever* quote from the holy books again." He recovered and slowly sat down. "Every word you speak is a blasphemy."

"And why is that?"

Realizing that there would be no straight answers or direct statement from the man in front of him until he was ready, Avidol resolved to wait him out. For seventy-one years he had studied law, philosophy, theology, morality, and ethics. He was prepared to play the man's word games back at him if that would get him closer to the answers he now desperately needed.

"You have no soul, Mr. Stone. It withered and died many years ago."

Herb played with his cigar. "But it was a grand funeral, I assure you. Please, do continue."

"You equate the ability to inflict pain with strength. You believe that a lie told with noble intent is the truth. You think that lives are yours for the taking, if you are strong enough, smart enough, to get away with it."

"Everyone has to have a talent." The ancient spymaster began gesturing with his cigar. "Yours was hypocrisy, as I recall. Jerry's was playing the piano, feral violence, and exquisite mendacity." He seemed to relish the memory, then caught himself. "But isn't that why you disowned him?" Herb asked as he lit his cigar.

"Are you the devil, Mr. Stone?"

Herb grinned. "Not in years."

"But you believe in Hell?"

For the first time, an air of seriousness crept over the spook across from the scholar. "Intimately."

"And would you consign my son's soul to it?"

"We make our own Hells, Mr. Goldman. Mine in marble buildings; your son's on volcanic islands." He took a deep drag on the cigar. "Yours, in your heart."

Avidol nodded. "There is truth there. But there is a fundamental difference between my Jerry and you."

Herb laughed. "A great many, I'm sure. Care to be more specific?"

"What my son did, whatever crimes against his fellowman and his God he may have committed, he did in the name of love."

"Love?"

"Love," Avidol said softly. "Love of country, of freedom; love of ideals you whispered into his ear even as you were perverting them. Jerry was a romantic warrior who might've been brought to understand, in time, that the true warrior—in the Jewish tradition —is the man who stands up for what he believes in, but never breaks God's laws."

"Thou shalt not kill and like that?" Herb sucked on his cigar. "*Ever?* Seems a bit limiting."

"Now you will tell me about my son," Avidol said after a moment's silence.

"I will? Why?"

"Because you have been entertained, and because you have learned what you needed to know."

"Which was?"

Avidol sadly lowered his head. "That I am an old man who— when confronted by sad realities and the stain of my loved one's blood—cares more about his son than his God's laws." At that moment, he seemed far older than his eighty-four years. "That I, like you, must bear my pain silently while seeking to end it."

Herb moved to the edge of the couch. "I don't know what's happened to your son. Not exactly anyway."

"But . . ."

Herb held up a cautionary hand. "What I do know is that something is very wrong. That *someone* is very wrong. And *that* someone has your son, for the moment anyway." He rolled the cigar in his mouth as he concentrated. "And I would very much like to know who that someone is."

"What do you want?" Avidol sensed something, fear maybe, deep down in this blank man with the insincere smile.

"The reality is," Herb continued as if he hadn't heard the old man, "Jerry will either be dead or free in the next twenty-four hours."

"You know this?" Avidol almost reached out to the man across from him.

"I *know* Jerry," was his cryptic reply. "If he contacts you, I'd like you to call me." He handed across a card with only a phone number on it. "I can be reached there twenty-four hours a day."

"And my son can trust you?"

Herb shrugged. "Well, he can *count* on me. Let's leave it at that, shall we?" He stood, starting for the door.

Avidol followed him out. "Why would you help him?"

Herb knocked the ash off his cigar into the fireplace. "Because I was once a romantic warrior as well." He exhaled deeply. "It's just that I grew up."

At the door, Avidol noticed the three large bodyguards standing just outside. "He will not come to me, Mr. Stone. We were finished years ago."

Herb buttoned his coat and smiled. "One of our first rules—us murderers and sinners—is that the only ones you can trust are those who've already betrayed you." He smiled. "If he can, he'll make contact."

Avidol watched him start down the stairs, carefully watched over by his phalanx of bodyguards.

"Shalom, Mr. Stone," the dedicated religious pacifist heard himself say.

"Peace?" Herb rolled the word on his tongue, then sadly shook his head. "Interesting idea." He chuckled bitterly. "Shalom, Reb Goldman. Shalom."

"I don't think you're appreciating the finer points of the exercise, Valerie," Canvas said pleasantly.

She strained against the iron grip of the man who held her facing the beaten man hanging from the ceiling beam. "What *finer points?*" she spat out. "That you can beat the Hell out of an innocent man?"

Canvas shrugged, then nodded, and the beating began again. Two men, taking turns hammering Xenos in the face and stomach with broom handles. Each strike raising large welts, or splitting existing ones bloodily open. "He may be a lot of things, Valerie, but innocent *is not* one of them."

A blow under Xenos's rib cage.

"And I'd hardly qualify this as a beating."

A blow to the face.

"More like a warm-up for the real grotesqueries to come."

Valerie shivered as she tried to look away from the blood-covered face and the swelling injuries. "You sick bastard!" Her face was turned to continue watching. "What do you want?"

"Open the case," Canvas said simply.

"Or what? You'll beat a stranger to death?"

Canvas signaled for the beating to stop as he stepped between Valerie and Xenos. "I told you, this is just a warm-up." He smiled. "The main event comes when I let these rather talented gentlemen loose on your son and daughter."

He turned to Xenos, taking a towel and wiping the blood from his mostly swollen-shut eyes. "Somehow I don't think the tykes will stand up near as well as my friend here."

Valerie closed her eyes in the most tearing psychic pain of her life.

"What do you think, Jerry?" Canvas asked as he gave Xenos a drink of cool water.

"Let me down and I'll show you," the wounded man somehow whispered through the agony.

Canvas shook his head. "I know you would," he said almost sympathetically. He turned back to Valerie. "It won't be pretty, it will be prolonged, and I *will* make you watch every moment of it, I promise you."

"*Monstruo,*" Valerie cried.

The big man shrugged. "*Mi madre lo quiere.*" He waved the men from the room. "I'll give you a few minutes to think about it." He looked over at Xenos. "Give her some good advice, man. I don't think she gets it." He started out of the room.

"Colin?" Xenos's voice was surprisingly strong and clear.

"Yeah?"

"Let it go, man."

The man turned, regarding Xenos as he swung lazily in the air. "*You* wouldn't."

"I did."

A noncommittal shrug. "Which is why you're swinging and I'm making retirement bucks."

The door closed, locked, and they were alone.

"I'm sorry," Valerie whispered. "So sorry."

Xenos spat some blood from his mouth. "I don't really care right now."

"They're going to kill my babies," she moaned. "No matter what I do." She took in deep breaths, sobs mixing with calm until after five minutes she'd mostly recovered. "They're going to kill us all."

Xenos ignored her, staring up at the beam, the rope looped around it, the knots on each of his bloody wrists.

"I don't know who you are," Valerie continued with growing strength and resolve, "or if it'll make you feel any better"—she walked over to him, taking the towel and gently wiping his face clear of blood—"but when they come back, I'm going to end it."

Xenos studied her, thought about what he'd read about her, what he'd heard on his room tap. Despite the pain and his rapidly depleting resources, he easily slipped into analysis mode, then smiled.

Something about that smile chilled her to the bone.

"If you kill them, then you guarantee your children's deaths," he said matter-of-factly.

"But they'll . . ."

Xenos looked down at her through slits of eyes, a broken nose, and blackened, seeping wounds. "Let me help you."

Ten minutes later Canvas, the interrogators, and three guards returned.

"Time's up, Valerie." He held up her case. "Either you open it now, with no tricks, or you can watch the destruction of the kiddies. Your choice."

Valerie's mind was racing.

Her nightmare existence had changed into a pornographic hallucination into a demonic visitation. Sanity and madness merged, separated, mutated, and blew apart into billions of pieces all within the same second. Her ears filled with the rush-ing of her blood, her skin went cold, muscles tightened, eyes went in and out of focus.

"Valerie," Canvas said in an annoyed tone, "I'm waiting."

She took what she supposed to be a final breath, mentally said a private prayer for the souls of her children, then turned to the case.

First combination: 6-6-6.

Second combination: 0-1-8.

"Not that I don't trust you, dear," Canvas said as he placed the case on a chair in front of her. He waved everybody back to his side of the room, then nodded at the case. "If you please."

She closed her eyes for a moment. Then—her conscience clear, committed, ready—she snapped the latches up, turned each toward the outside of the case, then lifted the lid.

"Impressive," the First mumbled to Canvas as they watched her reach in for the files.

The butt of the cocked and loaded Browning slid easily into her hand, just the way she'd practiced.

First the one directly in front of you, then anyone to your right, then my shot—and don't freakin' miss—then the floor. Xe-nos's words echoed in her brain in the nanosecond between thought and action. Then she pulled back from the case.

The first shot exploded through the room, paralyzing every-one. It took off the top of the head of one of the interrogators. Before any reaction could set in, she'd already swung the gun around and fired a lethal shot into the chest of one of the guards. As she dropped straight to the floor, her arm flew straight up and she fired twice more.

Time seemed to stop, her mind expand, as she could plainly see the panic setting in across the room. The man they called Can-vas dived for the door. A confused guard had got his gun caught on his jacket lining and died from her next shot. Another shot and another of the interrogators died. Too late, she saw two more guards—their guns already out—move to her right.

There was no chance, she would die, but not before she slapped the security case from the chair, activating the document-destruct device. Three seconds after it had started, she prepared to die . . . as an animal's scream filled the air.

Something heavy fell on her, and she realized with a start that it was a body. She rolled out from under it just in time to see Xenos drop the second corpse—the man's head turned around facing backward with a stunned expression—on the floor by her. With a roar, he grabbed the man's gun and leaped out the door firing a nonstop barrage.

Praying she wasn't going insane, Valerie followed him.

They ran the length of the corridor, Xenos killing two more guards at almost point-blank range, their brains exploding over the fleeing couple. A door started to open behind them and Valerie fired three rounds into it. She heard something drop to the floor but never looked back.

They burst through the fire door onto the stairs, less than a minute after it had started.

"Up!" Xenos said in an urgent whisper.

"But . . ."

She never finished her confused thought as two men came through the door. Xenos threw her to the side and slammed into them. The first toppled over the railing, then caromed off concrete stairs for the next three floors. The other regained his balance—if not the gun, which had been knocked from his hand. He pulled a knife from his boot, but it was pointless. Adrenalized fury grabbed the man's hand, turning it up toward his face, driving it through his eye.

"Up!" Xenos yelled again as he grabbed the fallen gun and hurried up the stairs behind Valerie.

Two flights later they broke into the corridor, both taking deadly aim at the emptiness there.

Xenos led her slowly through the building.

"What now?" Valerie said, panting, trying to suppress the bile that had risen three-quarters of the way in her throat.

"Nice shooting," was all he said as he kept his eyes forward and moved slowly.

For the first time she saw the ragged rope at his right wrist, along with the wound she caused when she'd shot. The man was covered with blood—his and several others'—was wounded, broken in almost every possible way. But he seemed unaware of it, just a preternatural beast from Hell's depths wandering an office building looking for people to kill.

"They'll look downstairs first," he finally said as they paused by a drinking fountain. He cupped his hand and splashed water into his swelling-shut eyes. "We've got ten minutes, tops."

"Then what?"

Something across the corridor seemed to catch his attention. "Watch the elevators and the stairs. Anyone comes through"—he handed her his gun—"kill them."

Valerie couldn't breathe. Her heart was racing, the guns abnormally heavy in her grasp. "But what if it's some innocent guy coming to work?"

Xenos was closely examining a door to an office. "No innocents today," he mumbled. "Dentist's office." He tried the knob, studied the door frame, then stepped back. A deep breath, then he kicked the door open with a crashing splintering of wood.

And somewhere deep inside, a siren screamed to life.

"All exits locked down and covered by closed circuit; elevators shut down. Floors three through basement are clear. We're starting up now."

Canvas nodded as he listened to another report coming in on a radio. "Damage?"

The guard shook his head and bit his lips. "Too fucking much," he said in shocked tones. But the look on his employer's face quickly snapped him back to order.

"Five in the room including two of the players, but I think the Kraut got out clean." He took a deep breath. "Three in the corridor, two more in the stairwell."

"Personnel?"

"We're down to five not counting you and me and a medic." The man seemed to drift. "I mean, I'd heard stories, you know? But I never thought that, I mean, Jesus!"

"Hey!"

"Sorry, boss."

Canvas put his arm around the nervous man. "Pull the men back. I need those bodies out of there before the coppers show, right?"

The man seemed to regain himself. "No chance of that. No one could've heard the shots, and we shut down the building's telephone trunks as soon as it happened."

Just then an alarm from one of the upper floors broke through the otherwise silent darkness.

"Hello, Jerry." Canvas smiled up at the darkened building. "Get those bodies out through the garage now! We've got maybe five minutes." The man raced into the building.

Canvas changed the frequency on his radio, then pressed the call key for ten seconds. Finally, shaking his head, he spoke into the microphone.

"Point taken, Jerry." His voice echoed through the building's emergency intercom. "But this is just starting, right? Game on and all that." He swallowed hard, forcing all anxiety out of his voice. "No authorities, or the lady's children are done for. You know me, you know what I mean, right?" He released the button.

"Hey, Colin?" Xenos's voice sounded tinny and far away over the intercom's relay.

"Yeah?"

"Let it go, man."

Canvas looked long and hard at the upper floors of the building before answering. Even longer and deeper into the heart of the man on the other end of the radio.

"Fraid I can't. You take the money, you hook the fish."

A long, fanged silence.

"I understand," Xenos said flatly.

Canvas sighed, turned away, and started toward a waiting car. As in the distance red flashing lights and squealing sirens could be heard.

"How'd you know they wouldn't kill them?" Valerie looked shocked as Xenos hurriedly cleaned himself up in the dentist's office.

"Leverage," he mumbled. "With you in their control, your

kids were almost worthless and therefore expendable. With you loose"—he pulled a sweater he'd found in a desk drawer over his head—"the kids are all they have to keep you quiet; under control."

Valerie helped him adjust his clothes. "But what now? If I go to the FBI or anyone . . ."

"He *will* kill them. Guaranteed."

"So what do we do now?"

He threw some bandages and disinfectant into a canvas bag and headed out. "We leave."

"How? We can't talk to the cops, and the others are probably waiting right outside for us!"

Xenos took a deep breath, then turned to her. "Well, we just have . . . uh, we've gotta . . ."

Valerie barely caught him as he toppled over. His weight knocked her over and they collapsed to the floor.

"Swell."

The sniper scope's crosshairs moved steadily back and forth over the parking garage's mesh doors. Its infrared sighting mechanism casting the gate and the street around it in an eerie pale orange.

"Nothing," the sniper said as he continued to monitor the area. "Maybe they're gonna try another way."

Canvas just shook his head. "This is how they'll come."

"How do you know?"

The big man smiled spasmodically. "It's how *I* would do it."

As a child, they'd called it "shaft surfing." Valerie could still remember her mother's frightened expression the few times her only daughter had been caught doing it. She also remembered two neighborhood boys who had been crushed to death or electrocuted while crouching in the slippery darkness, waiting to "catch a ride." But she'd always been unafraid, and if the boys could do it, well, she had to do it better.

The elevator doors opened easily, the way she'd remembered

they did. And the car itself was just two flights below, maybe twenty feet. The trick now was the timing.

Made all the more complicated by the half-conscious man beside her.

"Hey! You ready for this?"

Xenos nodded, saving his strength for the next few minutes.

The two of them sat on the threshold of the elevator, their feet dangling in the shaft. Valerie leaned forward watching the car below them. After several minutes, it began to move up.

"Okay. Here we go. When you feel it hit your feet, just lean forward quickly and let it take your weight."

"I know."

Valerie held her breath as she saw the car start upward again. She'd been the 103rd Street Champion for an entire summer. Twenty-six cars ridden consecutively over one summer vacation.

"Here it comes. Wait. Wait. Wai . . . Now," she whispered as she leaned forward and half fell onto the top of the elevator. All the while praying that Xenos was conscious enough to do it right.

"Hey, Sarge. You hear that?"

"Hear what?"

"A thump. I heard a thump."

The Bristol police sergeant shook his head. "I didn't hear nothing. Now get ready. Larsen, Washington, you go left. D'Amico, you're with me on the right."

The elevator bell rang, and the doors opened on an empty floor.

Three hours later—after a perfunctory police investigation of a break-in at a dentist's office, amid the morning crush of arriving office workers—a limping man heavily leaning on a smaller woman casually walked out the front door of the office building and hailed a cab.

Six

Xi Lin Huan was a patient man, born of a patient people. A man of dedication, national loyalty, and pure—state-endorsed—vision. For forty years he had waited his turn, stood in lines, accepted his lot as his due at that moment. Forty years from private soldier in the border skirmishes with Burma to commanding officer of the Long-Range Study Organization of the People's Liberation Army.

At sixty-three, he was arguably one of the most powerful men in the People's Republic of China.

From his office deep beneath the Forbidden City he oversaw the most delicate, the most daring intelligence operations in the world. Plans that stretched across decades and shifting alliances.

Operations begun by men long dead; who died happily knowing that their work would one day bear fruit.

There were—in fact—seven such operations in place across the globe. Intricate intelligence warfares that were designed to leave the PRC the sole remaining superpower in a post–Cold War world.

And the one on his mind as he took his usual late night walk among the brightly lit gardens of the former Imperial Palace was code-named *Apple Blossom.*

Xi was followed by his aides as he strolled along the green paths. One by one, following a gesture or a nod, they would come forward, give their morning reports, receive orders, then fall back into the pack. None of the others ever close enough to hear a carelessly loud word or read the lips of the general.

Xi had spent nine years as a member of the pack, understood their nervousness and ambition—the problems they brought to him might have begun before they were born—but he still gave them little comfort or help. None had been offered him, and his country had none offered to it in the last half century. And if these younger men behind him were to carry on the work he stewarded, they must learn to be as hard as he.

He stopped by a small flower bush, kneeled down, and began a meticulous examination of the leaves. A moment later one of the packlings stepped forward, bowed, then stood beside him.

"Sir."

"Proceed," Xi said as he turned the leaves in his callused hands.

"The, uh, German reports that there has been an incident." The young officer stiffened. *An incident*—LRSO shorthand for a major disaster. And many a messenger had suffered for delivering such a message.

"Continue," the old general said as he brushed some aphids off the flower.

"Sir. It has been reported that Yü and Xuë have been lost."

The insects seemed to be coming from a colony in the dirt between two flower bushes. As he listened, Xi pulled out a pencil and began probing in the dirt.

"There were additional fatalities and a possible compromising of operational integrity."

The pencil traced a small trough in the dirt, which Xi spit into several times. As he expected, the tiny bugs began to swarm out of their nest along the path. Xi watched in fascination as they divided into forward scouts, flanking columns, and a main body that held back as the others moved into the trough or along its sides.

"Responsibility?" he asked distractedly.

"Primarily Congresswoman Alvarez, with assistance from Indigo One."

"Continue."

The young man almost hesitated. It was so short a moment, virtually unnoticed, but it spoke volumes to the man watching the insects prepare for battle.

And it guaranteed that the man's promotion had been put back for at least five years.

Xi had little tolerance for men afraid to act and accept the consequences of their actions.

"Sir," the man continued, "Canvas has confirmed that Indigo One is, as suspected, Gerald Michael Goldman, a former special assignment officer in the Defense Intelligence Agency's Operations Directorate. The American Registry reports that SAO Goldman was killed in an automobile accident ten years ago. We are, uh, pursuing the discrepancy."

Xi pulled out a small pocketknife, barely pricking his finger and allowing several drops of blood to fall into the path of the miniature army. Then he took out several wooden matchsticks, rolled them in the smeared blood on his finger, and dropped them in as well.

"Status?" he asked as the insects paused in obvious caution, then, forced forward by the smell of fresh death, moved over the unlit matches.

"Alvarez and Goldman are still at large," the aide said too quickly. "The reports on the traitor Pei's interrogation are still unavailable. But Canvas believes that Apple Blossom has not been *wholly* compromised as yet; that full containment will be restored within seventy-two hours." He stiffened as he awaited instructions.

"How is it that an SAO has remained unknown to Registry, to us, for ten years?" Xi's voice was a bare shadow as he leaned close to the insects as all elements came together over the bloody pile.

"Canvas reports that Goldman has been using the name Xenos Filotimo. Most probably living in an isolated part of the Mediterranean. What the Americans call a *shelved asset*."

"Who chooses now to make his return to the living. I'm not fond of the coincidence."

"No, sir."

"Inform Canvas he is to reestablish control of the situation and eliminate both Goldman and Alvarez at his first opportunity." Xi lit a match, held it for long moments as it burned close to his fingertips, then lightly dropped it into the milling, losing-interest insects. The matches beneath exploded into an orange sulfurous blaze, immolating the insects in its midst; drawing the remainder into the flame and death.

Sighing, he stood, dusted his trousers, and headed deeper into the gardens.

"I wonder if they've gotten to the lilies?" After twenty feet he stopped, seemed to look up at the stars, even deeper into the instincts that he so trusted.

"Xenos Filotimo." The light breeze brought his words back to the aides. "Stranger of Unbending Honor."

He turned back to his aides. "Full crisis management corps assembly in fifteen minutes, please."

The aides sprinted off to set the almost unprecedented orders in motion.

Xi slowly followed them, regretting that he would have to put off further inspection of the gardens. But there was something in that name—in its entry into the already thirty-one-year-old Apple Blossom plan at this moment, in this way—that reeked of chaos.

And, to a man like Xi, chaos was unimaginably bad.

The phone was answered on the third ring. "Paradise Café."

"I want to place an order for delivery."

"What's your phone number?"

"Thirteen."

A short silence. "Just a second."

Two minutes later another voice came on the line. "Quattro Cani."

"Filotimo."

"*Parla.*"

"*Mi chiami un taxi a New York.*"

"*C'è qualcosa che non va?*"

Xenos looked around the busy diner before answering in a near whisper. "You gonna help or what?"

"Where you at?"

"South of Waterbury, Connecticut; on eighty-four. I got wheels, but strictly short-term."

A brief silence followed by a whispered conversation in Italian taking place in the background.

"Conosci Bridgeport?" the Corsican facilitator finally asked. "I can find it."

"Prendi il Port Jefferson Ferry. Two-fifteen or 3:35. Any later you call us. You be met, okay?"

Xenos hung up and casually walked away from the booth.

After circling the diner twice, he stopped to check the cars in the parking lot. All Connecticut plates, none with casual couples eating or resting in them, none with the carefully concealed antenna that would indicate surveillance vehicles. But he couldn't be sure.

Xenos knew what Canvas knew and vice versa. Nothing could be taken for granted or left to chance.

Swallowing a handful of the aspirin he'd bought earlier, he climbed a low fence, dashed across the main road, and disappeared into a grove of trees. For ten minutes he watched the diner, the comings and goings, then left the grove another way.

Valerie sat behind the wheel of the car on a dirt road, engine running. She was more confused, more frightened, more drained than at any time in her life. The blood and tension of the last few hours now manifested as complete exhaustion and she fought to keep her eyes open.

Easy, actually. Since every time they closed, her mind conjured up images of broken and bleeding children crying for their mother to save them.

Cursing her for deserting them.

She jumped when she heard the passenger door slam shut.

"Let's go," Xenos said quietly as he slumped down in the seat. His wounds and injuries kept him perilously close to full collapse, only his will keeping him functioning. But for how much longer he wasn't sure.

"Where to?"

"South on eighty-four to Bridgeport."

Valerie dropped the stolen car with the stolen plates in gear. "And then?"

Xenos coughed up blood, his face paled, he began to sweat heavily. "They're looking, so until we can get out of the country or they stop looking, we keep moving."

"God," Valerie mumbled under her breath as she pulled onto the highway, "when does it stop?"

Xenos exhaled deeply, then painfully turned toward her. "You committed yourself when you put the gun in the case," he said flatly between coughs and blood bubbles forming at his nose and mouth. "No going back." He closed his eyes as he tried to settle himself more comfortably on the seat. "Never any going back."

"But it can't go on forever." Valerie concentrated on changing lanes every few minutes as she'd previously been instructed. "I don't think you realize what's going on. You see . . ."

"I don't want to know!" He opened his eyes, fury and something else—despondency, maybe—firing there. "Goddammit, I said I'd help you. I'll do that. But I *do not* want to get involved. I don't do that shit anymore. I'll get you safe and in contact with people who can help you, but beyond that, you're on your own! I'm just not involved in this, right?"

Not for the first time in the last few hours Valerie began to question the sanity of her companion. "How can you say that? How many people have you killed, have *we* killed? Do you really think that madman, that *Canvas* guy, is going to let you just be uninvolved?"

"He's not a madman."

She could barely hear him between the bloody coughs and his lifeless voice. "What?" She handed him a bottle of water.

Xenos drank half the contents in one swallow, poured the remainder over his head. "He's not a madman. Just a working stiff."

Valerie hoped the man wasn't becoming delirious. "Hey! Stay with me!" she yelled as he seemed about to pass out.

"Colin, er, Canvas," he said as he blinked himself back, "is just a guy being paid to do a job. He doesn't have any feelings about it. Won't take things personally or get angry. He's too good for that. He'll just—" Another hacking fit silenced him for the moment. "He'll just sit," he continued after a minute, "think, analyze, plan for all contingencies."

"Jesus."

Xenos somehow managed a smile. "Less prone to accidents than he was." He reached up and turned the rearview toward him, carefully watching the following traffic as he continued. "I was an accident. A minor course correction. A thing he'll make allowances for in the future that won't essentially change his plans." He studied the cars behind them. "Change lanes and speed up."

Valerie did as she was instructed while trying to comprehend what the man was explaining as though it were the most natural thing in the world.

"If I stay out of his way in the future," Xenos continued slowly, "he'll stay out of mine."

"Why the Hell would he do that?"

Xenos shrugged. "Call it professional courtesy."

"Who *are* you? How do you know all this? Christ! You talk about it like it's a couple of lawyers on a civil divorce case! Like it's all a Goddamned walk in the woods!"

Xenos smiled, painfully but fully. "I like that," he mumbled as he began to lose consciousness again.

The blood trail was strong, vibrant in the gray soil. Each droplet leaving an oval indentation, segregating a given footprint from all the others in the dirt.

Jerry moved quickly but smoothly. Gliding through the brush alongside the trail, eyes searching for more of the traitorous gore, ears straining to pick up any sound; mind counting down the time he had left before he would have to give up the search.

And fail.

But failure was not allowed in the program. Nothing short of complete success was accepted, so he continued on.

A pure predator on the scent.

The drops led off the road, toward a small barn behind an abandoned farm. Calculating how much time he had left, the possibilities of being observed and interdicted, the possible countermoves of his, well, quarry, he moved.

Kicking in a side door, he fired short bursts at every movement. His orders were completely clear: this traitor and his family were not to get back across the border into the deep East. The damage that they could then do, he'd been briefed, would be cataclysmic.

Lives would be lost, he'd been assured.

America, all America, was depending on him, he'd been conditioned.

In his first series of volleys two dogs, a horse, and a middleaged woman died. In the next . . . a running teenage boy.

Then the father, the traitor, the hunted.

The victim.

Jerry felt nothing, was numbed—by a rapidly depleting energy reserve, the adrenaline of the action, by drill. By something else as well.

These weren't people—he'd been trained—they were the enemy. To feel anything for the enemy was, in and of itself, a treasonous act.

Swallowing more of the Agency's unofficially encouraged (but officially banned) nepenthe—a highly addictive Middle Eastern drug that "tranquilizes the soul"—he paused waiting to feel the effects of the latest dose take hold before the last wore off.

Slowly he felt the drug—created in the time of the Pharaohs and improved by Nazi experimentation—crawl into his brain. He began to sweat and shiver, felt an erection grow then dissipate, felt the emotions of the moment slip away into a gray void that he was barely conscious of.

Men under the influence of "black mooders" were said to be able to do anything—torture close family members, kill lovers, spouses, children, anyone—without ever feeling a moment's guilt or psychic pain afterward.

Ever. As if the event were not a memory, but something dimly recalled from a news article read decades before.

But the body's tolerance to nepenthe began almost with the first dose. So, on each occasion, more would be needed to guarantee what Herb called "the freedoms of actions" necessary to "be a good soldier."

Some days, it seemed there would never be enough capsules in *the bottle, Jerry thought as he waited for his body's temperature to return to normal and his pulse to ease.*

With a deep breath, he quickly and thoroughly returned to the task at hand. He searched all three bodies, then began the next phase of the operation.

Cyrillic writing was spray-painted above the man's corpse, indicating that he was a traitor to the Soviet Union; his tongue was cut out and shoved in his pants. His dead wife's skirt was pulled up above her waist, her underclothes ripped away, then she was turned over as if shot trying to escape a rape. Cocaine was planted on the boy.

As the healing haze of the drug began to seep through him, Jerry surveyed his work, then turned to leave. A rustle behind and to his left caused him to throw himself to the ground. He quickly rolled to his knees, turned, and fired a burst . . . just over the head of a six-month-old baby hidden in the straw.

For twenty minutes, narcotics, orders, conditioning, and frayed humanity fought for control of the man who had killed twenty-nine times before.

Cleanly.

Professionally.

But never—completely—dispassionately.

Eight hours later the Stasi—the East German secret police—raided the barn, quickly concluding that the KGB had killed one of their own . . . for what would undoubtedly be their own reasons. They would carefully search the scene, gather evidence, then set the old building alight, an improvised crematorium for the man, his wife, and his teenage son.

The next day, an infant would be left at the gate of the Sisters of Hope mission in Toulon, France, with a note that read simply:

I'm sorry.

Valerie violently lurched the car side to side, forcing the man back up. "Goddammit, I can't do this without you! Whoever the Hell you are. Talk to me, dammit!"

More coughing, his features wincing from the pain. "*You're* what he wants, what his employers want. You stay loose and moving and dangerous, and they'll have to negotiate. Canvas will make that clear to them." Another fleeting, spasmodic smile. "If he doesn't kill you first."

Valerie shook her head in confusion and shock. "He sounds like a bloody robot to me. Put in your nickel and he kills, kidnaps, whatever."

Xenos nodded. "So long as you keep the nickels coming." He pointed to the left fork of an interchange. "Bridgeport off ramp."

"Then?" Valerie was beginning to sound as washed-out as the wounded man beside her.

"Just do what I say, every time I say it, exactly like I say it, and you and your children will be fine. I'll get you out of the country, someplace safe. Get you in contact with people that can help you."

"People like this Canvas bastard?" She laughed bitterly. "How many more like him can there be?"

"One," Xenos said as he closed his eyes. He began to drift off. "Just one," and he was out.

"Left, left, left, *left!*"

The attorney general of the United States was screaming to his personal aide as the man broke for the open spot on the field. He threw the football as hard as he could, his aide dived, but the ball bounced scant inches from his fingers.

"Shit."

"Fourth down, Jeff," Senator Buckley called from the middle linebacker position of his staff's team. "You gonna throw another wounded duck, or get surgery on your shoulder first?"

"Up yours." DeWitt laughed back. "I've got you just where you want me." His staff's team gathered around him. "Quarterback draw on three," he whispered. "Michael?"

"Yeah." His aide looked up at him in anticipation.

"Think you can knock that fat-assed senator into next week?"

The two men exchanged long, understanding looks. "Follow me, Mr. Attorney General, sir."

They broke the huddle.

DeWitt's and Buckley's eyes remained locked as he called out the cadence, then the ball was snapped.

Michael faked to his left, then cut back over the middle. Knowing that his boss was only a step or two behind, he lowered his shoulder, slamming into Buckley's groin with the full force of his 190 pounds. The chairman of the Senate Armed Services Committee doubled over, as DeWitt sprinted past for a touchdown.

"Some touch football game," Kingston shouted from the sidelines where his team was stretching and preparing for their game against the Commerce Department.

"Justice can be terrible swift," Attorney General DeWitt called back.

It was a typical fall afternoon in a suburban D.C. park. The usual mix of government workers, students, tourists, and military. The sun reflected off a nearby lake as it began its descent toward the woods on the other side. As the games—interagency or departmental—wound down, the barbecue pits were lit, and the smell of burgers slowly replaced the scent of sweat.

As one of the players started off on his usual postgame jog through the woods before eating with the merged staffs.

Halfway through the woods, the jogger stopped, falling into step alongside his weekly companion on walks through the Georgetown campus.

"This is fucking dangerous," the jogger said after they'd finished with the security rituals.

"No more so than usual," the older man replied calmly. "Just one of the president's favorites with one of the president's friends. What could be more natural?"

"I don't know, Old Man, fifty years to life in Leavenworth?"

The president's friend and adviser winced. "A not likely scenario, if we all keep our heads."

The jogger shook his head. "I can tell you personally, that's not happening. Ever since word got out about last night's . . ." The look on the Old Man's face stopped him. "After last night, a lot of us in the Apple Blossom chain are having trouble staying calm."

"Have there been specific problems?"

"Not yet," the jogger said. "But my cell alone is already starting to think crazy thoughts." He laughed bitterly. "And it's the smallest Goddamned cell in espionage history."

The Old Man nodded. "My reason for this meeting." He checked his watch. "How much longer can you give me?"

"I don't know. Ten minutes maybe; then I have to get back. I'll be missed."

"Very well, then, let me bring you up to date. The field controllers are dead. As are many support personnel. Canvas has begun search operations and expects to have the situation back under control within seventy-two hours.

"There has been no direct exposure of you or any others in the chain. The only one at risk is me, and the sword over her children's heads should keep the good woman silent."

"For the moment," the jogger added.

"For the moment," the Old Man agreed. "The toothpaste will be back in the tube in short order, I assure you."

The jogger took then exhaled a deep breath. "Sure," he said without confidence.

"What we need from you," the Old Man said carefully, "is to keep things on track, right? Keep everyone calm, everyone working, everyone on schedule. We are no more at risk than we have ever been. *That* is your message and must be your example."

The jogger bit his lips and nodded. "Okay. Just catch this bitch before anything else happens. I'd like my heart to start beating again in my lifetime."

The Old Man laughed openly. "As would we all."

The jogger began to stretch. "When do I meet the new field controllers?"

"You already have."

"You? How? They trust you that much?"

"Not really," the Old Man replied. "But they do *know* me. Since a confused twenty-year-old fell into their hands in Korea, more than half a century before." He hesitated, as if to reveal more would be to reveal too much. But the look of doubt on the jogger's face convinced him.

"I reached an accommodation with them then, and we have been very good to each other since. They know that I care too much about my payoffs to jeopardize anything. They know they can destroy me quite easily, at a whim, and they know that I am *painfully* conscious of the fact.

"More to the point, though, they have little choice." He shook his head sadly. "This was a terrible time for this to happen, things are just too close. They can't risk the delay of preparing new controls, then getting them into place. They are forced into using me, just as I am forced into taking ever greater risk."

He sighed deeply. "It's a vicious circle that will one day immolate both sides, I expect," he said with genuine sorrow. Then he brightened.

"But not today, or in the immediate future, right?"

The jogger studied the Old Man, paused, then started off down the trail that led back to the picnickers. "I'll pass the word." And he was off at a slow trot.

The Old Man watched him go, then turned and watched the sunset until he was completely surrounded by the dark.

As he had been for the last half century.

The Grand Republic was a resplendent sight on its worst days.

Gleaming white, rising over sixty feet out of the water, the ferry between Bridgeport, Connecticut, and Port Jefferson, New York, had two car decks, an inside observation deck, an elegant formal bar, and a weather deck that could hold over 150 people. It was the pride of the multiferry fleet that serviced Long Island and a virtual historical landmark.

But to Xenos and Valerie, it was simply a place to get to. The world's largest getaway car.

After parking their car on the murky, gray streets of the industrial section of Bridgeport, they'd walked the last three blocks. Weaving through six lanes of cars waiting to board through the boat's gaping raised bow, they made their way to the narrow gangway used for the few carless passengers that regularly fled Bridgeport for the fairyland resort of Port Jefferson.

They immediately climbed to the top weather deck, where

they both searched the oncoming cars and people that were seem-ingly devoured by the boat as they drove into its cavernous bowels. Only after the boat had backed away from the dock, made its tight turn around Bridgeport Granite Inc., and given its passengers a view of the fetid dying land around the harbor did they finally give up their watch and go belowdeck.

"Who are we looking for?"

Xenos shrugged. He'd slept a little on the trip over and was now experiencing his fifth wind of the day. "Just stay alert. They said we'd be met."

He gave her the last of his money—he didn't even have the fare for the tickets he would need to get off the boat—and sent her to the tiny snack bar to buy some coffee. Eventually they settled at one of the incongruous-looking picnic tables with the thin, rickety plastic chairs that groaned their objection to any weight.

Children ran around, people opened some of the large win-dows allowing cold winds from Long Island Sound to race through the relatively bare deck; some bought snacks and perched on ledges to watch the water go by or the other passengers. Some wandered into or out of the bar or up and down from the car decks. The usual mix for a late afternoon ferry ride.

But to Valerie, they all looked like threats, all sinister, deadly. Each man and woman waiting to catch them up and throw them overboard. Each child a smiling accusation of her failed maternity.

So she wasn't surprised when Xenos tensed, staring across the wide enclosed deck, and tapped on her tightly clasped hands.

"We have a problem."

Valerie shook her head. "Has it ever been otherwise?" She followed his gaze, sadly recognizing one of the guards from the building. "You think he's alone?"

"I doubt it," Xenos said as his gaze shifted to another man in his forties in an elegantly expensive suit who was smiling as he casually walked over to their table.

"Judging by what's left of your face, you have to be the man I'm supposed to be meeting." He pulled over a chair and sat down, as Valerie edged away from him.

"If I told you that I had a gun under this table," Xenos said conversationally, "you'd talk to me, right?"

The man seemed unfazed. "That's why I'm here."

"So convince me." Xenos's eyes never wavered from the casual man's.

"Okay," the man began after a moment of thought. "Let's see. What would be the best way to break the ice?" He suddenly brightened. "Franco says don't worry about transportation. He *never* walks."

Xenos slid his gun back into his boot. "He's okay."

Valerie exhaled deeply, then leaned in to hear the whispered conversation.

"How bad are things?" the man asked.

"Worse than you can imagine," Xenos answered. "We're hot, targeted, with no money and fewer options. We need to get out of the country."

"Not a problem."

The man's casual manner, confidence, almost carefree attitude, struck Valerie as just the latest lunacy in her lunatic day. "You do realize," she said urgently, "that people are trying to kill us?"

"Congresswoman Alvarez," he beamed, "I'm an admirer. Even thought about voting for you once or twice." He paused. "Does that make me a stupid man or a smart one?"

Valerie relaxed for a brief instant and smiled. "Can I let you know in a couple of hours?"

He turned back to Xenos, handing him two ferry tickets. "Call me Gary. It'll do for the moment."

He began nibbling on the corn chips Valerie had bought. "First things first. Do either of you have any contraband, any drugs, guns, documents, or anything else that could get you in trouble with the legitimate authorities?"

They shook their heads.

"Mr. Filotimo, before we leave this table, you're going to have to give me that gun you mentioned. I have a carry permit, so there won't be any trouble if I have it."

Xenos raised his swollen eyebrows. "And what about our friends over there?"

"How many do you make?"

Xenos never moved his head, but his eyes took in everything. "One stone pro, maybe two punks working with him."

Gary nodded. "Local hire, brought over from Hartford and Queens. And we make it one slick and four pussies."

He began to casually look around the deck. "Pro's moved over to the snack bar to try and hear what we're talking about. Local number one by the starboard staircase to the car deck. Number two's by the port one. Number three's in the bar behind us. Number four on the upper car deck."

Xenos easily spotted the men within view. "And you want me to give up the gun." It was a sad statement, not a question.

Gary shrugged. "Mr. Filotimo, Congresswoman Alvarez, I've been in this business for a long time and I've done hundreds of deals like this one. You have to trust me. I'm a straight shooter who's only looking out for your best interest."

He smiled again. "Listen, I live on repeat business. Let me impress you on this one and maybe you'll throw some other deals my way in the future. Right? We'll all have some fun, maybe make a couple of bucks."

Valerie looked questioningly at Xenos, who continued to study the man across from him. Slowly he pulled the gun from his boot and handed it—under the table—to him.

"Okay," Gary said comfortably as he tossed the gun into his open briefcase, "now watch how I look after your best interests." He brushed some hair out of his eyes.

They watched incredulously as men began to casually move next to each of the identified threats. Reading newspapers, carrying sweaters or gym bags, they each settled next to the armed men— who almost immediately stiffened with surprised looks on their paling faces.

"Step one," Gary said calmly. "Now if you'd come with me, we'll adjourn to my office."

He led them past one of the fuming but frozen gunmen, down

the staircase to the car deck; to a large cargo van parked in the very front of the boat. He knocked twice, then opened the door.

"We don't have as much time as I'd like," he said as he climbed in behind them, "so if you'd save your questions for later, I'll answer them all, I promise. Ms. Alvarez, if you'll join me in the front, I think the doctor will have more room to work."

Valerie moved into the front passenger seat, leaving Xenos in the back being stripped and tended to by an older man and an assistant. "Who *are* you?" she asked out of genuine curiosity.

Gary pulled a laptop over to him as he settled behind the wheel. "Most of the time? A real estate attorney. Pretty good one too."

"And the rest of the time?"

He continued to type as he talked. "Whatever my clients require. My partners and I run a full-service firm." He took a sheet of paper from the dashboard printer. "Would you sign this, please?"

Valerie read the paper, a routine attorney/client agreement combined with a power of attorney granting *Smith, Walker, Corson, and Bruno—a legal corporation—full authority to act on behalf of Congresswoman Valerie Alvarez on any and all matters other than financial transactions.*

Valerie signed quickly but looked concerned. "There may be a problem."

"Okay," Gary said calmly.

"There's this letter I sent to one of my staff that might—"

"You send it to their office or home?"

"Home."

Gary handed her a pad. "Write down the address." He seemed lost in thought as she complied. "When and where'd you mail it?"

"East Manhattan, late last night."

He thought some more and checked his watch. "Wouldn't have been picked up until this morning at the earliest." After another silence the smile returned. "Not a problem. We'll interdict it at the home."

They both felt the ship seem to shudder and begin a turn.

"How's it going back there?" Gary called.

"Best we can do without X rays," the doctor replied.

The lawyer spoke loud enough for both Xenos and Valerie to hear. "We're coming into Port Jeff now. Probably another reception committee on the dock. Everybody just stay low, in the back, and after we clear the village, we'll talk about where we go next, okay?"

He helped Valerie back, then joined her as the doctor and his assistant moved into the front.

Xenos's chest had been wrapped with a tight bandage and brace. A butterfly bandage held the wound above one eye closed, and the swelling was noticeably down in both. He also looked half asleep, but relieved of pain.

"You run a nice operation," he said in a drugged voice.

Gary just smiled back professionally. *"Grazie. Il fratello si prende il suo."*

The great mouth of the boat opened and they disappeared into the traffic nightmare of a Port Jefferson Village sunset.

The busy night had worn into a hectic day for Xi. The Crisis Management Corps had analyzed everything that they knew. Conclusions had shifted, changed, been abandoned or embraced as more information was received throughout the day. Psychologists had been consulted for profiles on the new player, Xenos Filotimo; to update and factor in the recent actions of the unexpectedly unpredictable congresswoman.

Finally they were done.

In classic Chinese fashion the corps had reached three mutually exclusive conclusions on what to do.

Now, as Xi sat in his office, watching a large tank of tropical fish, he reviewed them carefully.

The LRSO was not set up to deal with short-term, immediate solutions to long-range operations. Quite the opposite. And Xi personally detested hasty decisions.

But this time he knew one had to be made, and in the next few hours at the latest.

He allowed his mind to drift with the fish as he rolled the options around his mind.

The easiest solution—endorsed by eight of the fifteen corps

members—was to do nothing. Allow Canvas the freedom to run his operation his way and not jeopardize thirty-one years of work and a near victory by unconsidered reflexive actions.

Four of the fifteen had voted for a slightly more activist response.

They advocated the execution of one of Valerie's children as an object lesson. Although the woman was on the run, they were confident that news coverage of *a horrible traffic accident* would bring her out and bring her in. Once more the compliant eyes and ears needed to plug the holes the traitor Pei had created.

A small minority of the corps—three of the fifteen—had held out for the most radical of the possible solutions.

Their reasoning had the feel of correctness to the patient veteran of all of China's covert wars. But its audacity and speed frightened him to the core. To say nothing of the implications of even the slightest error in the plan's implementation.

But it felt right, and Xi couldn't ignore that.

"We selected Apple Blossom from a cluster of seventy-five possible," the three planners had argued. "Of this group, twenty-six remain active in the Apple Blossom chain in various critical positions in and out of the American government.

"While Apple Blossom himself was selected as the best possible carriage, several of the others are of nearly equal qualification and pliability. Any of whom could be elevated to a position equal to Apple Blossom's within five to ten years. This allows us a certain degree of flexibility in the boldness we may use in the current dilemma," they'd argued.

In effect: take a calculatedly bold risk. If it fails, or begins to fail, simply remove Apple Blossom from the chain and start fresh with one of the other twenty-six. It would add time and expense to the operation, but the LRSO was designed to spend both freely. And to win the prize they were playing for, what were ten more years?

There were complications, Xi thought. Short-term, intense, potentially disastrous if things spun out faster than Canvas could control them. But four assassinations—their planning already in place as a possible contingency—would remove all evidence of any LRSO involvement in the affair.

And the Americans would never react meaningfully without evidence.

Calmly Xi rose and began feeding his fish. Precise amounts of food carefully crushed between his thumb and index finger. He watched as they rose to the top of the tank, conditioned to the time and placement of the food, by their own natural instincts.

As he stared into the tank, even deeper into his own heart, he knew that he, too, was equally conditioned. To distrust speed, rapidly arrived-at decisions, actions that entailed more than minimal risks. It was both his strength and his weakness, and the hallmark of his administration of the Long-Range Study Organization.

He reached into his pocket for the bottle of medication he kept for a troublesome heart. Skimming up some of the residue of the tablets on one finger, he brushed a very few grains into the water. A brilliantly colored angelfish rapidly rose to the three grains that floated downward and swallowed them instantly.

Less than ten seconds later the fish convulsed and died.

Instinct, he thought as he scooped the fish out of the tank and walked back to his desk. He put the dead fish on the desk as he pressed the call button for his aide.

A moment later the man stood before him.

"On Apple Blossom," he said softly as he stared at the fish whose instinct had caused its death. "Inform the German that he is to expedite the operation. Fruition in one month, please."

"Sir!" The man hurried from the room to issue the order.

Xi stared at the dead fish for ten minutes before finally burying it in a nearby planter—typically taking advantage of the death to further something else . . . the fish's decaying form would add strength and resiliency to the plant.

As Xi's death from a disaster wrought by his casting instinct aside would strengthen the LRSO. They would never again risk such a precipitous act.

In either event—grand failure or spectacular success—the LRSO (and the People's Republic beyond) would benefit from his decision.

And that was all that mattered.

Seven

It looked like it wanted to die, but kept on out of habit.

Happy's Burgers and Playland sat alone in a brown weedy field, odd spindly-looking green things having consumed 80 percent of its former parking lot, wooden boards sealing every door and window as permanently as pennies on the eyes. But due to oddities and discrepancies in the land's title, it was never allowed to be euthanized. Just forced to remain in annually greater decay; a frozen monument to a time that must have been better since it was in the past.

But the life within the hollow building was far from frozen.

Tables were set up in the former Nerf Pit, on which were spread maps, photographs, a telephone. Cots and trays were in the cold kitchen; including a microwave oven powered by a car battery, several ice chests, and a neat pile of cans.

But it was the dining room that was the most jarring incongruity in the place.

High-powered lamps surrounded a glistening coroner's table that was draped with hospital-green sheets. Bloodstains browned on the floor around it, carts with surgical instruments were alongside, oxygen cylinders stood by IV stands, all connected—one way or another—to the man that lay on the table, watched over by a blue-jeaned nurse reading *Forbes*.

For two days the fugitives had rested at this improvised way station. Two days of sleep and alternating worry, panic, and relief for Valerie.

Two days of surgeries, follow-ups, and blissful unconsciousness for Xenos.

An armed man sat by the seemingly boarded front door, another sat at the rear; and Gary—constantly on the phone or checking on his charges—was everywhere. He would come and go, no explanations asked or offered. And he would return with fresh clothes, newspapers, and this morning . . . information.

"Valerie," he said as they talked in the improvised operations center, "this thing is spiraling out of control, and fast."

But she was taking such news better now, almost as though it had become the norm and nothing special to react to.

"What now?" she asked as she read a *Washington Post* article about the crisis of the week—Taiwanese nationalists had allegedly boarded a U.S. merchant vessel, robbing it, raping a female officer. The Taiwan government denied any involvement, but the evidence seemed otherwise.

As the world paid rapt attention, moving the disappearance of a congresswoman from Spanish Harlem to the back of the paper.

"Someone's ratcheted up the pressure." Gary referred to his hurried notes. "New York cops have received an advisory from the Secret Service to locate and detain our sleeping friend over there." He nodded at Xenos. "They list him as a possible terrorist out to kill the president."

He shook his head. "No one seems to know what set the Feds off on him, but everybody's giving it a very low-key but very high priority."

Valerie tossed the paper aside. "It just keeps getting better," she said as if she'd just tasted something unpleasant.

Gary handed her a fax. "You have no idea."

FBI DCHQ Nat'l Sec Desk Highest Priority
To: All Field Offices, Subdistricts, Branches, Divisions
From: The Office of the Director
Status: Extremely Urgent/Confidential—Maintain InfoSec on Need to
     Know strictly

Message Follows

A highly placed DEFECTOR from the Foreign Ministry of the People's Republic of China has informed USG that he has been in regular receipt of HIGHLY CLASSIFIED DOCUMENTS and briefings re: USG policy and intelligence efforts directed at his country.

DEFECTOR further states that primary source for this information has been CONGRESSWOMAN VALERIE ALVAREZ of New York City. CONGRESSWOMAN ALVAREZ and her family have been missing from home and office since news of the defection reached USG D.C.

Make every effort to locate and detain ALVAREZ and any others in her presence and hold incommunicado until resources from DCHQ and Central Intelligence can arrive.

Valerie turned ghostly white, her hand began to tremble, sweat poured from her forehead. "My God," she whispered over and over again. "My God."

Gary took the stolen telex from her unresisting hands and poured her a shot of something from a flask in his pocket.

"Like I said, someone's getting very serious about this." He returned to his notes. "We've got heavy surveillance on all ports of exit in the city and on the island. Cops, Feds, Coast Guard covertly checking pleasure craft under the guise of safety inspections. All with our friends from Connecticut still sniffing around."

He shook his head in a cross of amusement and desperation. "I've never seen anything like it. Gotta be costing a ton."

Valerie seemed to be slowly recovering. "So what do we do now?"

For the first time since she'd met him, the lawyer seemed uncertain. He caught himself, and the trademark smile returned.

"We deal with it. I've made certain arrangements, set some things in motion. But essentially"—he paused and looked her in the eyes—"we wait."

"I can't!"

"Valerie . . ."

The fear and panic seemed to recede as Valerie took the pad from him and began making notes.

"You don't understand the federal bureaucracy. I do," she said distractedly. "The longer this bullshit is allowed to go unchallenged, the more real it becomes. Second law of Washington survival." She continued writing/thinking. "Tell a lie loud enough, long enough, and it becomes the truth."

Gary was impressed as he saw the competent, tough, capable government official begin to emerge from shock. "What do you propose?"

"Four possibilities," she said as she scanned her notes. "One, I call friends in the media. Tell them everything I know and get our side of the story out, and fast."

"No."

"Why not?"

The lawyer adopted an almost scholarly pose. "Unless you have an intimate relation that owns the *Times,* you can't guarantee your story will get out. The government will be expecting something like that and have probably already briefed—on background —key editors and decision makers. You'd be exposing us all with no real guarantees of results."

Valerie scratched out that idea on the pad and turned to the next. "I could go in. Turn myself in, to the director of the FBI himself if I have to. Get my statement on the official record and safely into police custody before anyone knows what's happened. Then I become too hot to touch and can make contact with friends in Congress who I trust."

She looked steadily at the doubtful lawyer. "Just get me to the director, let me go into their custody, and they'll have to keep me safe."

Gary looked dark. "Like Oswald?"

After a confused moment Valerie shivered.

"Okay. Third option. I turn myself over to the secretary general of the United Nations and ask for asylum." She sounded more confident now. "I know him. He's smart, tough, and has granted *real* spies on the run refuge until he could sort out truths and lies. From there, I'd be able to safely talk to the media, to the FBI, to the world."

Gary seemed to consider this option. "I see two problems.

First, you think you know what he'll do, but you can't be sure. Whoever's behind this is going to bring massive pressure to bear when you surface.

"Second, and more troubling, I expect the FBI knows you know the secretary general. I doubt we'd get a hundred yards out of the Brooklyn tube before they'd snatch you up."

"But you're thinking about it," Valerie said as she studied the man.

Gary didn't answer right away. "I'm thinking about it," he said distractedly. "What's option four?"

Valerie shrugged. "A flare in the dark, but not exclusive of the U.N. idea." She leaned in close. "Let me call my chief of staff. She's tough, a veteran of the worst Washington can throw at you, and I'd trust her with my children's lives."

She hesitated, suddenly overcome by the emotion the last part of the statement raised in her.

"Let me call her. If nothing else, she can begin countering any press or inferences without revealing anything about where we are. I know her like a sister, she can do it."

The lawyer was quiet for a long time. He stared at the brightly painted floor and doodled on a new pad. Finally, after having analyzed it from all possible perspectives, he nodded.

"We'll try it. But only on my terms."

Two hours later they were ready.

A digital timer sat next to a telephone. A recorder was attached to the phone, and pads had been laid out for Valerie and Gary, who would listen on an earpiece wired into the phone.

"The call's being shunted through a series of forwards," Gary explained as Valerie reviewed the notes she'd made for her call. "It'll go to my office, then to a place I have on Fire Island. From there it'll be transferred to a safe line in Los Angeles, then to a Baltimore bar that does favors for us. From Maryland it'll go to your office."

Valerie shook her head. "I don't understand the twentieth century."

"Neither do I," he said as he entered a code on the telephone's keypad. "Which is why I pay Ma Bell for this service."

"Unbelievable." She took a deep breath. "What do I dial?"

"Just your office's general number," the lawyer warned. "No direct lines or dedicated numbers, they're too easy to trace. Go through the general switchboard and don't stay on longer than four minutes."

Valerie began dialing.

"The Honorable Valerie Alvarez, New York, Twenty-third District. How may we help you?"

Gary took the receiver. "Barbara Krusiec, please."

"Who shall I say is calling in reference to what?"

"My name's Darrow, and I'm calling in reference to"—he read a note Valerie passed him—"a mortgage application Ms. Krusiec has filed with our company."

"One moment, please."

Two minutes later Krusiec answered the phone and Gary started the timer.

"Mr. Darrow, this isn't a real good time. I can only give you a couple of minutes. So I hope you have some good news for me," she said lightly.

"Barb," Valerie said quickly, "it's me."

"Valerie! Shit! Where are you?"

"Calm down and listen." Valerie carefully read from her prepared, timed script. "Tell me what you know."

There was a too long silence on the other end. When Krusiec spoke again, it was in a near whisper. "FBI has been at your house, at two of the field offices. Very low-key, but with warrants and attitude."

"What are they looking for?"

"Won't say, but whatever it is, it must be bad. Where are you? What's happening?"

Valerie watched the timer roll. "Any press inquiries?"

"Nothing specific, but building interest." A brief silence. "Tell me where you are. If you're in trouble, I'll come and get you."

Valerie smiled at the commitment in her best friend/assistant's voice.

"Look, things are going to start breaking and we're going to need to start getting our story out fast." Valerie skipped the next notes and proceeded to the circled paragraph in her notes. "I'm being set up to take the fall in a conspiracy that's going to make Watergate look small-time. It involves—"

"Maybe you shouldn't be talking like this," her assistant/friend cut her off.

"It's our best shot. You'll need to call a press conference or something, but that's getting ahead of ourselves." Valerie was skimming over the next part, thinking how best to synopsize everything she had to tell the other woman.

"No," Krusiec said flatly.

"What was that?"

Krusiec's voice came through filled with dark concern. "If you whisper one word of what's happened, Drake will be dead before the press conference is over, you know that."

Valerie stiffened. "What? Have they contacted—"

"Listen. They say you need to come in, deliver the reports on Pei, and finish your questioning."

"My God." Valerie couldn't catch her breath or control her heartbeats. "They *did* contact you! What did they say about Cathy and—"

"Valerie. Listen. They don't want to hurt anyone. They say everything that happened before was a mistake and they can make it right. But only if you come in. I have assurances from the highest levels on that."

Before a pale Valerie could respond, Gary reached out and slammed his hand down on the receiver button.

"So much for your options," he mumbled as Valerie clawed at him to move his hand.

"Goddammit! Let me talk to her! She's talked to them! Damn you!" She desperately tried to pry the lawyer's hand off the disconnect switch, only to be restrained by one of Gary's gunmen.

"It's okay," he said to the man who released the furious woman. He removed his hand. "Call her. Go ahead, go to her . . . and you and your children can die together," he said in a cold but somehow reasonable tone.

"What?"

He looked her in the eyes, his own reflecting absolute certainty. "She's in it with them."

"No! Not Barbara, you don't know her!"

The lawyer's only response was to rewind the tape and play back the conversation.

"God in Heaven," Valerie barely whispered when it stopped. "My God in Heaven."

In a midtown Manhattan office building, Canvas put down the headphones that he'd used to listen to a replay of the conversation. He glanced down at his few notes, made a couple more, then looked up at the others in the room.

"Options, gentlemen," he said shortly.

"Not enough time for a meaningful trace," one said. "But the call did come from the continental United States."

"VSA showed high stress, but general truthfulness in her voice," another added.

"Wonderful," Canvas sighed. "She didn't say shit that was helpful, but she meant every word." He exhaled, as if he was trying to rid himself of the two problems that had kept him awake for over fifty hours so far.

Problem one: killing a member of the United States Congress —whether they could make it look like an accident or not—would draw the most intense heat possible. FBI, local cops, maybe a Justice Department task force and congressional investigators. Particularly now that his hands were tied by the floated traitor story. If the FBI believed Valerie a traitor, they would assume that those she worked for had killed her.

And redouble their efforts to expose them by solving the killing.

Canvas had argued for over an hour with the German that Beijing's order was impractical, unwieldy, and—frankly—insane. But the man had simply replied that these new orders came directly from Beijing and were unchallengeable. Valerie and Xenos were to be killed.

Which led to problem number two.

He'd had one opportunity to kill Xenos Filotimo, when he'd been suspended from the ceiling beam, beaten and half conscious. That he hadn't done it then was more a matter of reason and options. Valerie couldn't be touched in any meaningful way; actually killing her children was a final—unwithdrawable—option that would only serve to harden her attitudes. But forcing her to witness Xeno's torture had been a reasonable alternative. Which had led to Canvas missing his chance.

And he doubted if he would ever get as inviting an opportunity.

Even if—and that was strict conjecture—Xenos chose to uninvolve himself in anything further, he wasn't stupid. He would be aware of a potential threat against him. And that awareness—combined with his natural talents and learned abilities—would make him a deeply difficult, to say nothing of lethal, target.

Canvas had demanded an additional million dollars for the two killings.

The first half had been deposited within a half hour.

Which left him in this small office in New York City running out of time and guesses. In a few weeks his talents would be needed in another, even more critical phase of the Apple Blossom morass. And he would be forced to have second-stringers going after his old colleague.

Canvas shook his head as he thought about the men he would lose then.

"Somebody offer a suggestion," he said in an irritated voice.

The room remained quiet.

He stood, walking out on the small balcony, staring down Broadway with all the people moving along it, sublimely happy in their ordinary lives. Lives he both envied and despised.

"Mr. Collins?"

"Yes, boss?" One of the men came out to the edge of the balcony.

"Increase surveillance to third-level contacts of the subjects. Reports from all teams every fifteen minutes."

"Right away." The man returned to the office and picked up a phone.

"Mr. Lambeth?"

"Here, Guv."

"Let's start making some guesses."

The man behind him silently pulled out a pad and waited.

"If it was me," Canvas said in a faraway voice as he tried to picture himself in the van whose photos he'd so closely studied, "I'd limit my exposure. Drive an erratic, random course—doubling back and all—for, oh, say an hour at forty-five miles an hour."

His aide began making notes.

Canvas closed his eyes as he continued to travel in his cerebral van. "Then no more than another hour on back roads, staying off the highways. Too exposed. No. Just local routes and highways, speeds under fifty.

"I don't change cars, might be seen. No house—residential neighborhoods have too many eyes. I'm looking for a business. But . . ."

His lips moved silently as he began to drop into the deep meditation of the professional assassin/planner/spy that he was at his core. "How far have I come?"

Lambeth quickly did the math. "Seventy-two and a half miles."

"How far is Port Jefferson from Manhattan?"

The aide checked notes on his clipboard. "Fifty-six miles as the crow flies. Ninety the most direct practical route."

Canvas smiled; a small thing but triumphant nonetheless. He spun around and hurried into the office, circling Long Island on a wall map.

"He's still on the island," he said with psychic certainty. "I want a complete search of all abandoned commercial structures. Anything over, say, one thousand square feet—they'll need to keep the van out of sight. No residences nearby, still structurally intact, off the main roads."

"Boss," one of his aides said as he looked at the map of the large, sprawling island of over a million people, "that's one Hell of a lot of ground to cover."

Canvas crossed out the western and eastern ends of the island.

"Queens is too dense, too crowded, and that's where he

knows we operated earlier. Everything east of Twin Forks is too isolated. People would notice too many things they shouldn't." He crossed out other areas. "Forget the Hamptons, Oyster Bay, Northport. All of the North and South Shores from the Nassau/ Suffolk County line east. Too many environmental laws for the kind of structure we're going to need to still be standing."

He looked at his whittled-down map. "Stay middle island, Suffolk County line east to Twin Forks. He'll be there."

The aide shook his head. "Still . . ."

Canvas handed him a phone. "So, get help." And he returned to the balcony to breathe in the life of the city.

To picture two deaths on an island.

As night fell over Happy's, activity began to increase. Gary brought in "some guys I know"; four big men, bikers. All heavily tattooed and armed. The doctor arrived, changed Xenos's bandages, and remedicated the semiconscious man. Gary made calls.

Valerie slept, or tried to.

"I'm not happy," the doctor said as he came over to the improvised operations center.

"Take a number," Valerie growled as she reluctantly got up.

The doctor looked questioningly at Gary, who shrugged.

"What's wrong?" the attorney asked without really wanting to know.

"He's running a fever, probably an infection from the collapsed lung. He's still in a lot of pain, maybe from a pinched disk. And I'm worried about the swelling around his left eye."

Gary glanced over at the coroner's table where the nurse was sponge bathing a barely aware Xenos. "What do you want to do?"

"Hospital out of the question?"

"Afraid so."

The doctor thought for a minute. "I've pumped him full of antibiotics and painkillers, lanced the eye twice. But he needs an ophthalmic surgeon, a good ortho man, maybe a neurologist. Unless you get him better care than I can give, well, I can't guarantee that the man won't be crippled for life." He paused ominously. "Or worse."

"And?"

"Can I at least get him to an X-ray unit at Mather or Saint Charles?"

Gary walked the man back to his patient. "We'll see, Frank. Just keep on with what you can for the moment and we'll see what we can do about the rest. Okay?"

The doctor sighed and returned to work.

Gary walked back to Valerie without ever looking at the mangled man on the table.

"I hate to admit this," she said rather sheepishly, "but I'd sort of forgotten all about him."

Gary busied himself with some notes. "You've got a right to be a little distracted right now."

Valerie realized that she hadn't seen the lawyer's trademark grin for a great many hours. "You're at risk now too. Aren't you?"

He nodded grimly. "I admit that this is the toughest deal I've ever been involved with." He looked up at her. "But it keeps life interesting, wouldn't you say?" And the smile returned.

"Movement in the lot!" one of the bikers yelled out. "And it *ain't* cops."

Gary grabbed Valerie and forced her under the table with him. One of the other bikers came over to them, standing between them and the door with his Ingram machine pistol at the ready. Another stood by the prone Xenos.

"In the building," an accented voice called out after an endless minute. "I'm a friend."

Gary looked at the biker nearest the movable board that served as a door. "What d'you have?"

"Man, olive skin, thick hair, T-shirt and jeans. Don't see no gun, but it's dark."

Gary grimaced, then slowly moved along the floor to the door. *"Ma chi t'ha pagato?"*

"La mia anima."

The lawyer stood up and peeked through the spy hole. "I can't tell," he muttered to himself. The bikers cocked their weapons.

"You gonna let me in or what?" the intruder called out in an irked tone.

"*Adoro la politica Italiana,*" Gary called out in an unsure voice.

"It's fucking cold out here, *cretino*! Forget the bullshit countersigns and let me in!" The man sounded furious.

"If he doesn't answer in one minute," Gary ordered the biker nearest him, "cut the fucker down." The biker nodded.

Long seconds passed. Finally they heard a deep exhaling of an angry breath.

"This is bullshit, Gary!" A sigh. "*Si. Prima o poi tutti vogliono fare il presidente per quindici minuti.* Okay?"

Gary pushed down the biker's gun and nodded. "He's okay."

A moment later Franco was let into the building.

Staring daggers at the lawyer, he was escorted first to Xenos's side, where he crossed himself as he looked down at him. Then he was brought over to Valerie.

"Congresswoman Alvarez," Gary said formally, "I'd like you to meet—"

"An ally," Franco said brusquely as he reached out and perfunctorily shook her hand. "I understand that you know my brother?"

Valerie sounded as confused as she looked. "What? Brother? Who are you?"

Franco looked over at Gary, who shrugged. "I didn't expect you to come yourself. I thought it was just too danger—"

"My brother," Franco said in a slightly less aggressive tone as he ignored the lawyer next to him, "was known to you as Paul Satordi."

"Paul?" She sat down heavily. "God, I'm sorry."

Franco stood over her. His presence at once threatening and comforting. "Do not be sorry, Congresswoman. Be helpful." He hesitated, but his voice never weakened. "Is he dead?"

Valerie looked up into the resolute face. "I'm not sure. He may be."

Franco sat down next to her. "Tell me what you know."

"Paul was working for me, researching a subway station redevelopment plan," she said, unable to look away from the fuming man across from her. "I think, maybe . . ."

"Tell me what you know!"

She nodded weakly. "You know what's been happening to me?" He nodded. "Well, one of the meetings, about two weeks ago, was in a hotel off Broadway. I guess Paul must've been working there, 'cause I saw him behind the bell captain's desk when I went up."

Franco nodded without realizing it. "You told the bastards you'd seen him—your research assistant; a man who should not have seen you there, at that time with those men?"

Valerie heard Paul's murder in the man's voice. "Yes," she said weakly as she wondered how many sins her overburdened soul would carry to its inevitable Hell.

"*In culo alla balena*," he cursed under his breath. "I will kill them all."

Gary handed him a drink. "Can we get out of here first?"

Franco swallowed the drink, then nodded. "Can he travel?" He waved toward Xenos.

"Barely. You've got a way out?"

For the first time since he'd arrived, the Corsican strongman didn't look invulnerable. Instead, he looked . . . unsure.

"I always hated New York," he said with obvious sincerity. "The harbor is fine—big, open, like a Marseilles streetwalker on a Saturday night." He expertly spit on a cockroach crawling near his leg. "But the rest—bridges, tunnels, airports—too Goddamned easy to button up. And here on this island . . ."

He raised his hands in an act of frustration. "One way on, one off. Lots of Goddamn harbors, but all real small, easy to watch. Even if you make it onto the water, you got whole fucking New England off one shore, *three* Coast Guard stations and an American naval base off the other."

Gary looked concerned. "But you *have* found a way?"

"We're working on it."

"Shit." The suddenly morose lawyer poured himself a drink.

"Are you saying we can't get away?" Valerie blurted out as she began to understand who Franco must be.

The Corsican tilted his head to an angle as he talked, like it was the only way to see the world, which had shifted off its axis.

"There's muscle everywhere. Government, spooks, crooks. Even surveillance teams on Xenos's family, *proprio stronzi.*"

He accepted another drink. This one he sipped. "But this place is fine place," he nodded as he looked around. "Away from main roads, deserted, in the middle of the island. A place no one notices." Another sip. "You could be safe here a long time."

A commotion behind them caused them all to spin around.

"It's not safe," Xenos said as he stepped off of the table and tore the IV from his arms. He pushed the nurse away and stepped toward the group. "And we're not staying."

Franco got up and walked over to him. "What do you need, *amico?*" he asked as he studied the unsteady man.

He was pale, sweating, muscles contracting in his calves and upper arms, but Xenos stood steadily as he locked eyes with the Corsican. "Can you get us out through New York Harbor?"

"Is the pope a hypocrite?"

"Set it up."

Franco hurried over to the phone as Xenos began to dress.

"The doctor," Valerie said as she came over, "he said you were hurt bad. That you could . . ."

"Where are we?" he asked past her.

"Hauppauge, Suffolk County," Gary answered as he came over. "Middle island, away from everything and everyone."

Xenos winced. "Stupid." He pulled on a windbreaker over his bare chest. "Got a cell?"

"Yeah."

"Give Franco the number. Then get in a car—*not* the van we came in—and hit the road."

Valerie looked up at him. "Where?"

"Just get mobile and stay on the island until you hear it's safe to get off. Keep moving until you hear from Franco. Stick to the main highways, the larger population centers."

"I don't understand," Valerie said as Franco joined them and nodded to the bigger man.

"Why are you still here?" Xenos demanded.

Taking two of the bikers with them in the car, the other two riding escort—alternately in front and behind, several car lengths—

Valerie and Gary were on the Long Island Expressway fifteen minutes later.

"I got a Senegalese container ship leaving at dawn, with stops in Miami, Kingston, then Cartagena. From any of those we get home real sweet," Franco said when they were alone. "If we get to the warehouse intact, the rest is bread and olives." He took a deep breath. "But getting there, this is the trick I want to see."

Xenos just grunted and started out of the building. "You got a car?"

"Do I ever walk?"

They were no good, neighborhood thugs and knee breakers. But they were tough, didn't give a shit about consequences; and most important—they were expendable. Canvas had assigned four of the "local hire" to each of his handpicked field operatives.

Assigned to the five priority sites Canvas had identified, their job was simple and clear.

Observe and report. Take actions only if absolutely necessary; otherwise watch and call for reinforcements in the unlikely event either of the targets showed their face. But they were a back-shelf operation at best. Intended only to cover all *possible* contingencies. So that the "real pros" could continue closing their net on Long Island.

Two of the punks sat in a car in an alley across the street from Sarah Goldman's apartment. Two more sat in all-night coffee stands on either end of the block. Canvas's man sat in the window of a lower-floor apartment, dressed in black, lights out, never taking his eyes off the street below him. And calling in every fifteen minutes to report their futility.

Xenos saw them all from the roof of a building down the block. Shaking his head in sympathy with Canvas's plight, he pointed them out to Franco.

"Bottom of the barrel," the Corsican said softly.

"He's desperate," Xenos replied. "Somebody's pushing him for results." He turned and started for the stairway. "Given time to plan properly, we'd never have made any of them."

Franco shrugged. "Hard or soft?"

Xenos appeared not to have heard the question. His eyes were closed, his lips silently moving, in what Franco recognized as his analysis mode.

They'd left Happy's six hours before.

Strictly following Xenos's orders, Franco had driven them west toward New York City. Xenos had used an atlas that had come with the rented car to call out changes in directions, sometimes on four-lane highways, sometimes on unimproved shale roads. When they arrived in Queens, they'd abandoned the car and walked.

"You see," Xenos had said as he half leaned on the much smaller man, "their thinking is too systematized, too planned, too procedural. The FBI, the cops, they watch the tunnels, the bridges, the harbor, the ferries, the major airports. Colin deploys his resources on the smaller harbors and ports, the regional fields and airstrips, maybe rolling searches in the countryside.

"His resources are depleted, he's on the clock, whoever's pushing his buttons wants results and wants them fast. So he begins taking educated guesses."

They started down a dark staircase together, Xenos wincing from the effort.

"He ignores the obvious, because neither he nor the cops have the resources to deal with it." He'd actually managed a smile amid the pain and the wounds which had started bleeding again. "Xenos," the wounded man said in a professorial lecturing tone, "is a professional, wounded, dangerous, on the run. He would never take a risk like the subway."

Franco bought their tokens and they quickly passed through the turnstiles.

"And if you can think like this," Franco had asked, "how do you know he has not as well?"

They boarded the westbound train and Xenos collapsed to a seat on the nearly empty car.

"He will," he said as he zipped up his windbreaker to better cover the bloody bandages. "But he's not *from* here. He's acting on intelligence, not experience. I don't think he's thought of it yet."

Franco had been openly doubtful. "You don't think? *Gesù Cristo!* Why not?"

Xenos had shrugged. " 'Cause *I* just thought of it." He took a deep painful breath. "It's sort of like a psychotic game. I think him. He thinks me. One acts, the other *reacts.* My anticipation against his forethought."

Franco rubbed his forehead. "And you can think like, anticipate, him better than he can you?"

The unsatisfying answer had been a noncommittal grunt.

In the city they'd changed subways twice more, before emerging on Flatbush Avenue in Brooklyn. Franco stole a car, Xenos had popped some pain pills with two cups of coffee, and they'd arrived on the rooftop looking down on the street at the surveillance team.

"So?" Franco almost hated to interrupt, but sunrise was less than two hours away, and most of that time would be needed to get the others to the harbor and circumvent the Feds' surveillance net there.

"Hard. No time for the other," Xenos said with commitment and regret as he started down the stairs.

Franco nodded, pulling a large knife out of his boot before following.

Ten minutes later the two gunmen on either end of the block died silently, drowning in their own blood as their throats were cut through to the spine.

The men in the car never saw anything more than two black forms rising up in the dark by their windows as the carbide-steel blades slid obstructionlessly down, guided by the notch in their collarbones. Their aortas severed, heart muscle turned to mush, they quivered briefly and died without sound or movement.

As the black forms vanished into the building behind them.

It was almost time for the next bulletin. Canvas's man sighed, picked up his radio, and entered the comm code for the hour. "Site one, report." Nothing. "Site one, report." Again, nothing but static. "Site two, report."

He began to curse under his breath at the incompetents he was forced to deal with. He was going to kick some ass when they were relieved in a few hours, he decided. "Site three, can you see your asshole friends sleeping on the street?"

This time the silence was ominous.

He put aside the radio, pulled out his night-vision scope, and looked down at the car just below him. The men seemed to be asleep, slouched down in their seats. But zooming in revealed their eyes wide open, trickles of black ooze coming out of the corner of their mouths and a growing stain on their chests.

"Jesus, Jesus, Jesus," the man whispered as he clawed for his cell phone. "Oh Jesus."

"Go," a voice on the other end of the phone said flatly.

"He's here," the man whispered in open fear. "He's fucking here!"

A pause. "Unit number?"

"Uh, this is nine-four, dammit! The sonofabitch is here. They're all fucking dead and he's here."

Just then he thought he heard a voice behind him—somewhere in the darkened apartment—whisper "*Wait.*" He pulled his gun, waving it behind him, not hearing a thing, hearing too much.

"Nine-four, stand by for Canvas."

"Send help, dammit!"

Canvas rushed to the phone in the outer office, tearing it out of an aide's hands. "Talk to me, boy!"

There were sounds on the other end of the line; strange moving sounds without voice or substance. Then a too identifiable thud. Then more silence and moving sounds.

"Let it end, Colin," Xenos's voice came through the phone—tired but committed.

"Things have gotten complicated, Jerry," Canvas finally said. "We need to talk."

"Did you *need* to put people on my family?"

"Like I said, it's complicated." Canvas held up a hand to stop the flurry of activity around him. "It was nothing personal, it's not even about you. It's Alvarez. Let's you and me just—"

"Let it end," the voice repeated coldly. "Now"—a deathly pause—"or never."

The line went dead.

"I can have nine units in Brooklyn in twenty minutes," an aide screamed out as he picked up a telephone.

"No," Canvas said as he looked at the receiver in his hand. "He'll be gone before your people can drop their cocks."

He hung up the phone and moved to a map of the five boroughs of New York.

"He'll go for the old Brooklyn Navy Yard or the Thirty-ninth Avenue Helispot," another aide called out. "I'll—"

"Send the cops or the Feds, not our people," Canvas said as he blankly studied the map. "Where are you going?" he whispered at the map. "Where are you? Would *I* . . ."

His voice trailed off as his finger began tracing several possible routes on the map. All of a sudden he smiled.

"Pull all our people, everyone. Get them off the island and every assignment." His voice was calm but commanding. "I want everything—our guys, local hire, Feds, cops, anything that moves that we control—and I want it flooding the harbor now! Any ship or boat scheduled to leave in the next six hours. From a supertanker to a fishing boat; I want them searched, every building around them as well."

He turned to his stunned, silent staff. "Move yer arses!"

After giving new orders to a surprised Franco—leaving him talking rapidly on his cell phone—Xenos knocked on the apartment door. Two minutes later it was answered.

"Papa, I need you to . . ."

He half collapsed from exhaustion and blood loss into his crying father's arms.

Twenty minutes later—with his head cradled in his father's lap, with his sister and nephew trying to stop the bleeding and change the bandages, with Franco driving a hastily stolen passenger van from a nearby car lot—they drove away.

An hour later they rendezvoused with Valerie and Gary on the Jersey Turnpike.

Less than two hours later they boarded *Le Petit Gitan*—a French freighter in Philadelphia Harbor—and were at sea before dawn.

As Canvas was on the satellite link with Beijing.

Phase Three

Electronic Warfare

Eight

It never occurred to him that he might someday be his own guest.

Oh, he'd considered the possibility of dying alone and broken on some rocky plain or inner city's gutter. Had lain beaten and bloodied in hospitals and improvised way stations throughout the world.

He'd even fantasized about dying in some far-off field surrounded by flowers and green.

But a stiff—too short—mattress in a hospital of his own construction had never been a possibility.

Until it became reality.

For over a week now he'd been there. In and out of consciousness, barely aware of the concerned faces and shrouded looks, he'd lain and throbbed. But there comes a time in every recovery where the absence of tormenting pain must be replaced by real healing.

At least of the body.

Dr. Jacmil shook his head as he reviewed the chart. "How many years have we known each other, eh? Nine, ten?" He made a notation as he shook his head. "I always said you would one day end up my patient." He frowned. "But did you have to prove me right with such *joie*?"

Xenos would've shrugged if his upper body were not encased in a cast. "It took my being unconscious to make it happen."

"But, *mon patrone*, that is how I prefer your company." Jacmil put down the chart, then carefully began to test the range of motion of Xenos's legs. "Any pain?"

Xenos winced. "No."

Jacmil shook his head. *"Imbécile."* After examining the vastly reduced swelling around the man's eyes, rechecking the latest X rays (courtesy Franco's recently delivered machine), he made a final notation on the chart.

"So? When do I get out of here and away from your butchery?" But there was no humor in the sullen eyes or the dark voice.

The doctor shrugged. "We take the cast off this afternoon, then see how you do for a couple of days." He shook his head. "End of next week maybe. If you cooperate fully." He shook his head as he walked away. "As if there is any chance of that."

Xenos lay there, ignoring the sounds from beyond his screened-off part of the ward. Ignoring the doctor's muttering, the children's singing, the sound of construction just outside the window. The pain of the examination, of the healing wounds, of his life, all slipped into some nether place that he denied existence to.

For the moment, at least, all that existed was *the problem.*

Twenty-four hours on the French freighter had left them in Norfolk Harbor, then on a hastily chartered jet (through a well-camouflaged Corsican front company) that touched down at a discreet airstrip outside of Toulon—after filing four false flight plans and touching down five times as diversions. In the almost forty-eight hours of packed-together, high-tension travel, the improvised party had barely spoken to each other, so involved were they in their own problems.

Franco had been on the phone or radio constantly. Issuing orders, seeking advice, making arrangements, he was a flurry of nonstop activity until touchdown. In consultation with Xenos during the man's rare moments of consciousness and lucidity.

Valerie slept.

She'd neither intended to have nor had any control over it. After so many days, nights, hours of bone-chilling tension, her body had just shut down like a car out of gas. It blessedly denied her worries about her children—whom she had already begun to mourn—as well as the dozens of other things that tormented her every waking.

Understanding, somehow, that she was now safe and could be allowed this momentary respite.

However guilty it might make her feel each time she woke up.

Sarah Goldman and her son had both been enervated by the experience. Frightened but exhilarated by their glimpse into Xenos's world. As she had told her son, "Know someone before you judge them." And their knowledge was expanding daily. Bradley sat and studied his wounded uncle—whom he'd only heard alluded to in the past. Fascinated by the life that the man seemed to imply and angered by being cheated out of someone who might've replaced his long-absent father.

But for Avidol—as he sat at his son's side throughout the fevered chills, the pained moans, and the seemingly uncontrollable muscle spasms—the journey had been one of completion rather than flight.

And although he couldn't have known it, it was for Xenos as well.

Seventeen years before—after a decade of bitter arguments and running resentments—the men had severed all ties to each other. The older declaring the younger dead because of his betrayals of the precepts the old man held so dearly.

The younger denying existence to the older out of self-delusion and a naïve belief that his starting-out life was meant to be lived alone and would be made stronger for it.

So Avidol remained by his stricken future throughout the harrowing journey. Wiping his boy's face with cool, damp cloths. Holding him still enough for the bandages to be changed. Brushing hairs out of his face or readjusting a blanket during those few peaceful moments.

Remembering the pain of the past, even as he consigned it to the past.

All the while praying for his, for *their,* soul.

But all of this was secondary to Xenos at this moment. Bare flashes of memory or experience that mattered not at all in the face of the problem at hand. Instead, he concentrated on that problem, examining its contours, shapes, complications. Constantly turning it over and around and inside out to examine it as closely as a biologist his microbe. So that he might fathom its innermost secrets and possibilities.

To stay ahead of Canvas.

What would *he* do now? How would he continue the search? *Would* he continue? What were his resources, goals—immediate and long-term? Had he told the truth? Was Alvarez alone the object, or had it now become a scorched-earth operation to leave no witnesses to whatever was being planned?

The questions were, by themselves, impossible to solve. All except one.

Canvas would never stop.

So contingencies must be made.

As soon as he'd regained consciousness Xenos had reviewed their escape with Franco. It had been accomplished with typical Corsican thoroughness and skill. Unlikely to be followed or unraveled much beyond Norfolk. And they were now safely ensconced in either the clinic (Xenos and his family) or a Brotherhood safe haven (Valerie).

Guards—trained, experienced men—had a low-key but deadly presence in both locales with orders to "protect our sheep no matter what." The harbor, airport, airstrips, boat landings, and the narrow roads leading in and out of the smuggler's paradise were being closely watched for strangers. Descriptions of Canvas and those of his men that Valerie could recall had been given to the local police along with a generous bounty.

By all usual standards, the fugitives were as safe as they could possibly be.

But Canvas was not usual, as Xenos well knew.

So the wounded man had already begun making his plans to move them all again, this time to Corsica itself. To a friendly village in the interior where discovery was as impossible as life to a mannequin. A place where negotiations could be started to turn the whole thing off, once and for all.

Until then, Xenos would never stop thinking, planning, predicting.

Because Canvas wouldn't.

"Jerry?"

The tiny, timid voice called him back from his black thoughts. And the small face at the foot of his bed reminded him of a world beyond red death and black destruction.

So long as he didn't look at the artificial arm.

"Je entendre la petit souris?"

The little girl crouched down, her eyes barely showing above the big man's feet. *"Cri. Cri. Cri,"* she giggled.

"There *is* a mouse here! *Mon Dieu!"*

Gabi jumped up, laughing.

"Oh," Xenos gasped with a forced smile. "It's the biggest mouse I've ever seen." Then, after the blank look on her face, *"Le gran souris!"*

The girl exploded in laughter and hurried around the bed. "Jerry! Jerry!" She stopped when she saw the edge of the cast under the blanket. But this girl had been born into worse and it affected her for only a moment. *"Que apprit?"* Her voice was matter-of-fact, calm.

"I fell down."

"J'en suis faché."

Painfully—although he showed none of it—Xenos reached out and stroked the smiling face. "How are your English lessons going?"

"Mervill—"

"Dans anglais, si vous plaisez, mademoiselle."

"Jerry . . ."

He frowned in an exaggerated way. *"J'insiste."*

Gabi took a deep breath—looked at the man she'd idolized since she'd first seen him come over a hill into her burning village and he'd pulled her from the rubble of her dead family's house, like an angel from God—then slowly, laboriously, began.

"Mois English is very good, *merci."*

"Thank you," he corrected.

"Thank you."

"And how is your brother?"

"Mon frère, my brother is very well. *Thank you."* She stuck out her tongue as she emphasized the last words.

Jerry stuck his out back at her. *"Superbe, Gabi!"*

For a moment the two wounded individuals were silent, each lost in their own thoughts of pain and recovery; savagery and tenderness.

"Jerry?"

"*Oui?*"

The little girl frowned disapprovingly as she crossed her prosthetic arm over her real one. "*Dans anglais, si vous plaisez, monsieur!*" she said in a mimicked grown-up tone.

"Okay," Xenos chuckled. "Yes?" he said seriously.

Gabi seemed to look deep within him at that moment. "Why is the world so, eh, *démenté?*"

"Crazy?" he said after a moment of stunned silence.

"*Oui,* eh, yes. Crazy." She seemed to like the word. "Why?"

"I just don't know, sweetie. I just don't . . ."

"Have you forgotten everything I've taught you?" Avidol asked from the other side of the bed.

Xenos looked over at him, locking eyes with the man he thought might never speak to him again. He felt a tug at his sleeve, then turned back to the puzzled little girl. "*Mon père, Gabi.*"

"Ah!" she said with a mixture of surprise and amusement as she studied the man. She leaned over and quickly kissed Xenos on the cheek. "*Au revoir.*" She curtsied toward the older man. "*Excusez-moi, monsieur.*"

"*Au revoir, ma minet.*" Avidol smiled after her as she skipped away. "I didn't expect this place," he said as he watched her go.

"I didn't expect it either."

Avidol sat down next to the bed. "So?"

Xenos winced as he turned toward the old man. "The Russians figured that the only way to win a war of attrition in Afghanistan was to eliminate future generations of enemies. So they dropped bombs disguised as dolls or toys for the children to find. Those that survived ended up like Gabi."

"So?"

"The world still largely refuses to concede what happened there over ten years. The Taliban militia that took over hates the mountain people almost as much as the Russians did. So what little aid there is barely gets through to where it's needed."

Avidol stared into his son's eyes with fire and accusation. "So?"

"I know these people," Xenos said after a long silence. "Tried to help them then. Do what I can now."

Avidol breathed in the pure Mediterranean air. "Why is the world so crazy?" There was accusation in his voice.

Jerry closed his eyes. "Beats the Hell out of me."

"Is the truth so foreign to you now?" Avidol's gaze was changing from accusing to sheer astonishment. "Is there so little of my son left in you?"

Xenos met that look, that indictment, with an equally steely glare of his own. "What do you want from me?"

"Only the truth."

Xenos laughed bitterly. "Yeah. But whose truth?"

Avidol shrugged. "God's."

A deep sigh from the man in the bed. "God's. God's truth." He seemed to drift with the thought. He shook his head. "For that, you'll have to ask someone else. I only have my own."

His father seemed shocked. "You have completely forgotten your God?" He said the words as if he couldn't quite make himself believe it. Although he'd expressed the same thought aloud many times about his "lost" son.

"Oh, Papa. What's the point? You are who you are and I'm something else entirely. Can't we just leave it at that? Put it aside for a few days, at least, and enjoy being together again?"

"No." Avidol's voice was rock-solid. "You were lost to me, I thought forever, because we 'put it aside' before. Not again."

He reached out, turning his depressed son's face back toward his. The physical contact sent an electric tremble through both men.

"Gerald," Avidol began in a soft voice, choked in emotion, "you are my son and I will always love you. We may, I may," he said in a trembling voice, "not always be able to see that. But it remains nonetheless. A living bond between us."

Xenos looked up at him, anger and accusation flying from *his* eyes now. "You said I'd died! You said Kaddish, tore your clothes, and consigned me to eternity away from you! Away from my family! That's not love!"

Avidol shrugged. "A man sits on a stoop and watches his child playing catch. He misses a ball and it rolls into the street. The child runs after it as a truck which has lost its brakes rounds the corner." He paused. "The man cannot sit by and allow his son to die."

He stood, looking out the window at the breathtaking Mediterranean view.

"You were never an easy boy." He laughed quietly. "From early on you sought your own way in the world. There was little I could do to stop you from your headstrongness." He turned back to Xenos. "Do you remember the lake?"

Xenos nodded. "Of course."

Avidol nodded. "So little a boy, so large a lake," he whispered as he sat back down. "I told you that you couldn't swim beyond the restraining rope. We argued, we fought that entire summer. Then, one day, you were gone. When we pulled you from the water you were half drowned, exhausted, using your last strength to fight me in order to finish that swim. It was like you were a little stranger, fighting your father like that. Amazing."

"I would've made it," the man in the bed said softly.

Avidol smiled. "Still?" He sighed. "Perhaps. But at what cost? As is, you came down with double pneumonia which was made all the worse by your complete exhaustion. The doctors all thought you would die."

"I refused to."

Avidol studied his son. "That's right. That is exactly what you said to us. You were eleven years old and lecturing your father and the doctors about how you 'control what happens to me. Not some god or force I can't see or prove. I determine my own fate.' An amazing sight."

The old man shook his head sadly. "When the angel of death came for you the next night, we called for the rabbi and he told us what to do. We must give you another name, he said. To fool the angel of death. So that night, for that night, you became—in the language of your ancestors—Xenos Filotimo." Another laugh, this one more bitter than the last. "My little stranger with the iron self-respect and sense of honor."

Xenos busied himself sipping from his ice water. Anything but look into those sad eyes. "What does this have to do with—"

"I knew then that I could never stop you with an argument. Not my little Xenos. Not my headstrong little boy with such a dangerous self-confidence. Then you became a man. And mere words seemed to become meaningless."

After a deep breath, Xenos turned to face his father. "I don't recall your ever running out of them."

"Perhaps not," Avidol said sadly. "But then you turned your back on me, on our people, on your God."

"I never . . ."

Avidol held up a restraining hand. "We will not discuss what we have already exhausted. I didn't understand your arguments then, I won't now. I only knew, know, that if I allowed you to go your own way—to do these sinful things in the name of national glory—then I would be as guilty as you in the eyes of God."

"The eyes of God," Xenos repeated wistfully. "I remember that phrase well enough."

"I know you do." Avidol shrugged. "My words could not stop you, I could only pray that my actions would. So you became as dead to me."

"It didn't work," Xenos mumbled regretfully.

Avidol suddenly smiled. "Didn't it? Then why did you come back to me?"

Xenos quickly recovered his anger. "You hypocritical sonofabitch! How *many* times did I come to you? How many times did I *beg* you to talk to me? To let me explain! Damn you and damn your God! You both left me alone and naked in a world that was trying to devour me! You never even once tried to see me through that bullshit piousness of yours!"

The old man was strangely calm, almost smiling. "And in those times, all those terrible times, were you ready to start again? To see your life for the tragedy that it had become and start anew?"

"Serving my country was no—"

"Tragedy? Of course not," Avidol said reasonably. "But did you *serve* it? Or did you just follow its orders? Further politics and personal agendas, or further ideals and principles? Serve your country or serve some men?"

Xenos stiffened with the slap of truth. "I'll never make you understand."

Avidol nodded. "Especially if you do not understand yourself." His voice dropped low and seductive. "But you *do* understand now, don't you?"

"What?"

"You weren't ready in the past to admit that the grand design of patriotism and national honor you were force-fed was pure *tref*. Crap. A thing unwholesome and corrupt."

"No," Xenos finally said so softly that it might've been a thought.

"No." The old man looked triumphant. "Not until God sends faces to haunt you in your sleep. To drive you away from those who would mislead and betray you."

He smiled openly now. "To bring you back to *his* will. To me." He leaned back with a self-satisfied grin on his ancient face.

Laughter exploded from the tightened lips of the man in the bed. "This is God's will? His plan? All of this pain and death and torment and anguish, God's divine insight? Shit! Even *you* can't believe that, Papa!"

"Chuni, my son." Avidol moved closer to the bed. "Answer just one question. And you needn't answer it aloud if you don't want to."

"What's that?"

"If this is not all part of God's plan for us—for humanity, for our people, for you and me—then"—he hesitated—"why did you create this place for the children?"

Avidol leaned back, smiling a private smile that reeked of triumph and the universe being set right; as his son remained silenced, his emotions written across his damaged face.

"The Talmud tells us, my son, that there is chaos in the world —craziness if you will—because God allows it to be. And this he allows because he has also created men of honor and self-respect, self-sacrifice and righteousness, who will stand up and defend the weak from that chaos. From the powerful, depraved corrupted men who would use them in wicked ways or destroy them entirely.

"As I said," he continued after a minute of intense emotional stillness, "I did not expect this place." He stood, moving very close to his son: his dreams, his immortality regained. He tenderly leaned over, kissing Xenos on the forehead. "But I am overjoyed to see it."

Not far away from the clinic, truths of another kind were being brought out in front of a far different audience. It was in a house constructed of rocks and driftwood—even more of loyalty and tradition—that sat on the very edge of the Mediterranean. They had gathered—these men who lived by simple rules of honor, trust, and fidelity—to hear the story. And the listeners were intent that they alone would do the hearing.

Of course the three-foot-thick rock walls prevented any casual listening from the outside, combined with the electronic "shadow" that Xenos had loaned them to prevent high-tech eavesdropping. But thoroughness—in the Corsican way—meant four men on constant armed patrol of the grounds surrounding the small house.

Inside, the one large room was nearly full.

In the front were five chairs, facing the rest, for the Council. In front of them sat eleven more chairs, one each for the heads of the eleven Corsican Unions—which formed the Brotherhood throughout Europe—that had been summoned to this *tomba*.

This *dissection of the grave*.

Finally, two standing desks—both facing the Council—one on each side. At one was Franco, leaning casually, speaking confidently to some of the Union heads as he waited. At the other, Valerie. She concentrated on the notes she'd made in the last week, tried to remember the protocols that had been explained to her by Franco.

Distractedly accepting yet another bizarre twist in her nightmare existence.

The room hushed as five old men entered from the rear. They made their way silently to the front, arranged themselves in the chairs, then each, when settled, nodded to Franco.

"Fratelli; genitori; coluiche che è senza genitori giurerà lealtà al fratello," he began in the centuries-old way. *"Non c'è maggior dolore che ricordarsi la felicità nel dolore."*

All sixteen men in the room nodded somberly as Valerie remembered the invocation as Franco had explained it to her: "There is no greater ache than to remember the happy times in misery."

"O, Fratello," the old man in the center chair responded in the traditional way, *"quanto tormento è quello che v'offende?"* Although he knew well what torment was afflicting Franco at this moment. As did the rest, for it was the reason for the first full gathering of Brotherhood leaders in nine years.

But form—tradition—must be adhered to.

"Fratelli, posso parlare in inglese?"

The room nodded as one.

"Grazie per la vostra indulgenza." He sighed deeply. "A grave injustice has been done to my family. A brother's murder." He raised his hands in a gesture of futility. "I would not inflict this on my brothers within, except . . . this injustice is also a slap in the face of every man here. And of all the men that they represent.

"My brother Paolo—known to most of you in the past twenty years—was entrusted by the Council with a sacred trust. Six hundred thousand francs. He was to go to America, become a lawyer of merit and note, then return to us and serve the Brotherhood with honor and faith."

Another deep breath. His head lowered, his hand trembled the very slightest bit. "But, *amici,* my friends and brothers, he was murdered before he could fulfill this sacred task. Crushed like an insect. Obliterated from this world, his body lost in some unmarked, unhonored place in America."

The men looked appropriately impressed and sorrowful. But they still had not heard any reason for them to have been called together. The loss was a substantial one—but tolerable. And the death of his brother on only peripherally related Brotherhood business was Franco's concern, not all the Brotherhood's.

But they continued to listen.

"Brothers," he continued after what he considered to be an adequate pause for effect, "hear now the reason for Paolo's murder. The foul acts that bred such contempt and venom as I could heap upon the doers."

He looked over at Valerie. "I present to the Council the Honorable Valerie Alvarez, a member of the United States House of Representatives and a witness to these crimes against us all."

Valerie smiled (seriously), then began. "It is an honor to—"

"Un momento," the man in the center chair interrupted. *"Lei ha accettato Gesù Cristo come il suo salvatore?"*

Franco immediately translated. "Are you a Christian?"

Valerie looked surprised. "Uh, yes. A Catholic."

The man in the center chair nodded. *"Sappi questo. Se stai mentendo, sarai ucciso lentalmente ed in un periodo di settimane. Ti bestemmio nel nome di Gesù Cristo."* He looked over at Franco, then nodded.

"He says," Franco began slowly, "that you should know this one thing. If you lie to the Council, or are later found to be lying on any matter of import, you will be killed. Slowly, and over a period of weeks. This is his curse to your lies, in the name of God." Franco shrugged. "And I assure you he means it."

Valerie straightened, looking angrily into the eyes of the calm little old man in the center chair. "Does he understand English?"

"Sì."

"Good." She paused to gather her thoughts. "Sir, in coming to you I am not only risking my career, my life, the security of my country, but the lives of my son and daughter. I have no reason not to tell you the full truth." Another pause, this one briefer and followed by a withering stare at all of the five men in the Council.

"And if anything that *you* may do—any leak or gossip, carelessness or malignancy—threatens or endangers my children in any way"—she fixed the man in the center chair with a gunmetal look —"then I assure you, you'll *pray* that I kill you over several weeks. That, sir, is *my* curse. By God."

The old man regarded her for five silent, thoughtful minutes.

"Bene," he finally said. "You may begin."

Three hours later, three hours of uninterrupted talking, explaining, clarifying, and praying, Valerie sat down and waited. It had been explained to her that there would be no questions directly to her. That the procedure was for the assemblage to write down their questions, submit them to the Council, then to have Franco ask only those questions that the Council ruled were critical to the decision to be reached.

After forty minutes of silent discussion amongst themselves, the Council members handed the questions over to Franco. He seemed stunned by how few there were.

"Uh, Congresswoman, we have five questions for you. Are you prepared to answer them freely and truthfully?"

"I am," Valerie said as confidently as she could.

"First, this Pei, Source 24601. What was his exact position in this LRSO and what was his exact assignment?"

Simple enough beginning.

"Pei was the deputy director of the LRSO's Office of Planning Review. It was his job to supervise analyses and critiques of ongoing Chinese intelligence operations. In order to determine if the best methods had been used, if there were possible improvements that could be implemented in the future; to ascertain whether or not the operations had been or still were being run as efficiently and profitably as they could be."

"And what did he conclude with Apple Blossom?" one of the eleven interrupted, as she'd been told they might.

"He told me that Apple Blossom was as well run a plot as he'd ever come across. But that the operative was as unstable a lead element as he'd ever experienced. He even suggested that there might've been a flaw in the screening process that allowed this person to get through an otherwise tight net."

Franco looked over the room; no follow-ups were forthcoming, so he turned to the next question. "Why were you chosen to have such close access to Pei? Including but not limited to individual debriefings that were—by your own account—unsupervised and unrecorded."

Valerie exhaled deeply. "Pei had, at one time, been in charge of maintaining the LRSO's profiles of members of Congress. The CIA seemed to think that he had become, well, *enamored* of me at that time. They wanted me to encourage that in him. He was

scared, timid at first, kinda sweet really." She pulled herself back
from the memory. "He was raised to fear the CIA, so they thought
I could get him past that."

"Did you become his lover?" someone asked.

"No," she responded too quickly, forcing down the memories
of the slight brushings and touchings she'd allowed the basically
naïve defector.

Praying that the CIA *had*—as promised—destroyed the covert
videos that she would never admit to. Pei had been a find—a man
with virtually unlimited access to the inner circles of ChiCom intelligence. The benefits of his testimony in front of her committee—to
national security and to her career—had been worth allowing the
socially innocent man his fantasies.

There had been one other thing besides.

In the dark, sleep-deprived eyes of the man, she recognized
something painfully familiar. A soul alone in the world. A person
beneath the spy, who had risked everything to try to save himself.
A person who needed someone to tell him that everything would be
all right; that the myriad decisions he'd made that left him essentially alone and a traitor to his birth were the right ones.

As no one had ever consoled Valerie.

"The next question," Franco said immediately. "You said that
you were contacted by the Canvas Group *before* Pei was killed,
along with the three agents guarding him. Did you give the Canvas
Group the information on where Pei was being hidden and with
what security?"

All eyes in the room turned to her.

"No! I wouldn't do such a thing!"

The seventeen men sat quietly, calmly, their eyes locked with
her soul.

"Yes," she whispered. "They took my kids, my . . ."

"So you are responsible for their deaths?"

In her role as chair of the investigating subcommittee, Valerie
had been walked through the scene, even before the bodies were
removed. The look of surprise in the dead eyes of one of the agents,
the look of betrayal in another's, were seared into her brain.

She'd rationalized that her interrogators—the bastard traitor and his two Chinese assistants—would use the information to carry out surveillance of the defector. To try to listen to his interrogations, maybe to sneak a message of warning to him.

All bullshit, she thought as she faced this almost primordial tribunal who demanded instant truths with no exception.

As she faced her soul.

Were the seven children left without their fathers worth the lives of her two?

Mercifully Franco interrupted before she could find an answer.

"The next question," he said as he looked away. "This Canvas person, or any of the Chinese, or the men who worked for them, did they ever tell you specifically that they murdered Paolo?"

He whirled on the Council. *"Fratelli, questo è un oltraggio! Pensa quello . . ."*

"Silenzio!" the man in the center chair called out. "You will answer the question, Congresswoman."

Valerie took a deep breath. "No. No one ever expressly said that they'd killed Paul, Paolo." She sighed. "But I have no doubts in my mind. They would've killed anyone that they even suspected might compromise their operations. No question."

"Ultima domanda," the old man said to Franco.

Franco briefly bowed his head.

"Congresswoman Alvarez," he began slowly as he read the question over. "What, in your opinion, is the long-term goal of this Apple Blossom operation?" He looked up. "And please be specific."

For a full minute Valerie shuffled papers on her table—a meaningless act, since she was far more concentrating on the answer that was still forming in her head. The dark gooey thing that had never quite found its voice.

Until now.

"Pei said that they had spent decades working on the idea. Their top psychiatrists, behaviorists, theorists, had created profiles and tests to identify an individual that could be completely controlled merely by the manipulation of this individual's lusts, desires, wants, needs, inclinations. They no longer believed in brainwashing. Instead they believed that they could exploit an already existing amoral individual's weakness. They called it the, uh, *doctrine of sociopathy*.

"Their economists, political scientists, psychologists, and behaviorists had reasoned and evaluated; planned and projected until they were *certain* of the costs and procedures. Apple Blossom was the result."

She checked some notes, then put them away and looked each man in the room directly in the eyes.

"The Chinese reasoned that they would never develop an industrial base that could compete with the West's. They understood that technological proficiency and inspiration was not their forte, so they could never hope to win a *technical* arms race. But there was one area where they had an advantage over all other societies.

"People and time.

"The Chinese believe they must, as a matter of historical perspective, triumph over the Western democracies. And to that end, Apple Blossom was created.

"They screened hundreds, maybe more, until they found the one they needed. With an almost open-ended budget and the finest analysis and planning possible, they intend to manipulate their man—this Apple Blossom—into a senior decision-making position in the United States government. A position where this Apple Blossom could influence events in the ChiCom's favor. A position where—over time—he could, well, cede control over our government to the Chinese . . . with no one being any the wiser.

"A simple, bloodless, invisible coup d'état."

"Do you know who this Apple Blossom is?" asked one of the assembled.

"No, beyond Pei's contention that he was already 'deeply integrated into the government's fabric,' his phrase."

"Do you have any suspicions?" from another.

Valerie did—a great many. But none that would answer the specific question being asked. And Franco had warned her to be as specific as possible.

"I can only refer back," she began carefully, "to what I said in my statement. To the man who led the interrogation sessions." She took a deep breath, trying to control her evident anger. "That *he* is a traitor there is no doubt. But I don't know if even that *bastard* knows the real answer to your question."

The room was silent, nonreactive, uncaring. It startled Valerie to the core.

"Franco," the old man in the center chair said casually, *"finiscila."*

"Sono il tuo schiavo." He turned to the group, bowed his head to them, then straightened. "My brothers, the picture is clear. One of our own has been murdered. Savagely killed while carrying out the duties assigned him by our most precious Brotherhood, our Union. That he is blood to me is of no import. That he is kith to all of you is. This Canvas, these *Cinesi* behind him, they have robbed us of Paolo's counsel and brotherhood forever. I ask you to help me take my due revenge. And that as an instrument for that vendetta we use Congresswoman Alvarez, as she has offered."

He hesitated, fighting back his emotions. "For Paolo, for our honor, in order to live with ourselves as freemen of the island of Corsica, we can do no less. *Non ho più niente da dichiarare."*

It was early evening when the Council came to see Xenos. With his father and Valerie sitting nearby, they gathered around his bed, dutifully crossing themselves and offering him their prayers for recovery. Then they waited silently.

"Valerie," Xenos said after studying the men, "would you mind waiting outside with my father?"

Reluctantly they left.

"Dureté," Franco began simply, "the Council wishes to ask you about Canvas."

"I thought they might."

"You are well enough for this?" the man from the center chair asked cautiously.

With Franco's help, Xenos sat up, a stern expression covering the pain of the movement.

"I owe much to the Brotherhood."

The old man smiled. "As I knew would be your answer." He hesitated, though. "Dureté, we are troubled by the situation surrounding our lost brother, Paolo. Is it your belief that he *was* killed by this Canvas?"

"By him, or at his order, yes." His voice was strong, firm, committed.

"And that it is the *Cinesi*, the communists, that are behind him?"

"Absolutely."

"You believe this woman's story, then?"

Xenos nodded solemnly. "What I know of it, yes. Everything I saw was consistent with her tale."

The old man seemed to hesitate, as if something in what he would next say was personally painful. "Dureté, there is no bullshit between us, yes?"

"Yes."

The old man looked out the window as he continued. "Franco has told us about this Canvas. About the kind of man he is, what he has behind his balls."

"He has the Chinese military establishment behind those balls, old man."

The man nodded. *"Sì, lo so."* He took a deep breath. "Dureté, could the Brotherhood stand against such a man?"

Xenos considered the question. The organization, loyalty, and savage fury of the Corsicans butting up against Canvas—an unemotional, calculating planner/killer with the resources of a malevolent continent behind him.

"He's a man, and dies from a bullet in the brain like any man," he said after five minutes' consideration. "You *could* get lucky."

Franco flinched, but recognized the truth behind the flat statement of fact.

"And if we are not *lucky*?" The old man needed to hear the answer.

Xenos shrugged. "Then many more Paolos will die. Along with the Alvarez children."

"Could you take him?" Franco's voice reflected the near panic and fury that threatened to erupt from just beneath the surface.

"Maybe," Xenos said matter-of-factly. "With help, the right breaks, the right . . . luck."

The old man studied the man in the bed. "And the dead?"

Xenos merely returned his gaze.

"*Will* you take him?" the old man finally asked.

An hour later Valerie and Avidol were allowed back in the room.

"What happened?" she asked when she saw the expressions on the Council members' faces.

Franco spoke . . . *carefully*. "The Brotherhood has had dealings with the Chinese before. In Macao, in India."

Valerie looked from one face to another. "What does that mean?"

The man from the center chair nodded at Franco.

"It has been decided," the younger man said, "that any attempt by us—alone," he added, drawing a look of reproval from the older man, "would only result in more deaths, including those of your children. So we are sending an envoy to the Chinese to demand the following.

"One: the immediate return of your children, unharmed. Two: a guarantee that your treasons in the Pei affair will never be revealed. Three: a payment of six hundred thousand francs, our investment in Paolo's education, along with a five-million-dollar penalty. Four: a payment of five million dollars as an indemnity to Paolo's family for his death. Five: the turning over to us of the man known as Canvas."

"The Council has ruled," the old man said as he led the others out.

Franco lingered behind briefly, staring daggers at the man in the bed, unable to further meet Valerie's sickened eyes. Finally he walked slowly away.

"Oh God," Valerie muttered as if in pain. "It was all for nothing. Nothing."

Xenos looked up from whispering to his father. "They might well go for the deal. Negotiation makes sense, and the Chinese appreciate sense."

"And if they don't? What then?"

Xenos held out his hand to her.

At first she thought it a conciliatory gesture, then she noticed the business card in it. She took it, seeing only a phone number printed on one side.

"What's this?"

"Ask for Herb," Avidol said with an odd expression. "Tell him—" He thought for a moment. "Tell him . . . *shalom.*"

Nine

It had been a good day. Or at least no one had died, no new catastrophes had manifested themselves, and the Chinese had left him alone.

So Canvas relaxed as he walked down the quiet country road.

It was warm, walls of humidity greeted his every step, but a breeze off the water was cooling. The birds sang and the late summer foliage was spectacular. He closed off his mind from the myriad of decisions he had to make in the next few weeks and allowed himself the luxury of thinking of just one thing.

Xenos.

They'd never been friends—coworkers was barely accurate—but each man knew the other with a greater intimacy than they could a lover of twenty years. Because there had passed between them a shared, well, *life*.

Both men were products of a system that both men had rejected. Both understood that whatever it was that had caused them to be singled out, to be given the intensive training and experience that had completed their metamorphosis, it was not the gift that their former masters believed it to be.

Both knew it only as a curse.

As he wandered the country road, absently wondering which road led down to the beach, he began—as he occasionally did—to examine the realities of his life. The facts of who he had become and whether or not he'd ever had any choice in the matter.

Perhaps they were born with birth defects—men like Xenos

and himself—slight things, unnoticed at the moment of their nascency by the doctors who were more concerned with essentially meaningless issues like breathing, heart rates, and the numbers of fingers and toes. Maybe it *was* that simple. A thing out of anyone's control and impossible to correct or avoid.

The idea pleased him as he climbed over a guardrail to walk on the softer grass rather than the rock-hard road.

The concept had many attractive qualities to it. Giving God the blame/credit for everything they'd done or would do. For their coldness and passion, their calculations and mayhem. It was the ultimate get-out-of-jail-free card, allowing a clear conscience and complete freedom of actions in all things.

No, the man reluctantly admitted. That was too pat, too easy.

And Canvas had seen enough of the world to know that none of it was easy.

Well, if they weren't acts of a vengeant and lustful God, maybe the answer lay in Freudian terms. Dissections of personalities, foibles, habits. Idiosyncratic behaviors leading to an inevitable breakdown of the core personality resulting in antisocietal tendencies and a heightened awareness of the world around them and how best to manipulate it.

Not easy, but not right either.

He shrugged as he paused, for the first time scenting the salt water on the light breeze. He rolled his head to loosen his constantly (these days) tight neck. A squirrel froze halfway up a nearby tree trunk, regarding him calmly, cautiously. It evaluated his potential threat, examined possible solutions, then turned away and continued climbing into the upper branches.

He smiled openly, comfortably. Took in deep breaths of the nearby sea, rubbed his heavily tattooed forearms, then continued on.

Maybe it came down to just that, the squirrel and its life.

Certainly the rodents weren't superior to the other animals around them. No one claimed them as psychotic or particularly blessed by God. They were what they were.

Dynamically vulnerable and damned sure not going to make it easy for the world of predators around them!

He and Xenos had once talked about it, years ago when both believed that what they were doing for their respective governments had worth and importance. In a time when patriot pimps had so clouded their minds that they mistook *doctrine* for clarity.

"I think we're badly developed agoraphobics," Xenos had offered in a stilled voice from their place of concealment.

"We're outdoors, facing a rather hostile group of villains, in case you hadn't noticed, old son," Canvas replied as he swept his night-vision equipment over the vacant empty area they had to cross.

But Xenos had pressed the point. "That's what I mean by 'badly developed.' We're afraid of everything. Complete paranoids with enough training and experience to know just how dangerous and deadly a world we live in."

He'd smiled as he pointed out a passing patrol. "But instead of hiding in a room by ourselves—jumping at every sound—we plan every aspect of our lives to a degree and finiteness that precludes disaster. And we're able to do it like a blind guy hears better. We just overcompensate our basic living skills."

"Bullshit. I ain't afraid of nothing."

Xenos had just smiled at him, sighted down his rifle, calmly depressing the trigger, and watched the first man die.

"Sure," he said as he watched Canvas take his shot. "As long as you're in control."

Canvas remembered that smile.

In his adult years he had killed—personally—sixteen times; arranged or planned many more deaths than that. He'd carried out sophisticated intelligence operations for queen and country, and for money. Been a plaguelike cause of pain and misery for more people than he could possibly know.

He'd been well paid, decorated, lauded, and feted.

But in the end, in the times that he planned for his eventual retreat from a world that he both detested and feared, he'd done it for one reason and one reason only. To *know* the one thing that practically no other on the planet could possibly dream, yet all desperately yearned for.

That he was in control of his own life.

At least as long as the man with the smile wasn't in his life.

The feeling of ease and comfort vanished as he stepped onto the beach.

In the distance he could see them standing by the beached motor launch. Obscene spots on the drifting sands in their dark suits and $500 shoes. People of such inability that they were forced to humiliate themselves by turning to men like himself, like Xenos. Fools so haunted by their impotence that they could only come if other men did their fucking.

Only to fuck over their saviors in return.

As he drew closer, Canvas could see in their eyes a serious molesting coming his way.

"So?"

The German barely bowed his head. "I must protest this meeting. The plan called for individual briefings. The risks incurred by us all . . ."

". . . *being here* is entirely your fault," Canvas finished for him. "If you'd all been willing to stick to the original timetable, none of this *would* be necessary, right?"

"The decision to expedite was made by higher authority," the German said stiffly.

Canvas laughed. "Then we mustn't disappoint them, must we?" He looked over the people whose pictures he'd long ago committed to memory. "What you all need to understand is that our losing six months of planning means we have to do everything on the fly, yes?"

The others seemed less nervous than the old German as they nodded.

"Now, I don't expect this to be a particularly clean or well-fit operation, as we're rushing it through; but if we remain calm, do our jobs, it'll be all right. But you can't hold anything back, right? Any problems, any imponderables, anything that gets in the way because of the shortened schedule, I have to know now. It's improvise, adapt, and overcome time, my lovelies. So come to Jesus and confess your sins."

Silence.

As he'd expected from the too worried individuals. They were being asked—in days—to scrap years of preparation, of planning, and learn to juggle hand grenades, blindfolded in the dark during an earthquake.

"Come on, no fault being found. You all believe in this bullshit or you wouldn't be here. Me, I'm in it for the money and don't really give a shit, beyond my own personal safety, you see."

His voice dropped low and cautionary. "But since that personal safety depends on you true believers getting this stuff right, I'm going to help you as much as possible." The briefest, but noticeable, pause. "Or I'll find someone who can do your job *in place* of you."

Nervous shifting of weight between their feet, digging of toes into the brownish sand.

"Right, now who wants to start? Air?"

A man in his forties stepped forward. "For the most part, my end is unchanged," he said in a forced tone. "I'm confident we'll get the job done."

"I'm particularly concerned about forensics on the head and brain," Canvas said quietly. "We're not going there, but mistakes happen."

The man smiled nervously. "We've done three run-throughs to date. If the hospital guys can't get it done, all we'll need is four minutes alone (per wound)—at the outside—to debride and sanitize."

Canvas looked at a man in the center of the group. "Which brings us to . . ."

This man exhaled deeply. "The move-up screws us bad. We'd planned on using hospital politics and contributions to the board to get our people in position, but now, well, we've had to come up with alternatives." He handed a small piece of paper with three names on it to Canvas. "They're the ones scheduled to have the duty that day. They'll have to be stopped from coming to work."

Canvas never looked at the list as he pocketed it. "And then?"

"Our people will be the logical backups. And I'm the guy that makes the call."

He looked out at the water. "The problem is getting these guys out of the way without it looking like it really is. With the extra time, no problem. But right now, well, we're just not ready." His voice nervously trailed off.

"We'll start right away. Car accidents, mugging with injuries, maybe a family crisis." Canvas hesitated. "Hell, we still have a couple of weeks, right?" But the tone of bitterness in his voice undid anything encouraging in the words.

The other man studied him, then finally nodded. "We need things to go right, but if they do, we'll be there and get it done."

"Fine." Canvas pointed at a woman in her twenties, seemingly out of place among the older people around her. "Go."

"The schedule remains unchanged as of this morning," she said confidently, with just a hint of arrogance or anger. "The Secret Service has approved the route and begun their advance work. Athlete will have breakfast with contributors and high rollers in the hotel ballroom at 0800; get his usual intelligence briefing right after, oh, say 0930 to 0950. He should enter the kill box around 1000 to 1015."

"That's bloody approximate."

The woman shrugged noncommittally. "Give me more time and I'll put him on the dime at the instant you want," she said angrily. "A year from now I would've been his appointments secretary, not just a personal aide! Then I would've shown you something."

Canvas wasn't sure if she was angrier about the coming improvised operation or the loss of her eventual promotion. He shook his head. "What about a vest?"

"Kevlar, level four. But he hates the damn thing, thinks it ruins the line of his shirts when he's in shirtsleeves. Thinks he's got the body of a twenty-year-old and all that." She sighed deeply. "Which I've encouraged. Half the time, he doesn't wear the damned thing."

The German looked concerned. "Will the vest be a problem?"

Canvas shook his head. "Thanks to Teflon and *her* gracious charms, I doubt it." But he made a mental note to switch the large .444 Marlin jacketed rounds from Teflon to porcelain Dynex jacketing, to ensure maximum penetration.

"Media," he demanded.

"We'll be ready. A nonsourced wire-service story will break exactly seventeen minutes after zero that unidentified Asians were involved. We'll need help after that, though. Witnesses, on-camera interview ops, stuff like that."

"Yeah," Canvas said as he thought about the months of work that were being compressed into the next few days. "We'll see to it," he said with more confidence than he felt. Then a thought hit him. "What about your experts?"

The man looked uncomfortable. "None in position. Zip. Nada. If we had more time . . ."

"How gullible are the ones you'd use normally?" He looked deeply concerned. If the disinformation aspect of the plan went awry, then the rest was a fragile house of cards in a gale wind.

"Our biggest break, actually. I've already sent our two best off on assignment to Myanmar. The one I've got left tends to rehash the latest wire-service copy with his own flare. We'll feed him phony teletypes and faxes, spin him before he gets on the air."

"And if you can't?"

The man shrugged. "Then he doesn't get on the air and I'll do the commentary myself."

Canvas shook his head. "Bloody fire drill," he mumbled. He looked up at a woman in her fifties who stood a little apart from the rest. "Remind me why I love you, Lissy."

The woman smiled supportively. "At ten minutes to zero we'll crash the local telephone system in a ten-block radius. Can't do anything about the police and sheriff's nets on this short notice, but . . ." She barely suppressed a grin.

"But . . ."

"There's going to be a bloody great fire at an elementary school a mile and a half outside of the box. It'll start eighteen minutes before zero and they'll be pulling as many coppers off perimeter duty as they can when they hear about the little kiddies being barbecued and all." She paused as the others flinched or looked away. "How's that for love?"

Canvas laughed. "Marry me."

"And be unfaithful to my Mitch? Never. What kind of girl do you think I am?"

"Okay," the big man said after a moment of appreciation of that question, "this is our last meet, right? From now until zero we operate on a descending schedule that *cannot* be recalled. Any problems, anything unforeseen that might create a no-go situation, must be immediately reported to your chain link. And, people"— his voice lowered, eyes narrowed, and death became his face— "there will not be a no-go. Am I understood?"

They all nodded. Some reluctantly, others enthusiastically. But everyone understood the message.

The German joined Canvas as he walked away from the group.

"And your end of these . . . arrangements?" he asked.

Canvas winced, surprising the man who considered him un-flappable. "My end is the most screwed of all. No time to train proper, no physical simuls, barely time to get my facilitators in place."

"Then, what will you do?"

Canvas looked out at the water as they talked, longing to be in the South Pacific, on the island for which he was meeting with a broker that afternoon to make the first payment.

"Canvas?"

He turned back to the German. "I've walked the box four times. Given videos and stills from all nests to each of my people. And I've given instructions to my primary that if the target is still intact after the nests speak, then he's to use his RPG to settle the matter properlike." He smiled. "Made in Taiwan, if you're inter-ested."

The German nodded sagely. "And if that fails?"

Canvas smiled spasmodically; a sickly, convulsive thing. "Then we have the team at the hospital—either in initial treatment or during recovery."

"And if the worst happens, if the target is completely intact when he leaves your *box*."

The German had been handpicked by General Xi for his *coloration,* true enough; but more important, for his thoroughness and eye for detail. "If there is no need for the hospital or they go to a *different* hospital? What then?"

The assassin/planner slowly shook his head. "No chance of that, is there? Not with my boys in the nests. At worst, the target comes out wounded and we get him at *our* hospital."

"Still," the German pressed, knowing that Xi would ask the question later, when he reported by satellite burst transmission.

"Well," the bigger man said pleasantly, "I imagine you'll have me killed then, won't you? Or will it just be a refund with penalty?"

"And if you were in our position?"

Canvas nodded. "Of course."

They started back for the boat.

"I still am not completely comfortable with all these faces knowing each other," the German said, looking over at the group that was talking among themselves. "After, uh, zero, pressures could be brought to bear."

"I know." He exhaled deeply as he thought of himself swimming naked in his private lagoon. "Been taken care of already." He stopped a little way off from the group. "I've got a question for you." He looked deeply into the German's eyes. "Can *you* do this thing you have to?"

The German nodded solemnly. "As with the others, it would've been nicer, certainly more convenient, if I had another six months, or even a year. But . . ." He looked into the woods behind the beach. "This is the fruition of thirty-one years' work. I have been in place—waiting—for the last seven of them. If I cannot do it now, I could not do it better fourteen months from now."

Canvas looked at the committed man, thought about the fanged demons that drove him, the long-bred discipline of his people, his culture. His sellout/buy-in with the Chinese. A merging of their ideology with the man's lack of any true belief.

Then he laughed.

Because with all of that, they'd still had to come to him when their geometric logic had threatened to come crashing down around them.

"Your daddy really a Nazi?"

The German shrugged. "Not in a noticeably provable way. But what if he was?" The man seemed relaxed for the first time. "In this country, every man is judged as himself; not as his father's son."

"God bless America," Canvas said affably to the German's discomfort.

Ten minutes later he watched them reboard the small boat. Standing on the beach—watching silently, thoughtfully—until they disappeared around the point for the covert rendezvous. Knowing that—other than the German—he would never see any of them alive again.

"I will miss Lissy, though," he mumbled as he turned and started back.

Clearing his mind of everything but squirrels, vulnerabilities, and Pacific islands for the rest of the afternoon.

3 Hours 40 Minutes to Zero
Washington, D.C.

"Where are we supposed to be, Michael?" DeWitt asked as he straightened his tie.

"Car's waiting, sir." The personal aide had already made his —as usual—thorough preparations. "Twenty-minute drive, then the seminar, then brunch with selected members of the host committee."

The attorney general nodded. "Right." He exhaled a deep, cleansing breath. "Any updates?"

"No, sir. Not on anything."

DeWitt nodded. "Okay." He started to pour himself his second vodka of the early morning.

"Uh, sir. Maybe not today?" Michael braced for an outburst.

Instead, the man looked down at his hand on the bottle, then slowly drew it away. "You're right."

Thirty minutes later, joined by an equally tense Buckley and Kingston, DeWitt took his place on the dais.

"Good morning," the youngish moderator said pleasantly. "And welcome to our third in a series of meetings with"—a dramatic pause—"our leaders of tomorrow. Our guests today are Attorney General Jefferson DeWitt; the junior senator from Colorado, Rod Buckley; and the director of the Peace Corps and former counsel to the president, Lane Kingston."

After the applause the man sat down. "Before we begin the questioning, we'll hear briefly from each of our guests. Director Kingston?"

Kingston smiled. "I'm very pleased to be here today, Carl. My job is directly linked to the topic of these meetings . . . addressing the future of the world. A thought never far from my mind. Because it is the next generation that will lead us through the early days of the new millennium. And it is the youth of the world—which I hope I'm not too far removed from"—light laughter from the crowd—"that we must turn to for new ideas, new appeals, new ways of looking at things in order for us to move forward into the new, American century."

Enthusiastic applause, as the moderator turned to Buckley.

"Well," the senator said as he checked a note from his aide, "leadership *is* what this is all about. Isn't it? But the *form* of that leadership is what concerns me. Will the next wave or whatever you call them merely be parrots of the old strictures and tired concepts, or will they be able to see things with new eyes? Young, *fresh* eyes, which will recognize that in our uncertain future old enemies might become our friends, and old friends might well become enemies."

Sage nods from around the room. "Personally I hope for a new generation of leadership that is both flexible and thoughtful. A generation that will lead America forward, and not remain too trapped in the past."

"Mr. Attorney General," the moderator said, nodding to DeWitt.

DeWitt grinned. "Sounds like a presidential debate to me."

The moderator smiled. "Perhaps in a couple of years." The crowd laughed, along with the panelists.

"God help us all." DeWitt smiled back. "What do I see for the leaders of tomorrow?" He seemed to think the question over. "New ideas? Sure. Flexibility? Absolutely."

He suddenly grew deeply introspective. "But what strikes me is that we've heard the same thing for each of the political generations that has come before us. And the more they call for change, the more things seem to stay the same."

He sighed deeply. "What I would like to see, what I pray to see, is far simpler than all the lofty declarations of all who have come before us.

"The challenge to the next generation of leaders must be to create an America where no child goes to bed hungry or illiterate or abandoned at night. Where no man or woman loses self-respect through work that demeans and doesn't provide a basic living wage; or through the plague of racism. Where every American's basic dignity is not only protected by their government but embraced and worshiped by it as well."

Loud applause and the slightest mocking applause from Kingston and Buckley beside him.

Buckley leaned over and whispered to DeWitt, "Nice speech. You write it or did Michael?"

"Jealous?"

Buckley shrugged. "Just thought I might steal the one person in your office who knows what he's doing."

"Cynic," DeWitt said out of the corner of his mouth. "Michael and I *are* the same person."

And the questioning began.

2 Hours 25 Minutes to Zero
The Safe House

Canvas sat in a fully extended recliner, feet up, head back, eyes closed. A cup of coffee sat ignored on a table next to him. Maps of *The Box* on the walls in front of him, charts, tables of organization, the nuts and bolts of an elaborate plot laid out within easy reach.

But he didn't need any of it. In his mind he was already in the kill box; moving with the growing crowds, examining, accepting, rejecting, adjusting things until they fit the pattern he'd designed.

The operation had been forced to become fluid, not planned so much as felt, so his instructions to his teams had been general at best, mirroring his relaxed, "go with the flow" state of mind in the chair.

"You all know your nests, but we're not married to them," he'd said at the final briefing the night before. "You want to move, do it. Just make sure your facilitators know where you've gotten.

"And all of that goes for post-zero as well, right? We all know what we *want* to do, what we *planned* to do, but after zero use your own best judgment. Instinct says 'split,' you just split! Call in at the approved times to let us know you haven't run off with the family silver."

Then his voice had grown solemn, quiet, concerned.

"Don't none of us like this cowboy nonsense, but there's where we sit, lads. In it up to our exposed throats, we are. So make sure you get your shots off, as many as you can without putting yourself at maximum risk. Then get the bleeding Hell out of there! And if you have to drop Mr. or Mrs. Nosy Pants to get it done or on the way out, then you drop 'em, mates."

He'd smiled easily then, as he'd handed out the small five-round clips he'd personally loaded with rounds he'd personally manufactured.

"Can't afford any more insurance payments on this here thing, can I?"

But that was hours ago. And although he'd heard nothing since they'd wordlessly left, he knew the teams and their facilitators were in position, waiting.

Ready.

Just as he now knew it was time to check that knowledge.

He picked up the microphone from the handie-talkie on the table next to him, sighed, then pressed the call key.

"Zhè shì qù jînán de liè-chë ma?" he said firmly into the radio.

A long, static-filled silence.

"Yï." A voice cut through the white noise.

"Líng."

"Èr."

"Sän."

"Sì."

"Wû."

"Liù."

The primary on-site supervisor and the five teams were in the box with clear fields of fire.

"Chü shì le," he said simply.

And his mind drifted away from the shooters to other problems of the day.

1 Hour 47 Minutes to Zero
The Hospital

"Hey! What are you doing here?"

The surgical resident shrugged as he shook his colleague's hand. "Got called back from vacation a couple of days early is what. Immerman got a job interview at some high-line body shop in Palm Springs, so I gotta fill in."

"The way it's running, I guess."

"What d'you mean?"

They started down the corridor together.

"Well," the first doctor said, "I'm covering for Singh, who got his knee broken in a mugging last week."

"Shit," the second doctor said. "They got to do something about security out here. It's like a war zone."

"You're talking about Darlene."

"Yeah. I mean when the senior scrub nurse gets raped and beaten in our own parking lot, you know things are getting out of control."

They shook their heads and began to discuss the latest hospital gossip as they entered the emergency room.

35 Minutes to Zero
A Bed-and-Breakfast

The renovation work had been going on for over ten days.

There was the usual jumble of pickup trucks, vans, concrete mixers, and tools spread across the front lawn. An eyesore, but the people of the neighborhood didn't mind really.

A reopened Pleasantry B&B could only mean fresh business for their arts and crafts shops.

So a little inconvenience of workmen and their lewd comments or slovenly habits could be put up with.

And besides, none seem to be around right now.

Other than two men, bent over the open hood of the truck, mostly hidden from view.

15 Minutes to Zero
John Dickinson Elementary School

"Goddammit, get those doors open!"

The men leaned against the double doors, kicked at them, but they refused to move.

"Sonofabitch!" one yelled as he began to choke on the growing black smoke. "There's no way out!"

A woman came running up. Slapping at her blouse, trying to put out flames, she screamed out at the men.

"Fire's worse back there! God in Heaven," she cried as children's screams could be heard over the ringing alarms and approaching sirens, "what are we going to do!"

"Everybody to the roof," the principal ordered, praying they had time and no one would be left behind.

5 Minutes to Zero
The Safe House

Canvas turned down the television, answering his cell phone on the second ring. "Candle."

"Proceed." The line went dead.

He brought the microphone, already in his other hand, up to his lips.

"Käi mén," he said clearly. *"Käi mén."*

He put down the radio, started to leave, then stopped, turning up the TV for one last look.

"Reports are still sketchy, details still coming in," the announcer was saying as he shuffled several papers in his hands, "but this much, at least, is clear. About twenty minutes ago there was an explosion at the factory of American Banners in Kaohsiung, Taiwan. The factory—which makes U.S. flags and sports pennants—is said to be fully engulfed in flames, with the bulk of its workforce trapped inside.

"An anonymous call to WIN's Taipei Bureau claimed that the bombing was, and I quote here, 'the first blow, of many yet to come, against America for its gradual sellout of her Nationalist Chinese allies.' We go now to . . .'"

Canvas shut the set, studied the blank tube for a moment, then moved into another room.

Five minutes later he was gone, the house an inferno—accelerated by solid rocket fuel spread throughout. The most that would ever be found was a soft, white ash.

Zero Plus 9 Minutes
Chevy Chase, Maryland

"My point is, Mr. Attorney General, that your generation just has never appreciated the sacrifices those of my generation made in order to give you the chance to turn on and drop out."

DeWitt laughed easily. "I'd hardly say we've dropped out, Mr. Williams. Three-quarters of the president's cabinet is made up of men and women of my generation. At the polls, we voted in greater numbers than did yours, in business we have become CEOs and COOs of half the Fortune 500 companies."

"Still, y'all never seem to get it right! You may have the numbers for the moment, sir, but . . ."

"Well," Kingston added between bites, "let's just say our generation and yours don't see things the same way, although our motivations are the same. A better, stronger America."

The lunch with senior members of the Democratic National Committee had been going on for about half an hour. The committee members challenging, testing, *evaluating* the three men who were the leading candidates—if undeclared—to replace the lame duck incumbent.

"Motivations by whose definition, gentlemen?" another committeeman interrupted. "The hippies or the fogies?"

Buckley laughed. "I vote with the hippies, Robert, but *deeply* respect my fogy constituency."

"Excuse me, Mr. Attorney General." His aide—Michael— hurried up to him, a concerned look on his face. "It's FBI Director Hayes for you. Quite urgent." He handed him a cell phone as the table moved onto another argument.

Zero Plus 18 Minutes
The Hospital

"Goddammit, I am not going to lose this man!" the first doctor shouted.

"Pulse is too fast to count," the scrub nurse called out as she gave the horribly wounded man an injection. "He's shutting down!"

"I got eight holes in his back and chest. Maybe five of them entries," the second doctor called out. "Hang two more units of whole blood and push 'em! Also all the Ringers you can get!"

"V-fib," a nurse called out.

The first doctor grabbed a cardiac needle and plunged it straight into the man's heart. "Dammit, what next?"

Zero Plus 29 Minutes
Chevy Chase, Maryland

The table was hushed, stilled. All eyes stared at the attorney general, silently begging not to hear the news they'd all heard before—too often—in their lifetimes.

"Ladies and gentlemen," he said in a voice choked with emotion as he handed the phone back to Michael. "Director Hayes informs me that the vice president died of his wounds approximately five minutes ago."

"Sweet Jesus," someone gasped.

DeWitt shook his head—stunned—as he stood up. "I have to get back to Washington."

Zero Plus 4 Hours 15 Minutes
Lafayette Park, Washington, D.C.

In his life, the German would never face more danger than he would in the next few minutes. He'd hoped to have more time, more practice, a closer relationship with the old man he must now move into place. But orders were orders, so recriminations and doubts were for another time.

With a sigh, he straightened his suit and crossed the street.

Zero Plus 7 Hours 30 Minutes
The White House

The two men sat in front of the television, comparing their private notes to what they were hearing.

"Let me repeat that," the anchor was saying. "There are now confirmed eyewitness reports that three to five Asian or Oriental men were seen leaving the area of the shooting at a high rate of speed. One of them was described as having—and I'm quoting from the wire-service copy here—a tattoo of a green tiger on his left forearm.

"We turn now to our expert on Asian terrorism, retired Army Special Forces Colonel Clay Merit. Colonel, is there anything you can tell us from this new information?"

The camera pushed in on a middle-aged, paunchy man who quickly looked up from the printouts in his hand.

"Well, Bernie," he said, shaking his head, "it is difficult to say this out loud, but the green tiger has always been a symbol for the covert operations wing of the Dàn Jì. Taiwan's secret intelligence service."

The anchor looked shocked. "Are you saying, Colonel, that this man the police are seeking may have worked for our allies, the Nationalist Chinese?"

The man nodded. "Unfortunately, as this and previous administrations have moved closer and closer to fully normalized relations with the Communist Chinese, our friends in Taiwan have grown more and more militant in their opposition to this. And I'm reminded it was the vice president who served as the chief negotiator in setting up the recent summit between the premier of the People's Republic and the president."

He paused, trying to decide whether he should put on his *serious* or *concerned* look. "When taken in concert with the flag factory bombing earlier today, there seems to be little doubt left for anyone. However much the FBI might withhold direct comment."

A Secret Service agent interrupted the men. "The attorney general, Mr. President."

The president muted the TV, then turned to shake the hands of the younger man. "Jeff, you know George Steingarth."

"Mr. President. George, how are you?"

The son of German immigrants shook his hand as they all sat down.

"Well," DeWitt began without preamble, "here's where we stand." He handed a copy of his file to the president. "The FBI has confirmed that the hit team was Asian and staying in a dilapidated old bed-and-breakfast very near the assassination site. A title search shows that the building had recently been purchased by a dummy corporation that *has* had ties to Nationalist Chinese intelligence."

"Swine," Steingarth said under his breath.

"Can we prove they came from Taiwan and were acting on their government's orders?" The elderly president squinted as he continued to read.

DeWitt shrugged. "There's knowing and there's proving, Mr. President. Unless we catch one of them, unless he talks, we may never be able to actually *prove* what we are all certain of. At least not in court."

"I'm not fucking interested in courts," the president growled as he finished reading. "I've got a hundred and seventy-five dead—thirty of them Americans—in a factory in Taiwan, a dead vice president, and the military all over my ass! We have a Crisis Management Committee meeting in ten minutes, and I need some fucking answers!"

DeWitt nodded. "Director Hayes is preparing a full presentation of the evidence to date for them."

"Good." The president seemed distracted. "Jeff, you're a pro, you understand the real world . . ."

"Yes, Mr. President?"

"Senator Buckley and Director Kingston, Mr. President."

The president waved the Secret Service to admit the men. Two minutes later, after DeWitt brought them up to date, the old man gestured at the muted TV.

"We have a terminal situation, boys. Getting worse all the time." He took a note from DeWitt that had been handed him by his aide, Michael. "And I am now informed that a van with the green tiger symbol painted on the side just fired on a group of American tourists in Manila."

He looked exhausted as he handed the note to Steingarth. "We are about as close to war as this nation has ever been, and will get all the way there in an instant if we don't act, and act decisively."

"What do you need, Mr. President?" Buckley asked—hoping he knew the answer.

"I've ordered all our workers back to barracks, sir," Kingston said firmly. "We're making arrangements with the host countries to provide extra security for all Peace Corps workers in Asia. But if there's anything more I can do for you?"

And he prayed that there was. One thing, specifically.

DeWitt, busy on the phone, covered the mouthpiece. "Mr. President, Director Hayes and the CIA director are downstairs, along with the Joint Chiefs, sir. Other staff and advisers are en route. They'll be ready for you in ten minutes."

If you're not ready for me before then, he hoped.

The president looked them each in the eye. He'd never really liked the young, idealistic lawyer, the politically correct politician, or the social-climbing administrator. He'd supported them, advanced their careers and expectations as much to please the more moderate wing of the party as for their qualifications.

And he knew they were all considering running to replace him in fourteen months, at the end of the president's second and final term. A prospect that depressed him.

He personally didn't care for the idea of these young, admitted former pot smokers with foreign educations and no military records—but winning smiles, charm, style, and a very high approval rating—replacing him.

But this was politics—all about making the hard, distasteful choices above personal desires, he'd been reminded within the hour —and the men in front of him were the champions of the young moderates that were gradually taking over the party.

Also, the president frankly admitted to himself—if no one else —he was tired.

Exhausted in his eightieth year of life, of defending the ideals that had been bred into him, that gave him chills each time he saw an American flag. The job of the last six-plus years had been draining and dispiriting, particularly since his wife had died of cancer.

The president had come to realize, in the private isolation that included only *true* friends like the German American banker beside him, that he was slipping away—like a faded melody—and would need their youth, energy, and strength if he was going to face what he knew would be the greatest crisis his administration had ever seen.

"If what we think has happened," the president said after too long a pause, "has *in fact* happened, this country cannot afford to appear weak. Not even for a second!"

Buckley agreed. "Of course, Mr. President. But what does—"

"George and I have been talking. There are niceties and there are political realities. And our reality—at this moment—is that we could be in combat in Taiwan within the week."

Steingarth leaned forward. "Gentlemen, what we are saying is that there must be no appearance of a vacuum in the national command authority."

The president looked uncomfortable but determined. "Look, I

know old Bobby's not cold yet, but I have to act for the good of the country, dammit! And George agrees. Hell, his instincts are almost as sharp as mine at this."

"I know the Taiwanese," Steingarth said. "They will deny, obfuscate, plead communist plots and sinister conspiracies. We must not be perceived as even tolerating any of those lies."

"I understand," Kingston said slowly. "But what does this—"

"The Oriental mentality is such," Steingarth continued, "that they will believe they have dealt a crippling blow to our government. Even before I became a member of the President's Foreign Intelligence Advisory Board, I detected this growing animosity from them. This need to have a high-profile, world-shattering victory."

"He's been telling me about it for years," the president added emphatically.

"But we will deny them their moment," Steingarth said with surety.

"Jeff," the president said as he reached out and touched the younger man, "I want to nominate you for the vice presidency the day after Bobby's funeral."

"Mr. President." DeWitt sounded in shock. "I don't know what to say. You need to take more time, sir."

"There is no more time to take," the president argued forcefully. "We must demonstrate to the Nationalists that we are firm in our resolve and will not be bullied or frightened into abandoning decades of hard work at normalization with the mainland."

The president looked at the other men. "Rod, you're the new attorney general. I'm ordering you to immediately convene a special commission to investigate what's happened and provide definitive answers within two weeks."

Buckley, equally shocked, slowly nodded. "Sir."

"Lane, I've spoken to Governor Free. We can't afford to lose a vote in our thin margin in the Senate. Not with some of the things that will need to be done. She'll appoint you to replace Rod as soon as I announce Jeff and these moves."

"Thank you, Mr. President," Kingston said as he quietly exulted at his new power—even as he resented the others theirs.

"Mr. President," DeWitt said softly, instantly getting the other men's attention, "I think you should take more time. A decision like this . . ."

Steingarth looked at him supportively—privately appreciating the man's control. "Jeff, you're a moderate, with no clear China policy, but a proven history of loyalty to the goals of this administration. You know everyone on Judiciary and Foreign Affairs intimately and are a certain confirmation."

"You must do this, Jeff," the president said. "If not for yourself, then for history."

DeWitt was silent for a long time while the other men studied him, absorbed by their own private thoughts of ascension.

During the silence, Apple Blossom looked around the room, saw the trappings of the office, the history, the nervous Secret Service guards, aides on the phone getting further updates.

Their minds flashed over a lifetime of decisions, over decades of fear and avarice merged into a single, undefinable but overpoweringly lusty emotion. They thought of the stark reality of what this moment would bring with it.

Of the universe that had been implied by the old man's words.

They looked into the eyes of that desperate old man and of the blank German adviser who had replaced the first lady as the president's only intimate; both begging in their own way to fulfill his and their destinies.

"Mr. President," DeWitt said with sober sincerity after a brief, whispered conversation with Michael, "for the sake of the nation, I accept."

Ten

It was a small theater, steeply tiered, with three-quarters of the seventy-five seats surrounding the tiny stage. The stage itself had two comfortable chairs, a lectern with a microphone, and a floor-to-ceiling mosaic of a small man—holding a bamboo spade—slowly chipping away at a massive mountain.

And above it, in large red letters trimmed in gold, the motto of the Long-Range Study Organization.

Time is our ultimate ally.

The room was packed, filled with men and women in faded gray or dark blue shapeless uniforms. Each with pad, pen, and laser pointer. All carefully arranged and undisturbed as they waited for the event to begin. There was no talking among themselves, no restless rustlings, just calm patience and anticipation.

On the stage a man in a suit—older than the rest, somehow different—sat in one of the chairs. He looked them all in the eye, making mental notes as to the comportment of each for correction or compliment later.

To his right was Xi. Hands folded in his lap, the slightest of smiles; he looked every inch the humble farmer waiting to be congratulated for a bumper crop of rice.

Nothing anywhere in the hall or on the stage indicated that the group was over one hundred feet belowground, surrounded by a company of elite guards and state-of-the-art anti-eavesdropping gear.

As the hands on the antique Chin dynasty clock struck twenty minutes past the hour, the man in the suit stood, as if propelled by the minute hand. He walked to the microphone, bowed his head toward the audience, then toward Xi.

They all stood, bowing deeply toward him. Then, settling back in their seats, they uncapped their pens, opened their pads, and waited.

"Friends," the man began in his strained, emphysemic voice, "these are dangerous times. Our enemies would seek to destroy us at every turn. Our allies become corrupt and useless, the unaligned continue to be seduced by the falsehoods and promiscuity of the West.

"But we remain stalwart in our defense of our people's honor and pride."

He paused, looking over at Xi, then back at the assemblage.

"I am well pleased at our progress on this score. General Xi."

Even as the suited man began applauding the approaching general, the rest of the group leaped to their feet and wrapped an enormous ovation around the tiny man. Shouts of "Xi!" and "First chair!" rained down on the man, who took it stoically.

Xi shook the suited man's hand, then paused while he sat down. The applause instantly ceased.

"Friends, I am unworthy."

Again applause led by the suited man.

"Friends," Xi finally continued, "this is a progress report on Project Apple Blossom, as of 0515 this date."

He opened a file—which he knew by heart—and began reading.

"Since the assassination of Vice President Kroll, the American FBI and CIA have concluded through the Buckley Commission's investigation, as intended, that the *Dàn Jì* is responsible for the crime. This belief has been bolstered by the discovery of appropriately incriminating evidence at the sites of the factory fire and the tourist massacre. Taiwan has officially and unofficially denied all complicity, have offered complete cooperation to the American investigators in the case.

"After initial proclamations of the PRC's probable hand in this, they have even retreated on that score. Now even the Taiwanese traitors are beginning to believe that the operation was carried out either by renegade members of the Green Tiger, or by the Green Tiger itself without government sanction." He paused. "We are encouraging that belief both in Taiwan and the United States.

"Three American Naval Task Forces have taken up positions in the South and East China Seas and the Philippine Sea. They are flying freedom of navigation exercises in the Taiwan Straits and have moved B-1 and Stealth aircraft to their base in the northeast on Okinawa. While no strike appears likely in the short term, the pressure continues to build among American popular opinion for a retaliatory mission of some kind."

He moved ahead several sections in the file before continuing.

"Vice President Kroll will be buried this afternoon—Washington time—in his home state of Wyoming. The president and full cabinet will be in attendance under maximum possible security. Upon his return to Washington, he will address the nation from the Oval Office and announce he is placing into nomination the name of Jefferson DeWitt—his attorney general—to become the next vice president, and Senator Rodney Buckley to replace DeWitt. The nominations will be approved within the month."

This time there was no prompting for the applause. Shouts, cheers, genuine love were thrown down at him.

For nearly five minutes he luxuriated in it, then raised his hands for silence.

"This is the people's victory, not one man's. It is a victory that was won due to the hard work of a great many. I stand here for them, to accept your thanks and answer your questions." He turned to the suited man next to him. "Mr. Chairman?"

"Has any connection been made between our man and the operation?" he asked carefully from a list prepared by his staff after Xi's private briefing earlier.

"Canvas has reported that the shooters and their facilitators escaped unwitnessed or marked in any way." Xi seemed completely at ease. "The associate support drawn for this operation performed well and was never suspected. Their supervisors have been eliminated in two automobile crashes and a commercial airliner explosion. Those few voices that cry 'conspiracy,' cry 'Taiwanese conspiracy,' nothing more."

The chairman nodded as he read the next question. "What are the prospects for Apple Blossom implementing some form of policy control and on what timetable?"

Xi pretended to deeply ponder that question, although he and the chairman had fastidiously crafted the answer hours before.

"It *is* a forked element of the plan," he said slowly, as if the words were drawn from deep thought. "We *can* do nothing but rely on momentum and judicious tappings. This, in and of itself, will almost certainly deliver the Democratic nomination for the presidency to Apple Blossom in ten months. With proper funding, he cannot lose the general election and would rise to the presidency within fourteen months.

"However, I am still cautious of the situation. There are the traitor Pei's allegations; Congresswoman Alvarez is still a figure of concern; there is the very real possibility of exposure—in some form—prior to November of next year."

He clasped his hands in front of him, the picture of deep concentration."

"The other fork available to us—in light of this information—is to continue to expedite the situation. President Brackens is an old man in ill health. The pressures on him are enormous. It would be a simple matter to eliminate him, thereby giving greater policy control to Apple Blossom in the inevitable political confusion that would follow." He looked contemplative. "From any number of positions or tangents, the elimination of the president *must*, of itself, give us more, perhaps total, control."

"Another assassination?" the much older and sicker chairman said in shock, not from the prepared cards. His tone was both disapproving and fearful.

Xi shook his head in the finest tradition of grand Chinese theater. "A natural death, Mr. Chairman. A stroke or heart attack at a fortuitous moment."

The room seemed to relax.

The chairman didn't.

"You mentioned the congresswoman as a continuing threat," the chairman said stiffly as he struggled to read his staff's enlarged typing. "Is there anything new on that score?"

Xi nodded firmly. "There is, Mr. Chairman."

Technically, at least, it was a beach. Really far more rocks than sand, it was an uncomfortable, if breathtaking, tableau to walk on, around, through. With sheer cliffs on one side, the pounding Mediterranean on the other, and the eons-old shining smooth rocks looking back at you in quiet mocking at your turmoil.

Valerie carried her shoes as she picked her way around the obstacles, concentrating as hard as she could on picking a path around the stones. It was the way she'd found—the only way—to escape thinking in general. Thinking, and crying.

She felt cursed, betrayed, abandoned by God and the devil to roast in a purgatory of her own making. With the ghosts of her children calmly, sadly, looking out at her from every shadow.

So she walked on the rocky beach, and didn't think, for longer each day.

The tide was going out at the end of another of the interminably beautiful days of this place. Another day of warm breezes, sweet scents, and no news.

She knew the negotiations between the Chinese and the Corsicans had begun, but had heard nothing beyond that. Assumed they were going badly, that her children had already been made to pay for the headstrongness of their insane mother; that the Chinese were delaying to cover that fact.

But the head of the Council had urged patience. And since she was a wanted fugitive in her own country, in this one illegally, as powerless as a human being could be to stop the events she saw unspooling on the evening news nightly, she just grit her teeth and walked the beaches.

Her own limbo in paradise.

When not on the beach, Valerie had been keeping mostly to

herself. Despite the debt she owed him, she couldn't bring herself to talk to Xenos anymore. He'd refused to involve himself any further—as he'd told her in the midst of the chaos—and she'd been led to believe that this was the primary reason the Corsicans chose to negotiate rather than fight.

She understood him, in her mind—he'd been drawn into this thing unwillingly and accidentally—but these days she was ruled by her heart, not her mind.

And her heart couldn't forgive him.

Avidol had been nice, solicitous, talking to her every day—the weather, her health, small talk meaning nothing—and she understood that he was legitimately concerned for her. But he was an old man from a different time, and she was unwilling to educate him about the kind of man his son was, and the men his son knew that he refused to confront.

The Corsicans were . . . polite. They saw her, she believed, as an inconvenience. A tool necessary to propel the negotiations for the compensation for Paolo's murder. A club to hold over the Chinese's head. But beyond that, she was simply and purely the instrument that had caused Paolo's death in the first place.

A thing that kept her from looking Franco in the eyes, in the soul, the few times she encountered him.

So she walked.

She looked up from the thin strip of sand, in order to better pick her way around a boulder, suddenly surprised to see someone else on this deserted stretch of ocean's edge.

Franco, staring out at the water, unmoving, silhouetted by the setting sun.

Embarrassed, she quickly looked for a way off the beach, realizing that her only options were to go back the way she had come or to continue on, past the man. She turned around to go.

"Alvarez!"

Valerie winced when she heard her name called out, freezing with indecision as to whether or not to answer or hurry off the beach.

"Alvarez!"

The voice was closer now, coming toward her. Reluctantly she forced up a nonfrown and turned to face the brother of the boy she'd betrayed.

"Franco."

He came up to her, his face an angry blank. "It is dangerous for you to walk alone."

She shrugged. "I need alone."

He seemed to study her closely. "Me also." He turned away from her, again looking out at the water, beyond the water.

"Are the, uh, negotiations going well?" She felt she had to ask.

He raised his eyebrows in an expression of both doubt and *I don't really give a damn*. "Everything with the *Cinesi* is time. They analyze, dissect, repeat, and probe. Then they ask for clarifications."

"But at least they're talking, right?" Her voice was strained as she longed to be gone, to not be so physically close to the man she'd so soul-wounded.

The man she had so much in common with.

Franco never looked away from the blue water that reflected the reds and oranges of the sunset as if it were on fire.

"We all die."

"What?"

He took a deep breath, exhaled it even more deeply, then pointed out at the water. *"Moriamo tutti.* It is an old Corsican belief."

Valerie felt sick to her stomach. "I, uh, I promised Dr. Jacmil that I would . . ."

"What it means," Franco said, ignoring the clearly distraught woman, "is that death is inevitable. We will all, at length, return to the sea that gave us life. It's comforting somehow. Don't you think?"

A chill raced through Valerie. An unclean hand clenching her soul to the brink of extinction. Slowly, almost against her will, she moved closer to the Corsican strongman.

"You've heard something." A statement, not a question. "My children . . ."

Franco shook his head. "No. I've heard nothing." He laughed bitterly. "But then it doesn't matter, does it?"

Valerie had looked down, saying a private prayer of thanks, but she snapped her head up at that. "What! What did you say?"

Franco just looked at her blankly.

"You bastard," she whispered. "You unfeeling sonofabitch!" Her anger found its voice and exploded over the man. "It amuses you to play head games with me? To tell me that it doesn't matter if my babies are dead! That it's inevitable?"

She reached up and slapped his expressionless face. *"Boca de gusano!* We all die? You heartless bastard, what the Hell do you know about it?"

She swung on him again. This time he easily caught her blow, then the one from the other hand. She began to struggle, spitting at him, cursing him, kicking; using him as the effigy for all the men, all the users and killers and brutes, who had turned her into what she'd become.

A mother who had killed her own children.

Her fury grew, anger becoming rage becoming an unquenchable fire. She screamed, tore at him, tried to hurt, disfigure him as harshly and painfully as possible.

Finally, his eyes still reflecting nothing but a quiet calm, he hugged her arms to her sides, lifted her off her feet, and threw her into the retreating surf.

"Bast—" she cried out, then froze as he stood over her menacingly.

"Do not ever think," Franco began slowly, "that I have forgotten what *you* did to *me*. Huh? How you destroyed me when you betrayed my sainted brother."

His face reddened, his breathing became raspy. "If it were not for a promise I have made to Dureté, I would have wrung the life from your body days ago."

He stood with the water washing around his calves, looking down at the woman who lay half covered by the warm tide.

"Your children are your life? My brother was mine. Now I must go to our mother and tell her that her baby is dead, buried somewhere we can't find, without the sacraments or the witness of those that loved him." He paused. "I would *gladly* trade the lives of your precious children to avoid looking into my mother's eyes at that moment."

Valerie tried to get up, but he pushed her back into the water with his foot.

"Listen to me carefully. I believe that your children live. I *want* your children to be alive. Because if they are, then it is more likely the *Cinesi* will negotiate in good faith, as far as they ever do. And it is more likely I will get a chance to avenge my brother's death."

He grew quiet, still, turning back to the water and the deepening bloodreds reflected there. "It is my only reason for not blowing my brains out. And yours."

Valerie—stunned, confused—sat up. "I'm so sorry," was all she could think to say.

"Moriamo tutti."

"We all die," she repeated.

Franco nodded as he started off, down the beach.

For a long moment Valerie watched him go slowly off, understanding, for the first time, that in his grief Franco had dedicated himself to living—albeit for his revenge—rather than dying in his mourning for a soul he could not return to this plain.

Ten minutes later—in a secluded, sandy cove—all memories, pain, recriminations, guilt, and doubts were washed away (for the moment) by the mutually violent sex.

As Franco violently expelled his anger and his fury at Valerie's equally rough, savage, mountingly *alive* frenzy, the two found something within each other. A commonality of the most primitive level of existence.

As the Corsican's thrusts threatened to split her apart, as her kicks and scratching bruised and gashed the man, as their blood spilled into the raging surf, was thrown up into their faces, something inside her died.

Was reborn.

"Moriamo tutti!" she called out at the height of the violent tenderness.

And she began to live . . . not for ambition or self-improvement; not to provide her children a perfect world; not to gain power, ascendancy, or control.

But simply, and completely, for revenge.

The Champ-de-Mars is about as far removed from the quiet beauty of the French Mediterranean coast as possible. It is pageant and poetry, neon and subtlety, a tribute to Paris's elegant past and its cacophonous present. Running almost the length of the city, it is the magnet that draws almost all visitors and residents of the glorious metropolis, if only for a moment, if only to say, "I was there."

But Herb Stone wasn't interested in tourism or history. The crowds of passersby he found both comforting and frightening. Coloration and threat. But even this he largely ignored as he wandered through the music-churning, flashing-lights experience. His eyes remaining locked on the statue about a half-block ahead.

With the Eiffel Tower behind it, the statue of *Mars Ascending* seemed somehow out of place, its smooth pale pink marble contrasting against the copper giant. But there was also something very right about the placement—the god of war and destruction serenely looking up at a monument to peace and prosperity.

"Only in France," he said aloud as he stopped at the foot of the statue.

"You have no appreciation of art, Mr. Stone?"

Herb didn't turn to acknowledge Avidol Goldman. "Well, this one piece perhaps." He gestured toward the lightning in the angry god's left hand. "He has purpose, commitment, dedication to mission. I *appreciate* those qualities, Reb Goldman."

He turned to face the old man. "I was expecting Ms. Alvarez."

"We all must learn to live with disappointment," Avidol said as he studied the man with equal frankness.

"Yes, I know," Herb said somewhat sadly. "The story of my life, it seems." He followed Avidol through the crowded park. "Do you know Paris, Reb Goldman?"

The old man nodded. "Very well. When my family came from Greece to the United States, we stopped here for several years."

"Really?" Herb sounded genuinely interested. "When was that?"

"Oh, just before the war. We lived in the Twenty-third Arrondisement for three years, I think. We left for England, then America, around 1939."

Herb was impressed. "I would've killed to see Paris back then. It must've been so . . . alive!"

Avidol stopped, a dour look crossing his strong face. "Can you hear yourself, Stone? Even in admiration, you mix death and life."

Herb laughed. "My apologies, sir. We're not all lifelong pacifists like you."

Avidol gestured to the right, by a noisy carousel. "I was not always a pacifist, as you put it."

"No?"

"No. You will please hand me your overcoat and jacket."

Herb did as he was requested. "Oh, don't stop. Please."

Avidol sat down on a bench and methodically checked the pockets, patting down and squeezing the lining, the padding, as he'd been shown.

"There is little to tell. I was a boy, full of myself and the world. Convinced that right must triumph over wrong and that I should be the tool of that."

"Admirable sentiment."

Avidol shook his head. "A foolish one. There were fascists in Greece even then. Bullies in their black shirts that also believed they were right and instruments for correction."

Herb studied the old man as he put on his jacket. "You killed one," he said in an astonished tone.

Avidol sighed. "Three of them attacked a young girl from a neighboring town. I came across the outrage as it was just beginning." He paused, a tear appearing and working its way down into his full beard. "I stopped it."

Herb froze as he was shrugging on the overcoat. "You killed all three." It was a statement, not a question, so sure was he of the answer.

Avidol got up, walking around the carousel. Herb followed.

"It was why we had to leave Greece. It took many years, many prayers, much thoughtful study and soul-searching before I felt my God's forgiveness for that irredeemable act." He shook his head. "I don't think my father *ever* forgave me."

He gestured at a coffee kiosk in front of them. Herb nodded, took a last look at the old man, then walked over.

Xenos stepped out of the shadows. "Hello, Herb."

But the spymaster just stood there, staring deeply at, into, the younger man.

"What the Hell you looking at?"

Herb seemed to snap out of it. "Just never noticed how much you resemble your father."

"Whatever." Xenos began to walk, Herb following after a moment. "What do you have for me?"

Herb laughed. "Not a damned thing, my boy. I came to see Alvarez."

"You'll see me first."

Herb shook his head. "Do you really think I'm here to harm her?"

"Somebody is."

"Yeah. They sure as shit are. Which is why I have to talk to *her.*"

Xenos studied his face, his commitment, then shook his head. "Good-bye, Herb. It's been fun."

The older man watched him go. "Trust never *was* your strong suit, was it, son?" Xenos kept walking. "What do you know about Apple Blossom?" he called out in a black whisper.

Xenos stopped, turned, allowing the old man to come up to him. "Obviously a helluva lot less than you do."

"Don't count on it." He lowered his voice still further. "I *have* to talk to Alvarez, Jerry. Only her."

Xenos shook his head. "Me first."

Herb casually ran his fingers through his thinning hair. "Let's not make this more complicated than it has to be, okay? Just take me to her, or bring her to me."

"Hey, Herb?"

"Yeah?"

"How many guys you got around us?"

The man froze. "Why's that?" he said cautiously.

Xenos smiled, an evil smile of teeth and suggestion. "You know me, Herb. You know who I am and how I think. Hell, you helped teach me, right?"

"Right," he answered as his eyes searched the crowd around them.

Xenos casually placed his hand on the smaller man's shoulder. Herb never flinched, but was surprised that it was so light a touch.

"Look at my shoulder, will you?"

Herb looked at the big man's right shoulder. Suddenly a small red dot appeared on it.

Then a second.

Then a third.

The dots, as though they were living things, seemed to dance and play as they slowly moved down the length of that powerful arm, onto the smaller man's shoulder, then finally coming to rest in the middle of his chest.

"It don't matter how many men you've got," Xenos said conversationally, "how they're equipped or trained." One of the dots traveled up to Herb's cheek, another dropped to his groin. " 'Cause they'll never get here in time."

"You'll never get out alive," Herb said perfunctorily.

Xenos nodded easily. "That'd be a favor."

Amazingly the targeted man smiled. "God, I've missed you."

"Apple Blossom, Herb. Remember?"

"You're so, uh, enlivening, Jerry. I always liked that about you."

"Apple Blossom."

"Yes," the old man said wistfully. "Apple Blossom." He seemed distracted for a moment. "You heard about the vice president?"

Xenos just watched, listening. A Swiss instrument precisely ticking down to mayhem.

Herb took a deep breath. "Everybody's hot for a war, son. The factories have gone to golden time, politicians getting their best suits cleaned and pressed, the public crowding round to see the flags and plumes.

"The President's Foreign Intelligence Advisory Board has been tasked with selecting economic and strategic targets in Taiwan. Defense is deploying first-strike capabilities. State is being muzzled, and the White House is a limp dick using a corrupt little Spanish fly to get it up one last time."

Xenos thought about what the man in front of him *was not* saying. "You *know* who Apple Blossom is?"

Herb shrugged. "Not so's I can prove it. And I've looked at the smiling little pricks real good too. All three of them."

"I can imagine." He thought for a moment. "What about this guy Steingarth?"

"I've never liked him," Herb said casually, "so I'm willing to take the good congresswoman's word that he's a rat bastard. It pleases the aesthetic in me." He smiled. "But he doesn't fit the role —miscast, you might say. I can see him as the organizer, but his power base is too limited to be the star."

Xenos looked into the crowd around them. "If Steingarth's not Apple Blossom, where do you go next?"

Herb frowned. "Me? Not *us?*" He shook his head. "You're not abandoning your country again, are you, son?"

The hand moved so quickly, grabbed the old man around the throat so tightly, that it might have happened in an instant. Herb never moved as Xenos pulled him close, slowly squeezing the older man's throat.

"Don't you ever call me your *son* again," a mythical savage voice growled out at him. "No more."

Despite being shaken to his core, despite feeling his windpipe being crushed, the amoral man slowly brought his cigar to his mouth, then exhaled a puff of blue smoke in the leviathan's face.

Deliberately, Xenos released him.

The former Cold Warlord took several deep breaths, then looked back up at his creation/find.

"You're not getting soft, are you, Jerry?"

Xenos took a deep breath. "You have one last chance to convince me that I should let you anywhere near Alvarez."

Herb thought for a moment, then nodded at a Gypsy family that was telling fortunes out of a cart on the side of the road.

"Want to know the future? Get a look into *my* tea leaves?"

Xenos nodded.

"Within two weeks there'll be a massive cruise missile strike on Taiwan. They'll respond with a shore-to-surface barrage at our vessels in the China Sea. The president'll order air strikes to suppress the Taiwanese missile capabilities."

He paused, his eyes disconnecting from the conversation, drifting with the pictures in his mind. His voice became soft, almost disbelieving. But there was iron behind the words.

"Then there'll be a bright light along the Mainland China shore. Wenzhou maybe. Maybe Xiamen. A military-industrial complex of little strategic importance but a dense population of civilians.

"The ChiComs—in their righteous indignation at this horrid attack—will launch a massive Silkworm attack on Taiwan. Then, in a coordinated action with U.S. forces, we'll jointly invade Taiwan, crush its forces, and China will be united once again." He paused. "Hallelujah."

He shook his head sadly, as though in mourning for a death that had yet to happen.

"Sometime after, oh—after the parades and speeches are done and a new China/U.S. mutual love pact is passed into law—our beloved president (exhausted from the pressures, from grief over his wife and so many dead Americans in the *Great War*) will pass away peacefully in his sleep. And a brave new world of Sino-American relations will begin."

He looked deeply into Xenos's eyes. "Amen."

"You have any evidence of any of this?"

Herb smiled back at the man. "Of what? A paranoid old man's wild fantasies?" He shook his head. "If the first rule is win, then the second is *don't get caught*. You know that." His shrug became a shroud. "No evidence, no plot. You can't stop what doesn't exist, can you?"

Xenos heard the truth in the old man's voice, saw his frustration, felt his anger.

"What are you doing about it?"

"Me?" Herb asked innocently.

"You."

"Well"—he smiled a secret smile—"I might've had a thought or two, but . . ."

"But?"

"But then"—the older man's eyes narrowed, his voice became an angry growl—"I don't *fucking have Alvarez*!" The face immediately relaxed, the voice returning to its usual calm, peaceful nature. "Do I, *son?*"

Canvas bounded off the Exec-jet and raced to the waiting jeep. "Go, damn you!"

The Philippine heat was oppressive, slamming into the man in the back of the open car as it raced along the dirt road. His clothes were soaked through after five minutes. But he never moved, never showed any sign of the discomfort they all felt. His mind was so disconnected from his body that it wouldn't have mattered if it was one hundred degrees above or below zero just then.

All that mattered was the news.

A representative of Chinese intelligence in Macao had been contacted by one of the leaders of the Corsican Union, the non-European branch of the Brotherhood. The man had offered a deal, with Alvarez and Canvas as two of the most critical terms.

And that had galvanized Canvas into a flight halfway around the world in the middle of the night.

The jeep screeched to a halt in front of a corrugated tin building in a jungle clearing.

Heavily armed men openly displayed their machine guns and machetes in defiance of the local law. Two stretch limousines sat off to one side. And a helicopter sat, its rotor turning lazily in the almost nonexistent wind, just on the other side of the clearing.

Canvas leaped off the jeep and rushed into the building.

"What the fuck is this about a deal?" he demanded of the tropical-suited men at the table.

A tall Chinese stood, bowed his head toward the angry man,

then gestured at an empty seat. "If you would care to join us, Canvas. We would be happy to explain."

Canvas looked the room over. Three Chinese, three olive-skinned Europeans. "Talk to me, Yin."

The Chinese sat down calmly. "It was you who first suggested negotiations, I believe. We are merely carrying that thought to its logical conclusion."

The Corsicans stared at Canvas with undisguised hostility. "He has been pleading for your life, *sporco parassita*!" one of them spat out.

"An exaggeration," Yin said simply. "We have simply been attempting to discover if there is a common ground available that will satisfy all interested parties." He seemed satisfied. "We've settled on financial terms, now we're discussing human terms."

Canvas nodded. "You going to kill me, or let them? Stuff like that?"

"We hope it won't come to that. We are, after all, civilized men here at this table."

Canvas shook his head as a laugh escaped his lips. "And those, uh, *human terms,* they take old Jerry Goldman into account?"

"Dureté is not involved in this," a Corsican said angrily. "This involves only tribute for Paolo DiBenetti, guarantees for Congresswoman Alvarez and her children . . ."

"And justice," the third Corsican said between clenched teeth.

Canvas nodded sagely. "That would be about me again, right?" The men ignored him. "Yin, do you honestly believe that you can trust these boobs? Or that Goldman will just stay out of things?"

Yin nodded. "You have told us so yourself."

"That was before we brought his family into things. Before you and your people managed to fuck things up so completely."

The Chinese diplomat/spy shrugged. "You overdramatize, Canvas."

"Dureté will not interfere in these matters if his family is no longer disturbed. You have his word on this," the lead Corsican said to Yin.

"That is acceptable to me. Now then, about Mr. Meadows here."

Canvas laughed bitterly, shook his head, then turned to leave. "Idiot."

"Mr. Meadows!"

Canvas turned back to the Chinese. "Yeah?"

"I must ask you to remain until these negotiations are completed. If you attempt to leave, my men outside will stop you."

"I'm trapped?" Canvas asked pleasantly.

"Essentially," Yin said firmly. "It does have the convenience of saving me the trouble of sending for you."

He turned back to the negotiations, hesitated, then suddenly turned back to the big Englishman. "How *did* you know about these negotiations?"

"How indeed?" he repeated affably.

He smiled, as automatic weapons fire erupted from outside the hut. The men inside threw themselves to the floor. Except for Canvas, who stood there, looking down at them, still smiling.

Armed, uniformed men burst into the hut, quickly searching the men on the floor, then lining them up along the far wall. Canvas accepted a .45 from one of the men and casually walked over to the shocked men, two minutes after it was over.

"I hate amateurs," he said as he blew the brains of two of the Chinese through the front of their faces onto the tin wall. Then he took the gun, placing it under Yin's quivering chin. "To say nothing of second-raters with delusions of grandeur." He pulled the trigger three times.

"Watch the Corsies," he said as he handed the gun back and stepped outside.

The bandit toughs were all dead, blown apart by the disciplined, concentrated fire of the mercenaries. He picked his way through their corpses, casually taking a machete from one. Then met a limousine that was pulling up to the hut.

Xi lowered the window, ignoring the bloody scene. "The negotiations are over?"

"Quite."

The general sighed. "Our chairman and general secretary has been a brilliant man in his time. Quite ruthless, intelligent, uncompromising." He sadly shook his head. "But age brings out caution in many."

"But not you."

Again, Xi shrugged. "A matter of perspective, really. I have been bred—not for caution, as the West so often misunderstands—but for long-term strategy. And when that strategy calls for boldness, I am quite prepared to employ it."

"So I've noticed lately." Canvas leaned casually on the open window so he could feel the cooling air-conditioning from inside. "So the negotiations were the chairman's idea."

Xi nodded. "An old man's desire to preserve the status quo. Apple Blossom is in place, so we must take no further risk, merely trust to momentum and time to finish the job."

"How very Chinese of him."

The general frowned. "Do you know bezique?"

"Card game."

"Yes," Xi said flatly. "It is very popular in my country. Many consider it a true test of one's patience and self-control. The only way to win is to closely husband your most strategic, most important cards until the most critical moment, then play them all at once."

"So?"

"The truly gifted player, however, will not wait for that critical moment to come to him. He will force it to happen at a time of his own choosing."

Canvas was quiet for a long time. "And now is *your* time?"

"It is my country's time, Canvas. My people's. I just see that more clearly than others."

The Englishman shook his head. "What do you want me to do?"

"Can you now find Alvarez and the other one, this Xenos?"

Canvas glanced back at the hut. "I imagine."

"Then destroy them, please." The window was raised and the limo pulled away into the jungle.

He watched it go, pleased to have clear orders at last; but shaken to his core at having to try to directly confront the one man he could least control.

He tested the heft of the long blade in his hand, laid the flat of it on his shoulder, then started back toward the hut.

"All right, gents," he called out conversationally, "who wants to be the first to tell the truth to their Uncle Colin?"

He stepped inside, closed the door, and a minute later the screaming began.

Eleven

"The sum of all our answer is but this,
We would not seek a battle, as we are;
Nor, as we are, we will not shun it."

Bradley stood in the doorway, watching his uncle read aloud to the empty room, not certain whether or not to intrude on so private a moment.

"Come on in," Xenos said to his nephew without looking up.

"I didn't want to disturb you."

Xenos smiled. "You? Not possible."

The boy settled in a chair opposite him. "Everybody's so tense, I was just looking to get away, you know?"

"Oh yeah." Xenos leaned back in the overstuffed chair. "Something I've dedicated the last few years of my life to." He studied the sixteen-year-old. "How're you holding up?"

The boy laughed. "Are you kidding? This is great! I mean the trip, this place, these people! Shit! It's the best time I've ever had." He suddenly looked very guilty. "Except for you getting hurt and all," he said sheepishly.

Xenos shrugged it off. "I'd always hoped to get to know you in somewhat calmer circumstances." He paused, glancing down at the book in his hands. "It just never worked out, you know?"

"Mom says . . ." But he hesitated rather than finish the thought.

"Bradley," Xenos said supportively. "You don't ever have to

choose your words around me. Never. Just say what you mean and do what you say. That's all I'll ever ask of you."

The boy laughed. "Sounds like a lot."

"It is."

A moment of comfortable silence wrapped itself around them.

"Mom says you and Poppy didn't talk from before I was born."

"Yeah."

"She says you had a horrible fight when she was just a little girl and you left."

"Also true." The man leaned painfully forward. "Just say it, kid."

Bradley reached for Xenos's can of beer, surprised when the man just smiled and pushed it over to him. "Why'd you run away?"

Xenos studied the clear eyes, the smooth skin, the face that reminded him so much of the nightmare/visitation of his pain.

"My father and I disagreed about how I should lead my life. And neither of us was willing to work hard enough to get around it, I guess."

"Not that," the boy said as he sipped the beer—obviously disliking the taste, but determined to drink it nonetheless. "I mean afterwards. After you quit."

"What did your mother tell you about me?"

"She said you worked for something like the CIA, but not the CIA. That you were a very important person there, that you did a lot of bad things for good reasons, and that you split."

Xenos chuckled bitterly. "Bad things for good reasons," he repeated. "Makes it sound like cheating on my taxes to pay for Grandmother's operation." He shook his head. "Close enough, I guess."

"So why didn't you come back to us? To Poppy?"

Xenos flipped through the book on his lap as he talked. "I left when I was around your age, I guess. Full of life and ready to change the world. You see"—he hesitated—"I was a *true believer*. There was good and there was evil, and as long as you were on the side of good, you couldn't do anything evil."

He looked into the fireplace, losing himself in the flames.

"Don't ever believe in anything, Bradley," he said wearily. "It hurts too much when you're proven wrong."

But the man's grays were lost on the boy's clarities.

"Why didn't you come home afterwards?" he persisted. The answer was clearly important to him.

"Oh, I don't know. Got lost, I guess."

"Bullshit," the boy said clearly and carefully.

Xenos grinned. "You got a lot of your grandfather in you."

The boy just sat there, silently demanding an answer.

"All right. Truth." He thought for a moment. "What I did—good, bad, or indifferent—I did because other men told me to do it. They convinced me that democracy was better than totalitarianism or communism or whatever ism we were fighting that month. Or I did it because it was easier than not doing it.

"I hurt a lot of people, *a lot*!" His voice trailed off. "Maybe helped a few, I don't really know. Like to think I did."

He took a deep breath. "I was going to *change the world!*" he almost yelled out in sarcastic exuberance. "Through me, the Maccabee Code was going to be reestablished. Milk and honey would flow, swords beaten into plowshares, evil men beaten off." He hesitated. "*Peace* made a real thing, not a goal or ideal." When he spoke again, his voice was still as the grave.

"I didn't figure out, until it was too late, that *peace* is just a fairy tale, bait to catch people dumb enough to believe in it."

He managed a strained laugh. "And, God, how I believed."

"Two-six to Car Wreck."

Jerry keyed his mike. "Two-six, this is Car Wreck."

"Two-six to Car Wreck, in position."

"Copy that, two-six," Jerry whispered as he peered through the binoculars at the encampment below. "All units stand by."

The encampment was just west of the Pakistani border, filled to capacity with Moujahadeen gunmen, Taliban militiamen, and Russian deserters. All distracted by the daze of their afternoon meal and the unconfined joy of unloading the crates they'd stolen from the U.N. convoy.

Jerry'd planned the raid with his usual precision.

For three weeks in a row—on random days—the cable, which carried electricity and communications to the camp, had been cut in different places. Now they were getting used to the outages.

He'd surveilled the camp for a month, had memorized every building, path, vehicle, and procedure there. Had gamed it out in his head endlessly.

Explosions were set off in the old Soviet garrison in the nearby town of Charikar. Knowing that the authorities in Kabul would immediately pull back all their roving patrols into the city—believing this to be an attack in force.

Rumors had been floated that a Soviet Spetsnaz commando group was hunting this particular band of guerrilla/thieves, so that anything that would happen would be laid at their door.

And something was about to happen.

Herb had given him the mission with his usual casualness.

A band of guerrillas—in the pay of the DIA—had recently crossed the line by hijacking U.N. humanitarian shipments; raping the women and torturing the men who had volunteered to bring "a degree of humanity and hope" to the survivors of the endless guerrilla war.

It was one of Herb's most sincere moments as he ordered that they were to be eliminated—out of righteous indignation, as a point of national honor.

As an example to other such groups not to cross the line from freedom fighter to marauder.

But the operation was to have complete deniability.

And in these days of greater media access to the former battleground of Afghanistan, with 60 Minutes regularly exposing embarrassing intelligence connections, that meant one thing.

A Four Phase operation.

Jerry swallowed a handful of nepenthe, washed it down, then closed his eyes and waited for the effect to begin. As he felt the warmth and calm rise up in him, he opened his eyes, looking back down at the target.

There was more activity now. A group of the ragged band was herding three men and a woman in U.N. uniforms toward the middle of the camp. Jerry decided to wait until they were distracted by the attack on the men and the rape of the woman before he would give the go code.

"Car Wreck, Car Wreck, Car Wreck, this is ground."

"Car Wreck."

"Car Wreck, this is ground, all units at IPs."

"Ground, this is Car Wreck. All ground units are go for action in one-zero minutes from my mark."

"Car Wreck, this is ground. Copy. Ground units go one-zero minutes from your mark."

As the time ticked down, Jerry watched the camp closely. The sentries were where they were expected. No aircraft or ground traffic could be seen. His men had inched within striking distance. Time to give the order.

But something was wrong.

Again, he carefully searched the camp. The guards, the trucks, the hostages . . .

The hostages.

No one was being assaulted, no one being brutalized. They were laughing with the Afghans! Coffee and food were being doled out. There was a general sense of relaxation and ease.

Then one of the crates was pried open, and Jerry finally understood. Slowly he worked his way closer to the camp to confirm the awful truth.

The crates were stenciled in German, not English; and what was coming out of them was far from humanitarian aid. Rather, it was Heckler & Koch assault weapons in their original factory wrappers. Each arm-length weapon coming complete with its triple-forked banana clips.

And the relief workers wore the pale blue uniforms of the Grens-Schutz Gruppe III. West German GSG-3 counterinsurgents, not U.N. workers.

Jerry cried.

Because these people—their wives, children, animals, homes, their very existence and any traces of it—were to be wiped out simply because they had changed allegiance from one Western power to another. And Herb Stone—as well as the people behind him—were going to send that message to the other groups.

"We buy you, you'd better stay bought."

"Car Wreck, Car Wreck, Car Wreck, this is ground."

"Car Wreck."

"Car Wreck, this is ground, all units at jump-off. Go/no go?"

"Ground from Car Wreck." Jerry took a deep breath. *"Abort, abort, abort."*

"Say again Car Wreck."

"Abort! Abort! Abort," he almost shouted into his radio as the tears of this final betrayal filled his eyes.

Disaffection from service to country almost never comes about apocalyptically. There are almost never crashes of thunder, streaks of lightning, or great sudden realizations.

Instead, it's a gentle, a quiet thing. A moment—if a moment could be identified—when you realize that you're being used not to protect God and country, not for lofty ideals or flags waving in the wind; but to get someone a corner office, enhance an invisible's career, defend an essentially meaningless whim, or merely the transitory personal agenda of middle management.

These are the things that lead to apostates and burnouts, suicides and men shooting from towers.

But at this moment (being asked to destroy innocent allies in the name of proprietary office politics)—torn between the pull of his twin addictions (nepenthe and blind patriotism)—Jerry Goldman simply and completely chose to blink from all existence.

Hoping God and the devil wouldn't notice.

Xenos pulled himself back from his dark center.

"I finally realized," he said to the rapt youth, "that the only thing these men wanted was power. For themselves, for their power structure, for the Hell of it. Right and wrong were mere abstracts to them. Tools." He paused. "Like I was."

He exhaled deeply. "Anyway, I quit because—whether he wants to admit it or not—your grandfather taught me to hold myself to a higher standard. To demand truths, real truths of the world, and to defend them whenever and wherever I found them.

"Trouble was . . . I couldn't find them. So, after a while, I stopped looking."

He shrugged, like a helpless child. "How could I go home to a man like your grandfather after that?"

Bradley shook his head. "You just could've. I know him."

Xenos sadly shook his head. "Sixteen," he said with a sad laugh. "Talk to me when you're forty."

Bradley stared at his uncle, then suddenly stood up and walked to the door.

"There is some soul of goodness in things evil, would men observingly distill it out," he recited carefully, thoughtfully. "For who could bear the whips and scorns of time, the oppressor's wrong, the proud man's contumely, the pangs of despised love, the law's delay, the insolence of office, and the spurns that merit of the unworthy takes . . ."

Xenos looked up abruptly.

". . . but that the dread of something after death," he said as if going into or coming out of a trance, "the undiscovered country from whose bourn no traveler returns, puzzles the will and makes us rather bear those ills we have than fly to others that we know not of." He hesitated. "Thus conscience does make cowards of us all."

He looked stunned. "Where did you learn that?"

Bradley shrugged as he went through the door. "Something Poppy taught me." And he was gone.

Slowly, as if drugged and fighting through it, Xenos turned the pages in the old book, not checking numbers, knowing by the feel where it was.

By Jove, I am not covetous for gold, nor care I who doth feed
  upon my cost;
It yearns me not if men my garments wear;
Such outward things dwell not in my desires;

But if it be a sin to covet honor, I am the most offending soul alive.

And beneath it, in a tiny, childish scrawl, the words:

It is my sacred trust as a Knight Eminent to never give up my honour! This I swear upon my very soul.
Jerry Goldman
10 years old

And he stared at those words for the bulk of the next hour.

"Six, in position."
"Copy six. Twelve?"
"Twelve, in position."
"Copy twelve. Thirty-four?"
"Thirty-four, in position."
"Copy thirty-four. Vulture, Vulture, Vulture, this is ground."
"Vulture."
"Vulture, this is ground, all units at IPs."
"Ground, this is Vulture. Inbound one-five minutes to LZ. All ground units are go for action in one-zero minutes from my mark."
"Vulture, this is ground. Copy. Ground units go one-zero minutes from your mark."
"Ground, ground, ground. My mark in three, two, one. Mark!"
"All units, all units, all units. This is ground. You are go for action in nine minutes five-zero seconds."

In his third day at the clinic, Herb was getting his balancing act down to a science.

Shuttling messages to his Washington headquarters through information-blind intermediaries in half the capitals of Europe; answering queries from other government agencies as if he were still in Washington; fending off the suspicion of Alvarez and the Corsicans with a natural charm and glee. He was alive, functional, awake after decades of disuse and bad habits born of boredom.

But, chillingly, he was no closer to stopping Apple Blossom than when he'd first arrived.

"Your reputation seems to have been inflated, Mr. Stone," Alvarez snapped at him.

He shrugged. "You're the politician, Congresswoman, not me. I just try to do my job."

"You don't do it very well!"

For one of the rare times in his life, Herb allowed his anger to show.

"What would you have me do?" he demanded. "If my suspicions and your allegations are even *half* right, then this Apple Blossom thing's penetrated almost every organ of the government. If George Steingarth's involved, if they're in *your office* for God's sake, I'd better Goddamn assume they're in mine! And that means taking no chances, going damned slowly, and restricting access to the truth as much as possible."

He shook his head in exhausted fury. "Even without these handcuffs, I'll be damned if I know how to go about this without getting us all killed, committed, or disappeared!"

He began counting on his fingers.

"One, figure out who Apple Blossom is in provable, concrete terms.

"Two, find your children—God knows where—before exposing the traitor or risk losing them.

"Three, find a way to use this impossible to find proof to bring down Apple Blossom, whoever *he* is when he's at home.

"Four, find a way to expose the remainder of the Apple Blossom network. And let's not forget number five."

He paused, clearly for effect. "Do all this with no budget, no trustworthy, experienced personnel, no planning staff, and damned little else!"

"Xenos! You said—"

Avidol interrupted her. "My son has done what he's willing to do. What he *can* do, in good conscience." He shook his head. "Asking for more than that would be futile." He sighed. "I know."

"As do I," Herb added firmly.

Valerie looked at them—her mouth moving, but no words coming out—then whirled and stalked from the room.

Franco watched her go, then turned back to the men. "But you haven't given up."

"No," Herb said flatly. "Not likely either."

"Call if you need anything," Franco said as he headed out the door. "Just not in the next couple of hours, okay?" He smiled and hurried off.

Herb studied him. "You suppose that smile of his is ever sincere?"

"As often as yours is," Avidol said simply.

Herb smiled, then went back to work.

Franco caught up with Valerie at the door to her cottage on the edge of the clinic's grounds. "Hey, slow down. I hate running after a woman. It's demeaning."

"Go away." Valerie's voice was harsh and bitter.

"Sure, sure." But he didn't move.

There's a moment that comes at the end of every battle; an odd quiet that descends on the field and on the men and women in it. They hear the wind blow, the strange rustle of a dying flame, dirt settling, their own hearts trying to begin to beat again. As if the world—as they've known it—has stopped, and they're completely and utterly alone.

Like Valerie.

Like Franco.

Their combined guilts, angers, failures, becoming a distant but piercing howling in the wind—like a banshee's warning.

The soldier looks around, sees the odd abstracts that his best friend's brains and blood have made on a nearby wall. The way the angles of an imploded chest are almost beautiful; the strange dichotomy of a shoe—laces still tied and cinched—sitting by itself away from any possible bodies. And one thought sweeps over them like a gel, slowly enveloping them in its demand for . . .

. . . *Life.*

And like it or not, Valerie and Franco had either become soldiers . . . or victims.

"What are we going to do, eh?" Franco said after a long moment. He took a step toward her. "You going to lie in your bed, alone, and think about your boy and girl? I'm going to lie in my bed, alone, and think about Paolo?" He shook his head. "Stupid."

"I don't want to think at all," Valerie said angrily.

"So let's *not think* together."

Valerie was quiet for a moment.

How can you allow yourself a few minutes of freedom, her mind tortured her, *of physical joy, while your children are dead or dying . . . alone.* Whore!

She didn't think she liked Franco. There was a smell about him, physically and morally. A thing that stank of her own past. And he was most certainly no bastion of a gentleness and tenderness she so longed for. There was nothing about the man she liked, let alone loved!

But he *was* here, and he *did* understand.

And in those next few minutes of pain/pleasure, despair/ecstasy—the world of the dead and the dying and black tomorrows was gone. Replaced by flesh and warmth, forgiveness for surviving; and a blank, unwritten future where anything was possible.

The things that were necessary—not for living, but for *surviving.*

As soldiers.

"I got two perimeter guards, fifty meters at two o'clock."

"I see 'em. Wait till they get a little closer. I got a lousy angle."

"Forty meters at one o'clock."

"Wait for it."

"Thirty-five meters at twelve."

"Good."

"Ground from thirty-four."

"Ground."

"Splash two; perimeter, North Six."

"Thirty-four from ground. Move to point two."

"Thirty-four."

. . .

"And the wolf got very quiet . . ."

"*Qu'est-ce?*" the little girl asked sleepily.

"Uh. *Le loup,* you know . . . grr!"

Gabi laughed and yawned at the same time. "*Oui!* Grrr!"

Sarah laughed, stroked the nearly asleep little girl's hair, and continued. "Anyway, *le loup* got ve*rrr*y quiet and got ready to jump out and eat the little girl. Then, all of a sudden . . ."

She stopped as she saw Gabi was sound asleep.

"Didn't I used to tell you that when you were her age?"

Sarah quietly stood and faced her older brother. "Sure. But not as well as I do. I got a lot of practice with Bradley. It was his favorite."

She checked Gabi's covers, then started walking through the ward.

"I had a talk with your smart-ass son."

Sarah smiled. "I wonder where he gets *that* from?"

They walked silently through the room of sleeping, injured porcelain dolls.

"You going to be okay when we split for Corsica?"

Sarah shrugged. "You tell me. You're the one who kidnapped us out here in the first place."

"I think everything's had enough time to calm down; and for Colin to get his people under control." He smiled spasmodically. "Yeah. Everything will be fine." He seemed to relax. "No, what I meant was money. You okay? That deadbeat jerk you married keeping up his end?"

"Sure. With a little prompting, he comes through not too late. And the shop's doing well."

"If there's any problem with him, remember, I know people," Xenos said offhandedly.

Sarah barely suppressed a loud laugh. "So I'm learning!"

The dimmed lights in the ward began to flicker, then went out entirely.

"You should get yourself a better generator," Sarah said after a moment. Her answer was her brother's almost stilled breathing.

"I did."

. . .

Three teams of four men each swept in on the clinic's buildings from the north, east, and west. They moved silently, coordinated, deadly. They'd come up to a building, two would remain on guard outside, the others would enter the building, spray the rooms with automatic weapons fire, then move on.

The only sound in the night, the *pfft, pfft, pfft* of the noise-suppressed shots, mingling with the occasional muffled scream.

"Check left, check left!" a team leader called as they approached the third cottage in their zone.

"Got it," another gunman said.

Two of the men braced themselves by the front door, nodded to each other, then—three seconds later—burst through, filling the room with the deadly fire.

Ten seconds later they stopped to survey the damage. Only an unmade bed, crisscrossed with bullet holes.

"Empty. Let's go," the leader called out as he keyed his microphone. "Thirty-four, target North Six C-1 empty."

"Thirty-four proceed," came his reply.

And they moved on to the next cottage.

Never seeing Franco drop, naked, from the rafters.

"The next time you think you hear something," he said as he caught an equally naked Valerie, "remind me to listen to you." But there was no humor in his voice.

They dressed quickly.

"What's going on?" Valerie whispered.

Franco's moves became catlike, light, agile, darting. After pulling on his jeans he made one quick circle of the small room, coming up with a carving knife and a fireplace poker. He gave the poker to Valerie.

"Stay here," he whispered. "They probably won't come back." And he was gone—shirtless and barefoot—into the night.

There were more screams now, the shooting more constant. Valerie nervously gripped and regripped the poker.

"Fuck this," she mumbled, then headed out into the deadly night.

. . .

Two of the teams converged near the entrance to the main house, just behind the clinic itself. With hand gestures and nods, they deployed at two of the doors, and at an agreed moment, burst inside.

Herb's first shot caught the lead mercenary in the forehead and threw him backward into the next. His next three sprayed the doorway and anyone beyond it. Then he dived behind the sofa as a torrent of fire responded to him.

"Taking fire," one of the mercenaries called out. "West Two H-5. Taking fire!"

The other team entered more slowly from the back, having heard Herb's .45's reports.

"Carefully, lads," their leader whispered as he peeked from the kitchen into the dining area. "Carefu—"

A gurgling sound replaced the rest of his thought as Avidol's carving knife nearly severed the man's head.

He took four rounds—all grazing him in the side—before he got all the way back to the living room.

Three new teams were dispatched from their staging area in an olive grove just below the clinic enclave. The twelve men ran to the scene, four reinforcing the men at the main house, the other eight breaking off into the clinic itself.

Silence and stealth were history now, as a satchel charge blew the double doors off the front of the clinic. Flash-bangs were tossed through, exploding in blue light and smoke, followed by a two-man entry team. Unsilenced automatic fire pierced the night, then, abruptly, stopped.

"Trevor?" one of the mercenaries called out. "Ian? Is it clear?"

"Look!" another mercenary screamed as he pointed at the roof of the building.

But there was no hesitation, no shock on Xenos's face.

Just pure rage!

He squeezed both triggers on his captured weapons, holding them tight and long, as he demolished the six men below him. Then a commotion on the other side of the clinic called him and he left the barely human remains of the gunmen behind as he ran across the pitch roof.

One of the mercenary teams had cornered four children and a nurse on the edge of the southern bluff. They shined bright lights on them, checking the woman's face before reporting in.

"Twelve, South One Bluff."

"Ground."

"Four locals, none targeted. Request instructions."

"Clean sweep."

"Twelve, copy."

The men sighed, straightened their aims, then fell to the sides as Franco leaped into them.

The knife flashed—into the eye of one, the armpit of another —and he rolled to his feet grabbing one of the guns as he moved.

"Allez! Allez!" he screamed as the children scattered and he found the third gunman. He emptied the clip into the overwhelmed man's face. He realized too late that the fourth man was behind him, and he threw himself to the ground as a disciplined burst caught him on the left side. He lay on the green grass, looked up at a beautiful moon, out at the peaceful Mediterranean, and prepared to die.

Puzzled why it was taking so long.

He looked over in the direction of the shooter, a man who stood there stiffly, his gun hanging limply in his hands, the end of a poker barely showing through his bloodied chest.

"Vulture, Vulture, Vulture, this is ground!"

"Vulture."

"We're getting the Hell kicked out of us! Request air!"

"Ground from Vulture. ETA thirty seconds."

The helicopter climbed quickly from its below-radar, surf-skimming altitude. The pilot, remembering that he had to clear the eighty-foot bluff, concentrated on his instruments as the man in the seat next to him concentrated on making sure his two door gunners with their belt-fed .50-caliber machine guns were ready.

"Come up fast and quiet," he commanded. "Straight down the middle and we'll rake everything we see, right?"

The pilot and gunners nodded.

"When we reach the olive grove, bank left and start orbiting at fifty feet," Canvas yelled to be heard above the engine. "We'll take it one building at a time with the RPGs, then sweep back and take out anyone left about, got it?"

One of the gunners picked up a rifle-propelled-grenade launcher. "What about our guys down there?"

Canvas turned back to studying the approaching bluff with his night-vision goggles. "They been paid in advance."

Sarah was trying to get as many children out of the partially burning ward as she could. Somewhere behind her, she heard gunfire. Somewhere ahead, she heard explosions. And she hadn't seen Xenos in long minutes.

"Down," she commanded as a helicopter swept in low from the sea. She and Dr. Jacmil tried to keep the oddly calm children together. There was no screaming, little crying, most of them trooping along following orders like little soldiers.

Then she remembered the nightmare that they'd come from and she cursed God for giving such innocents such unique skills.

Five of the seven buildings were burning heavily now. The high-explosive and phosphorous grenades more than doing their jobs. The helicopter would come up on a building, hover long enough for the gunner to aim, then fire the lethal missile. A .50 would rake the inferno and they'd move on to the next target.

Killing anyone moving on the ground as they flew.

"Main building," Canvas called out. "Give her three RPGs and rake her good!"

The helicopter slowed, then hovered less than thirty feet above the building's roof.

"*Jesus!*" Canvas screamed as he instinctively reached over and jammed the pilot's stick to the side.

But before the helicopter perilously banked out of the way,

Xenos—his clothes on fire, silhouetted by fire breaking through the roof—emptied a clip into the chopper's cockpit.

The helicopter shook and trembled, threatened to overturn and break apart, but somehow the pilot got it down.

Canvas, the pilot, and the one living gunner threw themselves flat on the ground, barely in time to avoid the spray of automatic fire from the inferno roof.

"Can we get it up again?" Canvas screamed at the pilot, who was crawling around, checking his ship.

"I think so."

Canvas turned to the gunner. "How many RPGs left?"

"Five, if they're still working, Guv."

"Give him all of 'em!"

The gunner was cut in half by a burst from behind after he'd fired the first two. Canvas grabbed the third, fired it into the dark, hitting something as an explosion ripped the air behind him. He turned, sighted in on the devilish figure on the roof, and fired his last two grenades.

A sheet of flame erupted from the roof, a roar of explosion and the sounds of cracking beams filled the air.

As no more firing came from the room.

Canvas crawled back to the helicopter, not having to give the order for the pilot to take off. As they flew back toward the Med, he tore the ground with the heavy rounds of the .50, killing men—his and Corsicans—women, and children. Finally they were back over water and the firing stopped.

He struggled his way back to the cockpit.

"Ground from Vulture! Pull back! Pull back!"

"Pull back what?" was the pained reply.

Canvas tossed the microphone aside, realizing for the first time that he was wounded in the upper arm.

"Bloody carp," he mumbled as he tried to slow his breathing. "All they ever give me."

It was known only as *La Sortie.*
The Exit.

It was a place the Corsicans of Toulon had been coming to for over three hundred years. A place of refuge, safety, survival. A tightly held secret which was never referred to or mentioned at any time.

But in those days when the world—the outside world—had decided that Corsican lives were cheap enough to take at will, it was the place they all came to.

A natural grotto, invisible from the sea in its tiny, unnavigable cove; reachable on foot only at low tide, the rock ledges, stalactites and stalagmites would've been a geologist's dream. Over two football fields in depth, over forty feet high in the central chamber. It always held provisions for thirty people for a month, and first-aid supplies to match.

Which were being sorely strained at the moment.

Forty-two people crowded into the central chamber. Most of them children, they cried softly, moaned to themselves, died without disturbing the others. Many of the women of Toulon moved among them, rendering what care they could. A Corsican medical student who had survived the attack had learned more about emergency medicine in the last two hours than he had in three years of med school. And he knew the worst was still ahead.

Avidol, wounded, in pain, did what he could to help. Comforting frightened silent children, helping a few of the soon-to-be lost to say their final prayers. Praying himself with all the vigor he could muster while still being useful to the destroyed lot.

Trying not to think about his missing son.

Sarah and Bradley were in the back chamber of *La Sortie*. Uncrating clean clothes, food, blankets, that had been stored in fifty-five-gallon oil drums against a disaster like this.

As if anyone could have ever prepared for something like this.

They marveled at the resilience of the Corsicans as they calmly, with undisguised anger, distributed the supplies while muttering epithets to themselves and curses to their God.

In the front chamber, not far from the opening, grim-faced men carrying many guns stood and faced the entrance, prepared to vaporize anyone who might try to gain entrance. Behind them, the

Council sat—where other councils had sat—on a rock ledge in the dim light.

As they tried to take in the scope of the disaster.

"We have no choice," the old man from the center chair said sadly. "The *Cinesi* have left us no choice."

Franco—broken, bloody—struggled to his feet. *"Ma sei pazzo?! Hai perso il cervello?!* They kill our people, the children we have given our protection to, and we bend over for these *serpenti! Disgraziati!* I am ashamed to be called Corsican!"

"Be careful, Franco," the old man warned. "Do not let your feelings for this woman—"

"Lupo, sono il tuo schiavo. Sappilo. But you cannot give them this victory. The crying of the widows, the mothers, the newborn ghosts of our finest men demand vengeance. *Taglia quelle teste!* Cut off their heads, don't suck their dicks!"

"Basta!" The old man was furious. He gestured and two of the gunmen turned on Franco, forcing him back at rifle point.

The old man turned to Valerie, who was watching quietly from the side. "Congresswoman, understand me. If there was any other way, I would not do this thing. But—" He shrugged as if the weight of the world sat on his ancient shoulders. "But we have no other way. Understand?"

Oddly—as if the world had gone completely mad—Franco saw her stand, then nod.

"I understand completely," Valerie said in a quiet, somehow changed voice. "It's enough. I want no one else to die because of me."

The old man nodded in respect. "But know this. The day will come—in God's time—when the Brotherhood will take its revenge. For Paolo, for the children, for our men . . . for you."

"Thank you," she said quietly as she sat down again.

"No!" Franco screamed out. "You *cannot* do this!"

"It has been decided," the old man said simply. "No further discussion of the matter will be allowed."

He closed his eyes, gathered himself, then spoke in a strong, clear, commanding voice.

"It is the decision of the Council of Unions of the Brotherhood that all requests for compensation from the *Cinesi* be withdrawn; that it be made known to them that there will be no disclosure of information from the Brotherhood about their affairs. And that the congresswoman Alvarez will be turned over to them at the earliest opportunity. *Non ho più niente da dichiarare.*"

At that moment a cold wind swept through the chamber, an unclean thing that chilled each man down to his soul. Then the light from the narrow chamber entrance was suddenly obscured.

"*Il Diavolo!*" one of the gunmen called out in primitive fear when he turned around.

"*Chi è il diavolo?*" another said in a terror-filled whisper as he crossed himself.

A man, smoke still rising from his smoldering clothing, blood covering much of his exposed body, skin blackened in oozing patches, stood in the entrance, a destroyed little girl in his arms.

Armageddon in his eyes.

"Dureté," the old man said after crossing himself. "There is nothing to say. It has all been decided."

Xenos tenderly handed Gabi's dead form to Franco, then took a threatening step into the cavern.

"Not by me, it hasn't."

Phase Four

Assassination

He lay on the spot overlooking the Afghan camp for three days.

His team couldn't find him, so followed his abort order and fled the country. Herb Stone wouldn't look for him—a missing, presumed dead Four Phase Man was regrettable, sure, but not completely unexpected; no searches were mounted. And he was already dead to his family.

So he lay there, completely alone, waiting for an unforgiving God to take him.

Waiting for the release that his unprotesting death would bring.

The Moujahadeen found him on the morning of the fourth day.

Normally an unconscious European would've meant little to them. He wasn't Russian, so there was no trade value. The English and Americans never acknowledged their sources in Afghanistan, so there was no profit to be made there. He was just another un-named fatality of an unknown war that no one cared about.

But their leader—a man who believed the Moujahadeen were commanded by God to return the faithful to Allah—ordered them to take the mostly dead man with them.

As a "blessing."

There was nothing left in the man—no hate, no love, no fear, no sense or emotion of any kind—and he allowed himself to be carried to the nearby camp.

A week later, after these bare survivors had sacrificed their water and food to nurse this horrifically sunburned man back to life, their leader came to see him.

"Who are you?"

The man didn't answer.

"Why are you here?"

No answer.

"What is your purpose?"

"To die," the man wheezed out.

The leader thought about that for a long moment. "Will your death have a purpose?"

"What?"

"It is the time of the demons on earth," the leader said simply. "If your death purposes those demons ill"—he pulled out his razor-sharp dirk—"I will kill you myself. But if your living will more trouble them"—he shrugged—"I will see you well." He smiled simply. "Is same. Is time of demons, when each man must do what he is placed here to do. To give the world of the demons back to the humans as Allah—the God of us all—intended." He picked up a canteen of sweet water in his other hand. "So which is . . . what is your name, Mr. . . ."

His words were cut off by the first explosion.

If Herb couldn't make his point on the ground, he would do it through the air; and the F-111s screamed over the camp, their supernatural growls echoing the death they so easily released from their wing pylons. Within moments the entire camp was ablaze, the smells of napalm and high explosives mixing with charred flesh.

The early after-action bomb damage assessment was "100% destruction, 100% killed."

But Herb was a thorough man, and ordered a second photographic pass the next day.

And in his office, hidden away from the prying eyes of Congress, the people, and God, he trembled as he saw the last frame taken on the last run. A man, holding two small children by the hand, leading them up into the hills.

Staring directly into the lens of the drone recon aircraft.

For over a decade, Herb would wonder why he pulled that photo from the file and locked it away in his private safe. Why he had declared Jerry Goldman dead and closed the file.

Maybe he was worried about God's judgment for his life of apostasy and wanted one good act in his record.

Maybe he was afraid of the wrath of the Four Phase Man he had abandoned and tried to kill.

Maybe it was all of that and none of that.

But the letter he received one month later made him glad he had.

Administrator Stone:

Jerry Goldman died of his life in the Chakira Valley, Afghanistan.

Leave him in peace, or join him in pain. The choice is yours.

Xenos Filotimo

Black ops were ending; covert wars had become bad taste. Lies and deceit, manipulation and sabotage had become passé. Herb could see the day down the road when all human intelligence operations would be phased out.

The Four Phase Men most of all.

So he let him go, let Jerry Goldman pass into obscurity and espionage myth. What other choice did he have? Whom could he send after him, anyway? How could he explain to Congress and a Boy Scout administration the body count and damage that going to war with the last of the Four Phase Men would mean.

The decision was actually quite simple.

But every now and then—when the growing paperwork load and lack of "great goals" would wear the old man down, when the "special ops" he'd be asked to handle had to do with spying on Eurorail's new high-speed train design, or what the new Liechtenstein monetary policy would be toward the Bretton Woods Agreement—he would dig through his safe, pulling out the high-

resolution photograph of a man staring defiantly into the lens of a reconnaissance camera.

And raise a toast to Xenos Filotimo, endangered species— hero, conqueror, romantic warrior.

And to the soul of the man he'd helped create and destroy . . . Jerry Goldman.

Twelve

"There are three Corsicas," the saying goes. "The pilferers of the seas, the bandits of the ground, and the Brothers of the Unions.

"They are the water, wind, and fire, but—for the mercy of the world—they shall never unite.

"Until the *day of the plague* is called, and the world brought to its knees."

But that was just legend and myth, rhymes without reason. Or so the few people that knew the inhabitants of the small island, closer to Italy than France, prayed.

Because to know the Corsicans was to fear them.

The island is ruled by that fear, always has been.

In 550 B.C. the Romans conquered the island, only to be slaughtered legion after legion for decades until they left, a beaten and shattered empire.

The Vandals, Byzantines, and Moors all arrived, all *seemed* to conquer, all were driven away bloody and broken. Italians and French both tried, both died.

In the Second World War the Germans lost more men and matériel in their brief occupation of the less than 3,500-square-mile island than they did to the French, Greek, and Polish Resistance movements combined.

And Corsica remained.

Oh, some things changed—the harbor at the mouth of Girolata still had the Roman sentry tower and German artillery emplacements—now a church and school.

The Haute-Corse still used Moorish roads and Vandals' field
canals—to tend to the thin crops of olives and wheat that the island
produced.

Sartène, Corte, and L'Île-Rousse still carefully maintained the
French underground storage grottoes—if storing things *other* than
wine and olives in these more modern times.

But the heart of the island and its violent people who lived by
vendetta and blood feuds remained essentially as it was in the days
of the Lombard Kingdom. True to the other well-known saying of
the Corsicans.

"My enemy may bleed me, but I will learn from that blood
and it will drown my killers."

In the heart of the island—amid the almost jungle under-
growth and rock formations of the maquis—the small village of
Cammeo sits as a virtual doorway to the imposing Mount Cinto.
The ancestral home of all the Unions of the Corsican Brotherhood,
Cammeo grows olives, processes wheat into thick black bread, and
allows no strangers within.

There are no hotels, hostels, or inns here. No one will offer
you a room or a bed. There are no restaurants, gas stations, hospi-
tality centers, or attractions to draw the casual tourist. And any
that might be found in the sleepy, harmless-looking village come
nightfall will be significantly the worse for wear by morning.

It's not that the people aren't friendly. Like most island people
of the Mediterranean, they are easygoing and casual. But they have
protected themselves in this manner for generations and have
thereby become known as the safest safe haven in the world.

Which was why many of the people of Cammeo looked with
open concern and violence at the six outsiders that had been
brought to refuge in the cave homes halfway up the mountain behind the village.

But they'd been brought with the blessing of the Council and
that ended all *open* discussion. Besides, a more controversial topic
was sweeping the dusty, dark streets of Cammeo not even an hour
after the strangers had settled in.

The Council had called for a *tribunale*—a meeting of the leaders of all the clans of Corsican Unions on the island and around the world. They would all be coming within two days to the church hall. Not just a meeting of Union heads or a convening of the Council itself, the *tribunale* was a centuries-old tradition for settling disputes *within* the Brotherhood itself.

The word had circulated quickly that Franco DiBenetti—clan leader of the Cammeo Brotherhood—had directly challenged the Council.

And that he had enough support within the various factions and Unions of the Brotherhood to force this tribunal, where the world's Corsican leaders would decide the outcome.

Where the losing side would die painfully.

Three heavily armed men sitting in the rocks outside the small house carefully studied Franco as he came up. Never, in their lifetime, had a man directly challenged a Council ruling. It was a nearly unthinkable thing to do.

But the man was of Cammeo, so must be taken seriously. And his argument—snippets of which had been circulating in the hours since their arrival—was such that their Corsican blood boiled, and their warrior souls called out for vengeance.

But to challenge the Council . . .

They nodded noncommittally toward him as he passed.

Franco ignored them as he walked up to the house. His mind was far from the coming political/life battle, distracted from issues of ethnic ritual and tradition. Instead his mind wandered over the problem of how to deal with the men waiting for him inside.

He pounded three times on the door, then let himself in.

The central room was empty. A table with five chairs at its center; on the table a cork mat with a loaf of black bread, a spread of olive paste and loose olives, and a razor-sharp knife with an eight-inch blade.

Franco hesitated. The loaf was intact—imperfectly round, crust hard and smooth—which meant, in Corsican parlance, *This place is safe for our friends. But we do not yet know if you are our friend.*

Had the loaf been sliced, it would've meant that he was welcome, among allies. If one piece was missing, it meant friends open to persuasion. But intact . . .

He closed the door behind him. *"In bocca al lupo,"* he said in a strong voice to the emptiness.

"Crepi il lupo," a smallish man responded as he stepped out of the one bedroom. Everything about him seemed measured, planned; every step, gesture, or expression planned out to the most infinite detail.

"Crepi il lupo," a second man said as he stepped out of the kitchen. He was huge, well over six-five, 240 pounds. He held a cold leg of lamb in his hand, and it wouldn't have surprised Franco one bit to find the rest of the dismembered animal just behind the big man.

Franco turned as a third man moved out of the shadows to his right. He'd come from no room, no alcove or closet, must've been in the room within Franco's sight all the time. But he'd been invisible to the cautious Corsican leader, completely still and part of the shadowed woodwork.

"Fuck the wolf," he mumbled in English. "Let's talk business."

"Thank you all," Franco said pleasantly as he sat at the head of the table. "I owe you each a favor in return for your coming. You have my word on that."

"What makes you think you're going to be around long enough to do me any favors?" the small one said.

"Show's not till tomorrow," the big man mumbled. "You could be a memory by then."

Franco shrugged. "But what a happy memory, eh?" He smiled. "What does it hurt to talk?"

The quiet one looked him in the eyes. "Council'll have the balls of anyone who's with you if you lose. I say we should wait until it's over."

But no one at the table got up.

"Well, the Council has their schedule. I have mine," Franco said lightly. "Now, are we done with the bullshit, or what? None of you would be here if you gave a shit what happens tomorrow."

"We're not here because of you," the big man said clearly.

"And the Council is full of *zucconi odiosi*," the quiet man said without moving.

"As you are, Franco."

Franco smiled at the small one. "Let's not get personal."

"We're here *because* it's personal," the small man continued. "We each lost someone at Le Sangue Bambini." *Il Luogo dei Bambini che Sanguinano.*

"And we're going to fucking know why, before we hear another word from you." The quiet man's eyes narrowed, he grew cold, detached . . . lethal.

For long moments Franco thought about the answer. He considered and rejected retelling Valerie's story, railing against the Chinese conspiracy or invoking democracy versus communism. These men wanted simpler answers. Who was responsible, why? No shades, degrees, or cutouts.

And, more important, could all the deaths—thirty-two in all, mostly children—have been avoided?

It was a question he'd asked himself over and over again in the hours since the attack.

The clinic *was* under his protection. He'd brought the fugitives safely out of America and into what had become ground zero for the butchery. Hell, it'd been him that had coerced Xenos into looking for Paolo in the first place. It *could* all be considered his fault.

If the men around him came to that conclusion, he would never live to possibly be executed by the Council tomorrow.

"*Fratelli,* what happened in Toulon was caused by two things. First, a mother trying desperately to save her children; and second . . ." He sighed deeply. "My brothers, you know the second as well as I. The second reason is that we are Corsican.

"While we hold ourselves to standards of civility and protocol, do things in the proper way through the proper channels, the rest of the world never has. The *Cinesi* betrayed us, even as we offered them a way out of the crisis. A way that would have been equitable for everyone."

He shook his head. "But we now know, from the depraved tortures they inflicted on our men, that they were never serious about the negotiations. Why should they be? We are just Corsican, and when has the world wept bitter tears at the death of any of us?"

He paused, taken up in his own emotions and memories of that night. "Or at the wrecked bodies of children of color from an embarrassing war?"

He took his time, looking each man at the table in the eyes, in the heart. "It happened, my brothers, because the *Cinesi* care no more for us than the dirt beneath their feet; it happened because this man who works for them enjoys pain and blood.

"And it happened because we are Corsican, and the world allows their Corsicans, their Jews, their people of color or strong beliefs other than their own to die alone and forgotten.

"Because it is easier than doing anything about it."

The big man nodded solemnly. "The Council should never have negotiated in the first place. After Paolo, the rest was already written."

"You remember Serge and Bern Collatino?" the small man asked.

"Sure." Franco remembered them. Serge had been laced from groin to shoulder with automatic weapons fire. Bern's head had been blown into two—oddly balanced—halves.

"My wife's brothers. Not that the fucking Council gives a shit, but my wife is home crying." The little man's every aspect dripped anger and death.

"Fuck this," the quiet man said calmly, distractedly. "What do you want? You're sitting under the executioner's blade and you're giving moving speeches, but you aren't saying shit, Franco. What do you want from us?"

Franco smiled spasmodically as the man sliced the loaf and left the slices on the mat.

"Vendetta," he said simply.

The small man shook his head. "You aren't good enough."

Franco took no offense. The pyre of the clinic was grave silent witness to that fact.

"Twenty-one children under my, *our Brotherhood's,* protection lay torn open on land that was blessed by the church as a refuge. Nine of our finest men, two of our most virtuous and sacrificing women lay butchered by a man—by a system—that tortures and murders three of our elders."

He hesitated. "Have you lost your balls, along with the Council? I *will* see this vendetta satisfied."

The men ignored the insult, such was the passion of the moment and it could easily be forgotten. But the central problem remained.

Passion, pain, commitment, and anger couldn't counter the mentality, resources, and organization that had pursued the fugitives halfway around the world and organized a massacre that the world's press was calling a "terrorist attack by Afghan separatists."

"How are *you*, little lost Franco," the big man spat out, "going to see this done? Eh? I've heard of this man who works for the Chinks. He's an *inglese* spook with unlimited resources and the most malignant genius that ever crawled out of Hell's depths!"

Franco smiled—a strange, odd, broken, deceptive thing. "This Canvas is *not* the most malignant, *diavolo pericoloso* even of my acquaintance."

"No?" The quiet man gestured angrily at the man in front of him. "Tell me, then! Huh? In your *vast* experience with these things, who is worse, more reeking of the devil than this man who rapes our souls for *la Cina*?"

"Dureté."

The men might have been hit with an icy blast.

"Will you talk with him, then?" Franco asked after a full silent minute had passed. All the while fighting a temptation to slap them and laugh in their faces.

They looked at each other, then nodded.

Franco stood, walked to the door, and opened it. A moment later Xenos limped in.

His hair—much of it burned in the fire—had been cut extremely short, blackened patches of skin showed on his arms and neck, a hastily sewn closed laceration slightly oozed pinkish fluid through his T-shirt.

His face seemed devoid of all human feeling.

The other men stood when he walked into the room. These were among the toughest, most capable, most intelligent men of any of the Corsican Unions.

But they were, well, *uncomfortable* at facing this legend sitting vulnerably.

"In bocca al lupo," they all mumbled.

Xenos took a step into the room.

"I need three specialists," he said without preamble, "men who speak accentless English, are familiar with the States—who will not be made as foreigners. I need these men to be able to take orders and carry out complex tasks, but be able to think for themselves and improvise. I need three men with special skills, men of iron and commitment—willing to die, but smart enough to stay alive—to get the job done.

"I need a man of water.

"A man of wind.

"A man of fire."

The small man—Ugo Albina—a man wanted in seven countries for his seemingly supernatural abilities to get into and out of the most secured places, bit off a piece of skin from his left little finger.

"Ecco! Un uomo d'acqua!" He held the hand palm-up toward Xenos.

The quiet man—Constantin Vedette—known to the police of four continents as "the Watcher," bit his little finger and held it out.

"Ecco! Un uomo di vento!"

"Ecco!" the big man—Lucien Fabrè—assassin, demolitions expert, martial artist, said with passion and commitment. *"Un uomo di fuoco!"*

Xenos nodded, bit his own finger, then fully and deeply shook each man's hand—gripping them tightly for long moments each.

"Uccidi il lupo. Kill the fucking wolf."

Franco watched intensely, feeling the long-healed wound in his own finger from the years before when he had become a brother to these men.

To Xenos.

"And if the *tribunale* rules against us tomorrow?" Vedette asked him.

"Well"—he shrugged—"then God is dead," Franco said flatly. "And there is nothing that can then happen to us in this world that matters."

In the back of the presidential stretch limousine, surrounded by Secret Service and press, Apple Blossom made his final . . . checks.

"You're sure they're dead?" he said simply.

Steingarth nodded. "Without question. All final impediments have been removed."

The man across from him looked skeptical. "You said that before, with the college kid." He paused. "What does the man say?"

"Well," the old traitor said to the younger one, "he's susceptible to the insecurities that are part and parcel to his profession. He's not *completely* convinced. But that's just him."

Apple Blossom considered that. "Then I'm not either. It's too damned late in the game to take chances."

"And it's too late to change our plans significantly." Steingarth's voice contained the slightest parental hint of reproach. "They're waiting for you in there."

"Contingencies?"

"In place, *and* unnecessary, as I said." Steingarth reached out, supportively tapping the man's knee. "Haven't you caused your own inquiries to be made as well? Relax." He smiled encouragingly.

"I'll relax," the man said as he checked his tie, "when it's over, and not one damned minute before." He opened the door to the flashes and buzz of the press.

"Relax, my boy," Steingarth said happily. "These are your winnings."

Twenty-five minutes later the show began.

"Do you swear to tell the truth, the whole truth, without mental reservation or purpose of evasion, so help you God?"

Jefferson Wilson DeWitt—attorney general of the United

States, nominee for vice president of the United States—held his left hand high, held a corner of the American flag in his right, and answered in a strong, deep, committed voice.

"By almighty God's divine wrath, I do!"

The Senate Committee Room echoed with thunderous applause. Packed beyond capacity with congressmen, aides, security men, and three times the usual press, the sound bounced off the marble floors and ceilings, wrapping itself lovingly around the man facing the combined Senate/House Judiciary Committee.

DeWitt stood proudly, strongly—as he'd practiced for hours in front of a mirror. His expression set, firm; his posture ramrod straight and a little arrogant.

His eyes set firmly and completely on the future.

"Please be seated, Mr. Attorney General," the aging committee chairman said brusquely.

Frankly he could think of ten men more qualified for the number two job in the country, maybe fifty men that he *personally* liked more than the young AG.

But the world was in crisis, and the president entitled to have his own man at his side. Reluctantly the chairman had agreed—in the interest of national security—to expedite the hearings.

"Mr. Attorney General, let me be the first to thank you for your appearance before this committee; and to assure you, sir, that we will do everything we can to accommodate your schedule in light of the current, well, events."

DeWitt looked up from a whispered conversation with Michael. "Thank you, Mr. Chairman. As you know I *am* on call to the White House but will, of course, do all I can to stay before this illustrious group and answer all your questions to the best of my abilities."

Considering all the questions have been cleared in advance, the traitor thought as he looked stoically at the committee.

"Very well, sir." The chairman leaned back in his extra-padded seat. "You may begin."

DeWitt nodded, sipped his water, then opened his notebook, glancing at a note at the top of his aide's pad.

Patience! Pace!! Power!!!

"Mr. Chairman, Chairman Ruskin, Senators, Congressmen, assembled guests, ladies and gentlemen, my fellow citizens of the planet's greatest hope for true freedom and democracy; it is a sobering honor to appear before you. An honor, because the president has seen fit to entrust with me a part in the future of this great land. Sobering, because of the tragic and horrid circumstances that led to this nomination.

"My life," he said with the vaguest crack in his voice, "has been proof of the American dream. Testimony to the greatness that is still available to any- and everybody living under the banner of liberty. That it has led to this moment—when our nation stands so sorely tested and requires so much more commitment from all of us—is the grandest fulfillment of my immigrant grandfather's favorite phrase: 'Only in America.' "

Grandfather, he thought bitterly, *the old man that smelled of piss and couldn't be left alone with little girls.*

"My mother—God rest her soul—raised me in the midwestern traditions of loyalty to God, family, community, and country. A schoolteacher, a cook for the poor and deserted, a shining example of what Americanism means, was *all* to me. It was at her feet that I first heard the stories of Washington and Lincoln, Jefferson and Teddy Roosevelt. Was taught that *country* was not just a word, but a faith and a dedication requiring sacrifice and hard work.

"From my father I learned discipline. Many thought he was not an easy man—and as a veteran of too many trips to the woodshed to smile about—I can attest to that. But he was a man, all in all, who asked nothing from anyone. Who believed that hard work *was* its own reward, and that dedication to something larger than one's self is what defined a man."

Mommy and Daddy. Oh what teachers they were.

He continued reading from the well-rehearsed statement as his mind journeyed back to years he would deny any existence to.

Mommy—the belle of Racine—seldom home with her causes

*and missions. A woman so disdainful of her blue-collar husband
and albatross-around-the-neck son that she sought* **divertment** *in as
many other places—with as many other men—as she could.*

And Daddy.

*He'd found his own . . . diversions. The private pleasures
that he'd share with me at—oh, what was I? Eleven? Twelve? The
booze and the hookers; the beatings . . . and the touchings.*

"Mr. Attorney General?"

DeWitt pulled himself back from the memories. "My apologies, Mr. Chairman. But as I stand on the brink of this pinnacle of life, I'm overcome with emotion at those two giants of my life not being here to share it with me."

To choke on it.

"If I may return to my statement," he said after a long drink of cold water.

"Of course."

"My friends," he said, returning to the text that had undergone twenty-three drafts in the last two weeks. "It was in college that I think I began to fully appreciate how best I might serve my country."

And he smiled.

It was in England—in the late sixties—that the future vice presidential nominee felt alive for the first time in his life.

His father's suicide had left the boy some money, his mother's "social work" had gotten him some connections, and an affair with a high school counselor only five years older than himself had accomplished the rest.

The pain of the semirural existence, of his parents' violations, was quickly forgotten among the green, the cool, and the foreignness. England was eye-opening: here were others his age—shouting in the streets, protesting a war he knew or cared little about—all of them seeking to prove their individuality by aping their fellow individualists.

He learned quickly.

Naturally bright, and taught from childhood the finest arts of manipulation, DeWitt found Oxford and environs a ripe hunting ground. There were the free-love American girls on adventure (for the summer); the English girls, who seemed inordinately turned on by the Huck Finn/Karl Marx/John Kennedy persona that he'd affected for his stay; the European girls, who just wanted to make an American boy to annoy their parents.

He'd attended enough classes to keep from being thrown out, made enough of an impression to attract girls and possibilities. The possibilities were almost more tantalizing than the girls.

He'd known from the start that he was smarter than the others around him, but a life academia sickened him. An Oxford diploma was merely a means to a higher social stratum, more connected friends, higher-class lays. But what he'd soon discovered was that there were many other—more exciting—possibilities in the air at Oxford, and later at Barnsdahl (where he'd transferred after "an outright lie by a girl who slept around with everyone" had forced the move).

The governments of the world viewed the volatile English campuses as a breeding ground of "radicals, communists, anarchists, and pinkos." And they were anxious to identify which of the world's future leaders were simply *unsuitable.*

But DeWitt understood that a snitch—no matter how much patriotic fervor you wrapped around it—was still a snitch.

He'd also reasoned that there had to be a way—through charm, contacts, payoffs, or less traceable *favors*—to use the expensive education he was getting (inside and *outside* the colleges) to move up. Move out.

To win!

And midway through his junior year, he found it.

The camera pushed in tight on the attorney general's face. "While my college education prevented me from enlisting in the armed forces, I did see much of Asia in my travels. And while I never saw communist Asia, I can tell you from its impact on the noncommunist nations that it is not universally viewed as a sleeping dragon or monster, waiting to devour the rest of the region. In fact, there are many in Asia who would welcome a larger, more community-of-nations role for the People's Republic."

The camera was tight now, his face filling the tiny screen on the mountainside.

"And my friends, we must always remember that it *is* the warlords who founded Taiwan."

Valerie looked up as the television was switched off from behind.

"It's time," Avidol said as he started for the door.

Valerie sighed, ran her fingers through her hair, straightened the borrowed dress—she would not be allowed to appear in slacks —and slowly followed.

It was a stupid waste of time, she thought. For all the posturing (sincere or otherwise) of Franco's act, power systems just don't reverse themselves. Ever. It's what maintains their power, she knew, having been a part of one of the biggest power systems in the world.

A thing she no longer felt *any* part of.

So Franco would die tonight, and others who openly supported him—if there were any—would die alongside him. And Valerie would be given over to the Chinese.

Xenos, well, whatever moral outrage he'd mustered in the hours after the attack seemed to have calmed in him. Now he spoke quietly, in monosyllables of generalities. Not the man to put his life on the line to do a job that couldn't be done, anyway.

But at the door to the church hall, she straightened herself, put on a strong expression, and started in.

It would be good practice for when she faced the Chinese.

The "hall" turned out to be a large rock amphitheater with a constructed roof over the back half, giving the impression of a building. Over five hundred people lined the seats and rock ledges, sitting quietly looking down at the well of the theater where Franco stood . . . alone.

Each person in the place had a white card and a black card. Some kept them in their laps, others folded in pockets or laid carefully under their seats. But none were far from hand.

Franco wore tight leather pants and a loose, open-to-the-waist red silk shirt. His hair slicked back, his manner insolent, he looked confident, arrogant . . . almost noble.

A glass bell was rung from somewhere in the amphitheater's depths and the crowd stood solemnly as the Council walked in.

After they were seated, a long table was carried out and placed in front of them. In front of each man was a six-inch-long stiletto.

Franco bowed to the Council, bowed insolently to the crowd, then sat down. A table with a stiletto was brought before him.

The bell rang again, and the crowd sat down.

Il tribunale had begun.

For over an hour three survivors of the attack (all suitable to both the Council and Franco) gave gruesome, impartial accounts of the night that had become known as *the place of the bleeding children*. Members of the Council asked questions to bring out just how deep Franco's involvement had been in bringing the fugitives to Toulon, in setting up the security, in opposing negotiations with the Chinese.

Franco asked no questions, just polished his fingernails on the side of his spectacular shirt, the picture of disinterest.

For another hour a Corsican investigator (again, acceptable to both sides) recounted the history of the Council meeting in *La Sortie*, where Franco had openly challenged the manhood of the respected elders, where he'd had to be physically restrained when they'd decided to submit—for the moment—to the Chinese.

Franco asked no questions but seemed deeply involved in peeling the skin from each of the grapes in a plate that had been handed him.

Finally a report was given on Canvas himself, his background —as was known—his connections with the Chinese, their plan as Valerie'd outlined it. With emphasis placed on the resources of the Chinese and the malignancy of Canvas himself.

Franco still asked no questions, just spit out some grape seeds as the investigator walked past him.

The audience was getting nervous now. The case against Franco had built step by step, with overwhelming evidence, with no rebuttal of the facts by the man facing the knife's edge.

But there was something in the air, something from the man's casual disregard, the disdainful shaking of his head, the contemptuous look he gave the witnesses and the Council.

Finally the old man in the center chair stood and addressed the groups in Corsican, a rarity since most of the audience spoke primarily Italian or French.

"My brothers," he said in the ancient dialect, "the case has been made clear. The Council's orders were directly challenged and this has not been denied. The Council's judgment was questioned and this has not been denied. The Council's honor was most clearly savaged and this has not been denied. The evidence is clear.

"For centuries we have survived as a people by using our power judiciously, carefully. Doling it out in spoonfuls, not great promiscuous buckets. All who have come to this island have been defeated—in time—by our tradition of remembrance and slow retribution. Had we, had they (our sainted ancestors) attempted to attack in force, to overthrow in one night the might arrayed against them, most of us would not be here to meet in tribunal.

"This *was* the Council's judgment, this remains the Council's judgment—our life's traditions—and it will remain ever so. We therefore ask you to raise the black and reclaim clan honor and dignity."

He sat down.

The audience took a deep breath, then turned to Franco, anxious to hear him present his case.

After two long minutes, after a murmur of discomfort and unease went through the crowd, Franco looked up, confusion in his eyes.

"Oh," he began in a genuinely surprised voice. "Is it my turn now?"

Some laughed, others were shocked because he was speaking in English, a language never used before in any tribunal.

"My apologies, my friends, brothers," he said as he stood up and casually began wandering through the well of the theater. "But my ears were full of wind." He exaggeratedly put a finger in his ear as if to clear out an obstruction. When he pulled it out, he carefully examined the fingertip.

"Dusty." More laughter. "The wind was filled with the dust of the ages. The breaths of dusty old men who see distant history as not lessons, but *requirements* for the future."

All laughter instantly stopped.

"These old fools"—he shook his head and chuckled—"well, what can I say?" He smiled at the Council. "Fools who have outlived their usefulness to us all."

People leaned forward, moved to the edge of their seats. Something in the soon-to-be-dead man's voice compelled them, forced them, invigorated them.

Franco turned back to the audience. "A young boy is entrusted with money of the Brotherhood to secure a valued service for the Brotherhood. He disappears and they do nothing.

"The young boy is savagely murdered only because he becomes an inconvenience to a plot that he cares nothing about, and they do *nothing*."

He seemed to suddenly remember something. "Oh yes, they send three of their own to *talk*." His voice took on a deeply sarcastic tone. "They dearly *love to talk*. But then you've witnessed that yourself. Those of you who remained awake.

"Finally . . ." His tone lowered and became a dangerous living thing that moved among them on a knife's edge. "Finally, when eleven of our brothers and sisters are slaughtered defending children in a hospital under our protection—when twenty-one of those angels are torn apart by these savages—they stop talking and act."

He was quiet for a full minute.

"They act . . . *and the ghosts of our brothers back to the beginning of time rise as one and spit on their soon-to-be graves!*" His voice echoed off the rocks, through the people, becoming a part of the air.

"Brothers, I stand in opposition to the Council. I deny them their authority. They are not Corsican. They are not men. They are not human.

"For no human, no man, *no Corsican*, could possibly allow all these crimes against God and the Brotherhood to go unpunished. Join me and we will tear out the throats of the monsters who have raped our souls and the old men who are allowing it to continue."

There were whispered conversations everywhere. Angry discussions. Livid hushed tones. Then a chill went through the crowd.

Franco pulled off his shirt, picked up the dagger from his table, and made two deep diagonal cuts parallel to each other over his heart.

"I call for *the day of the plague*." He held the bloody knife out to the crowd. "I call for you to join me in the day of the plague on *la Cina*."

The old man in the central chair jumped up, red-faced, furious, pounding on his table for attention.

"Franco, *scaricatore di porto*. *You* yourself have said that you cannot defeat these men! Have you suddenly been endowed with magical spirits? Would you lead these people into inevitable destruction? *Stronzo!*"

"No," Franco answered in a strong voice that rang off the rock. "*I* cannot lead them to their just revenge."

"*Chi, allora?* Who, then? Or will you answer that only after more of our people have been led down the road to slaughter and ruin? *Chi, allora?*"

Slowly Franco raised the knife toward the cliff behind the Council seats. Higher and higher he raised it as the crowd followed with their eyes and hearts and hopes.

"*He* will," was all he said in the dreadful silence.

And standing on top of that sheer cliff, the full moon behind him—as though he were a holy symbol on a consecrated Corsican shield—was a man, his bare chest still bleeding from the recent cuts of dedication.

"Dureté!" someone yelled out.

"Il Diavolo," others—men who had known him—whispered as they crossed themselves.

"The day of the plague!" Xenos's voice carried to the heart and soul of every man in the crowd.

Franco forced down a smile as he turned back to the assemblage. His voice was soft but strong, and carried to the farthest reaches of the amphitheater. *"Il giorno della peste."*

The crowd stirred as Fabrè stepped out of the audience, took the knife, and boldly cut his chest. *"Il giorno della peste,"* he said with emphasis as he held the knife out to the crowd.

"Il giorno della peste." The crowd gasped as Vedette stepped forward, accepted the knife, and marked himself as a holy warrior.

"Il giorno della peste!" Albina . . . and the die had been cast.

It took thirty minutes of shouts and proclamations before more than three hundred of the men had marked themselves for battle.

Amid it all, no one noticed the Council led quietly away.

Their time was over.

The day of the plague had begun.

Thirteen

It was almost enough to make her question her commitment to the cause.

Almost.

But then the coming payoff was so great, the possibilities so exciting, that she could probably put up with yet another day of madness, chaos, and debris.

Since Valerie's disappearance, Barbara had been doing a balancing act—appearing the loyal staffer trying to put the best spin possible on her boss becoming a fugitive.

Working to undermine Valerie's credibility wherever possible the rest of the time.

Running the office on her own, reporting irregularly to her next up in the Apple Blossom chain, had left her tired and irritable. She wasn't sleeping, was eating sporadically, snapping at everyone she came in contact with.

But tonight was Friday—nothing loomed over the weekend that was urgent—and she hurried to her car in the House staff parking lot with high expectations.

Barring last-minute calls from staff, constituents, or spymasters, she would spend the weekend in Atlantic City, gambling with the constantly replenished account that was a small part of her reward.

As she picked her way through Dupont Circle traffic, she saw the White House rise up in front of her.

She smiled.

Everybody had a price, her mother had been fond of saying. And she thought that was about right. For the handsome traitor in the midst of his confirmation hearings, that price would soon be the presidency.

But that was too short-term a power for Barbara. Eight years, and then what? No. *Her price* held more permanence to it, more of a long-lasting high. A thing that she would wallow in, cover herself with, for the next few decades at least.

With the inauguration of President Jefferson DeWitt, Apple Blossom would end for the ambitious young woman.

As *Chrysanthemum* would begin.

Then, six short years later—after stints in the Treasury Department and Securities Exchange Commission—Barbara Krusiec would become a senior vice president at the World Bank. From there—with advance *inside* information on the major economic developments of a planet—it was a short step toward never having to have anyone replenish *any* accounts.

All for being willing to help here and there, now and then.

She smiled as she pulled out of traffic onto the large superhighway as she headed for a suburban shuttle airport.

It wasn't treason—what she would do now or in the future—she felt. Treason required an initial allegiance to something. A thing Barbara had never experienced.

Born into the "noble poverty" of the South of the fifties, her mother had worked four jobs to provide for the three children without a father among them. Elaine Krusiec had taken her children regularly to the ramshackle church that promised redemption and salvation, but never explained why the minister had two cars and the congregation was starving.

Barbara ran away at twelve and immediately began reinventing herself. Bright and intuitive, she figured early on who and how to manipulate—emotionally, intellectually, sexually (just another currency to the jaded young girl)—in order to get whatever she wanted.

Which was—primarily—to be someone else.

As she pulled into the exit lane before Rodney & McKean Regional Air Park, she had almost accomplished that. Just a few more days, and her future would be—inalterably—set.

A van pulled up alongside her town car, close to the boundary of his lane, but still legal. Normally Barbara would've honked or sped up or slowed down, but there was another van in front of her (slowing down, it seemed) and yet a third behind her.

Muttering the foulest expletive she could think of, she settled in to wait for the exit . . . as the side door of the van to her left slid open and a ski-masked man let loose with both barrels of his shotgun.

Her windshield and left rear window exploded in a spray of glass and smoke as she jerked the car hard over to the right. Crashing through the railing, she heard two more shots echo behind her as she careened down an embankment. Gripping the wheel with white knuckles, her head barely peeking through a jagged hole in the front glass, she struggled to control the car's slide.

It came to a stop with a sick thud against four water-filled traffic barrels that had—thankfully—been placed at the bottom of the hill exactly where she'd skidded. They threw up a wash of soapy water, drenching car and driver.

Slowly Barbara checked to see if she was still alive. No broken bones, a slight cut on her left cheek, and with a life expectancy ten years less whatever it had been a few seconds before.

But she *was* alive.

She quickly climbed out of the car, looking back up the hill. The attack had happened at close to sixty miles an hour, so there'd been no chance for the gunman to turn and follow her down the hill, even if he'd been crazy enough to do that.

She was on a service road, chain-link- and barbed-wire-fenced industrial parks across from the embankment. No traffic, people, or phones.

Shaking her head, daubing at her bleeding cheek with a piece of tissue, she returned to her car, pulling out her purse and cell phone.

The battery indicated it was fine, the phone looked undamaged, but there was no sound—even static—on the device. She tried several more times, then gave up. Throwing her purse strap over her neck and shoulder, she headed down the service road.

Then froze.

As a van slowly appeared and accelerated toward her.

She saw the puff of smoke a moment before she heard the shot, but it didn't matter. She was off and running at the sight of the vehicle.

There was no place to run to, though. The steep hill on one side, the dangerous fencing on the other, and the van behind. Her high heels flew away, her feet tore and ripped on the unimproved asphalt. Her heart seemed about to fly out of her chest as she heard the van get closer and a shot roar through the air around her.

Then, as if in response to her silent shouting prayers, she saw a thin hole torn through the fencing just ahead.

Dodging another shot from the van, she dived through, propelling herself into a maze of abandoned Dumpsters and Porta Pottis.

She hid in and among that putrescence for the next three hours. Never seeing two of the vans pull back to her car and load the lifesaving water barrels.

Or a flatbed almost immediately arrive and haul off her car as other men smoothed out the tracks of her car's slide.

Or a man remove a cellular line disrupter from under a chicken bucket less than twenty feet from her car, and move it to near the spot in the fence she'd disappeared through.

Three hours after dark, still terrified, breathing heavily and unable to stand her own stench, Barbara climbed out of a Dumpster. Carefully looking around at the deserted storage facility, she took a deep breath and headed for where she hoped the entrance would be. Ten minutes later she found it—using a nearby ladder to climb over the fence and jump onto the trunk of a conveniently parked car.

Which way to go? The street was well lit, light traffic, no people or businesses; just other warehouses or storage yards. Then she saw a van—maybe *the van*—slowly move through the intersection to her left.

She started off to her right.

The first three pay phones she got to were out of order. The fourth, in the back of a deserted gas station, worked. Her fear rapidly being overcome by her anger, she dialed the 800 number from memory.

"Bayshore Imports, night desk, this is Lou."

"Somebody tried to kill me," she said in an angry whisper.

"Who is this?" the mystified voice said in a light tone. "Is this George down in Shipping?"

"Somebody tried to Goddamn kill me and I want some help now!"

"Identify yourself," the voice said suddenly in a cold whisper, "or the connection will be terminated."

Barbara took a deep breath, trying desperately to remember a procedure she'd had no cause to use in eight years.

"This is Chrysanthemum," she said with bile. "I've been hit."

"Stand by, Chrysanthemum," was the last thing she heard before the phone was ripped out of her hand.

The man with the receiver in his hand leered at her. "She's a little dirty. But that's a tight little body under that shit."

Two more men moved in front of her.

"We could always take the clothes off her," one said.

"Clean her up some before," the other said.

The man behind her dropped the receiver, turned, kicking open the nearby bathroom door. "Bring her in here," he ordered.

As the first man reached for her, Barbara ducked and took off on the dead run. A moment later all three men were after her.

She turned the corner, praying to find some help, or just a group of people standing around that would scare off the bastards gaining on her.

As she collided with a man in a cheap suit.

"Hey!" He peeled her off him.

She looked back, seeing that the men had stopped, were arguing among themselves, then turned and left. "Thank God!"

The man stepped back from her. "Are you okay?" he asked as he viewed her with disdain.

She tried to dust some of the filth off, to pull her hair back. "Uh, yeah. I've been in an accident. Sorry."

The man shook his head. "What'd you do, hit a fertilizer truck?"

"Uh, something like that." She looked around, suddenly seeing the open trunk of the car next to them. "I, uh, could really use a ride."

The man looked suspicious. "Listen, I could call the police for you or something. But I don't think it'd be right . . ."

"Listen, I just need to get out of this neighborhood, okay? It's not safe," she said, looking back over her shoulder.

The man seemed unsure, then nodded. "Of course. I'm sorry. I should know better, I guess." He offered her his handkerchief. "The Lord says we must treat the most humble as the most exalted."

He opened the passenger door for her, then moved to close the trunk. "And be charitable to the most wretched of his creations."

"Thank you, uh, Mr. . . ."

"Oliver. Oliver O'Neill."

She hesitated before getting in the car. "You some kind of a minister, Mr. O'Neill?" The interior of the car was neat and tidy, a small crucifix hanging from the rearview mirror. On it was an icon of Saint Margaret, the patron saint of lost, hopeless, and abandoned women.

Her only companion on many nights alone in a hungry past.

"Not exactly," O'Neill said as he rummaged in the trunk before closing it. He handed her a book. "I sell study Bibles to religious schools."

Exhaustion and instinct conquering her rampant fears—the vans and the men somewhere behind her—Barbara collapsed into the comfortable car.

"Where do you need to go?" O'Neill asked.

"Which way you headed?"

"Next stop is Saint Barnabas's Academy in Georgetown."

For the first time in hours, she breathed a relaxed breath and nodded, thinking of the safety of the Georgetown apartment.

"Works for me."

They pulled away, Barbara never seeing a van pull up to the corner behind them to pick up the men who'd chased her.

"Beautiful," Vedette said as he hung up the phone. "We got a full trace on the phone and the target is securely in the jar." He made some notes on a clipboard. "Exactly as you drew it, my friend! *Molto bello.*"

Xenos ignored the praise as he studied the computer display in front of him. "People seldom surprise me," he mumbled as he called up another display. "It's a punch game."

"What?" Vedette walked over to read the display over the big man's shoulder.

"Punch game," Xenos repeated as he gestured at the monitor. "A sophisticated set of interconnected phone relays. Based on an old con game of the twenties. Merchants would be sold punch cards for a quarter apiece. The idea was that their customers would get four punches for a dollar. And somewhere on the card was a prize of one, five, or ten dollars.

"But the merchant would see that there was really no way for the customers to win, so it was pure profit. Especially after their customers got hooked on playing." He started another program and watched as the second examined the readouts from the first. "Kinda like lotto scratchers."

Vedette studied the man who was still recovering from his wounds, but seemed to ignore the pain and slight immobilities as an inconvenience rather than an injury. "And this is like that . . ."

Xenos made a note of some figures.

"They've tied together the relays from several distant areas— in this case four or five cities within one hundred miles of D.C.— into the one receiving station. Direct calls come through, but tracer tones or burst transmissions could go to any of the other numbers while at the same time alerting the actual receiver of the trace attempt."

"Then we have accomplished nothing." The Corsican looked positively depressed.

"Well." Xenos half smiled. "Yes and no. The other con of the punch game was that the con man had a partner who knew which holes to punch in order to win the big cash prizes. Moral being there's always a way to . . ." He paused, then nodded in satisfaction at the new readout. "You see?"

262,398 numbers searched for active measures
250,065 show positive impedance gains
12,333 show negative impedance drops
Working . . .

"Meaning?" The Corsican surveillance expert had worked with much of the highest-tech equipment in the world. Things that could "see" through walls, listen without being present, phone taps of every description and nature. He'd even invented a few "nuances" of his own.

But the technology and understanding of it that he was experiencing in this Virginia warehouse was like going back to school.

The *first day* of school.

"Emergency lines like Krusiec called *never* make outgoing calls. You can't risk the line being busy when an operative needs you. So I asked the computer to trace the relays for lines that had *only* received calls in the last eight hours. Now it's narrowing it down further by duration, transfer activity, sophistication of the receiving equipment. Stuff like that."

Vedette nodded as he made a note of the program name and version, surprised that it was an over-the-counter application. "So it will eventually give us the final relay."

"No. But it'll narrow it down to no more than ten possibilities. Those we check out other ways."

Xenos walked away from the computer when he saw Albina come into the room. "Talk to me."

The small man looked unhappy. "I have three teams, twenty-six men in all, sitting on a Greek freighter off Montauk, New York. They are good men, blooded, well equipped. But I still cannot land them."

"Why?"

"I've heard nothing from the negotiations. Those we have

here, those we have on the outside, are enough of a risk. There will be war if we bring in three hit squads and the Sicilianos find out about them before the talks are complete. We must wait for Franco."

Xenos checked his watch, then nodded. "Give him two more hours, then land your men."

"Dureté . . ." But the look in the man's eyes was enough to silence Albina. "God's mercy on us all," he said as he pulled out his cell phone.

"What about the other thing? Can you do it?"

Albina glanced at a table behind him strewn with photos, maps, and diagrams.

"I never worry about getting in," he said with more confidence than he felt. "It's staying in that bothers me."

Xenos nodded his agreement, then walked across the warehouse to a small office, a tiny room empty of everything except a chair and a small table. On the table was a pen-and-ink sketch he'd been working on for the past three days.

He closed the door behind him, picking up the pad, continuing the delicate work of sketching the face.

The hard eyes.

The scarred neck.

The perennial five o'clock shadow.

The hint of tattoos at the shoulder.

It was still unfinished, still forming, recognizable only to Xenos. But as he worked, hour by hour, moment by moment, it became clearer, fixed, more understandable.

As did the man it represented.

At some point the picture—physical and mental—would be complete. Then the time would come to look into those eyes, to challenge the mind and the flesh behind it. But that was still remote, removed, distant. A thing not considered or planned for.

Because the sketch wasn't yet ready.

In a small New York restaurant—little more than a storefront —the future was now.

Franco sat relaxed, confident, and comfortable. Despite the three gunmen standing behind him.

He'd been kept waiting for an hour, as he'd expected. Relations abroad between the Corsicans and the Mafia were strained at best. But here, in a country even more native to them than their precious Sicily, the relationship was openly hostile.

Members of the Brotherhood were banned from all illegal activities in cities controlled by the Mafia. And violation of this twenty-five-year-old "treaty" would most likely lead to an international war between the two deadly groups.

Not that there weren't members of individual Unions operating in "open cities" in the States.

Franco had drawn from Unions in San Diego, Los Angeles, and Houston for his initial personnel. But none of them were working for the Brotherhood as a whole—all of them independents —or in cities where the Mafia had no clear leader or leaders.

And they needed to be free to work—without interference—in New York, possibly New Jersey or Connecticut, as well as Washington and its suburbs.

So Franco sat and sipped coffee as he waited for this third and final meeting to begin.

There was a shuffling of men and chairs as the sixty-year-old, bathrobe-clad Mafia chieftain walked over and sat down.

"You got balls, DiBenetti. I'll give you that."

Franco shrugged. "My balls I've gotten better compliments on than from you, old man," he said easily. "You finally ready to do business, or you want to keep playing crazy for the Feds?"

"You Corsies blow me away."

"It could happen," Franco said with a smile. "But let's assume the best for the moment, okay?"

The Mafioso nodded. "Okay. I got two problems. You solve them, I give you my blessing. You don't," he sighed, "I have Leopold here cut off your magnificent balls and bronze them for my Christmas tree."

The Corsican never moved.

"First problem," the old gangster said in a rock-steady, almost accusing voice, "is that you Corsies don't never share. That's always been the fucking problem. You don't pay tribute, you don't show the proper respect, and once we let you in somewhere, we got to whack out maybe half a dozen or more of you bastards before you get the message and leave. Cockroaches, that's you. You either wipe 'em all out or they foul the whole house!"

He laughed uproariously at the picture, immediately joined in by the three gunmen behind Franco.

"Second problem," the Corsican leader prompted.

The man calmed, leaned forward, and spoke so softly he could only be heard by the man across from him. "We don't do politics. Never. It's like a holy order, see? And this here thing of yours stinks of it."

Before Franco could say anything, the old man held up a hand. "The only thing I know about Chinks is that I don't like the food. Too much tasteless oil."

But the look on the face of his adversary banished the laughter before it began.

"The G," the mob boss continued, "they barely know we're alive these days. They spend their time dealing with each other, white-collar guys, assholes beatin' fags, and rednecks burning niggers. Us, they look at as part of the landscape. Not pretty maybe. But acceptable, so long as we stay out of certain things." He shrugged. "And politics is number one on their shit list."

"You done?" Franco sounded annoyed. "I mean if you're gonna make another speech, I wouldn't want to interrupt. I know how hard that is for you."

The man across from him gestured for Franco to begin.

"First, I don't give a shit for your little civics lessons. You and me and who we stand for got nothing to do with governments or what they want. In the Brotherhood, we have *men,* not politicians." He looked around at the other men. "Maybe you guys have changed, eh?"

His voice hardened and his manner became more deliberate. "So I don't want to hear about your troubles with the G."

He leaned back. "As for the other, well, you do business your way, we do it ours. We don't share. Why should we if we do all the work?

"But this one time, to avoid misunderstandings and wrong impressions, we're willing to give you a taste." He paused, waiting for the man across from him to lean slightly forward in anticipation. "Fifteen percent of the San Diego and Houston operations for six months, and the use of Port Girolata as a transshipment point for your heroin processing for one year at no charge." He smiled. "Beyond expenses, of course."

"You really *do* want these Chinks."

"Even more than I want to send you to Hell."

The old man thought for a few minutes. "And at the end of the year?"

"Five percent biannually for the continued use and protection of Girolata."

"Jesus."

Franco shrugged. "I don't think he'd be interested."

After ten minutes of total silence, the don nodded. "And the Council will confirm the deal."

"I *am* the fucking Council. What about the commission?"

"Done."

The two men stood, shook hands, then kissed each other on the cheeks.

"*Buona fortuna, Corsicano,*" the don said with a smile.

"*Vaffanculo,* old man," Franco answered as he casually strolled away.

A quiet knock at the door caused Xenos to close the pad. "Come."

Valerie walked in. She looked nervous. "We're getting ready to leave."

"Right."

She took a step forward. "I just wanted to say, uh, that is . . ." Her mouth moved spasmodically, but nothing came out. "I never really thanked you for what you're trying to do."

Xenos studied her, the strength covered by the fragile look; the resolve beneath the worry. "I'm not doing it for you."

"I know," she said quietly. "All those children . . ." Her voice trailed off into the pain they all felt when the memory would —unbidden—gnaw at their ignoring consciousness.

"It's not for them either, really."

Now she looked truly confused. "I don't . . . But I thought . . . The girl . . ."

". . . is dead," he finished for her. "Nothing I'm going to do will ever bring her back."

"Then why?"

Xenos stood, looked at her, then started for the door. "Forget it."

Then he stopped, his back still to her, and spoke in a somehow *different* voice.

"I see . . . everything. I look at a situation and can immediately tell you what the outcome will be, what it *could* be, and how to make it come out the way you want it to."

"I've heard of the Four Phase programs," she said with a slight awe. "I heard that . . ."

"Forget what you heard," the bitterest laugh she'd ever been witness to responded. "They teach technique, not vision. That's why the programs turn out maybe two graduates every twenty years or so.

"Four Phase Men are born, not created. We're different— more perceptive, less caring—and all the training does is heighten that difference. That, and one other thing.

"It's drilled into us—at least it was to me—that we're not responsible, the planners and the doers. Oh, the politicians are sometimes responsible, the bad guys are *always* responsible, but not their instruments. By definition, the planners and the doers have clean souls and light hearts." He laughed again. "Just ask them."

He slowly turned to face the stunned woman, who had never expected to ever reach through to this man who had become so important to her and her children's lives.

"That was the basic problem between my father and me," he said simply. "He'd chosen to live a life absent violence. He accepted that mantle and that burden and remade himself in what he perceived as God's plan for him. But he'd never insist that anyone else do as he did. It was too personal a choice."

"Then, what happened?" Valerie asked quietly, trying to respect the moment but captivated by the soul-unveiling taking place in front of her.

"Papa knew what I was even before I did." Xenos began to pace. "So he tried to teach me the code of the Maccabees, the Jewish warriors who threw the Assyrians and Greeks out of Palestine, despite being outnumbered one hundred to one. I just never quite got it. I saw the tactics, the heroism, the glory, the pride in country and purpose; but missed the point."

His posture, body language, tone of voice, all begged Valerie to understand.

"The Maccabees, you see, believed that once you do a thing— large or small—all the future consequences of that act were your responsibility. No justifications, doublethinks, or rationalizations to it. Simple: do it, and the fallout belongs to you. Period.

"For years, I allowed the flags and the medals and the pomp and the *words* to obscure that. To take me off the hook. Until finally my soul was gone. Withered, irredeemable, damned. I ran away from my job, my family, I hoped from God."

He shook his head. "But you can't, not really."

He rolled his head, stretched, was the picture of a man whose body was slowly being taken over by cramps, muscle strain, or . . . guilt.

"You've met Herb."

"Sure." Valerie spoke quietly, afraid to break the mood.

Xenos shook his head. "Helluva guy. Really. I owe him a lot that I *am* going to pay back to him one day." He breathed deeply several times. "He found me in college, I was on a music scholarship."

"Really?"

He tilted his head to the side as if to see a cockeyed world around him. "I was young, desperate to change the world, without a clue as to how.

"Herb showed me."

Settling on the edge of the table, Xenos seemed lost in himself, looking not at Valerie, but at some moment in a distant past.

"I don't know how he found me, how he picked me." A bitter laugh. "Just came looking, I guess.

"Oh, he understood me so well." His voice grew, well, absent. "Knew I was different, knew that I knew it. Knew how to reach me like nobody else in my life." He shook his head. "He promised me that, together, we could change the world."

He stood up, shoulders bent inward, head down, his voice barely audible. "We changed it." The big man seemed to be shrinking in front of her; seemed one giant lump of pain.

Then, suddenly, a strange thing happened.

He straightened, as if forced away from the memories by some inner drive to hold himself up and face the woman a foot or less away.

"I never intended to do any of this," he said in a stronger voice. "It's just that recently, I've needed to, I've been, well . . ." He took a deep breath. "When Gabi died in my arms, when I looked around at all the children lying there like broken toys . . ." He shook his head sadly, mystified by himself, then turned and walked out of the room.

"Please!" Valerie called after him. "Please."

He stopped, then came back to her.

"When I saved you, even before—as soon as I became involved in looking for Paolo—everything that followed became my responsibility. Herb wouldn't agree. I doubt that Colin would even agree, although he'd understand." He shook his head with finality. "Now I have to live with that, somehow make it right again."

Valerie shook her head. "But what you did saved lives. Mine, others, maybe—please God—my children. How can that be a bad thing?"

Xenos never moved, never blinked or breathed. "I should've let them kill us," he said flatly. "You, me, your children."

"How could you?"

"Easily," was the atonal reply. "But because I didn't, the Chinese takeover of the government which would've happened peacefully—without fuss or bother or notice—has become the prelude to war. Because of what I did, a hundred thousand people could die. Maybe more. I can see it! Lay it out in detail to you with numbers, throw weights, troop movements, and strike contours! Christ!" He picked up a newspaper from a nearby table. "It's all there if you want to see it!"

He threw the paper across the room.

"And I *always* see it," he muttered sadly.

His shoulders dropped, his head bowed, he began to shuffle away. "And it's my responsibility. I started it. I'm the only one who can stop it."

Torn between thinking of Xenos as a madman or as a prophet —as both—Valerie looked down at the paper, then back at the man who seemed covered in blood and guilt.

"*Can* you stop it?" she asked weakly.

He sighed. "Don't be late," was his only comment as he sat down at a computer terminal and began to work.

She watched him for a moment, shivered uncontrollably, then hurried out to Fabrè in the waiting car.

In the subbasement of his headquarters, in a room protected against nuclear attack and twenty-first-century eavesdropping, Herb turned to the attorney general designate, eyeing him suspiciously.

"It's your dime, Senator."

"Where you been, Herb?" Buckley's answer was an expressionless stare. "Let me put it another way. How close are you to figuring out the shit that's been going on?"

"I'm sure you're more on top of that than I am," Herb said easily. "It *was* your commission."

Buckley smiled, an oddly unsettling expression. "I also sat on a committee with access to the Pei interrogations." A brief pause. "Interesting reading in light of recent developments."

"Whatever are you suggesting?" Herb was going to make the man commit himself before reacting.

A fact the senator seemed to understand. "My commission," he began easily, "dealt with evidence, not conjecture. The FBI, the CIA, the president, and the American people all believe the Taiwanese are responsible for this crisis. Who am I to argue?"

"Yes," the old intelligence chief agreed, "which makes you a wonderful candidate to be Pei's traitor—this Apple Blossom."

Buckley smiled, charmingly, happily, completely at ease. "But I'm not, and I think we both know that."

"I only know what I read in the papers."

"Then read these papers—originals with no copies—from my commission's, uh, *parallel* investigation."

Herb began flipping through the files. "And why would you investigate Messieurs Kingston and DeWitt?"

The senator stood to leave. "Call it a hunch. Call it jealousy. Call it anything you want."

Herb looked up at the man. "These are exactly the kinds of things I'd expect the real traitor to come up with."

Buckley chuckled. "Yeah. I thought of that." The door closed behind him.

Hours later Herb turned to the two other men who had been with him since Buckley left.

He knew them each intimately, had recruited them individually out of the service or college, had personally investigated them each time he'd advanced their careers.

Had done so again in the days since his return to Washington.

"Simply put, boys, I'm asking you all to commit treason on the most serious levels possible."

Nobody moved, spoke, or even raised an eyebrow. They just sat, waiting. Each man had a copy of Buckley's files, and there were nine cartons of other files stacked against the far wall.

Cartons labeled: Buckley, Kingston, and DeWitt.

"I want ideas," the old man said with pride as he looked at their professionally receptive faces, "propositions, thoughts. Three areas.

"One: how do we slow down the Kingston nomination?

"Two: how do we slow down the DeWitt confirmation?

"Three: which one of them is Apple Blossom?"

One of the men looked up from the papers. "How do you

know you can trust Buckley? He fits the profile as tightly as the other two."

"Four," Herb answered quickly, "can we trust the good senator?"

"How long do we have?" the taller one asked.

"Almost no time."

"Assets available?" the other asked calmly.

Herb shrugged. "The three of us. Whatever resources we can steal or subvert."

"Why don't we just kill all three, take no chances on guessing wrong?" one of the men who were pale knockoffs of the man in the warehouse asked.

"I'd like to avoid that. At least for now."

The men thought about it for a few minutes. Then the talking began.

Within an hour, a favorite emerged. Within another twenty minutes, they all began to believe in their choice. Two hours after that, a general plan had been agreed on.

It was raw, without sophistication or contingencies—but Xenos would add those, Herb knew. And it was risky beyond measure.

But, with a little luck, it would *work*.

Avidol found Xenos sitting on the warehouse roof. Looking up at the stars, fiddling with a pad, distracted in the way he'd become ever since he was a child when he was deep in thought.

"Jerry? How are you?"

Xenos jumped up and helped his father to one of the several lawn chairs that had been set up there. "Papa, you shouldn't be up here. You should rest."

Avidol shook his head firmly. "My place is where I am needed." He kissed his son on the hand. "And you need me, no?"

"I, I've hurt you. Got you shot, made you violate your strongest principles and values. I'm surprised you're even talking to me."

Avidol patted the hand he wouldn't release. "We are all free wills in this world. God's only promise to individual men. We make our choices. You chose to save your family when running away again would've been easier. I chose to kill a man rather than be killed."

He sighed. "It is a thing I will remember until I die. An irretrievable act that violated my most basic beliefs." The slightest hesitation. "But I am prepared to take responsibility for that act."

He moaned as he adjusted himself in the seat. "Maybe we both compromised, but our choice was life, and there can be no sin in that."

"I'm not so sure."

"You must be, Chuni."

The old man reached over, turning his son's face to him. "Evil has many faces, many guises. Few can recognize it beneath its beauty. But you can. You have."

Xenos nodded. "And I've started something worse because of it."

"You think so? I wonder."

"What is there to wonder about?" the morose man asked as he leaned back and stared up at the starry night.

"Let me ask you, not as a father—but as a teacher—do you still believe in God?"

"Yes," came the delayed response. "I just don't think he believes in me anymore."

"Really," Avidol said in a professorial tone. "Then why has he made you responsible for so much?"

"He didn't. I did."

"No!" It was an unequivocal statement of fact. "Einstein said it better than all the Talmudic scholars in all the centuries of our history." He paused. "God does not play dice with the universe.

"We are, to God, strange creatures. Capable of gaining Heaven or creating our own Hell. But it is always our choice. He set us in motion in Eden, and the rest has been of us, alone. He will not interfere in our lives, other than to place the tools of Heaven or Hell within our grasp. And always in equal balance."

He frowned. "God does not want a suicide any more than a murderer. If I do not kill, then I allow myself to be killed. God's paradox."

"Papa, it's cold. We should go inside."

But the old man refused to move.

"You see, Chuni, God offered these same tools to the Chinese and this Canvas fellow. They chose the path to Hell. But he also gave *you* the tools, the responsibility. You have chosen Heaven and accepted the responsibility."

"For a situation I created." The younger man sounded beyond bleak.

Avidol shook his head as if trying to explain the alphabet to a child who refused to believe *F* followed *E*.

"Jerry, whether lives would be lost now or in the future, the same lives would be lost. This is the inevitability of evil. The rest is only timing. This Canvas was born to be the right arm of the Chinese at this time in this place. His entire life—for good or ill—is what has placed him here. Not the money or bad breaks or political beliefs.

"But," and the old man smiled warmly, "God has also given you your life. A thing of twists and turns, blackness and pain and isolation. But a thing that has given you what you need to stand up to this evil. As God's strong right arm!"

Xenos stared into his father's intense eyes, inhaling the strength and purpose he saw there.

"And from the moment of your birth," Avidol said flatly as if God had told him himself, "the responsibility has been yours." He shrugged. "Everything that's happened in the last weeks has been mere details."

A young Corsican appeared on the roof. "Dureté, the jar is opening."

Xenos nodded and started for the door. "Are you going to be all right?"

"Sure, go."

A moment later, when he was alone on the roof looking up at the magnificent pageantry of the constellations and planets, Avidol sighed deeply and closed his eyes.

"Dear God, give my boy the strength he needs." He paused, almost unwilling to give voice to the thought that was almost a betrayal. "And let me be right."

. . .

O'Neill watched the young woman until she turned the corner. Smiling and waving to her as she disappeared from sight. Then he picked up a cell phone from under his seat.

The phone was answered on the first ring. "Yeah?"

"The jar is empty," O'Neill whispered.

"We're ready," was followed by the click of the line disconnecting.

Barbara had gotten out of the Bible salesman's car a block away from the house. After the night's battles and terrors, she was taking no chances now. She didn't *see* any surveillance on the street, everything looked calm and normal. But . . .

Twice she'd thought about calling the emergency number again. Each time deciding against it. Because the more she thought about it, the more she began to realize that it was a damned short list of who would want her dead and who had the resources to put together a professional hit team like the men in the vans.

And the Apple Blossom chain was at the top of that list.

It could be that she had outlived her usefulness to them. Or maybe they were just tidying up before anything could go wrong at the sonofabitch's hearings.

It also occurred to the young woman as she fished in her purse for the keys to the co-op she secretly owned with Valerie (*her* house was out of the question for now) that it could be other, even more sinister forces that were trying to kill her. A vengeful CIA or NSC that had discovered the plot and were cleaning house to avoid a public scandal.

But—in either event—she would clean up, get something to eat, *definitely* something to drink, then think about her next move.

She let herself in the side door, waiting to turn on the lights in the entry hall until she'd locked the door behind her.

"Hello, Barbara," a familiar voice called out softly from the dark behind her.

"What . . ."

She never finished the thought as her ribs seemed to explode with pain as Valerie's baseball bat crashed into them.

The furious congresswoman watched as Fabrè picked up the screaming woman with the broken ribs and tossed her on the couch. A quick search of her, a nod to Valerie, and the assassin stepped out from between the women.

"You and I have a lot of catching up to do," Valerie hissed as she took the bat and held it under her chief of staff's chin, painfully bending it back.

"Take your time," she said as Barbara struggled to catch her breath. "But you be thorough, like you've always been, old *friend*, when you tell me where my babies are. Get it right the first time."

Valerie paused, releasing the younger woman's chin and leaning in so close that Barbara could smell the rage on her when she spoke.

"We have the rest of your life."

Fourteen

Tony Grimes was a pillar and leader of the horsey set of northern Virginia.

Tony Grimes was a man of breeding and culture, an example proudly pointed to by the poor people of Bricks Hollow, South Carolina—the scene of his humble beginnings.

Tony Grimes was an internationally renowned artist, sculptor, composer. A man whose works had never pleased the critics but received an almost unprecedented public acceptance . . . giving him a "simple, humble" platform on which to hold forth on everything from the Super Bowl to international relations.

And, as he looked out across his large farm from the back of his prize American saddlebred stallion, he smiled.

Everything as far as he could see was his. The old-growth trees, the ten-thousand-square-foot mansion with the priceless Edwardian antiques, the vintage barn that held the even more vintage car collection, the small collection of guesthouses—barely visible in the distance through the trees—with his aspiring ballerina mistress and wanna-be sculptor mister. It was a multiglutton's paradise constructed from the blackness of a mind that still saw itself as shoeless, voiceless, powerless, amid a youth of terror.

As he gently urged the big horse on, the smile grew as he thought of the days to come, the days at hand.

Within a year he would be a nightly commentator on the largest network news show. Within three years, the de facto head of one of the most powerful communications networks in the world. Within eight years, the "de facto" replaced by permanence.

And all those from the years before Apple Blossom—those who had ignored, dismissed, or brutishly silenced the arrogant little boy who *knew* he was better than the rest—would be forced to listen! To obey! To follow!

All because he'd opted to attend college for a brief time in England.

The horse hesitated, sensing the electronic cable that ran just under the ground in front of it. Grimes dismounted, tied the animal to a nearby bush, and went on by foot.

Twenty minutes later—in a hollow of trees and rock in a left-wild part of the farm—he nodded at the guards.

"Good morning."

"Mr. Grimes," one of the heavily armed guards said into his radio. He nodded at the response that came through his earpiece. "Go ahead, sir."

Grimes pulled out a Havana Blanca Montefiore, carefully wet the end between his lips, then took his time lighting it. Ritual satisfied, he continued on into the first of five—connected—concrete and metal outbuildings in front of him.

"Sir," the guard just inside the door said as he opened the interior door for him. Grimes just nodded and walked on, the door shut and locked behind him.

The room was small—almost an antechamber—with three steel doors on the far wall, a desk with a television monitor on the near wall.

"How are they?" he asked the guard at the desk.

"Still not eating right," the guard said as he logged Grimes in. "Stubborn. The boy's lost maybe fifteen pounds since he got here. The girl just sleeps, mostly."

Grimes bent over the monitor, watching the split-screen picture of a young boy and a younger girl—both staring blankly across their bare room of a cot and little else.

"What about ice cream?" he offered. "Kids love ice cream."

"How would you know?" a voice asked him from behind.

"I was a kid once." Grimes smiled as he turned and held out his hand. "How're you doing, Jeff?"

DeWitt looked angry. "How the fuck do you think I'm doing? Taking a chance like this at this stage!"

Grimes led the vice president designate into a comfortable side room and poured them both a drink.

"What's to worry about? The great man needs a moment of retreat in his moment of trial and triumph. What more natural way than to spend the night with an old friend—a national treasure— who by just standing next to you gives you the Good Housekeeping Seal of Approval."

DeWitt downed the drink in one long gulp. "If the Secret Service got wind of what's going on . . ."

Grimes sighed and shook his head. "You always worried too much."

DeWitt poured himself another drink. "Why the meeting, Tony?"

Grimes settled into an overstuffed chair. "It's decision time, old friend. And certain, well, *others* thought you ought to be included."

"Go on."

"The committee votes in three days, the full Senate the following Monday. Our Eastern friends feel that all loose ends should be wrapped up before then."

Now DeWitt made a show of sitting down in a deeply relaxed way. "And . . ."

"Well," Grimes said easily, "there's still the issue of your *playmates.*"

DeWitt sipped his drink. "Any of them even *seem* to be about to cause trouble and they're gone. Period." He smiled; a pleasant thing, yet filled with sharp teeth and the slightest drool. "They're just pussy anyway."

"And my houseguests?" Grimes looked steadily into the handsome man's eyes, wondering what he would've done if the positions were reversed.

"Get rid of them."

Grimes shook his head. "Whores are one thing. Kids are another." He paused, leaning close to the other man. "No euphemisms, Jeff. You want something done, you're going to have to come out and say it."

DeWitt studied the artist for a long moment, then nodded. He leaned forward, then suddenly grabbed the man by the throat, throwing him to the ground. His left hand held Grimes down while the right roughly searched every inch of the man's body for a hidden microphone. When he was done, he pushed his face into the other's and virtually growled.

"You wouldn't be doubling on me, would you, Tony?"

"There's no wire."

DeWitt nodded and thrust his hand into the man's groin. "I know," he said as he felt around. "But convince me anyway."

"I'm not wired," Grimes almost whispered. "But I'm also not going to take the responsibility for killing two kids—high-profile kids—on my own."

He took a deep breath. "And fucking Canvas says one of us has to. So I figure it might as well be you." Another pause, this followed by an expression of commitment and fear. "There's some things I'm not real comfortable doing, you know?"

DeWitt nodded, patronizingly patted the man on the cheek, then got off him. "I do know." He straightened his clothes, ran his fingers through his hair, then reached down and helped the artist— would-be media king—up. "That's why I'm going to be president and you're just going to watch."

Grimes didn't move. "You still haven't said anything, *Mr. President*," he said with bite and vitriol.

DeWitt smiled and nodded. "Then listen to this. After my confirmation, after my swearing in as vice president, as soon as I'm in a position to move on the old man"—he seemed to consider something—"Tuesday, Wednesday would be even better." He picked up his drink. "Kill the little fuckers." His voice was calm and steady. "Grab them by the hair, pull their angelic little faces up to Heaven, and cut their fucking throats."

He raised his glass in a toast. "God bless America."

. . .

In another room, less than twenty feet away, another man—a man who seemed to always be there (in an invisible sort of way)—stopped the video recorder that was connected to a tiny camera in the ceiling light, then pocketed the "edge" he'd promised Steingarth, to help keep DeWitt in line.

"Amen," he said softly as he started out of the room. "Amen."

One by one they met with Xenos, told their stories, and conveyed their information, given their assessments. They'd walked into his small workroom, spoken briefly, answered terse questions, then been asked to send in the next. No questions entertained by the man who continued to sketch as they talked.

He kept the room dark, illuminated only by a pale blue bulb, the sound of midnight jazz quietly filling the air. He never looked up at them, never changed expression, took no notes. Remained a blank cipher with no key—with no reactions—to even *begin* interpreting.

Herb ignored it. He'd known the man the longest and had at least a rudimentary education in "Xenos 101." Years ago, Xenos had called these moods *sponge time,* and the veteran of all of America's cold wars had come to respect them. He saw it as a time of sifting, shifting, screening. A time that would eventually lead to action . . . and someone's death.

So he busied himself reworking *the package* he'd prepared at Xenos's direction, trying to decide which order what facts should be in for maximum effect. Knowing that the man in the room would have still more changes when the time came. Knowing that the requirements his former star pupil had given him were next to impossible to fulfill. But knowing that his dedicatedly amoral staff would somehow fill them.

And he never looked up at the clock.

Because times like this just couldn't be rushed.

Franco had briefed his friend on the arrival of the Corsican hit teams. Twenty-six of the toughest, most violent, most feared men in the world. All wanted by the police of most of Europe. He'd personally selected the eighteen he would work with, assigning the others to Fabrè.

No specific plans could be made yet—actually Franco expected only to be involved in the final details of the planning—but their time was well spent . . . breaking down and cleaning their weapons, whetting their blades and appetites.

Valerie and Vedette had jointly reported to the Four Phase Man. Barbara's admission had been vague but probably truthful. She knew the children were being held on a farm in northern Virginia. The Corsican surveillance expert knew that the trace on the call Barbara had made led to one of five farms in that part of the state.

But beyond that . . . nothing.

It was frustrating beyond belief for Valerie. To be so close to her children—all the while not wholly believing they were still alive —was maddening. She alternately felt energized and exhausted. Filled with hope and despairing beyond gloom. But her assistant had sworn through broken ribs and spit blood and teeth that they *were* alive.

Valerie clung to that.

As she was sure that the clock had stopped moving out of pure spite.

Albina's had been the strangest briefing of them all. The infiltration master—who they said had gotten into more places than Mediterranean cockroaches—had arrived at the warehouse in a spectacularly expensive suit, leather briefcase to match, and credentials around his neck showing him to be *Eleventh Floor Special* —*Cleared,* bearing the seal of the Department of Justice.

He'd been brought straight in to see Xenos, had stayed the longest of any of them. When he'd finished, he hadn't waited around for the coming meeting. Instead he'd quickly changed into a maintenance man's uniform, then sat for an hour at an embroidery machine, comparing his work with several pictures from a magazine or program. Finally, with Velcroed shoulder patches that said *Veterans Stadium—Event Staff,* he'd hurried away.

Fabrè had taken his eight men in to see Xenos for three minutes only. They exited almost as soon as they'd arrived and now sat in the back of the warehouse—calmly reading pornographic magazines while occasionally readjusting the knives or guns strapped to their waists and ankles.

Waiting like the cocked weapons that they were.

The waiting was the hardest for Avidol. He'd nothing to contribute beyond his emotional support; had no clear idea of what was happening around him. But he could smell the tension, the fear, the unknown demon that floated through the large room, tapping them each on the shoulder at unexpected moments, then moving on.

He knew the stakes: he knew that two small children waited to die or be reunited with their mother. He knew that a world stood poised at the brink of a war that could kill hundreds of thousands. He knew that America—the place that his father had called *the world's only hope*—was faced with a betrayal that would go unnoticed by the over 250 million that would suffer for it.

He knew that a God less generous than Avidol had always believed had given his son this burden.

So he would sit, wait—ignore the pain that radiated down his neck, the growing numbness of his arms and legs, the occasionally blurring vision—and he *would* be there for his boy, his Chuni.

His immortality.

Inside the small room, Xenos put the finishing details on his sketch.

The facts, figures, possibilities, and abstractions floated somewhere in the back of his mind. Things that some other part of him dealt with. His *consciousness* was directed down to the sketch in the half-light. To the delicate flicks of the pencil, the slight smears of the eraser, the blank expression of the face that looked back up at him.

Then he was done.

Letting the pencil drop from his hand, he stared down at the portrait, curiously examining its twists, turns, knolls, and crags. It was less an expression of the man who was the subject than it was a representation of the man's mind. A thing of angles, turns, false paths, and unlimited options.

Xenos looked into the eyes—so much his own—tried to feel the man who might have been his brother. Tried to know his soul.

If he still possessed one.

For Xenos no longer did, he was sure of that.

But souls were for dreamy-eyed poets and limp-wristed priests. People that had no measurable experience in the *real world* of living demons and killer angels. People who still believed that life was superior to death and that the differences between good and evil mattered.

He cried.

Oh, the pain that still racked his healing body could have been the cause. The guilt he felt over the death of innocent orphans or the near killing of his family would have been more than enough to evoke the tears. And the pain he'd inflicted on the world in the last twenty years or so *did* well up in him as a wrenching reminder of a lost God and life.

But none of that really explained the silent tears that dripped off his stubbled face and onto the page, smearing the sketch.

It was the simple, inexplicably rational pain of knowing that he would never see Jerry Goldman in the mirror again that made it feel as if something was breaking inside of him.

For long minutes he sobbed, slowly gaining control, using deep breaths and the disciplined mind that he'd always had. He put the pain in its proper place—the home where it would emerge in nightmares and life—then reached into his pocket.

He watched the match tip flare to life, momentarily caught up in the blue-orange fury of the flame, then touched it to the sketch.

He watched the merged face of Colin Meadows and Jerry Goldman slowly consumed and obliterated by the cleansing fire.

Herb stopped dialing a secure phone in midnumber.

A card froze in Franco's hand in the midst of his game of hearts.

Valerie's heart stopped.

Avidol slowly stood . . . as the door opened and Xenos stepped out.

"We go on Saturday," he said simply to the silenced warehouse. "It ends on Saturday."

Thursday

The committee members casually settled into their chairs, arranging staff-prepared notes, sipping ice water, slouching down. This was the last day of testimony on a slam-dunk nomination. The president wanted DeWitt, no pictures of him playing golf with Charles Manson or raping Mother Teresa had surfaced; the man had been equal parts charming, stirring, self-effacing, and arrogant. His poll numbers were higher than the president's or any member of the joint House/Senate Judiciary Committee, and with war probably less than a week away, each person behind the green baize table felt it was a personal responsibility to make the DeWitt confirmation his or her part in the coming war effort.

Well, not *each* person.

Senator Shawn Roberts of California had his doubts. DeWitt was too slick, too *prepared*. There was something basically unlikable about the man when you met him close up. But these were not things you denied a man the second highest office in the land for.

Still, Roberts had his staff make extra inquiries into DeWitt's past, just to satisfy his feelings of, well, *discomfort* at the prospect of Jefferson DeWitt being a heartbeat away from the presidency. But nothing had been found. The man was as squeaky-clean as any child of the sixties could be.

So, moments before the members began their final round of questioning of the man they would vote unanimously for tomorrow, Roberts was literally and figuratively washing his hands of the business when he heard the bathroom door open and close behind him.

He looked up to see Herb Stone standing just inside, studying him.

"Director Stone."

"Senator."

The two men just looked at each other for long moments.

"Is there something I can do for you, Mr. Stone?"

Herb had thought long and hard about that question. If he answered it, he would be committing an inarguably treasonable offense. If he didn't, his sin of omission might be even greater.

The "evidence" he'd come to deliver was carefully false. A construct—by his amoral but deeply loyal staff—that had been perfected, fine-tuned by Xenos, himself. The former intelligence prodigy had then studied the classified psychological profiles of the members of the committee, conferred with the ambitious Senator Buckley (through Herb), then decided whom the package would be presented to and how.

But if this went bad, if the man in front of him began to suspect, then a lengthy prison stay would be the least of the concerns Herb would have for the future.

"Mr. Stone . . ."

Taking a deep breath, Herb began, as he listened to the gentle breathing coming through his hidden earpiece.

"Senator Roberts, do you believe in monsters?"

"Excuse me?" Roberts dried his hands and started pulling on his jacket.

"Monsters, Senator. Slavering beasts which lurk in the dark waiting for an unsuspecting innocent to wander by."

Roberts smiled easily. "If politics has taught me anything, Mr. Stone, it's that there are all kinds of monsters." He hesitated as he studied the old man in front of him. "The trick is to know one when you see it."

Herb nodded. "And to know whose side they're on."

"Good afternoon," the senator said brusquely after a long pause as he stepped toward the door.

Herb moved in front of him. "Monsters, Senator, come in all sorts of shapes and sizes. Some even wearing Armani suits and welcoming smiles."

Roberts froze. "What do you have?"

Herb hesitated, then handed the thick file over to the cautious man. He watched closely as the man began reading. First casually flipping through the mixture of forged, composited, and real documents and photographs, then slowly taking in or reading each one completely.

These are dangerous times, Xenos's voice whispered through Herb's earpiece.

"These are dangerous times, Senator," Herb said softly. "Times when words such as . . ." He paused, seemed to cock his head slightly, then continued. "Words such as duty, honor, country must be given their true meaning or banished to oblivion."

Roberts nodded absently as he read. "Unbelievable," he muttered.

They said terrorism in America was unbelievable.

"They said terrorism in America was unbelievable," Herb continued. "That it could never happen here."

"I was at the World Trade Center," the senator mumbled, "trapped for two hours . . ." His voice trailed off.

Herb looked genuinely surprised. "Indeed?"

And they said monsters . . .

"And they said monsters are unbelievable. Fictions created by fevered imaginations and ignorance." He paused, listened, then continued. "How ignorant are you, Senator?"

"This will have to go to staff for further investigation . . ."

"So that it can be properly explained and cleared up," Herb interrupted, "without the public ever being the wiser?"

The man looked up at him, his expression a mixture of fear and anger. "What are you suggesting?"

Herb seemed to be distracted for a moment, then he smiled, a thing quickly put away in place of a stern, reproving look.

"Senator," he said simply, "are you the stuff that heroes are made of?" He hesitated. "Or are you too afraid of the dark?"

Two minutes later Herb stood alone in the bathroom.

"You have an obscene understanding of human nature, my boy," he said with a growing grin.

Wonder where I got that from, was the whispered reply. *Pickup's waiting at the South Portico. You have a plane to catch.* The connection went dead.

"The committee will come to order," the senator intoned emotionlessly. "This final round of questioning will be limited to ten minutes each. All members are requested to relinquish any time they may not require." He turned to DeWitt, who sat smiling in his new Armani suit, with a welcoming smile beaming from his clean-cut-image face. "Mr. Attorney General, do you have any final statements to make?"

"No, Mr. Chairman. Except to say that I appreciate the thoroughness, courtesies, and the fine job done by yourself and the committee. It makes me proud to be a part of such a fine and democratic process."

"Thank you, Mr. Attorney General." The chairman looked to the end of the table. "Senator Hawkins."

"Thank you, Mr. Chairman. I have only one question for our esteemed nominee. Mr. Attorney General, having experienced the confirmation process, can you give this committee—and through it the Congress as a whole—any advice on how we might improve it? With an eye toward rapidity of confirmation and fair treatment of nominees."

DeWitt thought about it.

"Essentially, Senator, I believe this committee has not only done a fine job, a complete job, and shown that when exigencies require it, it can move with alacrity and dispatch without sacrificing thoroughness. My experience with you has been pleasant, gratifying, sobering, and a privilege. I wouldn't presume to change a thing. Do your jobs, ladies and gentlemen. Probe, question, investigate, and compel those who appear before you to be equally forthright in their responses. In that event, I can see nowhere to improve."

"Thank you." The senator smiled back. "Mr. Chairman, I relinquish back the remainder of my time."

The chairman looked toward the other end of the table. "Senator Weiss?"

"Mr. Chairman, I have no further questions of my good friend from Wisconsin and gladly relinquish back my time so that we may expedite his confirmation."

The chairman sighed and turned to his right. "Senator Roberts?"

Roberts held the closed file in both hands. This was one of those rare moments that he believed came once or twice in a man's life. Those times when he must either accept his place as a power-less member of the silent majority or step off into the dark chasm of moral certainty and minority.

There was no way to know if the allegations contained in the file were true or not—although they had the veneer of truth about them—but there was no way to test that truth either. Not and allow the public to judge fairly for themselves.

If the file was accurate, then DeWitt *was* a monster. If not, then Stone was the monster. And the only way to find out was to shine the sun on them both and see who dissolved.

Or so thought the senator who had once written a paper in college entitled "Monsters: A History of Corruption in American Politics."

A paper—folded, yellowed, decaying—that had found a home in an ultraclassified psychological profile of the man.

"Good morning, Mr. DeWitt."

"Good morning, Senator."

Roberts opened the file, took a deep breath, then pulled out the last sheet. A list of questions and follow-ups.

"I just have a few things I'd like to clarify, for the record."

DeWitt nodded. "That's why I'm here, Senator." He looked completely relaxed, his aide slouched down in his seat, the other senators went about their business.

"You were a student at Barnsdahl College in Wilfordshire, England, is that correct?"

"For two and a half years prior to my obtaining my postgrad-uate degrees at the University of Wisconsin, Madison, yes."

"And at Barnsdahl you received a bachelor of arts degree in international relations?"

DeWitt nodded. "International justice, actually. But that takes in much the same turf as an American B.A. in international rela-tions, Senator."

Roberts made a note in the file. The first mistake in its con-tents he'd found. But that could just be a misinterpretation of titles. "You were assigned to the international section, a group of stu-dents mainly drawn from countries other than Great Britain."

"I think there were about eleven countries represented, yes."

"Who is Rupert Everttson?"

DeWitt looked surprised. "Uh, I believe he was one of my professors at Barnsdahl."

One fact proved.

Roberts handed two copies of a document (provided in the file) to an aide, who delivered one to the chair and the other to DeWitt.

"For the record, Rupert Everttson was a professor of European history at Barnsdahl for over twenty years. Barnsdahl records show that Mr. DeWitt took three courses given by him."

Michael suddenly sat up. "Why doesn't he use your title?" he whispered.

DeWitt ignored him.

"Who is James Fergét?" Roberts folded his hands and waited for an answer.

"Uh . . ." DeWitt seemed off balance. "If you mean Jimmy Fergét, he was a Haitian student. We were in some study groups together." His mind raced for any connection between the effete Everttson, the nigger savant Fergét, and Apple Blossom.

But none came to mind.

Another fact confirmed, and from DeWitt's manner, Roberts suspected that there were more to come. "Do you recall how often, or in what context, you would meet privately with Professor Everttson or Mr. Fergét?"

DeWitt was shaking his head without realizing it. He couldn't remember much beyond their names. But then he'd spent so little time actually in class or on campus it was hard to remember much about that time.

"Senator, all I can tell you is that it was a long time ago, many years. My time at Barnsdahl was exhilarating and hectic. Filled with constant new experiences, new faces. I, uh, am ashamed to say that I would be hard-pressed to remember many of the names and faces I encountered casually during those years."

"Perfectly understandable," Roberts said easily. "Maybe I can help you out." More documents were passed out. "For the record, will the committee mark these as Roberts Two, Three, and Four, respectively?"

The chairman glanced at the two black-and-white photographs and the one document, humphed, and nodded. "So
marked."

"Thank you, Mr. Chairman. Mr. DeWitt, do you recognize
yourself in the photos marked Roberts Two and Three?"

DeWitt never looked up from the casually taken photos of
himself with a fellow student and a professor. The kind of thing
he'd posed for dozens of times, as souvenirs for the other students
who wanted to remember their "great college adventure."

"Yeah, uh, yes. That is me in the center of Roberts Two, and
on the extreme left in Roberts Three."

He looked up and reconstituted his smile. These people had
nothing to do with Apple Blossom, and he'd had little to do with
them at the time. Wherever the senator was going, there was nothing there.

"If it assists you," Dewitt added, "I believe that the black man
in both pictures is Mr. Fergét and the older man Professor Everttson."

Roberts chuckled professionally. "You anticipate me, sir." He
turned a page in the file. "Did you stay in contact with either
Professor Everttson or Mr. Fergét after you left Barnsdahl?"

DeWitt noticeably relaxed, although Michael was talking quietly—but urgently—on his cell phone. "Senator, as I said, it was a
great many years ago. How many of us have maintained contact
with old college buddies or acquaintances? Particularly those that
reside in other countries." He spread his hands in a gesture of
befuddled frustration. "Perhaps if you gave a more specific context?"

Roberts made more notes in the file. Each question on the list
had accurately anticipated DeWitt's responses. As did the next one,
which was typed in red capital letters. Casually, Roberts read it
aloud.

"Mr. DeWitt, to *be* more specific, I'll quote from a certified
copy of a statement released by New Scotland Yard on March
twenty-sixth of 1973." He waited for the copies to be delivered,
then began in a strong voice.

"Professor Rupert Everttson, late of Barnsdahl College in

Wilfordshire, has been taken into custody on charges of serving as an intermediary for the KGB."

A rumble went through the room.

"It is alleged by the Crown Prosecution Service that Professor Everttson acted as a recruitment officer for the KGB at Barnsdahl and later as a 'post office' for those he recruited to send their stolen secrets on to their KGB masters.

"Also taken into custody was Professor Everttson's lover, a Haitian national, James Fergét. Mr. Fergét is actively cooperating in identifying those recruited by Professor Everttson."

DeWitt was red with anger. "Senator! Are you suggesting . . ."

But Roberts held up a restraining hand. "All I'm doing is seeking the truth, Mr. DeWitt."

The chairman pounded his gavel five times before order was restored. "Mr. Attorney General, you may finish your answer."

DeWitt hardly knew where to start. His greatest nightmare had been to be discovered as an agent for the Chinese. He'd lost count of the nights he'd wake up screaming in terror at the thought/nightmare. But this, to be tarred by the brush of something he'd never been involved in . . .

He glanced at a note from Michael. It said, simply and unmistakably: *Moral outrage!!!!!*

"Thank you, Mr. Chairman." He took a deep breath, then turned to face Roberts eye-to-eye. "Senator, this country has spent too much time in the past debating half-truths and innuendos. Joseph McCarthy and Ken Starr both used that despicable tactic—the whispered half-truth, the sourceless leak, the *knowledgeable source* —to destroy the lives and reputations of some good men and women.

"If you have an allegation to make, sir, make it aloud and specifically, man to man. But before you do, let me state this clearly and for the record."

He seemed to gather himself. Like a volcano growing quiet before the final eruption.

"My record, my life, my very being, reject your smarmy implications. That I have to say this aloud saddens me deeply, that the monument of my life is not evidence enough to the contrary, I find deeply disheartening. But let me say it now, for the record and for all time. I have *never been*—now or at any time in my past—an agent for the Soviets. And I am filled with repugnance at the insinuation in your line of questioning!"

Scatterings of applause filled the chamber as all eyes turned to Roberts.

The senator nodded, not in awe or respect for the brilliantly displayed moral outrage in front of him, but in admiration that the question list had anticipated that *exact* response—almost to the words.

He waited until he was sure he had the complete attention of the crowd, the nominee, and the committee before he handed another document for delivery. Then he read the next question, certain now that the file contents *must* be accurate.

"I am reading from an uncertified copy of a statement from Mr. James Fergét given freely to New Scotland Yard investigators in 1974. Quote: *I do not know their names, his name, but I am certain in my belief that there was at least one American recruited by Rupert in his time at Barnsdahl.* Unquote."

Roberts paused.

"Mr. DeWitt, please don't misunderstand me. I make no allegations against your sterling record. Your time as attorney general has demonstrated a deep concern for maintaining the national security of the nation. It is specifically because of that, that I ask the question."

Roberts smiled like a friend. "Help us out, sir, you were there, knew the other Americans at Barnsdahl and in Professor Everttson's classes. Help us solve a decades-old mystery."

He folded his hands calmly in front of him. "Who is . . ." He checked his notes. "What did they call him? Oh yes . . . who is Apple Blossom?"

"Senator Roberts," DeWitt said slowly after the excitement around him had died down. "My apologies if I seemed to overreact just now. The burdens of assisting the president in our time of crisis, I fear, has frayed my nerves more than I was aware."

He took a long, calming drink of water. "This news about

Professor Everttson comes as a shock and a complete surprise. Of course I'll do whatever I can to assist you."

"Mr. DeWitt," said Roberts, smiling back, "if any of my comments were misinterpreted, I apologize as well. But the synchronicity of this revelation—"

"This twenty-five-year-old revelation," the chairman interrupted.

Roberts nodded. "This twenty-five-year-old revelation *does* seem to have a startling synchronicity with our business here. Perhaps, since we are engaged in so momentous an event in our history, you would be willing to help us—within the confines of this committee's hearings—to clear up what I am sure is merely a dastardly attempt to besmirch a great American."

"I will, Senator."

Roberts continued reading. "Mr. Chairman, I request that the committee recess until Monday morning to allow staff to examine the documents and allegations contained in this report. To better assist the vice president designate in helping us unearth the truth to this . . ."

The sheet said to pause, and had been right so far, so he paused.

"This Apple Blossom."

On Grimes's farm, Canvas flicked off the set the moment the committee unanimously voted to recess for the weekend. He didn't need the talking heads' critique that would follow, probably for hours and days to come. He didn't need to hear the White House spin, DeWitt's protestations, or the dissection by the politicians.

He had his own analysis to make. And quickly too.

"Too pretty," he mumbled as he turned to Steingarth, who had watched the hearings with him. "Too bloody neat." He glanced at the hurried notes he'd made, then looked up at Steingarth. "You *don't* have any connection with this Everttson, do you?"

"None at all," the old man said hurriedly. "If he was a Soviet asset-in-place, we would have no knowledge of it. And if he was in the history department, the point is only reinforced. Our people were solely in psychology and ethics venues."

Canvas nodded. "Right." He shook his head. "There is a poetry there, though."

He actually smiled. "The Americans react to nothing quite so violently as the good old Soviet Boogeyman. Accuse, but offer an out—he's not the spy, but might know who the spy is. Provide evidence that is irrefutable and eminently checkable—except for the key piece, the Apple Blossom comment from an *uncertified* transcript." He nodded in appreciation. "Pure poetry."

"But who could be behind it?" Steingarth asked with obvious concern.

"Who do you think?" The German looked blank. "Xenos."

"But he's dead. You killed him yourself."

"God bless resurrections," Canvas mumbled as he walked into the next room, where three aides were working frantically. "What do you have?" he asked one.

The man looked upset. "Everttson and Fergét were who they said and busted when and why they said. Everttson killed himself within three months, the Haitian the next year. Two of the interrogators died in the last five years from natural causes, the third is senile and in a home near Baysingstoke."

"So nothing can be verifiably proved or disproved. Sweet."

His aide continued after looking over some papers that were handed to him. "Scotland Yard *will* confirm the generic facts of the case, but refuse to give any details to the press." The man thought about it. "My guess, they'll make a Senate investigator fly to London for a face-to-face; to go through the files. Could take days, maybe weeks, you know what Central Registry's like on old files."

Canvas nodded. "What about cross-checking Apple Blossom?"

The assistant looked positively ill. "Pei used it sixteen times in nine different debriefings. Always vague, general." He hesitated, then spoke in a barely heard whisper of almost physical pain. "Always an American educated in Europe, in the sixties, a sleeper asset designed to take over a senior role in the U.S. government."

"Shit."

"There's no way the investigators will miss the cross-reference."

Canvas sighed, then moved to the window. He looked out at the woods around him, the calm, pastoral setting. Vaguely watched some squirrels lightly leap from branch to branch on a nearby tree.

"Why can't you just die like other people, Jerry?" he whispered.

He sighed again, ran his fingers through his close-cropped hair, then turned back to the waiting men.

"We go on the offensive right away. Before they get a chance to throw another chain saw at us, right? Have DeWitt issue a statement saying as how he is *honored* and all that crap to help ferret out this Russki spy. But for God's sake, he is *not* to use the phrase 'Apple Blossom' in any circumstances. Get Grimes and whoever else we have in the media to dredge up a lot of old footage of Joe McCarthy and the like. Phrases like 'rush to judgment' and 'guilty by suspicion' and the lot.

"Walker?"

"Yes, Guv?"

"Let's have someone in Congress, several someones, talk about expediting the nomination so that the committee can concentrate on the hunt for the *real* spy. Patriotic duty to get DeWitt in office and all. Time enough for a quarter-century-old scandal later."

"On it."

Canvas walked a few paces away from the group with the man. "Anything from Krusiec?"

The man shook his head. "Not since she called in an emergency. Nothing."

"Nothing," Canvas repeated sadly, then clapped the man on the back. "Get on it." The man raced off as his boss nodded for Steingarth to follow him into the next room.

"We have a problem, you and I."

"I've noticed," the German said morosely.

Canvas shook his head. "Forget DeWitt. Our problem is a bigger one."

The older man looked intensely curious but didn't say a word. Just waited.

"Xenos is out there somewhere," Canvas said in a low tone. "If he's alive, then it's only prudent to assume that Alvarez and the rest are alive as well."

"I see your point."

"You see half of it." He led them out the door for a walk among the privacy of the trees. "As long as we have her kids, Alvarez stays in line. But how long can we hold them? And if we lose positive control on Alvarez, the party's over."

"You want to kill the children now?" Steingarth sounded neither shocked nor eager, merely inquiring.

"Can't do that and keep control. But if he comes, we can't hold them either." Canvas sounded distracted. "And he'll come." Again, he thought about Barbara Krusiec's panicked call.

"But surely he could not find them here? Or get through your perimeter and defenses."

Canvas shook his head, laughed bitterly, then started walking again. "Time is what we're about now. Xenos doesn't move full tilt on DeWitt until the tykes are safe, right? So if we can buy enough time to confirm your boy, we still have a chance. Once he's in the White House, the rest takes care of itself." He paused. "So we go defensive on this and play for time."

Steingarth looked skeptical. "And your suggestion is?"

The Englishman knelt by a motion detector and checked its wiring. "Three things. One, you pressure the president to vocally and politically support DeWitt. Twist a few arms to get the confirmation back on track, with a thorough investigation of this other nonsense to be an administration priority as soon as the China crisis is over."

Steingarth agreed. "I see the president for dinner. He's tired and has convinced himself that a vice president must be in place before he acts in Taiwan. It presents some difficulties, but it can be accomplished."

"Good." Canvas was quiet for a moment. "I'll get connections in CI-5 in London to lose a few files. Slow the process down. When the committee sees the thing might drag on forever because of lost documents and extinct witnesses, they'll be less likely to want to press the matter. I'll also see what I can find on this Roberts fellow as well."

"My files are open to you, of course," Steingarth offered. "And your third step?"

As he rubbed at one of his tattoos—a struggling fish impaled on a stick—Canvas spoke distractedly. "I want the kids positively and finally out of Xenos's reach. Somewhere in China—rice field or prison cell I don't rightly care—but somewhere he can't get to them."

Steingarth considered for a moment. "A diplomatic flight leaves at 0830 Sunday." He coughed nervously, a violent act as if expelling a cancerous growth from deep in his bowels. "I keep track of them, in case of a, uh, necessary tactical, uh . . ." His voice trailed off. "If you can get them to the plane, I will see to the rest."

Canvas looked uncomfortable. "Nothing before then?"

The German shrugged. "In the best of times the State Department and FAA carefully control the Chinese comings and goings. With the climate we have helped to create, these are far from the best of times."

"Sunday," Canvas repeated absently. "Seventy-two hours." Finally he nodded. "Make the arrangements," he said with finality. "Call me on the secure line after you talk to the president."

Steingarth quickly left.

Canvas spent another ten minutes wandering in the woods, checking sensors and defenses, allowing his mind to drift and wander.

He played every scenario he could conceive of over and over in his mind. Thought of every contingency, every countermeasure, every move he might make to tilt this already lopsided table more in his direction. Knowing there would be no sleep, no rest or moments of distraction in the coming seventy-two hours, until the children were on their way to China and the threat was neutralized.

He took several brain-clearing deep breaths, looked out at the twelve-foot-high cinder block wall off in the distance, looked through it, beyond it, at all the threats and reasons for soul-numbing fear beyond, and slowly shook his head.

"Oh, Jerry," he sighed as he started back to his command post. "Where are you?"

Fifteen

"Where are you, Colin?"

Xenos sat in the back of a stretch limousine (the most inconspicuous transport he could think of, considering the area) slowly driving through some of the most exclusive roads in America. The multihundred-acre estates were worth millions, their owners worth considerably more. High-tech security systems were the norm—not telltale at all. And the country's "best, brightest, and most beautiful" regularly gathered at any given mansion in the area to decide the fate of the world.

Vedette, Albina, and Franco sipped their drinks and shook their heads as palace after palace (or the front gates thereof) passed in silent stately review.

"This place bespeaks a great deal of waste," Albina said, using his ultimate compliment for the highest level of riches attainable.

"Amazing," was Franco's only response.

Vedette looked up from his map, checked an address, then looked down again. "It's a pain in the ass. Every place here has state-of-the-art thugs and street-tough systems to get around. And most of them have no particular threat outstanding. Like other people have fancy landscaping. I hate to think what our place will be like."

Xenos just stared out the window. "Okay," he said as the

limousine slowly completed its circle of the area and headed back toward the interstate. "We've seen all the possibles twice. Five doors, only one right one, and we won't get a second chance." He seemed deeply distracted, as if his mind were out among the southern manors and carefully manicured grounds. "Any thoughts?" he mumbled.

"DeWitt's visited three of them in the last ten days," the surveillance expert, Vedette, said after checking his surveillance logs. "I say we eliminate the other two." He checked a computer printout. "The Collier and the Al Sheihala properties."

"*Three* doors."

Franco looked at the notes he'd made as they'd driven by the residences where Valerie's aide's emergency call could have been routed. "The Krusiec woman remembered a long curving driveway just inside the gate." He took a deep breath as if what followed was offered only with the most reluctance. Which it was. He didn't like this seemingly casual elimination process. He was a man who believed in careful analysis then overwhelming action. Not informal discussion.

But he also believed in Xenos.

"Number one has a straight drive with right-angle intersections off it," he finally offered.

"*Two* doors."

Vedette quickly pulled out the two files he'd compiled on the remaining possible targets.

"Briarcliff," he read aloud. "Owned by a television executive named Jacob Haft. Fifty-seven, married, three children. Educated at Missouri State University, two-year fellow at Cambridge and Manchester Universities in England. Inherited his money, parlayed the family capital into a thirty percent ownership of Wilkins International Network. Not a controlling interest, but enough to get what he wants. DeWitt visited him last Saturday night. Stayed over."

Albina checked *his* file on the place. A thing carefully pulled together from sources in both the straight and crook communities.

"Eighty-five-hundred-square-foot, seven-bedroom mansion," he began. "Four guesthouses, eight other outbuildings. Full-time, professional security—both automated and human. State-of-the-art and a lot of it."

He looked over at Xenos. "Media man, wealthy, English education, big estate, heavy security. Looks good, no?"

Xenos closed his eyes and slouched down in his seat. "Next."

Vedette began reading from his other file. "Heisenberg House, originally Maple Row Estate. Purchased five years ago by Heisenberg Assets, Limited—of Liechtenstein and Panama. Corporate purpose believed to be as a holding company to divert cash for tax purposes. But for whom I don't know yet. Current resident is Anthony Grimes, the Artist."

He shrugged as he closed the file. "Grimes is an open book. Politically conservative, wealthy, only six months in England when he was in his twenties. Some art school in the West End of London." He shook his head. "The guy's a pussycat. But DeWitt *did* visit him Wednesday night."

Albina continued the thought. "Very little security. A few cameras, a man at the gate, another in the house, one on the monitors, one roaming." He turned a page. "A lot of cameras, some lights with motion detectors." He shrugged. "The driveway curves, but so does Haft's."

Franco was studying the man who had the backseat to himself. Xenos seemed asleep, or at the least, deeply distracted. But his lips barely moved in soundless calculations, his breath became shallow, his movement almost nil. And Franco knew.

"You've decided," he said quietly.

Xenos never moved or opened his eyes. "I'm holding high-profile hostages in a rich man's paradise. I can expect a major effort if the congresswoman goes to the police. I want a place quiet, removed, but not a place where I would be noticed. A place big enough to establish a topflight security perimeter, without it being obvious. I don't want any of the neighbors to be even a little aware of it, but I'll need any queries easily satisfied by the given eccentricity of the owner or resident."

He opened his eyes and looked at the small infiltration expert. "Any buildings or cluster of buildings set off by themselves—ideally, connected—on either of the estates?"

His answer came a moment later.

"Work buildings well away from the main house and guest-houses at Briarcliff, maybe fifteen hundred meters," the little man read off his carefully prepared fact sheets. "Just inside the north fence." He turned to his file on the other estate. "We've got an old abandoned, sealed-up, fallout shelter in a grove of trees—maybe two thousand meters from the nearest occupant structure at Hei-senberg."

"How close to the fencing, Ugo?"

Albina pulled out a pocket ruler and checked the distance. "Close to two kilometers, a little over a mile from any fence. Almost in the center of the estate. The house and guest cottages are on the south end."

"Franco?" Xenos said in a faraway voice.

"Sì, amico."

"That's your target."

Franco nodded and took the files on Heisenberg House from the others. "Sì, amico." His voice was firm, committed.

Vedette looked less sure.

"Excuse me, Dureté, but I don't agree. Haft fits the profile better. His estate is better prepared to withstand an assault, his position in the community more useful to a man in Apple Blossom's position."

"I agree," Albina added. "With no disrespect, we will get only one chance at this, as you have said. Perhaps we should discuss this more, Dureté."

Xenos barely moved. "Before you go in, Franco, check the local photo libraries and real estate archives. There's got to be some aerial photos of Heisenberg House lying around somewhere. Make your maps from that and make sure every man in your team has one."

Franco continued studying the real estate maps and limited intelligence he had. "I'll get it done as soon as we get back."

Xenos finally moved. Sitting up, he gestured for the Corsican driver to head back to the warehouse.

"They're in there," he said to the other two in the back. "I know it."

"How?" Vedette demanded. "There is no room for error."

Xenos took a bottle of water from the ice tray, swallowing half of it in one gulp. "Two reasons. One: the name of the place. Heisenberg House. Named after the Heisenberg uncertainty principle, which says 'We can be sure of nothing.' It's Colin's sense of humor."

"Thin," Albina said with a little scorn. The man across from him in the car might be a living legend, the personification of death and destruction itself, but Albina was being asked to design a plan that would put nineteen brothers of the Union and two small children in harm's way.

And he would be damned certain they were hitting the right place before he did.

"What's your other reason?" he asked with toughness and resolution.

Xenos turned back to the window, closed his eyes, and slid down in the seat again.

"It's where *I* would hold them."

The discussion was over and the three Corsicans began planning the assault even before the car had reached the expressway.

"You shoot good for a woman," Fabrè said matter-of-factly as he took the pistol from Valerie's hand and gave her another.

"I've had a lot of experience lately," she mumbled as she tested the heft of the new pistol. "Heavy sonofabitch."

Fabrè adjusted her hands around the gun's butt. "Heckler & Koch VP 70, 9mm. No external hammer so it can't catch on your clothes. Eighteen-round clip, with one up the pipe. Very nice." He smiled spasmodically. "Longer trigger pull, but more accurate with more hitting power. Try it."

Valerie sighted in on the target—a mannequin of a man holding a doll of a small child in his arms—located in the basement of their temporary headquarters. She slowly squeezed the trigger, surprised at how long it took until the sound exploded around her.

"Loud," was all she said as the shot kicked up dirt from the pile behind and to the left of the target.

The assassin shrugged. "Big muzzle flash tells the bastards

where you are anyway." He nodded for her to fire again. "Every shot goes up and left with you. You're probably a natural shot, that tells me. So"—he took her hands and adjusted her aim lower and to the right—"we make adjustments."

Valerie sighted in on the new aiming point, then jerked the trigger. The round flew low and to the left. Angrily she slammed the gun down on the table in front of her.

"What's wrong?" the Corsican said patiently.

Valerie started pacing. "It's too damned close," she yelled. "You honestly expect me to be able to take a shot at a man holding one of my babies in front of him?" She was furious—at the Corsican, at herself for her inability to make the kind of shot she'd made on ranges for years.

At the terror of possibly being the cause of one of her children's deaths—*directly* instead of indirectly.

"It's an unusual trigger pull," Fabrè said quietly, understanding. Then he cocked his head to an angle and picked up the gun. "There is an old Corsican story," he began as he casually held the gun in front of him, wiping its blue steel exterior with a silicone cloth to ease its holster pull. "The story of Lucien Ècraser." He smiled openly, casually, a strange sight amid the smell of gunpowder and fear. "My papa named me for him.

"Ècraser was a secretary of the Nicosian Union of the Brotherhood. The man charged with settling the Union's accounts with those it transacted business with.

"Some *camorra* owed the Union a great deal of money and Ècraser went to collect. They refused." He spread his hands in a gesture of futility. "What could he do? He killed three of the five leaders and made his collection."

"What does this have to do . . ." But Valerie cut herself off when she saw a clouded expression cross the huge man's face.

"Six months later Ècraser returns home from business to find his house burned to the ground, his family dead or dying. His teenage daughter missing, taken into bondage by the Spanish bastards."

Again, the gesture of futility. "What could he do? He buried his family, paid holy obeisance to God's greater wisdom, then went in search of his daughter.

"He found her in a private *camorra* brothel in Málaga, near Gibraltar." He smiled suddenly. "Beautiful town, great hotel right on the beach if you like such things." Then the mood returned. "Anyways . . .

"Écraser shot his way in, finding the two men who had taken his daughter, hiding behind her nakedness on a bed." He paused, the objective voice returning. "She was lying on the bed, you see, and they were on the floor behind her, only their eyes and the top of their heads peeking out from behind, holding guns on her. You get it?"

Valerie nodded.

"Well," he continued, "what could he do?"

A silence filled the room, then the Heckler & Koch flashed up to shoulder level and two blasts shouted out.

Stunned, Valerie walked out from behind the table, over to the mannequin. Tracing her fingers over the still smoking, unquestionably fatal holes in its right eye and forehead . . . inches from the head of the baby doll.

Fabrè stood very still, looking not at the target, but deep into Valerie's shocked eyes.

"He could do . . . what he *had* to do."

For the next three hours Valerie practiced unflaggingly with the gun. Each round, each lungful of cordite and saltpeter invigorating her, cleansing her, hardening her for the night to come. Finally Fabrè seemed satisfied and took the gun from her swelling hands.

"You soak them in heavy salt and sugar water for an hour, then rinse with very hot water. Your fingers come alive then." He cleared the weapon, then nodded at the target. "Go get the baby, please."

After rinsing her mouth with cold water, swallowing some and spitting out the rest, she walked over and worked the baby from the terrorist's grasp.

"Another reason I like the H&K," Fabrè said simply as he

slammed a new clip into the handle. He turned the butt of the gun toward her. "You see this little lever, set on green?"

Valerie nodded. "The safety. What about it?"

The experienced Corsican weapons expert laughed loud and long. "In a manner of speaking only. On green you fire one shot per trigger pull. On red—"

"It won't fire, I know," she interrupted.

"Not quite." He flipped the almost invisible lever to the red pin spot. "Step away, please."

Valerie pressed herself against a side wall as she watched him take a tight grip on the weapon, sight in on the empty-handed mannequin, and then pull the trigger . . . once.

Three shots let go in almost instantaneous canon, neatly severing the head of the mannequin at the neck. It rolled on the ground, coming to a stop by Valerie's feet.

Fabrè laughed as if it was the funniest joke he'd ever heard. "Red means three rounds automatic fire per trigger pull," he said between roars. "For those less *delicate* moments."

A silent minute later Sarah knocked on the door, then let herself in. "They're back. Meeting in fifteen minutes."

Fabrè nodded and began cleaning the weapons. Valerie stepped carefully around the head, carefully placed the doll of the baby on the table, then headed for the door.

"Alvarez."

She turned back to the man who was quickly disassembling the H&K. "Yes?"

He never looked up as he pulled out solvent and cleaning patches. "What else could you do?" he said flatly.

Valerie took a deep breath. "I have to change."

The gunman nodded as she left. "A great deal, I imagine."

In his small room off the main area of the warehouse that he had made his, Xenos carefully reviewed last-minute notes, intelligence reports, and estimates. Everything was taken in, well chewed, tasted, then swallowed. His fingers flew over three pads in front of him—refining this plan, changing that operation, rescheduling another event. The final brushstrokes of the first Four Phase plan he'd fully assembled in ten years.

Vacantly he wondered if he still had what it took. If years of isolation had robbed him of the edge he would need to outguess—outluck—another of his kind who had stayed in the game, constantly sharpening his pestilential claws. Was his heart even in this abortion that he had fathered and now saw no escape from?

He shook his head at the notion.

Of course he was still good enough. What he had wasn't a learned skill—as he liked to claim—or the result of years of successful repetitions of arcane arts. It was a blessing/curse from a practical-joking God who had grown bored with the twentieth century and loosed the Four Phase Men upon it. Already he could feel the lack of emotion, the combat iciness working its way into him. That thing that activated as he did, the defense to protect him from any responsibility for what was to come.

But this time was different somehow, and he hoped God would be amused by that difference. Because this time, *he* was taking responsibility.

Complete.

Unqualified.

Undiminished.

Because he could no longer run away.

Then he glanced at the hard-to-get bottle of nepenthe on the table in front of him that Albina had obtained for him.

He heard its call, felt its pull; picked it up, testing the weight in his hands, shaking it slightly to hear the bare rattle the tiny black capsules made. Popped the lid, sniffed at the somehow rancid smell within.

Then he put it in his shirt pocket.

"It *is* God's work, you know."

Xenos looked up at his father, standing in the doorway. "Is it?"

Avidol smiled, walked fragilely forward, then sat in the one chair in the room. "Without question."

His son shook his head. "I wish I could be as sure."

"What kind of son doesn't listen to his father?" The old man laughed. Then he grew quiet, his face paled, he rubbed his arm, he coughed painfully, weakly.

Xenos rushed over to him. "Papa!"

Avidol reached up, cupping his son's face in his large hand. "Chuni, we are all here on this planet for a reason. Although many of us never see or fulfill that reason." A wince from a deep pain, then the smile returned. "And God has returned you to me, to us, for this moment."

Xenos looked anguished. "Papa! Let me get someone!"

"Why? I need no help to die. It feels . . . it *is* natural. Just be with me," he mumbled. A paroxysm of pain exploded in his chest, neck, and arm as Avidol stiffened, falling out of the chair.

Xenos caught him, laying him gently on the floor. "Sarah!" he screamed out.

His sister, followed by the others, rushed to the small room. Sarah ran to her father's side, took his hand, stroked his hair out of his eyes. "Daddy?" she whimpered as she clutched his hand with both of hers. "Oh, Daddy!"

"Shh," Avidol whispered gently. "It was my time even before our little adventure." He managed a laugh. "But it is worth it, in the end it is actually worth it." He looked from his daughter to his son to his grandson. "Family. It is . . . right." He stiffened again. "Be there for each other," he wheezed out.

"We will, Daddy," Sarah cried.

"Always, Papa," Xenos said with tears flowing freely from the scar-tissued eyes.

Avidol's face suddenly took on a strange, quizzical expression. He looked over to the side at a blank wall.

"Will they be all right . . . my children?" he asked the empty space. He nodded slightly. "Your will."

He turned, staring with a zealot's eyes into his son's. *"Shm'e Yisroyal, adonai elohaynu, adonai echod. V'imru osay . . ."*

He fell silent, gripping the hands of his children, a confidently tranquil expression in his eyes. A look of . . . triumph!

As Sarah moaned and was held by her son, Xenos reached down, gently closing his father's eyes.

"Yiskadal, v'yiskaddash," he began in a low tone, *"shme raboh."*

Behind him there were mumbled prayers, the Corsicans crossed themselves to a man, some falling to their knees and offering closed-eyes prayers for the soul of the man lying so peacefully calm before them.

Valerie cried silently, not understanding either the old man or his son, but grateful to the core for their existence. Grieved beyond measure—without fully knowing why—for his loss.

After finishing the traditional prayer for the dead, Xenos stood up, still looking down at his father. "Constantin?"

Vedette came forward immediately. "Sir."

"You're free for a few hours?"

The international smuggler nodded. "I will see to everything, Dureté. My hand upon my soul."

Xenos nodded. "Let's do this." He bent over, kissed his father's dead lips, then turned and strode purposefully from the room.

No one noticing the bottle of pills being dropped on the cement floor and being crushed under resolute feet.

Saturday
0121

Barry McNown had been a soldier and a good one. For seven years he'd served in the Royal Marines, a small-arms specialist. A career and a life to come of promotions, the right marriage, and eventual retirement with the rank of brigadier and ownership of a small hotel somewhere in the North Country.

But an incident with an illegally obtained Russian RPD led to a rash decision to lie and face court-martial.

Acquitted on the gun charge, but convicted of lying and conduct unbecoming an officer, he was stripped of his rank and served sixteen months in a British stockade.

Abandoned by the system he'd idolized, he immediately joined with Canvas upon being approached. If he couldn't soldier for queen and country, he would do it for the Swiss franc and personal satisfaction.

Even if it did mean—on this occasion—walking a lonely patrol on a wooded luxury estate in northern Virginia.

He stopped suddenly.

Nothing had changed around him, the night birds still sang and the dimly lit ground around him looked as deserted as always. But something didn't *feel* right. He shouldered his rifle and lowered his night-vision glasses.

The orange reflected world showed him windblown piles of leaves, gently hilly terrain, old-growth trees, and . . .

He would never finish the thought—as the ground seemed to rise up in front of him, almost instantly cutting off his view and life.

Clance Laughlin died while urinating behind a tree.

Bob Vincent's head was severed in one savage stroke that gave him—in his final moments of life—the unique view of his body reaching up to an empty neck.

Xenos rolled on.

He was pure instinct and mentality now. Virtually part of the grounds he moved through. An unseen, unheard, complete predator in search of an electronic prey.

And if the living should inadvertently cross his path, well . . .

The equipment he carried in his backpack and deployed carefully to the west of the fallout shelter was simple enough.

Signal absorbers that would suck in microwave search nets and spit them back at their receivers—leaving an undetected ten-foot-wide path cleared.

Thumpers—windup hammers that struck the ground at random, irregular moments and strengths—that would confuse motion detectors, seismic devices, and the such to the extent that men could move among them . . . so long as they tread lightly.

Mirror arrays that used sophisticated programming to reflect peaceful night scenes (seemingly in motion) at cameras that had been immobilized.

It was second nature to Xenos as he moved and studied and acted. All done on an autonomic level at best.

Then it was done. He moved off to the east as he activated the go signal for the others.

By the west fence, Franco and his eighteen gunmen—dressed in dark green and blue uniforms—heard the signal, cocked their weapons, and moved toward the fence.

"Perdonami Gesù Cristo, perché ho peccato." Franco crossed himself, kissed his thumbnail, then climbed over the fence. The others followed suit and were quickly on the estate side of the wall.

One hundred meters in, the silent assassins stopped.

"Alvarez," Franco whispered, "you will remain here with the rear guard." His expression was unequivocal and she nodded.

"Bring them back to me," she said in a near cry.

Franco nodded grimly. Then he signaled to his men.

And they were gone.

Valerie unholstered the VP 70, checked the clip, then took positions as instructed by the three men with her. Never stopping her prayers for a millisecond.

Canvas finished his cigar, just outside the command center, stubbed it out against the wall, then went back inside.

"Report."

"All systems on passive search," a man at a computer said as he checked the readouts. "No intrusions, no detections, everything functioning five-by."

Canvas nodded. "Perimeter?"

A man at a plastic map of the estate, who occasionally made notations on it based on what he heard on his headphones, smiled. "A quiet night in the country, boss."

"Right." The mercenary leader started into the next room. "Let me know when the patrol reports come in."

"Right, boss," the man said as he made a notation. "Gonna be a little late, though."

"What?" Canvas immediately reappeared in the control room.

The man looked very casual about it. "Patrols must've wandered into a dead zone. We're having trouble reading them."

Canvas took another step into the room. "You're out of touch?"

The man shook his head. "No, sir. They're reading us clearly enough. We're just not receiving *them* all that clearly. Garbled, kinda. Probably a battery problem, no sweat."

But Canvas had started to sweat. Just a little, on his upper lip. "Try them again."

His assistant nodded and picked up the radio. "Three, eight, two from base. Report please." Nothing. "Three, eight, two from base. Report please."

A phone rang a moment later. The man picked up the receiver. "Probably calling in on his cell." He turned back to the phone. "Bayshore Imports, night desk, this is Lou."

He froze and his face went white. Slowly, as if dazed, he held out the phone to Canvas. "He's asking to speak to Colin Meadows."

Canvas took the phone, holding it gingerly as if it were alive— almost reluctant to put it next to his ear. "Hello?"

"Hello, Colin."

"Jerry?" For the first time in years, Canvas allowed panic to flash across his face. He instantly banished the expression and wildly signaled for a trace to begin.

"This has to end."

"Save me the trouble, Jerry. Tell me where you are."

"Close."

Canvas walked to the door, shut the lights in the room, and opened it. "We need to talk," he said as he looked out into the night woods.

"No."

"I promise my offer will more than make up for any inconvenience or hardships you've had."

"Will it bring my father back from the dead?" Xenos asked in a subdued, committed tone.

"*Shit,*" Canvas whispered away from the phone. "Jerry, it was never my intent—"

"This has to end."

Canvas wildly motioned his men into action. Alarms were silently relayed, guards called on cell phones, locks thrown, and systems put into active mode. "What do you have in mind?"

"Do you remember Romania?"

"Sure. Last time we worked together."

"Remember those two Magyars?"

Canvas *did* remember. "The *pas de morts*. Sure."

"Two men, bound together by a large silk scarf, fighting to the death over a matter of principle."

"Beautiful bloody moment," Canvas said as he allowed the memory to come over him. The music, the passion, the two men locked in the *death dance* that would decide all issues between them. "You inviting me to dance, Jerry?"

"You made the invitation when you involved my family." Xenos sounded . . . tired, but resolved.

Canvas was handed a note that read "He's close!" Involuntarily he took a step out into the night. "Where and when, old friend?"

His answer was a volley of shots from the dark that barely missed him, but tore the door off its hinges. The experienced soldier dropped to the ground, rolled, and rushed into the woods.

Three Corsicans rushed each of the four buildings, the other four remaining outside. The night exploded in automatic weapons fire—weird flashes in the dark momentarily lighting up the woods, then disappearing. Screams mixed with the gunshots, explosions filled the calm air.

Franco and two others had stormed the command center, instantly killing the three men inside. A door was kicked in, a quick look followed by a fusillade of 9mm fire from inside.

Franco never hesitated.

He threw himself into the room at floor level, firing his .45s with both hands. *"Amici! In bocca al lupo!"*

"Crepi il lupo!" his sidemen screamed out as they followed him in. Two minutes later the room fell silent, the defenders dead or seriously wounded.

With the sounds of the firefight spreading around him, Franco wasted no time going up to the survivor among the defenders. He pulled out his knife, plunging it into the man's wounded shoulder.

"I bambini, the children, where are they?" He twisted the knife, and the man's screams drowned out the nearby shooting.

"Hall! Second and third doors!"

"*Grazie,*" Franco said as he pulled out the knife, cutting the man's throat in the same motion. He spit in the dead man's face as he kicked his body aside. "*Froccio!*" He checked through the door's peephole, then opened it and hurried through.

Grimes heard the battle begin. Saw the first explosions from the shelter's mesh-covered windows. Heard the gunfire from the outer rooms and knew that disaster wore a robe and carried a scythe in a skeletal hand.

And was actively looking for *him*!

He jumped as the door exploded inward and the men came for him.

"Another step and you'll see the girl's brains!" he screamed out as he pushed a .38 into Cathy Alvarez's seven-year-old ear.

Franco pushed down the barrel of his comrade's gun. A quick look behind to see that the third member of his team had Drake Alvarez safely in the hall, then he turned back to Grimes.

"*Disgraziato,*" he snarled at the man. "*Porco!* I give you one chance to let her go and face me like a man." He handed his gun to his comrade and pulled out his knife. "Come on, *Dolcezza,*" he sneered, "come and play."

"I'm not fucking kidding! I'll kill her! I will!" His face was sour-milk white, his hand trembled, his sweat formed pools on the floor, but he managed to thumb back the hammer on the gun.

Franco kissed the air in Grimes's direction as he rhythmically moved the knife from side to side. Slowly—almost floating—one foot closer each moment.

"Come on, *maschioni,* tough guy," another kiss, "let's dance," he whispered seductively.

Grimes couldn't take his eyes off the knife and the madman holding it. It wasn't supposed to be this way! He wasn't supposed to get dirty! None of them, it was just a game, money for nothing but a few favors. Just a game, dammit!

"Come and play."

"Wha—"

His words were stopped by a flick of Franco's wrist and the blade flying into his left eye. At almost the same moment, the Corsican threw himself forward, grabbing the little girl less than a second before Grimes's gun went off.

"Shit," he muttered as he looked down at the hole that went through his shoulder. Then he turned to Cathy—keeping his body between her and Grimes—as the other Corsican fired three times into the man's head. "Are you okay, little one?"

The girl seemed stunned, porcelain-like, a beautiful sculpture about to crack into a million pieces.

"Angelo mio," he said with a softened smile, "little angel, would you like to go see your mama?" He kept smiling as his hands searched her for broken bones or blood. He found none.

"Do you know my mommy?" she said in an impossibly weak voice.

Franco smiled as he lifted her into his arms. "We go to her right now, okay?"

"Okay." She buried her face in his uninjured shoulder as she caught a glimpse of the mutilated men around them.

"Shh, *bella.*" He kissed her tenderly on the top of the head. "Just some stupid men." He began to sing her a lullaby from his youth as he picked his way among the carnage.

He could either fight or flee. No other options. He knew that Xenos's plan would be flawless, his men ruthless, and the result inevitable. Although still stunned by how quickly they'd been found, Canvas nevertheless recovered rapidly in the dark and the pain that had become the night.

There were forces spread out around the compound on three sides, so he moved in the one remaining direction. He paused when he heard the gunfire coming from within his command shelter, then shook his head and started off again toward the east fence and safety.

He stopped. A frozen monument of introspection and caution. *The one way remaining.*

The only conveniently unguarded route away from the Hell and frenzy of the kill zone. Canvas turned to the east, seeing it all play out before him.

Somewhere ahead, Xenos was waiting for him. In the dark—

between this spot and the fence—they would meet. Canvas would take a step, then feel a fire explode within his chest as the hollow-point .44 slug found its home. Maybe he would live long enough to see Xenos's face as he came forward to deliver the coup de grâce.

For a full minute he considered continuing. Stealthily making his way forward—aware of the danger, but taking precautions. All for the chance to finally take out the man who haunted his dreams. When he *did* sleep.

Then he exhaled deeply, shook his head, and started toward the south.

To fight another day.

Valerie looked toward the sound of gunshots and running men, desperately trying to pierce the dark and see what she knew there was no hope of seeing.

Somewhere out ahead—in the heart of the thick woods—a fierce battle was taking place. No longer centered in the distance, it seemed to move toward her, groping through the black to reach the rear guard of the only way out that night. She fought to keep from running out, meeting it halfway, and ending her thirty minutes, her weeks, of waiting.

Then, without warning, the first of the assault teams appeared. Some were wounded, others bruised, all on the dead run.

None with what she needed.

Forcing back tears, she helped them over the wall, then froze. A thin voice called out from the dark—maybe, *must be,* imagined —and the voice melted all her defenses, her fears, her torment.

"Mom!"

She rushed forward as Drake and she collided in an ecstatic embrace.

"Baby, my baby! Thank you, God. Thank you, God. *Mi hijo! Gracias Dios por mi hijo,"* she cried. "Oh thank you, God." She smothered him with kisses. "Oh, Drake, baby . . ." Valerie cut herself off. "Where's Cathy?"

In answer, Drake looked back into the dark, just before he was grabbed by one of the Corsicans and almost thrown over the fence. They urged her to follow, but—satisfied that her son was safe—she turned and began jogging toward the nearest gunfire.

There were muzzle flashes everywhere in the fanged darkness. The reports filled the air like a typewriter's clatter. One hundred and fifty meters in, she stopped, not sure which way to go.

Then she saw them.

Franco, bent over and running full speed in a randomly zigzagging pattern, his arms wrapped around something clutched tightly to his chest.

With her heart bursting through muscle and bone that could no longer contain it, Valerie realized that the something was her little girl.

"Here!" she screamed above the violence in the air. "Over here!"

Franco looked up, saw her, and immediately altered his course in her direction. As one of the guards rose up behind him—unseen or heard—and pointed an automatic rifle at his back.

The Corsican fell to the ground, cushioning the child as he felt the shot whiz by his right ear. Then heard three shots in automatic-fire succession fly over him. A long moment later he looked behind him, seeing the guard with a neat hole in the middle of his forehead and three evenly spaced wounds stitched across his chest.

Valerie pulled her daughter from his arms, tossing him her gun in exchange.

Franco grinned—an insane sight amid the madness—as he looked at the smoking gun and Valerie's retreating form. Then, with a satisfied nod of his head, he followed them out of the battle zone.

As the first police cars arrived at the main gate, Xenos dropped out of a tree near the east fence.

He'd already heard that the children were safe and the Corsicans evacuated from the scene. They'd taken some hits—two were dead, three wounded. But the toll was less than he'd expected.

How would they explain the shooting and explosions? he wondered vacantly. Did Canvas have some contingency in place for it? Or would he have to improvise? It was an interesting problem.

And where *was* Canvas?

He hadn't been hit in the initial attack, hadn't been seen or heard from since he'd jumped into the woods in the first moments. And he'd obviously turned down Xenos's complex invitation. So he was still out there.

Somewhere.

As he climbed over the east fence, he put the thought aside.

Time enough to deal with Canvas after the immediate insanity was over.

The time for Apple Blossom, however, was now.

Sixteen

Sitting in a bathrobe, calmly sipping his coffee while watching the morning news reports, DeWitt was the picture of calm and cool. His hand was rock-steady as he poured. His expression placid. His manner aloof.

But Michael had known the man for ten years. Men like him for much longer than that. So he remained cautious, and out of easy reach.

"The media's been all over it since it broke. They're camped out in front of the estate like the Simpson trial. The neighbors aren't talking, but the press is getting nice gory shots each time a body is carried out."

"How many?" DeWitt asked as he changed to a different channel's coverage of *Massacre Among the Cottonwoods: Murder in Virginia.*

"Press knows about six so far. My sources say the final total will be more than three times that." He shook his head. "It's a bloody mess."

DeWitt looked up and smiled. "You're developing a sense of humor late in life, Michael." He returned to the broadcast. "Tony Grimes?"

"Dead."

"Canvas?"

"Missing." Michael shook his head. "The police are confused, asking for help from the Virginia Department of Justice and McLean Homicide Special. Also Quantico behaviorists. They suspect some kind of cult murder/suicide thing." He looked exhausted. "For now, anyway."

"Steingarth?" DeWitt asked as he shut the TV.

"Unaccounted for and unreachable." He hesitated. "Not connected to it . . . so far."

"My name come up?"

Michael sighed. "Not yet, but it's early."

The vice president designate nodded simply.

Oddly the destruction and death of the night before—first learned of at three in the morning by a panicked call from Michael —seemed to have quieted and strengthened the man. As if the combined blows of the Senate suspicions and the attack on the command center had loosed him from some bonds he'd been struggling against.

He poured himself some more coffee. "Since the children aren't there, we have to assume they were rescued and that the reports of the congresswoman's demise are less than thorough." He got up and started pacing, calmly. "What we need to do is *act,* get out ahead of all this before more silly accusations start flying."

Michael appeared less certain. "I think we should wait until we hear from Steingarth or Canvas."

"Don't think, Michael," DeWitt said without rancor. "You're no good at it." He opened a window and breathed in the dew-scented air. "We didn't get this close just because of foreign investment." He lightly tossed a pad over to his aide. "Take this down.

"For immediate release," he began after five minutes of an intense silence. "Attorney General Jefferson DeWitt is saddened by the death of national treasure and personal friend Anthony Grimes. But not completely surprised by it.

"In recent weeks, it has come to the attorney general's attention that Mr. Grimes was involved with an extremist cult called"— he paused, trying out different names—"the Heisenberg Effect. An organization linked to missing and feared mentally unbalanced Congresswoman Valerie Alvarez."

Michael looked up. "Linked by who?"

DeWitt shrugged. "Us. Continuing . . .

"As recently as several days ago, Attorney General DeWitt visited Mr. Grimes at his home to attempt to convince him to abandon this cult which had suicidal and murderous tendencies, along with reactionary political beliefs. The cult—which had been exerting more and more influence on Mr. Grimes in recent months —was suspected by the attorney general of attempting to engage in espionage against Western governments, not unlike the Aum Shoko Ritai in Japan.

"In retrospect, it appears that Mr. Grimes—who was educated in England—may well be this Apple Blossom whom the Senate Judiciary Committee has asked the attorney general to assist in identifying.

"Attorney General DeWitt prays that he is wrong, but fears he is not."

Michael looked up from the statement. "I thought he was your friend."

DeWitt shrugged. "No such thing as a dead friend."

His aide studied him, then started out of the room. "I'll try to reach Steingarth again before issuing it."

"Fuck the Nazi. Canvas too. We don't need them anymore."

Michael nodded reluctantly. "I'd still like to try."

"As long as it gets out before the ten o'clock talk shows." DeWitt started toward his bedroom to dress for the day. "What's on the schedule . . . besides damage control?" He chuckled.

"Filling in for the president at the Army-Navy game in Philadelphia this afternoon. Situation briefing at the White House and dinner with the national security staff at 7:30."

"Fine. Get the statement out, then contact as many of the others in the chain as you can. We've got to get them going on this cult idea." He pulled off his robe, admiring himself in a mirror. "Time they see who's *really* in charge."

Michael never looked back as he headed into his nearby office.

It took only a few minutes—and two more unanswered calls to Steingarth (and Canvas's cell phone)—and the statement was ready to be electronically sent out to the nation's media.

To an extent, he admired DeWitt's self-confidence. The natural arrogance that served as an understructure of strength to support him in the worst times. It was a large part of what made DeWitt the Chinese's first choice in the Apple Blossom plan.

But before he entered the sequence that would spread the gospel according to DeWitt out among what the attorney general truly believed were the naïve, the ignorant, and the just plain stupid that made up 90 percent of the American people, Michael read a fax that was being received on his private, secured machine.

It appeared to be a revised schedule for Justice Department staffers in the A.G.'s office. A jumble of names, titles, times, and hours. But ten minutes of *unwrapping* the code—which only he and his personal controller knew—left him with quite a different message.

Adieu O soldier
You of the rude campaign (which we shared)
The rapid march, the life of the camp,
The hot contention of opposing fronts, the long maneuver,
Red hot battles with their slaughter, the stimulus, the strong,
    terrific game.
Spell of all brave and manly hearts, the trains of time through
    you
And like you all fill'd,
With war and war's expression.
Adieu, dear comrade.
Your mission is fulfill'd.

Michael swiveled away from his keyboard, picked up the secure line and dialed a number that only *he* knew.

"Two, eight, one, three."

"Apple Blossom," he said softly.

"Countersign?"

Michael looked around to make sure he wasn't being overheard. "Blossom."

"One moment, please."

Thirty seconds later a new voice came on the line. "Blossom, it's been far too long."

"I have a problem," Michael said in a near whisper.

"How well I know, son."

"You seen the papers?" he asked softly.

"And the television," the voice responded with a concern and warmth that already made Michael feel a little better.

"He thinks it's a *good* thing."

"How so?"

Another furtive glance to be sure he was alone. "He's giving orders, bizarre stuff, wants to involve the entire chain in them."

A brief but noticeable silence on the other end of the line. "Well, we can't have that, can we?"

"No, sir."

A heavy sigh could be heard. "Michael, what's your assessment of the damage done him by the Roberts allegations?"

Michael thought about it. "Survivable, so long as we play like its meaningless. Don't legitimize it or give it any more power than it already has."

"Yes," the voice said in a happy tone.

Michael could picture the satisfied smile on the man's face. The look his real father had never shown him—except in those times when the belt would fly across the young boy's back and shoulders. "What should I do?"

"For now? Whatever the lunatic says. Do nothing that would personally endanger your position . . . or yourself, of course."

"Right."

"Apple's instability has been the topic of recent conversations. The cause of growing concerns. His, well, *boldness* of late is a thing that must be corrected. Perhaps he is not the one we need, after all." A long pause. "Do you understand me, son?"

"I do." It was said stiffly, reluctantly.

Soldierly.

"We'll need to consider the new circumstances," the voice was continuing. "Explore other possibilities."

"You'll stay in touch?" Michael's voice was plaintive, pained, longing.

"I'm only a phone call away, you know that." Another brief pause. "Help me out, Michael. I've been trying to remember something from U.S. history."

"Anything," the possible future White House chief of staff said happily. He remembered their discussions of obscure historical events as among the happiest times in his training and life.

"Who *was* the virtually unknown congressman that exposed Alger Hiss as a communist spy?"

"Richard Nixon."

"Ah! Right you are." Another, more strategic pause. "And he ended up president, did he not?"

"He did," Michael said in a suddenly hushed tone.

"Ah." The voice sounded deeply satisfied. "You always have such a current grasp on history." The briefest pauses. "And what makes it. Good-bye, Michael. We'll speak again soon, I'm sure." The line went dead.

As Michael's mind burst to life.

Twenty minutes later—the press release issued and with two hours to himself—he arrived at the offices of Attorney General Designate Rod Buckley.

A large box of tapes, videos, and documents in hand.

The Executive Office Building gate of the White House complex was always the least used on the weekends. Tourists and VIPs used the two gates nearest the impressive South Portico; weekend staff (mostly based in the Executive Mansion) used the west gate. So White House Police Officer Jack Kreiger was mildly surprised when a well-dressed woman walked up to the guard's booth.

"May I help you, ma'am?" he said professionally as he sized her up. Deeply tanned, a bruise under her left ear, a large briefcase that almost matched the off-the-rack—but expensive—business suit.

"I'm Congresswoman Valerie Alvarez of New York," she said as she placed her briefcase on the counter for inspection. "And I want to see the president . . . *now.*"

It was still late at night in the VIP lounge at Hòu-tiän Airport in Beijing. Chronically understaffed, the third and smallest jetport serving the largest city in China, it was filled primarily with traveling military, rich Hong Kong traders, and New Territory settlers seeking to bring family in or out of the People's Republic.

And, tonight, one other.

Herb sat patiently reading a spy novel—laughing at the absurdities it called fact—waiting for a response to his earlier request. He knew the risks he was taking—politically, personally—but he also realized that Xenos was right.

Only a face-to-face meeting would have the required impact.

Supposing that he wasn't arrested and deported for not having the required visas, or just arrested and interrogated for the secrets that he held, or just *disappeared* to face an uncertain fate that would never be known.

But it was worth it, somehow. Not so much to stop a war, and even less for the personal glory that would come with that act (in certain corridors of power).

No, he was doing it for one reason and one only.

Xenos had taken the nearly retired, certainly bypassed and forgotten, old man and put him back in the game. The ride had been a wild one, filled with terror and triumph, frustrations and victories galore. And for probably the last time in his life, Herb had meaning.

That was a gift that could never be repaid . . . except, perhaps, by this lunatic's mission to the heart of the Dragon.

"Wô jiào Xuan Li. Hù-zhào zài når?" a uniformed lieutenant asked brusquely.

Herb smiled noncommittally and held up his passport. The man took it, checked it against the contents of a folder, and then closed the folder with the passport inside.

"Qing," the lieutenant said, gesturing at a door across the room.

Herb took his briefcase and overcoat, and started forward, followed closely by the soldier. The door opened as they approached, then closed behind Herb, leaving the lieutenant outside.

"Director Stone," a major from the Long-Range Study Organization said in perfect English, "it is an honor to have you in Beijing. How may I be of service to you?"

"You can't. I asked to speak with General Xi, personally."

The major shrugged. "Regretfully we can find no record of anyone by that name in the city registers," he said easily. "Perhaps if you were more specific."

Herb sat down in the indicated chair. "Shall I tell you about his birthmark, the scar behind his left knee, or his days in Manchuria, first?"

The major was completely placid, a painted smile on a doll's face. "The reason you wish to see this Xi individual would be sufficient, sir."

"Son, let me be completely honest with you."

"Please do."

Herb took out a cigar, taking long moments to light it. Then he opened his briefcase, rummaged around, finally pulling out a bunch of thin, scraggly twigs. Each with small white and red flowers on them.

He handed them across to the officer. "To General Xi, with my compliments, sir. Tell him . . ." He blew a thick, blue cloud of smoke into the functionary's face. "Tell him the apple blossoms are in season."

The major suppressed a cough, picked up the thin branchlets, then held them up to the mirror behind his desk. Thirty seconds later his phone rang.

"*Wéi?*" A pause. "*Xiè-xie. Duì. Wǒ dài le . . . Duì-bu-qì. Xiè-xie!*" He hung up as he grew paler by the second. "Sir," he said in a chastened voice, "if you will accompany me, General Xi's car will meet us at the private terminus."

Herb smiled, took another deep drag, again blowing the smoke in the other man's face. "I rather thought it might."

Veterans Stadium in Philadelphia was jammed to capacity. Rising in nearly vertical walls of gray or blue, the competing sounds bounced back and forth like a living thing—a prehistoric bird trapped within the confines of the arena, flailing against the sides in a cacophonous attempt to break free.

"*Go Army! Beat Navy!*"

"*Go Navy! Beat Army!*"

The parade of cadets and midshipmen into the stadium—in

their perfect unison and barely controlled passions—added yet another element to the maelstrom of combined national pride and tribalism.

Flags were everywhere!

Chants and cheers mixed with the bunting, the mascots' haws and bays, the raw, heady scent of naked idealistic youth. These were the men and women from whom would be drawn the leaders of the free world in decades to come. They knew it—exalted in it—but put it all aside for the next few hours of unrefined, bold aggression.

Because whatever else happened in their careers, whatever George Pattons or Benedict Arnolds, Lewis Armisteads, Winfield Hancocks, or George Custers they turned out to be . . . they would always have the memory of this day in common.

Win or lose, the triumph of American youth!

It was a few minutes before kickoff when DeWitt settled himself into the luxury box with his entourage. He would spend the first half here on the Navy side of the field—the guest of the Annapolis superintendent and senior officers. Then, at halftime, he would perform a ceremony on the field honoring the three best cadets and midshipmen at each academy, before moving to an equally luxurious box on the Army side.

Never a big fan of football, and personally antimilitary, much of the pomp and splendor of this hallmark of Americanism was lost on the man, however.

But not the symbolism.

The form of the thing—the rigorously adhered-to traditions in the pregame that was timed down to the second the parachutists would enter the stadium with the game balls, trailing brightly colored smoke—it was a link to a thing over a hundred years old. A thing that DeWitt viewed as anachronistic and dumb.

But useful.

For within the rapture of the moment, the passion on the faces in the crowd, the nonstop cheers, the complete celebration of America that the game was, there was a narcofying effect. Not just in the stadium.

The millions who would watch the game on TV would be swept along with the rest, and forever associate *him* with all that was the best in America! It was a bonding that even his Chinese handlers had overlooked.

But at his halftime speech—being covered live by all the networks—he would be once and finally free of his last connections to the Apple Blossom conspiracy.

DeWitt would call his own shots, re-create America in an image to his liking, and the system (Chinese or American, he didn't really care) would *have to* go along.

He would be a *great* president, he knew, and soon so would the rest of the world.

A cell phone began ringing, and everyone in the box began checking theirs. It rang three times, then stopped . . . unanswered.

The game kicked off, the box filled with cheers, groans, and the natural excitement that this event always engendered, and DeWitt was surprised by how much the passion—for the teams, of course—affected him.

On the top of the stadium, under a cement-gray tarp behind a large plastic cutout of the Liberty Bell, Fabrè waited. He'd been in place for over five hours, calmly passing the time listening to Mozart through one ear of his Walkman, the communications net in his other.

If he was caught—he thought without much concern—he would be killed. There was little doubt of that. But he'd been well paid, his insurance was up to date, and he was doing "grand service to the Brotherhood."

It was enough.

He didn't need to site in on the luxury box that was his target. He'd done his run-throughs and had grooved the needed physical actions to a fine edge. But he was curious at the source of all the noise.

He peeked out through a less-than-an-inch slit in the tarp at the section just below him.

He could see groups of midshipmen—young men and women

sprinting around the end zone in a vain attempt to tear down the taunting banners that the cadets had hung there. He saw the cadets hastily pull up the banners, to frustrate the midshipmen.

Directly below him, the Army band played loud, raucous rock and roll—more noise than music. The fans cheered with a primitive vibration that shook the place as they pressed up against the thin guardrails.

And no one looked up.

Satisfied, he returned to Mozart and waiting.

Late in the second quarter, the cell phone rang again. This time, a navy steward found it—neatly tucked away—in the drawer of a writing desk at the back of the box. After answering it, he smoothly moved through the crowded box, handing it to a surprised Michael.

"Culbertson."

"Mr. Culbertson, would you mind moving to the back of the box and retrieving the sunglasses from the bottom drawer of the desk?"

"Who is this?" Michael said in an annoyed voice.

"Well, sufficient to say this *is not* Canvas." Michael froze in abject terror. "Please get the sunglasses, Mr. Culbertson. Then sit down again."

Slowly, surprised that his limbs had the strength to move, he retrieved the glasses and returned to his seat. "I have them."

"Please put them on."

Michael did as he was told.

They were dark, the darkest he'd ever worn, almost like welder's goggles. But there was enough light to barely see around him . . . and what he *did* see made his heart stop cold.

Two narrow beams of blue light came through the luxury box's window, coming to rest in the middle of his chest.

"If you move, or attempt to warn anyone, you'll die instantly. Do you understand? Answer now."

"Yes," Michael said in as natural a tone as he could.

"Look at DeWitt."

Two beams played on his chest and hairline.

"I see them," he said as he began sweating despite the coldness of the day.

"Write a note to DeWitt, explain the circumstances to him in an unmistakably clear fashion. Then hand him the glasses and the phone. Do not leave your seat or attempt to communicate with others until DeWitt hangs up. Then do what you like. Do you understand? Answer now."

"I—I understand." He pulled out his pad and began writing.

From a concourse behind the upper row on the Army side of the field, Xenos watched the frightened man through binoculars. Standing among pleasantly unaware fans, he waited until he saw the note passed to Apple Blossom. Then he got up and moved to a quieter spot. He put the phone in his jacket pocket and pulled out another, quickly dialing a number. Vedette answered on the first ring.

"So?" Xenos asked casually.

"One, two, three, and four are in position and ready on your command or an unexpected movement. Five and six are in position to exfiltrate one through four, if necessary. Seven and eight have the vehicles in position." The briefest pause. "We are go in all respects."

Xenos hung up, then looked down at the field, at two figures there that captured his attention.

A young man—no more than nineteen—was standing in jungle cammies, his face painted up, fully outfitted with pack, night-vision equipment, and multiple weapons. But despite it all, despite his fearsome exterior, he was a clear-eyed, callow youth who—Xenos's experienced eyes told him as he focused his binoculars—had never fired a shot in anger. Still pure, still clean, still morally alive.

And next to him, one of the Army's mascots—a man in black medieval armor from head to toe. Waving a black sword, with a bright golden plume in his helmet, he was simultaneously malevolent and inspirational. A thing to be feared, as he mockingly menaced Navy fans with his sword; to be admired, as he helped lead cheers in the Army section.

With considerable effort, Xenos turned away from these twin effigies of himself, centering the crosshairs of the binoculars on the frowning visage of Jefferson Wilson DeWitt.

Pressure makes diamonds, DeWitt repeated over and over in his head. *Pressure makes diamonds. If he wanted me dead, I'd be dead already. He—whoever he is—wants something other than my life. Pressure makes diamonds. Negotiate, delay, think. Pressure makes diamonds.*

"This is the attorney general," he said firmly.

"There are three minutes and twenty seconds left in the first half," Xenos replied. "At the halftime gun they will ask you to get up to go down to the field. At that moment we will have reached an arrangement, or you will die. Do you understand? Answer now."

"What can I do for you?" DeWitt asked casually. "Is there something specific . . ."

"Answer now. Or die now." The voice was flat, emotionless, not giving a damn.

"I understand," DeWitt said calmly, his eyes trying to follow the two beams across the open field to their source.

"Apple Blossom is over. The Alvarez children are safe. The congresswoman is with the president telling him everything. Grimes is dead, along with the command and control center. Canvas is running. The Chinese are about to disavow you. Apple Blossom is over. Do you understand? Answer now."

DeWitt fought to control himself. His anger was an ogre, pounding on his chest demanding voice. But the tiny blue dots kept it silenced, for now.

"I understand. Even if I don't entirely agree with you." He smiled at the superintendent as if in exasperation at the call.

"There is no other interpretation of the events."

"I think there is."

"How so?"

He turned to the superintendent, with an embarrassed look. "I'm dreadfully sorry, Admiral Hayland, but could I have a moment alone, it turns out this is a secure call."

"Of course," the admiral said as he instantly stood up. "Ladies and gentlemen, would you join me in the corridor for a few minutes," he said to the group.

Two minutes later DeWitt and Michael were alone in the box.

"I'm back," he said into the phone.

"You have two minutes, thirty-three seconds."

"I'm prepared to offer you ten million dollars, American, in any account of your choice." DeWitt looked out across the field as he talked, as if making eye contact with the voice on the other end of the phone. "Take the money and save yourself. You can't win." He paused, then smiled convulsively. "Answer now."

"I've won already, or hadn't you noticed?"

DeWitt shook his head. "Not even close. Grimes knew very little. There was little or no paper trail in the command center. As for the resilient congresswoman, well, she's just another member of the Heisenberg cult, you see. A traitor, trying to save herself by libeling a great American hero."

There was a long silence on the other end of the line.

"They chose you well," Xenos said sadly. "When you leave the box, you will be escorted to the field for the ceremony. At that ceremony you will announce that you are withdrawing your name from nomination and retiring from public life. The excuse is up to you." A short silence. "Make it health, if you like. It will be quite true."

DeWitt laughed. "Go ahead, kill me if you like."

"What?"

"I'm not suicidal, Mr. *Filotimo*." He rolled the name on his tongue. "Merely realistic."

"Really."

The attorney general nodded without realizing it. "You're a patriot, Mr. Filotimo, I've read your file. America is going to war— for whatever reason no longer matters—the war will soon be a fact." He shrugged. "And the old man in the White House is incapable of winning it.

"There are any number of reasons you might kill me, I think," DeWitt said matter-of-factly. "But my death leaves the lives of thousands of American men and women in the tender keeping of a half-senile old man who is so gullible that he has nominated a communist spy as his successor.

"Think of it. The blood of so many"—he looked down at the field—"so many that we are watching today, no doubt, spilled out upon the banner of your own vengeful impatience." He shook his head. "A waste of your talents and of life, sir."

Xenos was quiet for a long time. "You have fifty-four seconds to make your proposal. I assume you have one."

"I do." He gathered himself.

"Ten million dollars for you, five million dollars compensation to the family of that Satordi boy. Complete vindication of the Alvarez woman and her appointment to the ambassadorial post she chooses. Or my complete overt and covert support in any election bid for any office. And another ten million dollars to rebuild that clinic of yours and pay any compensations you feel I've left out."

"You really think you'll live long enough to pay out all that?"

"That, Mr. Filotimo, is up to you. I have a speech to make." He shut off the phone with an arrogant snap. But didn't move until the light beams disappeared from the luxury box.

"Call the Secret Service," DeWitt said as he stood to leave. "Tell them there's a sniper in the stadium. But tell them I'm making the speech anyway."

"Jeff! Don't you think—"

"For God's sake, Michael, he's not going to shoot! Not today anyway. Maybe after he gets to thinking about it, but not now. That offer's too damned good to turn down flat. He's a mercenary and they never turn down money without thinking about it first."

He started for the door. "Just make the call and join me when you can." He glad-handed his way into the corridor after tossing the cell phone to his aide.

Michael looked at the closed door, thought about the insanity that was soon to be president. An insanity that would—he was now sure—find him eminently expendable at the slightest fit of pique after he'd gotten what he wanted.

He thought about all that he would never get to do, all the dreams and time that would then be wasted.

He looked out at the stadium, knowing that Filotimo was out there somewhere, but knowing him better than the arrogant shit that had just left possibly could.

He had worked for years, swallowed loads of shit and more self-respect than any man should ever have to, and he would be *Goddamned* if he allowed either man—the preening ass or the outraged weapon—to take it away from him now that he was so close.

He looked down at the phone, dialed *69, and waited.

A moment later Xenos's voice came over the line—firm and clear.

"What do you propose?"

"A confidential act of amnesty," Valerie said to the president, his chief counsel, and Buckley.

"Not possible," the attorney general designate said. "Whatever your motivations, Valerie, you still turned classified documents and information over to a hostile foreign power. That's treason, maybe a lower degree, but treason nevertheless."

"And you've still only given us hints, snippets, possibilities about DeWitt, nothing we could take to court and get a conviction with," the White House counsel added. "You're going to have to do better."

"What about all that?" She pointed angrily at the box of evidence Michael had turned over to Buckley. "What's that, if not evidence?"

"That"—Buckley waved at the box—"is incriminating as Hell. Along with your testimony it's *damning* as Hell."

He hesitated, as if the taste of the next soured him. "But they'll argue everything in there is faked, forged, composited in a smear campaign. And your testimony will be viewed simply as the inadmissible ravings of a cultist coconspirator." He became uncomfortably quiet.

"Maybe you're the traitor," Valerie growled.

Buckley nodded. "I might've been. I do fit the circumstantial profile, but"—he tapped the box—"we now know it's DeWitt."

"We need more, Congresswoman," the president said softly.

For over an hour—since she'd told her story—Valerie had been arguing her case. Desperately trying to find an accommodation that would work for everyone and allow her to remain with her children. Because the one thing she now knew, beyond anything else in this whole muddled mess, was that she would never allow anything to come between them and her again.

"What more can I say?" she asked quietly. "I've come here willingly, to try and prevent an American tragedy of hitherto unknown proportions, and you're quoting the letter of the law at me!"

The president smiled and poured her a drink. "I probably believe you about your children. I've known you for years and I know what *I* would do for mine or my grandkids." He shivered at the thought. "But I still need more."

"Mr. President, I've told you everything I can. I've warned you about DeWitt, about the Chinese, about everything that's happened or about to happen. What more can I do?"

Buckley answered the phone, spoke quietly for a moment, then nodded at the president.

The old man smiled just then. "Show him in," he said casually. A moment later the door to the Oval Office opened. "Hello, George. We were just talking about you," he said easily.

George Steingarth nodded as he entered the room. "Mr. President, my apologies. But I was caught up in a series of international calls this . . ." He froze as Valerie turned to see who had come into the room.

"*Te voy a picar en pedacitos de salchica y dárselos de comer a tu madre,*" Valerie muttered in poisoned tones as she slowly stood up.

"Eh, Mr. President, I must . . . ," Steingarth said as he turned to leave—only to find his way blocked by two Secret Service agents.

Valerie launched herself at the man, her hands closing around his throat as they toppled to the ground.

"Bastard!"

The Secret Service agents started to come forward, but the president waived them off. "Leave her," he called out.

Valerie released her left hand and began methodically smashing it against the man's face. Apparently not satisfied with the result, she grabbed a brass ashtray from a nearby table and began using its corners on the man's groin.

"Help me," Steingarth moaned in a child's voice. "She's going to kill me!"

The president nodded and the Secret Service agents—both of them—barely pulled Valerie off of him. "Well," the president sighed, "you seem to have some explaining to do, George."

"I have . . . diplomatic immunity . . . from the . . . People's Republic of . . ." Steingarth's voice was a near thing, barely there as he gasped for lifesaving air and clutched at his groin.

"Of China, yes, George. I think we know that now," Buckley said as he sat down. "You have your corroboration, Val. The question now is: what are we going to do with you, both of you?"

"And what do we tell the American people?" the White House counsel added.

"Christ," the president said as he downed Valerie's drink.

It was still several hours before sunrise as the two old men strolled through the barely lit Imperial Gardens in the Forbidden City.

Below, in the tightly secured offices that no outsider had previously seen, they had said the facts, the brutish realities that would guide the decisions they must make. But here, among the willows and koi ponds and gentle floral beauty, contemplation only was in order.

They spoke little, then mostly about this plant or that tree. Both men knew the thoughts of the other, the ramparts that they would or would not cross. And neither was anxious to give voice to the realities that bore in on them.

But time—in all forms—was an ally to neither man.

"If what you say has happened *has* happened," Xi said calmly, "then I'm afraid our countries may be at war with the coming of the sun."

Herb shook his head. "I came here to turn off one war, not start another. We don't have to make it more complicated than that."

"And your country would seek no retaliation for the death of the vice president. Please, Director Stone, neither of us are young naïves."

Herb nodded. "But we *are* realists."

Xi studied the eyes of the man he'd made war on for over forty years. "Tell me your reality."

"War is made between men, not countries. So, too, the peace."

"Agreed."

"We want the names of all American citizens involved in the Apple Blossom project. We want the withdrawal of all Chinese advisers and military units from North Korea, Vietnam, Laos, Cambodia, and from within one hundred miles of the Indian border. We want, we *expect,* full and active support from the Chinese Mission to the United Nations on all U.S. proposals on human rights. We expect you to allow international inspections of all military facilities that can either stage to or directly threaten Taiwan and an immediate cessation of all hostile acts toward that nation."

Xi smiled. "Those are essentially political demands," he said simply. "Things for diplomats in their striped pants to negotiate." He gestured at a nearby marble bench. They walked over and sat down. "What do *you* require, Director Stone?" He waited.

Herb took his time lighting a cigar. "I want you to demonstrate, in some material way, your . . ."—he smiled—"deep remorse and grief over this horrible moment in our relations." He gestured with the cigar. "Something to do with drugs might help."

"And if all the opium fields in Burma, southern China, and Vietnam were to be verifiably destroyed by fire?"

"A good start. But nowhere near complete enough."

Xi looked off into the waning night sky. "If what you say has happened *has* happened—and you understand I cannot take your word for this?"

"Of course."

"In that event, I think I might take your proposals to the Central Committee."

They stood and began to walk again.

"It *was* a beautiful plan," Herb said sincerely.

"Thank you."

They stopped by a tree that seemed filled with fireflies—dancing in the last moment of the night in green shimmering brilliance.

"Will its failure go hard for you?"

Xi shrugged. "All failures are relative, I believe. While the acquisition of positive control over the fortunes of your country were not completely achieved, secondary designs—unrelated to your people—*were* reached."

Herb was too much of a gentleman (as much as any were in the intelligence community) to ask. "Will you be able to convince the general secretary of that?"

Xi almost—not quite but close—smiled. "Regretfully, our beloved general secretary has taken ill. The prognosis is not good."

"Indeed?"

"His illness seems to have affected his judgment, causing him to sanction certain operations that a healthy man in retention of all his faculties would never have done. Approved, it seems, by many misguided—similarly ill—members of the Central Committee."

He hesitated. "I'm afraid this *flu* epidemic may lead to a great many state funerals."

Herb studied the man's eyes, his soul—as much as he had one. "Pity," was all he said as he waited.

"In their benevolent wisdom, in the wake of these tragedies, the Central Committee has asked me to take over our esteemed general secretary's duties."

"My condolences and congratulations," Herb said deliberately as he locked blazing gazes with his Chinese counterpart. "When did all of this happen?"

"Approximately six hours from now." Xi gestured and a car came forward. "Your plane awaits you, Director Stone. A pleasure to have met you."

"A pleasure, *Secretary* Xi."

Xi remained in the garden until the sun was fully up, embracing him with its warmth and renewal. A strengthening brought about as he lost a country, and gained a country. And as the sun rose and strengthened in light and intensity, so, too, would *his* China.

That, after all, was the *real* purpose behind Apple Blossom . . . depending on perspectives, where you stood or who you were.

Finally, almost reluctantly, he got into his car to announce to the general secretary and the Central Committee that a "new age of China, as a member of the community of nations," had begun during the night.

And that they were no longer a part of it.

"Mr. Attorney General?"

DeWitt stopped at the mouth of the tunnel leading out onto the field. He turned to the men in the suits who had stepped between him and the throng awaiting him. "Who are you?"

"Inspector Lewis Peña, United States Secret Service."

"Oh, right. I remember you, you're the man in charge here, right?"

"Uh, yes sir." He seemed uncomfortable as five more of his men came up around him. "Sir, I can't allow you to go out onto that field."

DeWitt smiled bravely. "I know about the sniper, Inspector. But I won't allow a vague threat to silence me or keep me from the people."

"Yes, sir," Peña mumbled. "Very, uh, courageous of you." He hesitated. "But the president has instructed me to return you to Washington immediately."

DeWitt looked confused. "Has something happened that I don't know about?"

"Yes," Michael whispered as he walked away and disappeared into the crowd.

"What? Michael?" The agents began forcing DeWitt back into the tunnel toward a waiting car. "What the Hell is going on here? Michael!"

"Jefferson Wilson DeWitt," Peña intoned as they moved toward the parking lot, "you are under arrest for the crime of treason against the United States of America."

"What? Have you lost your fuck—"

He never finished his thought as they came out of the tunnel, into the sun of the parking lot, and two shots tore through his right eye into his brain.

If he still had a soul, it left his body before it hit the ground.

As Xenos Filotimo withdrew his rifle, rolled up his limousine's window, and gestured for the driver to leave.

Seventeen

"Mr. Chairman, members of the committee, assembled media, ladies and gentlemen of the nation and the world. My name is Michael Culbertson, formerly chief of staff to the late attorney general, Jefferson DeWitt. I would like it on the record that I appear before this investigating committee of my own volition, without subpoena or pressure from any quarter. I do this because it is my duty—however difficult—as an American citizen, dedicated to those most important principles of truth, justice, and fairness.

"Over the past seven months I began to grow suspicious of some of Attorney General DeWitt's actions. There were large unexplained absences in his schedule. He began to hold a series of secret meetings without myself or other staff present. There was the installation of an unlogged secure phone line in his home, and other occurrences which I found odd, inappropriate, and deeply troubling.

"Then, when he began to hint about his runaway ambitions, his quote *visions for the country* unquote, I began to realize the form of his madness. Unfortunately, not in time to prevent his plot to kill the vice president of the United States, insinuate himself into his place, foment a war with good and true allies, and eventually to seize control of the country itself.

"When I felt I had gathered sufficient evidence—primarily from video and audio recordings that the man himself had made, that I discovered—I contacted the office of Attorney General Designate Buckley, and, together, we set in motion the machinery that led to Mr. DeWitt's arrest.

"Unfortunately, those members of organized crime with whom he conspired learned of his imminent exposure and sought to obliterate all evidence of their connection with him. This led to the massacre at Heisenberg House, and eventually to DeWitt's own death at their hands, moments after he had been taken into custody."

The president clicked off the television, shaking his head. "I can already see someone running the little shit for Congress."

Valerie shook her head. "He can have my seat." She began to read off the titles of the papers she was signing. "Act accepting terms of presidential amnesty . . . Copy of terms of amnesty . . . Letter of resignation from the House of Representatives of the United States of America . . . Act renouncing citizenship in the United States of America."

She slammed the folder shut and dropped it in the president's lap. "Satisfied?"

The president sighed. "Valerie, bottom line, your acts of treason caused the death of that Chinese defector, Pei, the men guarding him, and probably more beside. Important military and intelligence secrets were given to the Chinese. Innocent lives were put at risk and the security of the country *was* compromised." He shook his head sadly. "*That,* my dear, is treason. Sorry."

Valerie collapsed in a chair across from him. "But you're protecting the citizenship and pension rights of my kids, right?" She sounded exhausted.

"It's in writing and over my signature. Your lawyers already have it."

She nodded. "Fine." Finishing off her drink, she stood and took a deep breath. "What are you going to do now?"

The president looked older than his eighty-plus years. "I've asked President Carter to come out of retirement to serve as vice president until the next election. The people need someone they can trust."

"Don't we all." Valerie began to gather her things.

"What are *you* going to do now?" the president asked with genuine curiosity.

"Not watch the news for a few thousand years," she said while holding back the tears that she knew would burst forth later that night.

"Actually, I've been asked to take on international fund-raising for a war orphans' hospital in Toulon, France."

The president stood up, extending his hand. "You have friends there? Any people?"

"I think . . . no." She didn't sound sad or beaten, more like —resigned. "No, I don't," she said as she shook his hand. "But I think I at least *know* some people there."

The president refused to let go of her. "Your nation and I owe you an unpayable debt of gratitude," he said seriously. "I hope you realize that."

"That why I'm getting the bum's rush?"

The president shrugged. "It *was* treason."

"And what would you have done?"

The old man was quiet for a long time. "Probably ended up raising money for war orphans."

And, for Valerie, it was finally over.

It was a place of warrior grace and poetic ugliness. A monument to greed, an achievement in futility. It had—in its distant past —been a critical piece of the puzzle that was London's docks, its gateway to the world.

But that had all been decades ago, a storied history of the tough men who hauled the freight that kept the great city alive.

Now the docks were gone, replaced by a glittering glass and steel construct, crowned by the tallest building in Europe. *The largest single office development in the world,* they said. A throne for the "new London" to sit comfortably on and look out at the world that must flock to it.

But they were wrong.

Recessions, Euro-unions, unrealistic and unrealized ambitions, had all left the place an empty shell; a place abandoned—that the tourists flocked to on the weekend to *ooh* and *ahh* at the magnificently polished gold statue in the courtyard that made as little sense as the development itself.

Whole floors of the grand tower had been left unfinished. The Docklands Light Railway station—capable of holding more people than Heathrow Airport—echoed with the few footsteps of photographers and a skeletal crew of maintenance.

Canary Wharf's dreams, ambitions, grand plans, and grandiose predictions gone.

But the tough men concerned with the life of the city remained.

They would come in the late evening, when midnight was a memory and dawn a thing they hoped to see again. The minders, the killers, the cops, the callous and the nonchalant. Anyone and everyone—men and women—who had the knowledge.

And the strength.

Some nights they would gather in the station itself, others in the plaza or on one of the desiccated skeletal upper floors with the magnificent views that went otherwise unappreciated. They would remain undisturbed, secure in knowing that some of their own controlled all security and surveillance in the complex.

Over steaming cups of coffee, cutting shots of whatever got them through the night, or pure adrenaline, they would gossip, exchange much-needed information and intelligence, or just take each other's measure.

There were other places like it throughout the world—Brevin's Hole in Las Vegas, Nevada; Two Dollar Bill's in Hollywood; La Rotunda in Rio—but Canary Wharf was the pinnacle. A place where acceptance as a friend (or enemy) meant you had arrived among the world's last remaining *truly* tough men.

On this rainy 3:00 A.M., there were about twenty of them gathered on the seventeenth floor. Thermoses of steaming liquid were being passed around; photographs of new babies, lovers, or victims being sought as well. As usual, the low hum of conversation stopped at the pleasant ding of the elevator doors as eyes casually turned to inspect the new arrivals.

"Shit," someone whispered as Xenos and Franco stepped off.

They stood for a moment, taking in the room, their bodies still, their eyes never stopping.

An older man, one of the few who had been coming to Canary Wharf when it was still a real wharf, walked over to him. "Goldman."

Xenos looked past him, into the crowd that had gone nervously back to their conversations.

"Who?" the man asked quietly.

"That would be me, I expect," another man said from the crowd behind.

The old man shook his head as he stepped out from between the two. Casually all conversations moved to the sides of the wall-less floor, opening up forty feet of space between the two men.

"Well, look who we have here, boys. Our American cousin, come back from the dead." Canvas regarded the two men carefully, missing no curve or lump in their clothing, no shift of weight between their legs. "I expected you yesterday," he said quietly.

"Flight was delayed."

Canvas nodded. "So?" he said after nearly a minute of silence.

Xenos just stared at him.

"*I Cinesi* send their regrets, *serpente*," Franco said in an electric tone. "They're going to miss the last payment."

Like a tennis match, those in the room switched their attention to Canvas.

One of only two living Four Phase Men in the world.

"Pity," Canvas said defiantly as he shrugged. "Their money's just as good as anyone else's." He laughed, ignoring Franco, but never taking his eyes off of Xenos. "Just a poor boy trying to make a living, that's me."

All eyes back to the *other* Four Phase Man.

"Could be a real short living."

Eyes on Canvas.

"An' why's that?"

Xenos unbuttoned his duster and the crowd took another step back. "Apple Blossom's over. Time to settle accounts."

For the first time, the bystanders smelled the putrescence of inevitable death settle over the room, floating between the two men.

Not yet decided which way to drift.

Canvas seemed genuinely nervous, but he quickly covered it with a professional braggadocio. "Apple Blossom was a joke from jump. I told the Chinks they oughta find themselves someone else." He hesitated. "Who's paying for the collection, Jerry? Certainly not this little Corsie?" He seemed relaxed, confident, completely at ease.

But he lowered his hands to his sides, split his weight evenly between his feet, relaxing his right arm. "No. You wouldn't do it for money, not pure and noble Jerry Goldman."

He shook his head sadly. "You must've started caring again, eh?" He frowned. "Pity," he said with genuine emotion. "When *are* you going to learn, Jerry? No room on the bus for sentimentality."

"It ends tonight." Xenos paused, and when he spoke again it was in tones that dripped finality. "For the Corsicans, for the children, for you and me . . . it ends tonight. Nothing more to worry about. Ever."

"I look worried to you, Goldman?"

Xenos sighed deeply. "You look . . . dead."

Franco walked over to the Englishman, hatred and murder in his eyes, and dropped a bloodred scarf to the floor in front of him. "Burn in Hell, *verme schifoso!*"

Canvas smiled. "See you there, darling."

Franco spit in the man's face, then turned, stalking back to Xenos.

The two men (Xenos and Canvas—once Jerry Goldman, talented young musician; and Colin Meadows, aspiring artist) looked at each other, into each other, then Canvas nodded.

"Pas de mort?" he asked quietly. "I always appreciated the romantic in you. Most didn't, I know. But I found it one of your most attractive qualities, old son." He picked up an end of the long scarf and tied it tightly around his left wrist.

Xenos walked forward slowly, picking up the other end of the scarf, tying it around his left wrist. "You won't suffer. You have my word."

"I don't intend to."

Xenos nodded, then spoke in a loud, demanding voice; directed not at Canvas, but at the rest of the crowd.

"Gentlemen, may we have this room."

They filed out quickly. Franco the last to go, flashing lightning stares at Canvas, whose eyes remained locked with the man tied to him, less than five feet away.

And they were alone.

In the silence of the never finished floor, they contemplated their lives, their sins, their gained and missed opportunities. And they deeply weighed the mirror in front of them.

"Good-bye, Colin," Xenos said as he pulled a ten-inch-blade Randall assault knife from his duster.

Canvas abruptly reached out with both hands, grabbed Xenos's head with his hands, and pulled it close for a long hard kiss on the lips.

"The only way for legends to die!" he shouted. He stepped back, pulling out a fourteen-inch Bowie knife.

Xenos stepped back until the scarf was stretched taut between them.

And the dance began.

Eighteen

The snow was falling harder as the Lincoln stopped in front of the hamburger stand just long enough for the heavily bundled-up person to get in.

"Do you need to come in?" the driver asked.

"No," the passenger replied. "I'm clean."

"Do you need to deliver anything?"

"No."

"Are you intact?"

"I've detected no changes in the flow across my desk, in my assignments. My phone was clean as of 1450, and I've detected no surveillance."

"Very well." Buckley pulled onto the lightly trafficked service roads that ran for miles from the rural airport. "How are you, Michael?"

"Good, sir."

"It's been an interesting time."

The star witness at the Buckley Commission hearings on Apple Blossom nodded. "It has."

Buckley concentrated on the rearview mirror. "It's hard not being able to talk."

Michael nodded his agreement. "After what's happened, I wouldn't feel comfortable with it anyway."

Buckley just studied the mirror. "Have you decided what you want to do?"

"Well," Michael said as he considered, "they're pretty much

leaving it up to me. But I think they want me to take the network commentator job with WIN for a couple of years, maybe the radio show too. Then run against Kingston for your old seat in 2002." He paused thoughtfully. "They've done right by me so far." He looked up at Buckley. "Been right for both of us."

"Agreed." The recently sworn-in attorney general frowned. "I've received new instructions," he said after a long silence.

Michael was paying close attention. "I thought maybe that was it."

"Our friends," the slightly older man said softly, "believe we might carve out the right identity by engaging in the morals debate."

"Gay bashing or church burning?" Michael answered easily.

"Neither, actually. They suggested that—given the mood in the country after Apple's fall—we focus on the lack of morality in our educational system. How Jeff was a product of the overliberalization of our schools and such." He hesitated. "Any ideas?"

Michael thought for a moment. "Teachers espousing the legalization of drugs, administrators allowing high school kids with babies to bring them to class, student athletes using steroids and such?"

"Sounds good."

"Maybe I can link it with administrators and teachers who went to college in Europe, make it a grand Chinese conspiracy to destroy the moral fabric of America," Michael said as he warmed to the idea.

Buckley held up a restraining hand. "Let's not push that too hard." He pulled up in front of the air terminal. "Your boss's recklessness didn't rub off on you, did it . . . Blossom?"

Michael smiled. "Not a chance . . . Cactus."

"To the next few months, then."

"To the eight years beyond that," Michael added soberly.

"To the eight, then," Buckley said as the man opened the door, letting some snow in, "and to *your* eight after that."

Cactus Blossom vanished, like a shadow on an X ray, into the snowy night.

And the possibilities beyond.

. . .

It was more atoll than island. A pacific paradise that mocked the winter that the rest of the world was shivering beneath. Warm gentle winds caressed pure white beaches, and crystalline blue water lapped at the few rocks, which added magnificent texture to the postcard scene.

"I hear they finally sell this place, but I no really believe it. They ask so much money!"

But the big man who stood solemnly in the bow of the small boat ignored the captain.

"You gonna build your house or maybe big hotel for all the rich fools pay to see this shit?" Again, no answer. "Hey! Mister! What are you, antisocial or something?"

But the glare that burned its way through the sunglasses the man wore above a bruised and scarred face was enough to silence the captain for the remainder of the trip.

In his life he had seen Pacific smugglers, Solomon Island pirates who would kill you for your fillings, and aboriginal islanders who still believed in cannibalism . . . and worse.

But, the captain decided, he would rather spend a weekend with any of *them* than anger the man behind the glasses.

They pulled up onto the beach, the captain was instructed to wait, and the man set off into the interior with only a backpack.

He walked for twenty minutes, following an inlet to a breathtakingly beautiful lagoon filled with fish, and flowers, and entente. He inhaled deeply, took off his glasses to prevent any filtration of the natural wonders of this Heaven on earth.

Here, the man believed, peace was a living thing. Still wild and untamed and undeterred by man's stupidities and pettiness. Here peace was a force of such dominance and majesty that all who lie in its wake must be healed and renewed. Here *was* Heaven on earth!

After ten minutes of taking it—inhaling it—in, the man shucked off his pack, reached inside, pulling out a simple aluminum box. He walked to the edge of the water, ignored the tears that were welling up in his eyes, and emptied the ashes and bone fragments into the water.

"Rest," Xenos said softly. "Find some peace, Colin." He watched the water and wind swirl the remains, drawing it off into the paradisiacal setting. "For both of us."

Then he stretched out next to that pacific beauty, closed his eyes, quickly falling asleep.

The dream came right away, before his breathing could shallow and even; before his body could settle and unwind. As always, it came with blinding speed.

He stood in the sanctuary of the hundred-year-old temple. The men in their dark suits, gray beards, *tallisim* and *kepas* in place, swaying to their own rhythms as the ancient prayers were recited. An odd cacophony of English, Yiddish, Russian, and German mutterings rising out of them.

Upstairs, the women sat. More still, more controlled than the men; they prayed with equal fervor but less demonstrably, as was the tradition. The old women in black, the middle women in navy or pale blues, the young women and girls in a few bright colors. But all had their shawls over their heads, their hands cupped over their eyes, their mouths moving almost silently with their prayers.

Xenos would move among them, looking into their eyes, tasting their breaths, inhaling the women's soapy-clean fragrances, feeling the submerged power of the men.

He stood for the longest time by his mother—who couldn't have been there, since she had died years before—watching as she tried hard to suppress a grin of pride and, well, ownership, in her son below. It was one of the comforts in the dream. A mother that he had barely known approving, supporting, loving.

He would move to his father, sitting proudly, stiffly, on the dais next to the president of the synagogue. His freshly altered suit —worn only for the most special occasions—paling in comparison to the other man's.

But he prayed with more fervor, with an extra something that had been reserved for this moment when he would sit in front of the congregation. A proud father's one and only embracement of his son's accomplishments.

Xenos would reach out, try to touch the old man with the scar across his forehead from a soldier's rifle butt. But he could never quite make it. Somehow, no matter how close the dream allowed him to move, it was never close enough. So his fingers would stretch and reach and beg; but never find the man whom he most wanted to please, whom he had most disappointed.

Then, quite unexpectedly, the old man reached out to him.

Embracing, nurturing him, tightly and warmly, for what seemed like centuries.

And as the big man slept beneath the palms in the warm pacific breeze, for the first time in ravaged years and a sordid adulthood, Jerry Goldman began to heal.

Acknowledgments

The Four Phase Man would not have been possible without the generous assistance, support, and belief of many people; both now and in the past. Too many to thank individually. So I'll take this opportunity to thank a special few; and through them, the rest.

Among the many are: David Schumaker; Hu Xiaoming; Sun Daqing; Paddy Jackson; Howard Tomb; Dr. Anthony Storr; Michael Newton; Steve Strasemeier, Sports Information Director at Annapolis; the wishing-to-remain-nameless aides from the staffs of Congresswomen Nancy Pelosi of California and Carolyn McCarthy of New York; Elizam Escobar and Guillermo Gomez-Peña for their inspiration; Stan Ridgley, who has what it takes; Dr. O. K. Burger, Ph.D.; Lieutenant Samuel Posner, LAPD (ret.); Dwight Chapin, Ron Sima, and Jack Liebling, who taught me to question everything.

Also: some special people who can't bring themselves to sit on the sidelines, watching and bitching. The strong men and women of the former Two Dollar Bill's in Hollywood; La Rotunda in Rio de Janeiro; Canary Wharf in London; and Brevin's Hole in Las Vegas.

Their professions and life choices preclude my using their names, but their contributions to *The Four Phase Man*—both now and in the past—are very real and I thank them deeply.

Thanks are also owed to: the United States Department of Justice, Bureau of Prisons; Communication Control Services (CCS); Tishman-Speyer Properties; Colt Firearms; Heckler & Koch Manufacturing; L'Direzione Soccorso di Corsicanos Internazionale; the Chinese American Foundation (San Francisco Annex); Dell Computers; Microsoft Encarta; Division of Geography & Environmental Management, University of Northumbria; the archives of the Central Intelligence Agency; Modern Military Branch of the National Archives of the United States; the *New York Times; Le Monde;* the *Times* (London); and the New York Public Library, Harriman Collection.

Also, far from least—the able men and women of the United States Naval Academy at Annapolis, Maryland, and the United States Military Academy at West Point, New York.

Less technically, and more personally, this novel would not have been possible if not for the kindness, support, friendship, and unwavering belief of a select few.

Particularly all of "Team Steinberg"—Jack and Marge Kratsas; Rolf and Detta Egelandsdal; Pat Glynn; Fred and Susan Boyce; Don Backer; Bill Gresham; Pat Nohrden, along with Roberta and Vivian; David Emry, and Peggy of course; Chad Bean, as well as Stan and Cynthia; Gary Smith; and, as always, my Angels on Earth . . . the Aguila family—Alex, Suzanne, Tani, Ama, and Adrian.

Bernard Kurman—along with Betty Anne Crawford—remains my most trusted face to the world. I don't say it often enough, but Bernie, trust me, what you do is deeply appreciated and valued.

If between the lines of *The Four Phase Man* you hear a distant voice lending passion, commitment, and calenture to my sometimes awkward prose, it is the voice of the magnificent Betty Buckley. I wrote every word of this book to her music, and without it the demons in the night might have won and Xenos Filotimo never found his way.

My mother—Gloria Steinberg—is a remarkable woman. Sacrificing, nurturing, leveling when I get too full of myself, praising when I get down; she has gone well above and beyond the call in all ways. What success I have or will obtain is due to the strength and freedom she has always given me. Now, Mom, sit back and enjoy. These are your winnings.

To the brilliant folks at the Brilliance Corporation—Eileen

Hutton, Max Bloomquist, Laura Grafton, Jeremy Spanos, and my "voice," as well as friend and partner in crime, Dick Hill—a heart-felt thanks! You bring my words to life and *that* is an incredible gift.

To the best, Jane Wesman Public Relations, especially Lori Ames Stuart, thank you for your class act.

And to Steve Rubin, Irwyn Applebaum, Erik Engstrom, Michael Palgon, Nita Taublib, Kate Miciak, as well as all the other stone pros at Bantam Doubleday Dell, my undiluted thanks. You make it easy, comfortable, and deeply satisfying and rewarding to be a part of the best publishing organization in the world!

Shawn Coyne—to whom this novel is dedicated—said to me in our first conversation, years ago, "All you have to worry about is the writing. Let me take care of all the rest."

A man of his word, through three novels together he has been a *painfully* thorough editor, an insightful counselor, and a deeply patient advocate on those *LOUD* (few) times when we butted heads. All my work—and there's damned little I care about beyond my work—has been significantly improved by his *nudges,* sense of humor, and insight. As I said in *The Gemini Man* . . . the editor of any writer's dreams!

The Four Phase Man had a troubled early life. Too troubled to detail here. It came about during one of the most hectic, chaotic periods of my life; a time of moving, injury, and pain—emotional and physical. That it *did* come about is a credit not only to the tolerance and caring of many of the people named above but to a special group of people at my Fifty-third Street fallout shelter in New York.

THE PINDER LANE ALL-STARS: Nancy Coffey, Roger Hayes, Jean Free, Dick Duane, and *most especially* Robert Thixton are far more than literary agents, they are my extended family, my quiet refuge in a cacophonous world, and the people who have given me my life.

They, along with you gentle readers, have—through kindness and patience—fulfilled my dreams and made my reality more glorious than any fantasy I ever had.

Thank you all.

Success!
Richard Steinberg
Somewhere in America
Spring 1999